Outcasts

Alan Janney

@alanjanney
ChaseTheOutlaw@gmail.com

First Edition
Printed in USA

Cover by Damonza
Artwork by Anne Pierson
Formatting by Polgarus Studio

ISBN: 978-0-9962293-7-1 (ebook)
ISBN: 978-0-9962293-8-8 (print)

Sparkle Press

A note from the author:

I recommend reading 'Kid' before you dive into Outcasts. In this short story, readers get a glimpse behind enemy lines into the daily life of a Chosen known to the Outlaw as Baby Face. It's not required reading, but it's fun, and it might shed light on a few mysteries.

Enter your email here and I'll instantly send you the short story for free. **http://eepurl.com/b1fquj**

I'll never spam you. That's the worst.

Happy reading.

The book is dedicated
to Larry and Debbie

Prologue
Special Agent Isaac Anderson
December 2018

We meet in secret because the President no longer trusts us. He cannot openly call for our arrest, so he monitors our group and phones our supervisors.

Because we support the Outlaw. Because we seek cooperation with his team.

And because the President is firmly ensnared by the Blue-Eyed Witch.

We're forced to operate in shadow, and now we meet in a vacant middle school just outside Los Angeles in one of the dark regions. No electricity. The power grid has been finicky since the hostile takeover of downtown LA.

The task force I've gathered is young. The Federal Bureau of Investigations, the Central Intelligence Agency, the National Security Agency, Navy, Army, Air Force, the Marshals, Los Angels Police Department, the Drug Enforcement Administration, and USSOCOM have all sent representatives that I trust. All military or law enforcement. No elected officials. No politicians. Quick thinkers, decisive, adaptable, and resourceful. No one in the room is afraid for his or her pension. Nobody is stodgy or inflexible. We all support the Outlaw.

And we're all in way over our heads.

I say, "Let's get started," and push a button on my iPhone. The battery-powered LCD projector flares to life, displaying my powerpoint on the wall. The rest of the room is dark. "I want to discuss four things in the next twenty minutes. The disease. The Infected. The Chosen. And the super drug."

A commander in the Navy speaks up. "Chosen and Infected are different things? I had no clue."

"I'll get to that. But first, I need to disclose that we have a visitor. I invited him." The members of the task-force glance at each other in confusion. "Say Hello, PuckDaddy."

The bluetooth Bose speaker on the table bursts to life. "Hello Captain FBI and his team of awesomeness! Thanks for inviting me, but I'd have listened in anyway. PuckDaddy rules."

The commander says, "PuckDaddy?? Isn't he the hacker I've read about?"

"Yes. But he's our friend and ally. I'll explain in a minute. I want to start our short meeting by discussing the disease. This won't take long, because we know almost nothing about it."

"Man-made?"

"Negative. It occurs naturally. We're almost certain of that. The Outlaw and his team agree on this. The disease has been around for centuries."

The bodies in the room shift and murmur in surprise. "Impossible. Hell, how are we just now hearing of it, then?"

"I'll get to that. Hold your questions."

PuckDaddy says, "Yeah shut up."

"We don't have much time. Here's what you need to know. It's incredibly rare, and usually fatal. US Bioservices believe it attacks the lymph nodes and various glands, overproducing hormones to a lethal extent. Any *body* that survives is…enhanced. Sped up. Stronger. Harder. Contrary to rumors, we're not dealing with supernatural beings. This isn't paranormal stuff. They aren't ghosts or angels or vampires. They're sick. And the result is that they…do stuff better than we do. Like think. And run. And jump. And shoot. No flying. No laser beams eyesight. No retractable claws."

"I wish. That's be SO cool!"

An Army colonel asks, "What do we call the disease?"

Bob, the FBI biochemist I brought with me, spoke up. "We don't have a sample. We know nothing about its chemistry. So we've dubbed it the Hyper Virus. Unofficially."

"It's contagious?"

"I'll cover that. More on the virus later. If it even *is* a virus. Moving on. Next, the Infected. This is the term the Outlaw uses for individuals sick since birth. Infected. Very few individuals are born with the Hyper Virus, and most die during infancy or adolescence. The survivors are-"

"Gods. The survivors are gods," the Navy commander grunts.

"Powerful," I correct him. "The survivors are powerful, and very secretive. That's how they've remained hidden for so long. Fortunately there aren't very many. We estimate fifteen."

"That's not an exact number?"

"No. An approximation. I'll show you their pictures in a moment. But the important thing to know is this: our real enemy is a small subset of the Infected. Not *all* the Infected. Our real enemy is not the Hyper Virus. And not the Chosen. We can handle them at a later date. Right now we need to focus on-."

"The Chemist."

"Right. Their leader is the Chemist." I push a button and a picture of a handsome, gaunt, gray-haired man comes on screen. "I hope you've all been following the online updates provided by Teresa Triplett, his captive. Fascinating stuff."

"Not the word I'd choose."

"You all know about him, but here's some new intel. His first name is Martin, and we think he's over two hundred years old." I progress quickly through a series of nine photos, starting at present day and going backwards. "NSA used what we know about him to comb through photographs, and they discovered these pictures. The earliest is from the 1930s." On screen is a black and white image, clearly of the Chemist, standing with a group of European military officials. "Another symptom of the disease. Longevity. And the older the Infected, the stronger he becomes."

"What...how?"

Bob the FBI biochemist answers, "Most likely advanced cellular regeneration. The sun's harmful effects don't *stick*."

"And because we're totally sweet," PuckDaddy interjects.

3

"That's why the Chemist is their leader. He's the oldest, he's the strongest. I can provide more information about him in a minute. But first, we have reason to believe his terrorist group isn't as monolithic as we once assumed."

"Which means?"

"It's fractured. Dissension among his crew, in other words." Another slide, this one of a beautiful blonde girl. Grumbles from the room. "This is Mary. Code named the Blue-Eyed Witch."

"She's the reason we're meeting in secret," NSA spoke up. "Intel reports that she's in the oval office at least once a week."

"Precisely. She knows we're aiding the Outlaw, and her control is growing. I suspect she'll have warrants out for our arrest soon. She's tearing our government in half. She's the reason I no longer trust Washington. The only person I trust in that city is the Secretary of Defense. He's reliable, thank God. Everything we know about Blue-Eyes is on the papers I gave you. No digital files." I push a button on my phone screen, which controls the projector. Another picture, this of an angry black man with cornrows. "This is Walter. He's much less well-known than Blue-Eyes but equally dangerous. According to a deceased informant, he and the Chemist are butting heads. The Chemist wants to control the world. Walter wants to burn it down."

"Yeah Walter sucks. Trust Puck."

Army asks, "Walter is the one leading raids on Houston and Seattle?"

"Yes. Extremely dangerous."

CIA says, "We got photos of him in New York City last week."

"What about the Chemist? Where's he?"

I say, "All over the globe. Not even PuckDaddy can track him."

"Isn't he barricaded downtown? How does he get out?"

"Bribes, most likely. He has multiple insurgents inside our forces, throwing around large sums of money. FBI is handling this investigation. One of our top priorities, but there are moles in the FBI too."

"Good grief."

"Additional Infected are working with the Chemist but we have no intel on them. We know they exist. But that's it. Just shadows. So for the sake of time let's move on to our allied Infected." Another slide. "This is the Outlaw.

Most everything the FBI knows, the media knows too."

"Anderson, does the FBI know the Outlaw's identity? I mean, who he *really* is?"

"No. The FBI does not."

"Do you?"

"Yes."

"Feel like sharing?"

"Not a chance."

PuckDaddy says, "You sneaky devil you. Puck had no idea. Good for you, Captain FBI. Keep it hush-hush."

"Next." I push a button. Another slide, this one of an athletic looking girl in a helicopter, holding a rifle. "This is Shooter. She and I worked together in Camino. Trustworthy. Very capable. All known intel about Shooter is printed on your papers. She'd follow the Outlaw into hell."

"Why?"

"I'm not sure. The same reason I would, I guess. But what you need to know is that she's on our side."

"She's the one who shot down the attack helicopters?"

"Yeah! That was crazy cool!"

I say, "She shot and killed the pilots of airborne helicopters while she herself was in an airborne helicopter, yes."

"That's impossible."

"That's the power of Infected."

"Damn freaks."

"Watch your mouth," Puck says. Perhaps his involvement was a bad idea. Too late now.

I say, "At least she's on our side. Next." Another picture. Laughter. On screen is an illustration of a smiling computer. "PuckDaddy. We have no photograph of him."

"Trust me. I'm hot."

DEA blurts, "You have proof the cyber terrorist PuckDaddy is working *with* the Outlaw?"

"I do. He's Infected, which explains the enormous gap he has on all other

5

hackers. Plus he assisted on the cargo plane capture over the Pacific."

"Wow."

The speaker rattles, "And don't call me a cyber terrorist. More like a cyber Robin Hood. Puck is running security for this little meeting of yours. Plus I have nude photos of all of you."

They laugh. Good. We need unity. I say, "My opinion is that these three, the Outlaw and Shooter and PuckDaddy, are our best bet to end this nightmare. But there are other Infected we don't know much about." Another slide. A bald man smoking a cigarette. "This is Carter. PuckDaddy says he's basically a mercenary and does a lot of work in the black market. He is enemies with the Chemist but that doesn't necessarily mean he's our ally. Is that right?"

"Yeah, basically. He's not a bad dude. Just a hard-ass. Don't tell him I said that."

"More information about him on your papers." New slide. A large man with a hard face and cold eyes. "Code name Russia. We know nothing, except he works with Carter and killed dozens of Chosen in the Camino College shootout."

Puck adds, "He lives outside of Moscow usually. Likes to ice fish. Sometimes dives in himself!"

New slide. I say, "You know this one. Tank Ware. We have him in custody."

The Army colonel says, "I thought you said we have no blood samples? Of the disease? You have an incarcerated Infected, for Christ sake."

"Getting a blood sample from this behemoth is not easy. We've tried. He's already killed one guard. It'll happen. Soon. Next." New slide. "The girl who set herself on fire."

"Anderson, a question. In the email you said she was the Chemist's most recent creation. Wouldn't that mean she's Chosen? Not Infected? I'm still confused on the difference."

"Good point. We know a little more about Hannah than the others. PuckDaddy doesn't like revealing much information on the Infected, but he explained Hannah Walker in detail. She was hurt during the Compton explosions, but the Chemist salvaged her body. She underwent a full blood exchange, which sped up her transformation. She's as strong as an Infected, which is why I've chosen to categorize her with them. But, whatever, we can categorize her however we like."

"How does she set herself on fire and survive?"

"We don't know."

"Scary as hell."

"Agreed. Those are all the photos PuckDaddy will share. There are other Infected. We know they exist, but that's all we know. That's why we estimate fifteen. Fortunately that is a fixed number. It's not growing."

"More than enough, you ask me."

"Next category. The Chosen. The Chemist's army." On screen were gangs of raving lunatics. "You asked if the disease is communicable. The short answer is No, except for the Chemist. Apparently his body produces contagious blood. The other Infected do not. Yet. They aren't old enough. And the Chemist is infecting people around their eighteenth birthday, creating his army of Chosen."

"Army of wild animals."

"Savages. Some of my officers have been *chewed* on."

"Move like cheetahs. Climb like monkeys."

I say forcefully, "The disease produces mild insanity. They are *people* with broken minds."

"When's the last time you slept, Anderson?"

"Been a while. Army R&D is working on non-lethal solutions to Chosen. They are vulnerable to electricity."

"Do we have more specifics about how the Chosen are being…produced?"

Puck answers the question. "The Chemist puts them into a medically induced coma and infects them using his own blood. Keeps them under for several months because the disease causes aneurysms otherwise. Headaches from hell! He calls them Twice Chosen, which is super confusing. We call them Chosen."

I say, "Keep this in mind; the Chosen were infected *recently*. They haven't had the disease long. So they aren't as strong as Infected. Nor as smart. Their strength is in their numbers."

Navy grumbles, "The Infected are gods, and Chosen are their wild animals."

Army asks, "Anderson, we've heard reports that Chosen are subservient to the Infected. True?"

"Meh," PuckDaddy says. "Kinda. The Chosen obey the Chemist, at least."

I continue, "There is a pecking order. We don't know how it's established. Remember, the Chosen are dangerous but they aren't the real problem. The real problem is the Chemist's terror group and his ability to *produce* Chosen."

"How many Chosen are there?"

A Captain of the LAPD says, "We estimated five hundred during the Los Angeles takeover."

"But that's just in Los Angeles. Doesn't account for Seattle and Houston and God-knows-where-else. Best guess is in the thousands. Okay, we're running out of time. Bob, tell us about the super drug."

"Sure. Okay. So, we got our hands on several pounds. Of the Chemist's super drug, I mean. We did a thorough workup. And it's astonishing. Very elegant, much more so than cocaine, although that's a primary ingredient."

"More elegant?"

Bob adjusts his glasses and says, "To be blunt, the powder is a viral vector."

USSOCOM asks, "The hell is a viral vector?"

"Well. For lack of better phrasing. A delivery system to the human body. Think of the cocaine as the delivery system. And there's a nasty surprise being delivered through said system."

The police captain chuckles. "Cocaine ain't nasty enough?"

Army asks, "What's the payload? What's the nasty surprise?"

"Genetic material." Bob the FBI biochemist enjoys dropping this particular bit of information. He always does it with the same dramatic flair.

"Holy…"

"What? What's that mean? I'm just Navy, someone explain."

I grin. "It means the powder alters their genome, Navy."

"Genome? Somebody use some damn English."

Bob says, "DNA. The powder is snorted and it temporarily changes the person's DNA."

"That's *possible?*"

"Not until recently."

PuckDaddy mumbles, "I'm not sure I knew that."

"Why? What's the point? If it's just a temporary behavior modifier, wouldn't other drugs do the trick?"

Bob continues, "There's more. We think we've located Chemist DNA inside the material."

"He put his own *genes* inside the stuff?"

I ask a clarification question for the benefit of the group, "So, say Jimbo snorts the powder. Some of Jimbo's DNA gets replaced with Chemist DNA?"

"Potentially. Temporarily. The delivery system is very crude. Because it's being mass produced. Well. Crude is a relative term. It's a massive leap forward in the biogenetic world, actually."

"What happens to users with their DNA replaced?"

"Still working on that. We think heightened aggression and faster mental processes. They become...more like him. Temporarily."

I move into the projector's cone of light. "We're out of time. I don't want our teams suspicious. Here's the point. The Chemist terror group has spies within our ranks and he's tearing our country in half while building these Hyper Humans. We have allies. Like PuckDaddy. We have enemies with powerful tools. And we have each other."

"Until Blue-Eyes has us arrested."

I press on. "I'm worried our military's infighting will get worse. Maybe a lot worse. But this group won't get distracted. Eyes on the prize."

"What's our next course of action?"

"Eliminate the Chemist. Or to be more specific, help the Outlaw kill him."

Outcasts

All good things….

…are wild and free
…must come to an end

We are united
We're undivided
We stand together never less
In any weather, a king's a king forever
We are Los Angeles
- The Goon Squad

Greater love has no man than this,
that he lay down his life for his friends - John 15:13

Chapter One
Saturday, December 31. 2018

"Everything is changing," I said. "And it sucks."

Cory grunted noncommittally. His mouth was full of brownie.

Lee raised his cup and said, "Cheers to change, bro! I'm a renaissance man. Adapt or die, baby. That's what I say."

The three of us stood on Lee's front porch, looking at faint stars. Inside his luxurious home, a party raged. He'd invited most of our senior class, and over a hundred kids were inside having a good time. Or pretending.

I wasn't good at pretending.

Besides, it was a sad affair. In addition to being a New Year's Eve bash, it was also a goodbye party. Approximately ten percent of our school's student body had already left for greener pastures. Glendale was simply too close to Downtown. Los Angeles could no longer be called the City of Angels. It was an insane asylum, a jungle, a haunted house.

Technically, most of the seniors graduated two weeks ago. The fall semester ended in mid-December, finals scores posted, and now we had enough credits to warrant our diplomas. Greater Los Angeles guidance counselors were processing graduation applications as rapidly as possible. With this final hurdle cleared, another twenty-five percent of the students would move next week. Maybe more than twenty-five. Rumors were, all Glendale schools could close soon, or at least make attendance optional until this part of southern California became safer. Cory's family was already packed.

My eyes stung.

Everything would've changed anyway. We were legally adults now. But. Something about this felt too abrupt, too scary, too permanent.

A familiar voice came howling out of Lee's open front doors, rising above the revelers. I intensely disliked that voice.

I said, "Can't believe you invited Andy Babington."

"Whatever dude," Lee shot back. "He's legit. His bowl game was televised on ESPN, and he threw two touchdowns. His baller status lends this party credibility."

"I was pretty good at football too," I grumbled, scuffing stone steps with my shoe. Cory thumped me on the shoulder, and gave me a nod of encouragement.

Lee continued, "Besides. S'not like I could invite the *Outlaw*, you know, Chase?"

"That guy is over-rated," I grinned.

"Noooooooo he's not, you shut up, dude. Never know. Maybe the Outlaw got my invitation."

"Nope."

"Maybe he did, bro."

"Nope."

"It'd be so cool if he showed up!"

"He won't. He's a punk," I said.

"Maybe. Any minute."

"No chance."

"ComeondudetheOutlawrules!!"

"I told you. He's lame. Never goes to parties."

Cory ruffled my hair and indicated the sidewalk. "Shorty fly, man. Yo' girl make it hard for a brother to stay pure."

Shorty. My girl.

Katie Lopez. Was here.

And my heart began to beat again.

The school where her mother taught had been temporarily commandeered by the government and transformed into a shelter. Katie was working there over Christmas break as an in-take receptionist for the displaced. She came straight from the shelter to Lee's party, wearing a tight skirt, tank-top, and carrying her flip-flops. Her brown hair was up, and I loved her so much.

"Hi boyfriend," she beamed.

"Katie, you're so freaking hot, dude!" Lee burst. He couldn't help himself. I knew the feeling. "I love your Instagram videos. So fly. And then, when you and Chase started hooking up, you *realized* you *are* hot and it made you even hotter, yo!"

"Thank you, Lee. I'm here to dance! Who's coming with me?"

She took Cory and Lee by their arms and pulled them after her. I followed my friends inside, down into the spacious main level, now a multi-colored and flashing dance floor where Katie posed for pictures with classmates.

Katie and I hadn't seen each other much recently. She worked non-stop at the shelter, and I helped Dad and the local law enforcement deliver emergency supplies. They gave me an official yellow vest and everything.

I tried to see Katie at night, but my other occupation kept me busy after dark. She understood. Cause she's the best. Two days ago she received her acceptance letter to Stanford University, her first choice. She'd probably get part of her tuition paid for, too. I wish she'd chosen a college away from all big cities and all maniacs.

Maniacs like the Infected.

Maniacs like me.

"There he is!" Andy roared.

Andy Babington is Glendale royalty, a high-profile athlete since elementary school. He just finished a very successful season playing college football at Fresno State. He and I had been teammates and enemies during his senior year at Hidden Spring, and we still not-so-secretly hated each other.

He draped an arm around my shoulder and breathed foul beer into my face. "There's the champ!"

"I watched your bowl game, Babington. You played well."

"Yeah," he laughed. So did a few of his buddies. "Yeah. I did. But you. *You!* You had a good year too." He pointed with a finger that pressed into my cheek. "You're not bad after all!"

"Uh huh."

"I think my brother is better than you. Unnerstand? But your season was good too."

"Uh huh."

Across the room, Katie caught my eye and grinned. I winked, and then lost her in the pulsating crowd.

He belched and said, "But I heard. I heard. I heard you're not playing in college."

I shrugged.

He said, "Good idea, sport. You'd get killed. I mean, totally killed."

"Yikes."

"You have the arm strength. Remember that? You're a nobody but wow! You can throw! Almoss' far as me! But you need to be a leader in college. Like, you know. You get it. A real leader. But you're jus' a kid. Unnerstand? Jus' a squirt. A nobody." I disentangled from his arm and pushed into the crowd. He shouted at my back, but I ignored him. "A nobody!"

As always, Katie danced in the middle of the crowd and she became its heart. She moved to the drums, strong, slender legs pumping, hips twisting, smile infectious, capturing the partiers inside her radiating joy, and I marveled again that this goddess had chosen me.

I am the Outlaw, trouble-maker extraordinaire, a globally recognized firebrand, beloved or vilified depending on the day, Time Magazine's Person of the Year, Los Angeles's masked avenger, and definitely undeserving of Katie Lopez.

After a few minutes, I joined the dance.

"About time, handsome!" she called above the throbbing music.

"Just enjoying the view."

"Close your eyes!" she laughed, our fingers lacing. "Listen to the beat and dance stupid, like no one can see you!"

So we did, with Cory and Lee, four friends colliding and laughing with closed eyes. For sixty minutes pretending like the world wasn't caving in. Like a madman didn't have full control of downtown Los Angeles. Like we were normal and happy.

During the final slow song, Katie grabbed handfuls of my shirt and tugged me close. Her mouth was hot in my ear. "You're wearing the cologne I bought you. I wish this dance would never end, mi novio."

"Except for all these people staring, my love."

"You're right. I want you. And I can't have you with these spectators watching."

"Maybe Lee can electrocute them all."

She snickered into my shirt and began nipping at my neck, small playful bites. "Grow for me, Outlaw. I like it when you swell. Get taller so your shirt rips."

"No," I laughed and gently pushed her mouth away. "Clothes are expensive. Plus, it's not time. People can't see me do that. Not yet."

Her resplendent face clouded a shade. "Soon?"

I nodded. Soon. Soon the world would discover Chase Jackson's dark side.

She sighed, "All will change then."

"It already has."

"You're still mine. Mine alone. But soon I'll be forced to share Chase Jackson with seven billion others."

"I'll always be yours alone."

"Let's never tell the world."

"The world is going to figure it out. Sooner or later. Regardless of what we do."

"Later, then. I covet my time with the world's savior."

At that instant, our hushed conversation was interrupted by screaming. Not the usual party screams; these were horrified cries. The crowd, over a hundred bodies, surged backwards like a tide. Katie and I fought against it, pushing towards the noise.

I smelled the nightmare before I saw it; the sharp bite of gasoline.

Hannah Walker.

The cheerleader was here, dressed in tight white linen pants and a white linen tunic. She wore no shoes. Her hair was a shock of short blond pixie spikes. Her limbs were rangy and strong, and she held Andy Babington by the throat.

Uh oh.

My fellow students freaked. The dead's come back to life! They stampeded into far corners, eyes wide, trampling each other.

Hannah, a beautiful and popular cheerleader during her time at Hidden Spring High, was dead. At least that's what the world assumed. I wept at her funeral, same as everybody else.

Unbeknownst to us, she'd been essentially murdered and remade by a mad physician. Not dead. During the previous couple months she made a handful of public appearances but no one realized it was the deceased Hannah Walker.

Her secret was certainly out now, however.

She was insane. She was Infected and impossibly strong. She could set herself on fire and endure the flames. And she was here for me.

Her eyes calmly inspected the multi-hued chaos. Andy struggled in vain, his tiptoes scrapping against the hardwood. Her grip was iron. He had ten or fifteen seconds left before losing consciousness.

Katie stopped me with hands on my chest.

"Let me go to her!" she shouted above the screams. "You stay!"

"*What?!*"

"You go outside and wait! Only come back if I need you!"

"No way."

She asked, "Where is Samantha??"

"Off somewhere with Puck!"

"This could be *bad!* She's here for Chase Jackson. If Chase isn't here, she might leave!"

"I can get her outside."

"And maybe hurt a hundred people! Let me try first! Please! I don't want the world to see what you can do. Not yet."

I hesitated.

She shouted, "Plus! We don't want Hannah to know…who you are. I'll stop her. Now go!"

I didn't go. But I did hide behind a corner, so I could watch. My stomach knotted and my hands shook. Her reasoning was sound, but I would take Hannah's head off if she threatened Katie.

She fought her way past terrified classmates. "Hannah!" she cried. "Hannah Walker!"

Hannah turned her cold eyes on Katie, and I nearly fainted. I squeezed the corner so hard the wall broke beneath my fingers.

Katie touched her. She took Hannah's face into her hands. "Hannah Walker. Do you remember me? I'm here. Katie. Katie Lopez." Katie was emotional. I didn't blame her. Tears spilled out of her eyes. "Hannah, sweetie? Can you hear me?"

Hannah spoke. "Katie Lopez." Her voice was a harsh rasp, painful syllables.

"Yes! Hannah, I thought you were dead. Do you remember me?"

"Katie. Lopez. I remember."

I whispered, "No. Hannah no. Please don't remember everything." Not everything!

Hannah's eyes whipped up and she scanned the room. Did she hear me?

"Hannah, sweetheart, can you let Andy go? You're hurting him." Katie had one hand on Hannah's face and the other on her arm. Hannah's face was a melted and rebuilt version of her former self. Still beautiful, but now waxen and stretched. "Hannah? Let go?"

"I remember him," she angrily indicated Andy. Andy was turning blue.

"Hannah, hold my hand. Please release his neck. Let him go and hold my hand. Hannah. Hannah now."

All our classmates huddled against walls, creating a circle around the two girls and Andy. No one breathed, including me. Pop music still throbbed.

Hannah threw the college quarterback with a flick of her wrist. He landed in the crowd, bowling over several seniors. She watched emotionlessly. Then she cradled Katie's cheek with her hand. I wanted to scream.

"Katie," she whispered.

"Yes." Katie's voice wavered. Her Latina accent was stronger because of the stress. "Your friend Katie. Do you remember? We were friends?"

"Where is Chase?"

"We were friends," Katie repeated desperately. Hannah appeared to be teetering on the edge of sanity, the edge of detachment and anger. "Do you remember being friends with me?"

"You are here."

"I am here, Hannah."

"The beautiful Latina girl."

"You're so sweet, Hannah. We were friends. *Are* friends."

"Chase's...friend. I was always jealous. And angry."

"We used to give each other advice about boys! Do you remember?"

"You were there, Katie. My last night. You were there."

By now a dozen kids had called the police. We had a very limited amount of time. I should probably text my father, the senior police officer on the Hyper Humanity Apprehension Team, but I didn't want him here. Hannah would kill him. Easily.

I wonder how many kids were recording this on their phones.

"I was there, Hannah. You were so brave. We went together."

Hannah said, "You were there. The fire. Where is Chase?"

"I'm glad you're here. Can we go for a walk?"

"Katie." She quit looking at the room and she locked her eyes on my girlfriend. Her voice was a scrape of steel. "Where. Is. Chase."

"Chase is not here."

"I smell him."

"Chase left, sweetie. He was here earlier."

"I get lost," Hannah said, and her voice broke. She dropped to a crouch, unable to support herself. Her face crumpled, and she spoke in strange sobs. Katie knelt and held her. "I can't find my house. I can't find him. I don't remember. So tired. So much fire."

"Don't be sad, sweetie. Sweet Hannah Walker. I can help."

"I followed. Him. Here. His scent."

"Hannah, can you let go of my hand? Please?"

"His house is close. But I don't..."

"My hand? You're hurting me."

"He promised."

"Hannah." Her voice was urgent with pain. "Let go. Now."

She released Katie's hand. I retreated back behind the corner, my heart a jackhammer.

Hannah whispered, "Don't leave. Please."

"I'm not, sweetie." Katie started waving the kids out of the room, using her injured hand. Carefully and quietly the high school students filed onto the back deck or up the stairs to the front door. "Where have you been living?"

"Where ever I want. I sleep a lot. I can smell Chase's cologne."

"Do you remember when we used to eat lunch together?"

"Yes," she laughed, a short rough snicker. "I remember. Before the fire."

"Let's go for a walk, Hannah. Out of this house. Maybe we'll see Chase."

My phone buzzed. PuckDaddy, the world's foremost computer hacker, was calling me. I slipped a bluetooth earpiece into place and answered the call, but I didn't speak. Hannah would hear.

"Chase? Hello?? You there?"

I tapped the earpiece twice.

"Chase? Can you hear me?"

Two more taps.

"Can you speak?"

More taps.

"Okay. I'm tracking these 911 calls and texts. Is Hannah Walker there?? That's what the calls are saying. Samantha is en route, but she's ten minutes away!"

"Hannah," Katie was saying. "Let's move outside."

"No."

"Hannah, let's go for a walk? You and me."

"No."

"I want to. It'll be fun. It's a nice night."

"He is here, Katie."

"Who?" Katie asked, growing frantic. "Andy? Andy is here, but you don't need him. Chase might be outside."

I stood near a wall of bookshelves. I retrieved two heavy metal bookends, projectiles in case I needed them.

"Katie," Hannah gasped. "Are you lying?"

"Hannah-"

"You're lying, Katie."

I moved into the room, ready to throw. Enough of this.

Hannah stood abruptly, facing the open front door, facing away from me. I heard it too. Sirens. The sudden move knocked Katie over.

"Katie, did you call police?"

"What? No, Hannah. I don't have my phone with me."

"We are friends, Katie. I will come back if I can."

Hannah *Moved*. She went through the front door, a white streak, a phantom, and the students screamed.

I rushed to Katie. "Are you okay?? Are you hurt?"

"No." She was still on the ground, crying. She flexed her fingers. "I'm fine. Nothing broken. That was *scary*."

"What??" Puck blurted in my ear. "Is Katie alright?? What happened?!"

I said, "That was incredible, Katie. So brave. I about hyperventilated."

She smiled weakly and touched my face. "Some secrets are worth keeping."

The distant sound of cars crashing came through the front doors. I bounded the stairs and slid to a stop on the stone walkway in the front yard. Lights flashed two blocks away, turning the night blue and red. Three cop cars were parked in the intersection. One smashed in, like it'd been stepped on by a giant. Or an angry cheerleader.

"She's gone," I said.

Puck asked in my ear, "Who is? Hannah?"

"Yes."

"Hey Nobody," Andy Babington called. He staggered onto the lawn, holding his throat. "She was here for *you*, freak. Where were you? Way to let your stupid girlfriend do the work."

"She saved your life, Andy. So close your mouth." I walked back inside to fetch Katie and take her home.

"You're an idiot, Jackson. I hate you. You ruin everything."

Well. He wasn't wrong.

Chapter Two
Tuesday, January 3. 2019

Hannah Walker, the pretty white girl from Glendale who died in the Compton fires, was alive and at-large. Although media outlets were overrun with wild stories and viewers grew somewhat numb to this bizarre new world, the Hannah Walker reappearance story dominated headlines, largely because she made a beautiful page one photo. Students were interviewed. Photographs examined. Puzzle pieces put together, and the conclusion reached that she had been the football mutant's attacker in November. She had somehow survived the fire, and now she roamed free.

"Dad stationed a patrol car in front of our house," I reported.

"Doesn't matter. Not enough." Samantha Gear shook her head. "You need to move."

"I don't want to move."

"She knows where you live, Chase. Well, kinda. Even if she forgot, she'll locate it again."

"I wish you'd just find her."

She growled, "I've tried. Tracked her everywhere. That scent of hers is hard to miss. Followed her for miles, but she slips away. Like she knows I'm coming."

Samantha Gear is striking. Like most Infected, she's ramrod straight and muscular. She is pretty the way an eagle is pretty. Her hair is short in a style that Katie once identified as a bob. She's also one of the most dangerous people alive.

We were sitting on leather captain chairs inside PuckDaddy's futuristic mobile headquarters. He'd purchased the nicest RV money can buy and invested another $300,000 transforming it into a rolling computer lab, constantly utilizing local wifi hotspots, ten different cellular signals and direct satellite feed. He paid four drivers to shuttle him around America. They worked in pairs, a week at a time, swapping shifts every twelve hours, paid so handsomely they never questioned the arrangement. From this data hub, Puck monitored and accessed all the digital earth.

He rarely used the bed, spending twenty-four hours a day at his machines. They brought him sanity, he explained. He slept once every four days, habitually in his chair. Only one time in two years had he ventured outside his RV, and that was to eat Thanksgiving dinner with us. Being away from his computers had visibly drained him and he returned after two hours.

Puck's legs were gone, starting at mid-thigh. He still hadn't explained. He sat on a swivel chair inside a cone of technology. Four keyboards, each with two monitors, at his fingertips. Above the eight computer monitors were ten television sets, tuned to news programs or security camera feeds. He could type on different keyboards with each hand while watching television. He was Infected, and the disease manifested itself in this bizarre fashion.

Samantha and I watched live satellite camera feed on the big screen television above our chairs. We could see the entire military barricade surrounding Downtown. Highway 101 and the Five bristled with patrolling jeeps and machine-gun checkpoints. This enemy-occupied territory was unlike Compton, which had been an entire city's populace taken hostage. Downtown Los Angeles was largely evacuated before the Chemist and his forces moved in. Instead of a hundred thousand captives allowed to freely roam the streets and live their lives, five thousand hostages were stashed in the towers and held at gunpoint.

The Chemist, an Infected terrorist and madman, had attempted demolishing the Downtown spires. His plans had been foiled by a devilishly handsome, swashbuckling high school senior in a wing-suit. And his cohorts. Almost simultaneously, the people of Compton had united and heaved out the enemy occupying forces, nonviolently freeing themselves from the terrorists.

Suddenly homeless and foiled, the Chemist had moved in and populated Downtown with his thousands of followers and Chosen. Now the city was a jungle, chiefly without power except for scattered generators. Commercial towers transformed into castles. Apartments into battlements. Entire streets were caved in, the 777 Tower was a pile of rubble, huge gashes ripped the surfaces of almost every high-rise, fires burned at random, and actual tigers prowled the alleys. But worst were the Chosen. They climbed buildings, screamed like howler monkeys, stalked the streets, and repelled invaders. He manufactured hundreds, and was adding to the number every day.

The American military conducted strategic airstrikes on targets they deemed safe from collateral damage, but there was no evidence the attacks hampered the enemy.

Despite being only seven feet from us, Puck's voice came through our earpieces. "Almost there."

Samantha replied, "Roger that." The RV rocked and hummed through south LA, near Inglewood.

I said, "Puck told me where you've been sleeping."

Samantha scoffed, "Good for you."

"You can sleep *inside* our house, you know."

"I won't do much good if I'm inside. And asleep."

"You don't sleep?"

She didn't answer.

"You stay awake the whole night??" I cried.

She scowled. "If you moved, I wouldn't have to stand guard. Too many people want to destroy you, and you're easily accessible."

"Who wants to destroy me? Hannah? Hannah loves me," I countered.

"Hannah wants no one else to have you, moron. She's insane and she'd kill you without blinking. ...not even sure she *can* blink."

"Who else are you guarding against?"

"Tank."

"He's in jail."

She shook her head. "Not for long. And the Chemist will find you sooner or later. You need to move."

Puck reported, "One mile out."

I asked, "Where would I move?"

She shrugged. "Don't care. Somewhere else. Richard needs to move too."

"Don't call my father Richard."

"Richard could move into my truck, now that I think about it."

"I will vomit. Directly into your lap."

She grinned. "What? My truck's cabin is comfortable! Two people could sleep in it. If we got creative."

"Samantha. I'm serious."

"It'd be nice and hot. Wouldn't even need the heater."

Before she could react, I undid the clasp on her shoulder holster. She caught the leather harness as it slipped but the movement distracted her; I put my hand under her hamstring and flipped her off the chair. She landed on her back with an angry grunt.

She hissed, "I *hate* how fast you are."

"Don't talk about my dad then, you big whore."

"Chase!" she laughed. "You may NOT call your future mother a whore." She stood and brushed herself off while I debated throwing her from the moving vehicle.

"Hey guys," Puck called. I heard his voice from his techno-cage and from the speaker in my ear. "Check this out. I'm putting it on screen."

The television changed to a different satellite picture. This video feed was zoomed in on an intersection inside enemy territory. An interesting conflict was developing. Chemist gunmen and Chosen were arguing about something we couldn't hear, but we could see them bickering.

"Five armed gunmen," Samantha said, indicating figures with her finger. "Three Chosen, I think. Wish we could hear them."

Puck groaned, "I know. It's like we live in the stone age."

I said, "The guy with the shaved head is the boss. Right?"

"Appears so. But they aren't happy with him."

"There's an inherent hierarchy within the Chemist's chaos. A method to his madness," I mused.

"I want to know how the chain of command is enforced," Samantha said, her mouth a grim line. "Who gets promoted. Who doesn't. How it's identified. And how discipline is administered."

"I don't think it's that complicated. I think it happens organically."

"That's what Carter says," she grunted. "But I want proof."

That got my attention. "Carter contacted you?"

"Twice so far. Just a general update."

"I thought he cut ties."

"Carter is in the business of resources and information. You and I are one of the many moving pieces on his chessboard. I think he sees me now like he once saw Martin. Not an ally, but not an enemy. A professional acquaintance."

"How does he see me?"

"As a threat. A ticking time bomb. If the Chemist captures you, the world will never be the same. Carter knows that. Plus, you're one of two or three people on earth capable of killing Carter."

"Are you capable?"

"No. I lose that fight ninety-nine times out of a hundred."

"How do you know?"

She shrugged. "Just do."

Puck called, "Agreed."

"See, that's how I think his Chosen work." I pointed at the intersection on screen. "They just *know* who's the strongest. And might makes right in their world. The Chemist allows them to toil autonomously because he built them with a...constitutional need to obey the powerful. The strongest is in charge, like in the wild."

"What do you mean 'built them'?"

"He told me he put his DNA inside those tigers. He's doing something other than just squirting his blood into people's veins. I think he's altered the virus. He wants the Chosen to be more...obedient."

She was scowling in thought, her bright eyes intense. "Infected are not obedient."

"Exactly! Carter has a mutiny on his hands because his Infected co-workers hate following orders. Plus, remember Carla? She wasn't obedient to the Chemist. Infected don't obey. But his Chosen do."

She sucked on her bottom lip a moment. "The disease interacts with us differently, the same way a common cold affects individuals with different symptoms. You're suggesting the virus gives us different levels of power, and the Chemist altered the disease cocktail so his new creations will inherently assume their place in a hierarchy? Without even being aware of it?"

"Otherwise they'd attack each other. We Infected don't like being around our own kind. Somehow, he solved this problem with the new ones."

"If might makes right then, because of your freakish power, wouldn't you be their natural leader? Or Tank? Damn, imagine how they'll react around Tank."

"They hate me. Attack me on sight. So Chosen don't obey everyone stronger than they are. The Chemist had a trigger which made the tigers attack me and no one else. Maybe he's doing the same thing with them?"

"Hannah Walker didn't attack the Outlaw. She seemed disinterested with you, on top of the tower."

"I think her mind is broken beyond tinkering. We're just lucky she couldn't smell Chase Jackson up there in the swirling winds."

Samantha shuffled restlessly in her chair. "So how does the Chemist make new Chosen obedient to him but hate you?"

"No idea."

She said, "None of this explains why Infected aren't repelled by you. We're drawn to you."

"Must be a rare side-effect. Watch, here comes another Chosen."

On screen, another girl approached the argument, which was now bordering on violence. The girl was small with dark hair. Possibly east Asian. She clearly had the disease inside her. A thousand attributes screamed it, even at this distance.

The men noticed her and stopped. She was the only girl. They backed away. We couldn't hear the conversation, but she was shouting. She gestured. They obeyed.

"Do you see?" I whispered. "The disease is stronger in her. They feel it."

"I see."

"She's the smallest, but the most powerful. She's naturally in charge, until a bigger and stronger animal comes along."

She chuckled. "You might be onto something, Outlaw."

PuckDaddy interrupted our thoughts. "Contact," he announced. "Samantha, your motion sensors detected movement and I confirmed with the camera. Target is coming up the corridor. Right on schedule."

"Roger that," she said. "Let's move."

"Girl, you KNOW I love it when you talk all tactical!"

I pulled my mask into place.

Puck's vehicle rolled to a stop and we jumped into a hidden alley. We were beyond the border of the Chemist's southern boundary, near the unfinished SoLA Village South Tower. We climbed the steel skeleton five hundred feet into the air as quickly as possible.

Other than the war zone, southern California is beautiful. The sky is an infinite blue, cool and crisp, and the distant ocean sparkles with sunlight. Ahead of us, the San Gabriel Mountains were tipped with winter snows.

Los Angeles International Airport was shut down. Zero air traffic. The Chemist had destroyed multiple pipelines, resulting in oil shortages. Gas was twenty dollars a gallon. All modes of transportation were struggling, not just air travel. Even the military cut back.

Lee finished Samantha Gear's vest two weeks ago. It was just like mine, complete with parachute and wings, except hers didn't have red Outlaw stitching. He practically hyperventilated while measuring her.

Puck spoke into our ears, "Military cameras spotted you two on the tower."

I replied, "Let them watch. I'm wearing my mask and Samantha is tired of hiding."

Soon we'd be forced to clarify which military we referred to. The American government (including armed forces) was split straight down the middle, being pulled apart by Chemist followers, including Blue-Eyes, the beautiful girl controlling Washington. Skirmishes erupted daily on military bases.

America was reeling. So was the world. And the culprit may or may not be sitting in the city below us, pumping more blood with impunity.

But we weren't here for him.

We *Jumped* and deployed wings, causing us to fall forward instead of downward. Our enemies could see us if they glanced towards the southern horizon. I hoped they saw. I wanted them afraid. To know the Outlaw stalked them. To give hope to the hostages. Samantha and I streaked east at a hundred miles per hour, released the wings and free fell out of sight.

The Alameda Corridor was a sparkling new railway system, connecting Downtown residents to Long Beach and the whole Pacific Ocean. A few months ago the train had shuttled thousands back and forth each day. Now it was useless, an empty passage twisting through Greater Los Angeles on raised platforms and through underground trenches. It was vacant. Except for the Priest and a small detachment of his cult, silently exploiting this ignored ingress into Downtown.

A bizarre religion was gaining notoriety. The worshipers proclaimed the Outlaw a deity, and they built a church and sanctuary for his adorers just north of Los Angeles. A man called The Priest headed the cult. A charismatic radical hellbent on causing trouble. He and small groups of followers kept sneaking into the Chemist's territory, sometimes with disastrous results.

We floated on parachutes above the zealots as they neared the end of the Alameda Corridor. They never looked up, so focused were they on potential dangers ahead. I gave the signal to Samantha. We retracted our parachutes and landed in their midst.

The rabble screamed and scattered. This was the first I'd seen them up close; men and women wearing dirty black vests and red Outlaw masks. Of the twenty, half had rods slung over their backs, cheap imitations of my powerful Thunder Stick (a stupid nickname Samantha thought up- I couldn't think of a better one). The other half had pistols.

On reflex, one of them fired a .22 at me. The bullet clanked harmlessly against my vest. I didn't even feel it. Their eyes widened further.

I pointed a finger at them. They cowered and trembled. "Bad news. Time to renounce your religion. I am a man with a disease," I told them. "Not a god. God wouldn't dress like this."

"Mighty Outlaw," came their cries. Some hit their knees. "Subjugate us in your mercy!"

"We seek to serve!"

"We seek your favor!"

"We only live to fulfill your will!"

I groaned. "Go home! I can't even legally drink."

"Bestow upon us your touch of blessing, inasmuch as you blessed the Priest!"

They were crying. Crying!

Samantha was already gone. So was their leader, the Priest.

"Supercalifragilisticexpialidocious!" I shouted. "Would a deity say that? No! Go back down the tracks and go home."

I *Jumped*. They screamed again. Ugh.

I rendezvoused with Samantha in the abandoned Coca-Cola Bottling building on Central Avenue. I found her upstairs in a ransacked meeting room. She hung a battery-powered lantern in the corner. The Priest struggled on the long table, his hands tied behind his back, a bag over his head.

She grinned. "I remember when Carter and I did this to you. I thought you were going to kill us both."

"My memory of it is less fond," I grumbled.

She broke the bonds with a knife thrust and yanked the Priest's bag off. He scrambled to his feet on top of the table.

The Priest was a handsome guy. He was tan, thin, had a strong jaw and a popular side-parted haircut worn by soccer players. His eyes blazed and he shoved his pointer finger into my face.

"You forget your place, apostate!"

"Better pull your finger back if you want to keep it," I growled.

Wisely, he did. "How dare you touch me," he sneered. "You defile me with your hypocrisy."

"Hypocrisy? Don't you worship me?"

"Worship a fallen idol? Pfah!"

Samantha apparently thought this was hilarious. She giggled and said, "Your worshipers hate you, Outlaw! What kind of god are you?!"

I glared at the Priest and admitted, "I am confused."

"Of course you are," he snapped, staring down his nose at me. I wish he

31

wasn't towering over my head. "Because you've turned your back on the truth."

"Your religion is based on my deification. I'm here to show you that I'm human. Like you."

"Our belief system is not contingent on you in the least," he said dismissively. His eyes were feverish. "I permit the lesser minded to worship you as a bolster to their faith until they mature. I hold out hope for your repentance, but we follow the truth. Not a sham. Not a puppet."

"Yeah. Well. Whatever. Stop using my name."

"I can no longer stop championing the truth than I could stop breathing."

Samantha dropped into a swivel chair and said, "Just curious, oh mighty Priest, but what is this truth?"

"The triumph of goodness and purity, and the downfall of arrogance and evil." He spoke to her over his shoulder, like she was not worth looking at.

"Sounds good to me. You and I are on the same page there, at least," I said.

"No we are not. You are a dissenter. A heretic who fell from your once prominent place." He lashed me with his words like a whip. I felt guilty but I didn't know why.

"What did I do? Why did I fall?"

Samantha stifled more laughter.

"You are not strong enough and gave yourself over to desires. We seek the Fire Angel now. Heaven's true Avenger."

"The Fire Angel?"

Samantha said, "I bet he means Hannah."

"Oh no," I shook my head. "Trust me. You don't want none of that mess. She's crazy."

"Jesus Christ seemed crazy during his day too."

"Yeah, but…he's Jesus."

"I am leaving now. I have a flock in need of a shepherd. But I will pray for you."

Samantha said, "You'll leave when we let you, Jesus."

The Priest pulled out a small black device from his stylish brown trench coat. I didn't like it. His thumb was on a red button. "I am leaving now. Else

I'll fill the room with electricity and we'll see if you are deities or not."

"We're NOT deities," I groaned. "That's the whole point! And what *is* that thing?"

Samantha stood up slowly, no longer laughing.

"This is an electric grenade. A device to protect us from false gods. Such as yourselves."

I looked at Samantha. "Electric grenade. Is that a real thing?"

"Dunno. Hope not."

"Listen, you stupid zealot," I growled. "Stop coming into the city. Innocent people are getting killed or captured. The Chemist is turning your followers into Chosen."

"They go willingly. They become moles. Informants. Saboteurs. There is much you do not know."

"No they don't. They become animals. Slaves. Stay in your compound and worship your Avengers there. Better yet, send your followers away. And stop using my name."

He locked eyes with me and for an instant I understood his growing infamy. He had a presence. A gravitas, a magnetic and feverish conviction.

"It's not too late for you," he whispered. "Repent. Find your conviction. Find your faith."

"I don't know what that meeeeeeeans!"

He hopped down from the table, brandished the electric grenade to stop Samantha's advance, and disappeared through the dark doorway.

I said, "I don't understand what just happened."

"You need to get control of your worshipers."

"He didn't seem to be worshipping me, Shooter," I pointed out.

"I don't blame him. Your zipper's down."

Chapter Three
Thursday, January 4. 2019.
Tank

"Food!"

I didn't move. Just stared at the ceiling.

"Big guy, you hungry? Chow time."

Still didn't move. Even though I was famished.

The short-haired girl had suggested starvation. The girl with guns. Keep him hungry. Keep him weak, she said. They took her advice.

I'm going to break her neck.

"Alright, big fella. I'll leave the food tray in your cart. Pull it through when you're hungry. Doc says you need to keep putting the cream on your face." He left.

I liked him. He started last week. Government's recent strategy, because the old one didn't work.

They want my blood. They need samples. Couldn't get the needles into my skin when I first arrived, so the short-haired girl told them to calm me down.

Don't feed him. Take the blood when he's asleep.

She's a dead woman.

They tried. Tried everything to knock me out. Tried gases. Didn't work; not even woozy. Tried shooting me with electricity, but I'm too fast. They don't dare come in here with me. They stay behind their electrified steel. I would break them, otherwise.

I'm at the Federal Correction Institute, near the Navy base. Locked in a cage inside a big room. I can hear the ocean through my one window. All four walls and the ceiling of my cage are steel bars carrying electrical currents. Smart. But they made it too big, gave me too much room to move.

It's dangerous. Guards are terrified of the bars. They won't get close to them. Neither will I. Electricity hurts. So does fire.

They want my blood. Study it. Figure out why I'm a freak. Diagnose me. Use me to diagnose the girl on fire. Diagnose the Outlaw.

My new handler is nice. Nice cop. Maybe that'll work. Last guy was the bad cop. I killed him. He got too close to the bars and I tossed my drink at him. The water splashed through the bars and connected with his face, transferring current for that single instant.

That was a good day.

I sat up in bed. So tired.

My bed is a standard size, not big enough for me. I barely sleep. Starving.

Miss my parents. They half-heartedly pursue legal ways to release me, but they're not sure what to think. I'm a freak. They're humiliated. Visited me once.

Miss Katie. She sent me a letter. And a care package with chocolate.

Katie. She'll be mine again one day. The Outlaw controls her somehow. Poisons her against me. But he won't be around much longer. Going to put my thumbs into his ears and squeeze until they connect in the middle. My body always relaxes with the thought of his death. Plotting his death is like meditation.

I dragged myself out of the tiny bed and walked across the cold concrete. The eight-foot high bars were only twelve inches above my head. They crackled with power and tingled my skin.

I sat down with an exhausted grunt at the cage's door and tugged on the string. A small wooden cart with wooden wheels rolled towards me, bringing food. Chicken and rice and juice.

Eating less than two thousand calories a day. I need over twice that. Maybe three times. The short-haired girl told them my body burns more calories

35

than normal, even for a big guy like me. Don't starve him but keep him weak, she said.

I've wondered what I'd do at full strength. Bust through the floor? It's possible. Charge and go through the bars? Wouldn't kill me. But I'd have to wake up before the other guards arrived.

Always one guard here. He stared at me from his stool, near the room's entrance. Maybe at my face, which will bear horrible scars forever. Maybe at my bulk, which is impressive.

They told me I'm the most famous prisoner alive. News vans park outside. So they said. They want to help. So they said. Interviews. Doctors. If I'd just cooperate.

I ate the food. Not enough. Never enough.

We just want a sample of your blood, they said. What's wrong with that? Give us a sample and we can feed you a little more.

What's wrong with that? I'm pissed, that's what's wrong with that.

I might, though. If I get more food then I could escape.

I lumbered back to bed and collapsed into it. The frame is slowly bending. So tired.

I woke up later that night, in time to see breaking news on CNN. The special was called, 'Opening Communication with Hyper Humanity.'

I knew that man. The man on the screen. The bald one. Pretended to be my doctor. He's got the same freak condition I do. He's on TV?

I sat up. "Officer. Turn the volume up, please."

First time I'd spoken to this particular guard. It startled him. My voice was still strong. He fumbled with the old television set until the volume increased.

"...and are you affiliated with the Outlaw?"

The bald man replied, "I'm not here to answer questions. I have a statement and then I'm leaving."

The text beneath the bald man identified him as 'Carter.' That's what

Chase Jackson had called him too.

Carter continued, "Your situation is more precarious than you realize. The man you call the Chemist is essentially creating biological freaks he can unleash on your population, and it's about to get worse. I've recently obtained proof that he is behind the capture of the world's foremost geneticists and stem cell researchers. Happened two years ago. He's crafting the destruction of the world while you and you government have your head up your ass."

He was being interviewed by a lady off-screen. They were on an airport runway in the dark. Tonight? Right now? She said, "What are-"

"This is a civilization-changer. A world-breaker. A society-collapser. The Chemist is infecting thousands with a disease, altering normal young adults into aggressive and powerful monsters. An army."

"Are you one of these aggressive and powerful people?"

"I'm not like his army. Neither is he. Neither is the Outlaw, we're all different. These new creations aren't as strong as we are. Yet."

"But-"

"Time for me to go. Listen. Listen carefully. The Chemist is a man named Martin Patterson. I know him better than anyone. I know he has multiple saboteurs and moles in every branch of your military and government. I know his tendencies. And I know his goal is to remake our whole damn planet before he dies. You need my help. Hell, you need all the help you can get. I'm willing to consult with your military for thirty days, and then I'll disappear. My price is ten million dollars a day."

The bald man turned and the video ended abruptly.

A visitor was in my room. I hadn't notice his entrance. He thumbed down the volume but continued to stare thoughtfully at the screen. The guard had disappeared.

My visitor was grotesquely thin. Old. Long gray hair tied in a ponytail. Wearing a long trench coat and leaning on a staff.

I heard him say, "Good for you, my old friend. Though you sell yourself short. You're worth more than that. Should have asked ten times that amount."

I stood up. I knew this man. But even if I didn't, all the hairs on my body still stood on end. Like he changed the temperature. Something about him churned something within me. Emotions long dormant flared to life. I hated him. And I loved him.

I growled, "Chemist."

He turned to face me. "Call me Martin."

"No."

"I'm glad Carter forwent cigarettes for his interview. Appearances are important, you realize." He turned back to watch the silent television. "That should stir things up. But I wonder just how many informants he can identify?" He spoke softly to himself. I didn't interrupt. This man was dangerous, despite his feeble appearance. My hands shook with the thought of hurting him. "A worthy opponent," he whispered, and then turned to face me. "What did you think of his statement?"

"Don't know. Don't care."

"Ah yes. Of course. Ogres can't think. Yes? You're just muscle?" He lowered himself carefully onto the stool. "Just a giant in full bloom."

"Why are you here?"

"I watched the videos, you know. Of Hannah attacking you on the football field." He smiled, indulging in my pain.

I'd seen the news. I knew the girl on fire was a cheerleader from Hidden Spring High come back from the dead and crashing parties.

The Chemist said, "I made her. Created her anew. Isn't she breath-taking?"

"Not the word I'd choose."

"Her skin can absorb small amounts of gasoline, and then burn like a torch for short periods of time. A fascinating side-effect. Unfortunately her hair always gets consumed in the flames, but her eyes and lungs and sinuses are impervious now. The virus is truly astonishing, yes?"

"I know nothing about it. No one has told me a thing."

"Well, truth be told, Ogre, we know very little. Even me. I just inject my subjects with it, and then tinker with their bodies while the virus burns. It's actually not even a virus. We just call it that. It works; that is enough."

"Why are you here, old man?"

"For your blood."

I shook my head. "You can't have it."

"Yes. Yes I can. You see, dear Ogre, I don't care if you live. If I must, I'll murder you in your cage and *then* get the blood. We can do either."

"Why do you want it?"

He shrugged. "You're a genetic abnormality, even without the disease. You're an outlier. A giant. A beautiful one. And I require your DNA for a project."

"What project?"

"It's a secret."

"Release me and you can have my blood peacefully."

"Forgive me, but I'd prefer you dead, in fact. I cannot control you. I'm not here to bargain with a man behind bars."

"Release me and you can have my blood *and* the secret identity of the Outlaw."

His breath caught. His face was already pale, but what color he did possess drained away. He gripped his staff with both hands.

"You possess this information?" he asked. His voice wavered pathetically, like he was faint.

"Yes."

"A former colleague told me the Outlaw attended Hannah's memorial service but there were hundreds of mourners. I couldn't divine his identity from the photographs."

I nodded. "I'm sure he was there."

"Do you know where he is now?"

"No. I'm in a cage, old man. How would I know? But I know his name. And his address."

He shifted in excitement and his eyes were wild. "I'm surprised you couldn't use this information to bargain with your captors."

"I tried. They weren't interested. I think he's got guys protecting him from the inside."

"Fascinating. Some of your jailers know the Outlaw's identity, and they aren't blabbing? He is truly the most remarkable man. Such loyalty! How does he do that?"

"Don't know. Don't care."

"We have a deal. You provide me blood and a name. In exchange, I provide you freedom."

I arched an eyebrow.

He smiled and said, "You can trust me, Ogre. No foul play. I am a gentleman. I *promise*."

"The Outlaw's name is Chase Jackson. He's a senior at Hidden Spring High. Now let me out."

Chapter Four
Friday, January 5. 2019

Someone pounded on my front door. Then did it again. And again.

I groaned and rolled out of bed. Nine in the morning. Too early for visitors, especially near the end of Christmas vacation. Probably Samantha. She wanted me to start jogging. I was going to throw the couch at her.

I stumbled down our townhouse's two flights of stairs to the main floor, full of sunlight and the remnant fragrance of Dad's coffee. I opened the door. Special Agent Isaac Anderson stood there, looking like a winded and worried FBI Captain America.

"Hey FBI," I grunted. "It's early. Come back later."

"Chase, pack your bags. We gotta go. Now."

"Aw, why? I haven't even had breakfast-"

I paused. Isaac Anderson was…here. At Chase Jackson's house. Not at the *Outlaw's* house. At Chase Jackson's house.

I observed, "You just called me Chase."

"I've known your identity for several weeks. I tracked you, but never told anyone. Get your stuff."

"Wha-"

He blurted, "Tank's loose. The Chemist freed him from his cell last night."

My heart turned cold. "Katie. Tank will try to see her again."

The world came crashing in. I had noticed sirens in the distance. Helicopter blades beating.

He said, "Even worse, a large force of Hyper Terrorists broke through the military's barricade fifteen minutes ago. Chosen. We're trying to track them, but they're fast. My guess is they are coming here. Soon"

I woke up in a hurry. Coming here. That meant the Chemist discovered my name. Tank must have told him. And my address. And now his Chosen were on the way.

Last autumn, the Chemist threatened to kill Katie in front of me. "I'll pack. You get Katie. The Chemist could have used my address to figure out hers."

He pushed me inside and towards the stairs. "I have an agent banging on her door this second, and a helicopter on the way. Let's go, Outlaw, get your gear."

I sprinted up the steps, my focus growing laser-sharp. I needed to alert Samantha. And Dad. Puck must be asleep. I yelled over my shoulder, "Call Shooter! Get her to Katie's place."

"Already done. She's on her way."

"How'd the Chemist get to Tank?

"Bribery, most likely, and three dead guards. Haven't had a chance to investigate."

I located my duffle-bag beneath a pile of clutter and started throwing clothes and Outlaw gear into it. Anderson inspected my bedroom with interest.

I asked, "Where did Tank go, any guesses?"

"Cameras caught him diving into the Los Angeles Harbor and swimming out to sea."

"You'll never get him. He could probably swim to Hawaii."

"He'll have a hard time hiding. Too big."

I froze. Something was…here. I felt it. Smelled it. My skin crawled. The disease inside flared to live, like a dog's hackles rising.

A kid about my age stood in the bedroom doorway, wearing a red windbreaker, jeans, sneakers. He pointed a gun at Special Agent Isaac Anderson's back.

I knew him. In my mind his name was Baby Face. He and I'd met once, six months ago, on the rooftop of Hollywood Presbyterian Medical. He was Infected, in the employ of my enemy.

His eyes were wide and wild, fixed on me. The gun in his hands shook, and his breath came fast and ragged. He didn't have the mental strength for violence.

"Hey kid," I said. My heart had jumpstarted to a thousand beats per minute. I wanted to help him. I wanted to kill him.

Isaac turned, startled. His hand dropped to the pistol on his belt.

"Don't," I warned. "He's faster than you. A lot faster."

Baby Face thumbed back his pistol's hammer. We didn't move. My body had begun swelling. Pants and shirt growing smaller. In another twenty seconds, his bullets would no longer matter. Fury and urgency were hurricanes inside my skull.

I said, "You don't want to do this."

He closed his mouth and pressed his lips into a hard line.

I continued, "I'm leaving. Someone important to me is about to be killed or taken. So I'm going."

He shook his head and tried to speak.

I said, "I want you to come with us. We need you. And you need us."

"Outlaw," he panted. He was sweating, close to tears, battling the same madness as me.

"You don't need him," I said. "You belong with me."

"They're coming," he whispered.

"Who?"

"All of them."

Anderson grunted under his breath, "Oh Christ."

I said, "You're better than them, kid. Come with me."

He shook his head and lowered the gun. "Go. Go now, Outlaw. Someone has to stop him."

"We need your help. You're with us," I said. I pulled the duffle bag strap over my shoulder and picked up the heavy Thunder Stick.

"Run," he said. "And remember me."

Below us, on the first floor, windows shattered. Howls of insanity throttled through hallways.

Anderson snapped a radio to his mouth and shouted, "Enemy on the premises! Requesting air support!"

We egressed onto the rooftop. The Chosen came like a deranged tsunami, sprinting backyards. Hundreds, still thin from their months in a coma, wearing rags, moving faster than humanly possible. They ran in frenzy, trampling the fallen, vaulting cars, screaming.

How did they all know where to go?? The sea of humanity surged over the road and spilled onto lawns.

"Air support is too far. We're trapped," Anderson noted.

"Where's that chopper?"

He pointed eastwards. Above the squat houses and commercial buildings and palm trees, a Black Hawk helicopter was climbing into the sky several minutes away.

Katie's apartment was half a mile north.

I had to shout above the screams. "Stay here! They'll follow me."

"I recommend remaining here. We can keep them off the roof."

"They'll swarm us. Some will be Jumpers. I'm getting Katie. Shoot anything that tries to come through that window."

I *Jumped* and landed in the street, barefoot. Savages poured from my home, disintegrating the front wall. They flipped over Anderson's car. If I didn't move I'd be swept away like a pebble before a wave.

I *Moved*, like an Olympic sprinter on speed with the throttle wide open. The Chosen were fast, but not Outlaw-fast. I raced down the street. Samantha's truck was parked on the grass at Katie's building, and her heavy pistols roared from within.

The Chosen were already there!?

The trap sprang. They fell on me from hidden spots in evergreen trees, all teeth and claws. Screaming and hitting and scratching. Bodies piled on until the sun blacked out. Dozens. The combined weight crushed me. I couldn't get to my feet. No leverage, face first, flat on the earth. My arms were pinned. Higher and higher the mountain climbed. My chest couldn't expand to draw air. The noise was obscene and loud. They bit and tore, white hot pain.

I couldn't hit. Couldn't kick. But I could elbow. I began pumped my arms backwards as far as possible, driving iron elbows into flesh. Harder and harder, faster, farther, like pistons, pulping and moving bodies trapped above me. I cleared space until I could pivot my torso. Finally, a little room. I bucked and shoved at the ground, breaking the human mountain's foundation, carving out a small cave, large enough to barely get my feet underneath my body. I exploded upwards, over and again, like a volcano trying to erupt, my shoulders and skull punishing anyone above me. Bones broke. Flesh surrendered. Finally I reached blue sky and fresh air.

The horde focused blindly on me. The two girls raced unseen to Samantha's truck. Katie still wore her pajamas, pink pants and white tank top, and her hair was tied up. She got behind the wheel and gunned the engine.

"Outlaw, get your ass over here!" Samantha shouted. She climbed into the truck bed and picked up an assault rifle.

I roared and tore free from desperate clawing hands. Leapt clear of the mountain. The masses turned like a singular animal and followed me. Truck wheels boiled into dirt and the vehicle leapt forward. Samantha opened fire. Bursts of three rounds each dropping a human being.

I reached the truck easily. But so did the Chosen. I anchored beside Samantha in the back and wielded the Rod like a sword. Any savage that survived Samantha's murderous hail of bullets met the Boom Stick, solid thumps to their cranium.

I needed to pick and stick with a name. Thunder Stick, maybe. I liked that one.

"Faster!" Samantha called to Katie. Our truck raced out of the suburbs, shedding bodies. The Five was dead ahead, under the distant Hollywood sign. Katie cut across a lawn, ruined a hedge of green boxwoods, and squealed onto the entrance ramp. "Faster!"

We tore onto the Interstate and brought the storm of chaos with us, a black dragon of bodies profaning beautiful Los Angeles. Nearby police sirens wailed. Two helicopters closed.

My phone rang. Somehow, in the midst of mayhem, I heard and felt it. I knocked on the truck cabin's rear window. Katie slid it open and said, "I'm a little busy, handsome."

"Eyes on the road! Phone's for you." I dropped the device onto the passenger chair.

"Who is it?"

"No idea. Might be important. Take a message."

I turned back to the nightmare chasing us, and heard her say, "Hello, this is Katie. Hi Puck! I'm good, how're you?"

My girlfriend is so cool.

We swerved into the HOV, barreling past slower traffic and accelerating to thirty-five miles per hour, forty, forty-five, fifty, and put some distance between us and our pursuers. They couldn't keep up. Samantha's rifle clattered to the metal truck bed and she reloaded a pistol. "One more magazine," she called above the wind. "THIS is why you needed to MOVE!"

"You were right."

"I *was* right," she snapped.

"I know!"

"You have bite marks all over you. Good thing they aren't zombies; I'd have to shoot you."

"I already have their disease."

"Yeah well. Maybe I should shoot you anyway."

We staggered and nearly fell as Katie sideswiped a Lexus. "Sorry!" she called.

"Easy on my truck, Lopez!"

"Puck is on the phone. He's coordinating with the FBI. A helicopter is landing a mile ahead to pick us up."

"Where?"

"In the middle of the road."

We inspected the pack of animals still chasing us, fifty yards back. Their eyes burned.

"This is going to be close," Samantha yelled, now eyeballing the Black Hawk settling northwards. "Tell them to warm up their fifty cal. We'll need it."

Katie's calm voice drifted back to us. "Hello, Puck? Would you please advise the pilot to prepare his or her fifty caliber machine gun?"

I observed, "She's handling this really well."

"Nerves of steel," Samantha nodded. "She's a tough one."

Thirty second later, the Black Hawk landed and immediately stalled northbound traffic. Instant collisions. Our truck ground to a halt three hundred yards away, at the backup.

I said, "Let's go."

Katie climbed down from the truck and I hauled her onto my back. "Hold tight," I cautioned.

"Always."

Samantha sprinted into the congestion, and I *Jumped*. Katie and I launched into the morning haze, twenty, thirty, forty feet high. She gasped and tightened her grip. We soared towards the Black Hawk and then plummeted back, my heart in my throat. I softened our fall, bracing and bending knees at the last instant, surging forward and crumpling car roofs. One more leap and we landed twenty feet from spinning blades.

"Move, move, move!" Samantha cried. I helped Katie into the metal gunner bay and turned to see Samantha leap over the final car. The closest Chosen were Jumpers and Sprinters, and they burst through the traffic jam twenty yards behind. The pilot swore loud enough for us to hear. Engines roared and we lifted off. There was no .50 caliber machine gun, but the FBI agent at the door began firing his rifle. At ten feet, Samantha *Leapt* the distance to our crowded gunner bay. She slammed into me but I held my ground, like part of the fuselage.

Three heartbeats later, the Chosen began *Jumping* but we were too high. They fell short. Our pilot kept climbing, as though he couldn't get far enough away from the freaks. We were safe.

The pilot yelled, "We're going to get Special Agent Anderson. I hear he's trapped and lonely on a roof!"

We sat and panted and trembled on the shaking deck. Below, Chosen scrambled and retreated as police moved in with weapons blazing. The trail of destruction we left was a stain across an otherwise perfect canvas, a rip in the fabric.

"Well," I said, taking deep breaths to calm my nerves. "Isaac will have his blood samples now."

The FBI agent in the gunner bay stared at me. I bet I looked ridiculous, covered in bites and holding a stick.

"Hey Outlaw," Katie said. She smiled sadly. "You forgot something."

"What?"

"To put your mask on."

Whoops.

I felt like I'd been dumped in ice water. The FBI agent was staring at Chase Jackson, inspecting him like a fascinating zoo animal. The Outlaw's true identity, now exposed. Hundreds of people saw me on the interstate. The media would figure out quickly whose house had been attacked.

My secret was out. And there was no going back.

Chapter Five
Friday, January 5. 2019

Our Black Hawk touched down at the Los Angeles International Airport, but media had already arrived. The dormant facility's skeleton crew couldn't keep out the swarm of incoming press, and we were forced to take off again immediately to avoid the circus. Not even the adjacent Air Force base was safe from cameramen and rabid reporters.

The pilot called back, "We're heading southeast. We'll outrace those bloodsuckers across the city."

I shot him a thumbs-up.

"I flew you last October, sir," he said. He grinned over his shoulder at me. The helmet visor was down so we only saw his nose and mouth. "Over the Pacific, up to the Greyhound. Special Agent Anderson and I, we make a good team."

I yelled, "Then I know we're in good hands."

"I'll fly you anywhere, sir!"

"Careful what you wish for."

"Name's Mike Matthews." He jerked a thumb at himself. "The Outlaw's personal pilot!"

His enthusiasm surprised me. One reason I wore the mask was because I assumed I'd lose everyone's respect when they saw my face and my youth. But Mike Matthews looked straight at Chase Jackson with unabated trust. That was reassuring. As if reading my thoughts, Katie nudged me and winked.

Anderson was on his phone the entire time, updating us with a hand over the receiver.

He told Katie, "Highway Patrol is escorting your mother to her sister's. They'll both be taken to a safe house near San Diego."

"Thank you," Katie said. She visibly unclenched, some of the stress draining out of her. Her eyes vacantly watched the palm trees below as wind tossed strands of her hair.

"Outlaw, we have a police detail staying with your father. He refuses to leave active duty, but he'll start sleeping at the station."

Samantha Gear sniffed her approval. She was texting with Carter and PuckDaddy.

Anderson continued, "He's seen pictures of your destroyed house. He says you're grounded."

We all laughed. Especially Samantha.

But it wasn't true. The days of being grounded were over. Chase Jackson was no longer a high school student. This helicopter would fly where I ordered, and everyone aboard would blindly follow my lead.

The blind leading the blind.

What would I do now?

Katie. She'd always been my north star. Keeping her safe, my priority. But she'd reject that now. She possessed an innate sense of right and wrong, of justice, and she'd never allow herself to be a distraction.

Her fingers found mine and squeezed. Samantha quit texting, crossed over to our side of the gunner bay and squeezed next to Katie, pinning her between us. "Now what, Outlaw?"

I shrugged. "McDonalds? I haven't had breakfast yet."

Katie pinched me. "Be serious."

"He is," Samantha said. "Our bodies burn calories at a murderous rate. He and I will go into shock soon unless we eat."

"What fascinating monsters you are," Katie commented. "I wish I could cook for you."

Anderson had apparently been listening in the middle of orchestrating a symphony through his cellphone and his two radios. He held one to his mouth and said, "Anyone got eyes on a McDonalds? Special request for breakfast sandwiches."

"And coffee."

"And chocolate donuts."

Katie said, "And yogurt and granola. ...*what??* I don't need all those additives. Wearing tight pajamas on a helicopter requires dietary sacrifices."

"You are quite eye-catching," Samantha agreed, inspecting Katie's outfit and then her own. Samantha wore cargo pants, a shoulder holster, and her black shirt was splattered with blood. "I'm as attractive as a garbageman in this."

"Not true," Katie protested. "You're so fit, you'd look good wearing actual garbage. I wish I could take video of all this. It'd be Instagram gold."

Anderson ordered food while I retrieved a pair of jeans from my duffle and tugged them on over my shorts. My red bandana partially pulled out from a side compartment. Should I put it on? I felt exposed without it, especially in a helicopter.

Samantha glared down at the rotating earth. "We're going to Los Alamitos."

"Where?"

"Los Alamitos, the Joint Forces base in Orange County."

Anderson covered the receiver and said, "Bingo. You'll be safe there. I know a guy."

We thundered straight towards a broad emptiness in the suburbs of eastern Los Angeles, a brown expanse of runway strips and military housing. The Los Alamitos campus was enormous and ugly. "It's perfect," Samantha observed.

"The whole world is wondering where this Black Hawk is going. Including my supervisors. And I'm not telling them. And these guys," Anderson jerked a thumb at the quiet agent with an assault rifle and at the pilot, "aren't spilling. The secret will get out soon, but I think we've bought a few hours. Maybe even a day or two."

"Perfect," I said. "Anderson, we owe you."

"Hell yeah you do. But we gotta hammer out a plan of attack. And soon."

I asked, "The Chemist is in Los Angeles?"

"He was last night," Anderson nodded.

Samantha frowned and said, "How do you know?"

"He freed Tank Ware from prison."

Samantha swore and punched the metal fuselage so hard her fist left an imprint. "I *knew* I should have ended that ape when I had the chance."

Katie's voice was quiet. "Where'd he go?"

Anderson held up his palms. "Out to sea. That's all we know. But he can't stay hidden long."

He appeared exhausted. I'd been so caught up in my own struggles I failed to notice his. His eyes were red, framed by dark circles, and he needed a shave. Katie noticed too. She squeezed Isaac's hand and said, "Have you heard from Natalie?"

He tried to smile but couldn't. "No. Not since the Downtown takeover. Teresa Triplett mentions her in the Chemist blog now and then, so I know she's alive."

Katie nodded sympathetically. "I read the updates. I met Natalie North once, did you know?"

"I didn't." He grinned, genuinely this time. "I haven't told anyone we're together. It's a hard secret to keep, because I'm so proud of her."

I said, "That settles it. That's the plan. We're going after the Chemist. And we're going after Natalie."

"That's always been the plan. Not working so far."

I said grimly, "This time is different."

"How so?"

"I don't have homework or English class. Samantha and I are going in and we're not coming out unless we've got his head."

Samantha pumped her fist, a small but fierce motion. "That plan makes me so happy I could cry."

We landed on the far side of a hot Los Alamitos tarmac, away from prying eyes. The four of us hopped off and Mike Matthews launched the Black Hawk into the firmament again. Anderson got behind the wheel of a waiting jeep and we climbed in.

He explained in the sudden silence, "I'm working with a small group of trusted individuals. Influential members inside all branches of intelligence, military, and law enforcement. We call ourselves the Resistance, and our main goal is to provide resources to our Hyper Human allies. With the military and governmental infighting, we don't advertise our existence. One of the Resistance is a colonel here. He allocated this jeep for us and a place to stash you." He ground the gears and gunned the gas, and we lurched down the runway. Like every nearby base, Los Alamitos bore scars from a recent Chemist rampage. This airfield was still being repaired so larger fixed-wings could land. We rolled through a graveyard of scorch marks.

I said, "I'm not crazy about being *stashed*."

"Me either," Samantha announced. "Infected are incapable of being stashed. We'll go crazy."

Anderson grumbled, "Just trying to keep you three alive. There's only so much help I can provide."

"You're doing great, Special Agent," Katie said. "And we're very grateful. Aren't we?"

"And you're hot," Samantha noted. "So that helps."

I said, "This place is perfect. Temporarily. We'll lay low until its time to move out. Where are we staying?"

"The guest room at the Infirmary. But I'm not positive where that is. I've never been here."

Our journey in the jeep did not go unnoticed. Four strangers in civilian clothes were uncommon on a Joint Forces base. Katie especially stuck out.

"Here," Samantha growled and stuffed a duffle bag into Katie's lap. "Hug that to your chest. You're too attractive and curvy, especially in your pjs. All these half-wits are staring."

Los Alamitos is not pretty. It's old and utilitarian and without adornment. No grass, just soldiers jogging in cadence over dusty earth. Anderson said there was a pool and golf course, but we'd never use them. We motored through cinderblock housing and offices and armories, all painted military grays and khakis, until we stumbled across the Infirmary. A small apartment was built into the back, just a bathroom and small bedroom. Several bags of McDonalds were steaming on the bedside table. I ate a sausage biscuit in one bite.

"One cot?" Samantha arched an eyebrow at the rickety mattress.

"I'm not your concierge," Anderson yawned. "Go check into a hotel if you want. See how that goes. Colonel Jordan should be here soon. I don't want to be spotted, so I'm leaving the base immediately."

The jeep roared, and he was gone. Samantha glared at the door, hands on hips, for a full fifteen seconds before announcing, "I look military. I'm not staying in this tiny room. Back later. And I'll bring clothes for Miss Pajamas." She grabbed a McDonalds bag and slammed the door.

The room was small. No windows. No televisions.

Katie said, "Well…"

"That was an interesting morning."

"Shall we eat?"

"Let's snuggle first."

She smiled. "We'd be fools not to."

Chapter Six
Friday, January 5. 2019

I couldn't stay quiet. I was too amped. Too juiced. Too much adrenaline. I paced back and forth until after lunch, when Katie grew tired of my simmering energy and pushed us both outside. We found a rec hall with a television but we could barely see the screen. The hall was standing room only, way above capacity, bodies crowding for a better view. The video footage of Chosen rioting over Glendale startled everyone, even me and Katie. Those freaks were *fast*. How on earth did we escape? The newscast displayed the wreckage which used to be my home, as well as the ten-mile backup on the interstate. Fortunately our names weren't being used, even though our helicopter dash had been caught on several cellphone cameras.

"It's only a matter of time," Katie observed. "A few hours. And then they'll be confident enough to release your real name." Katie did not fit in, even wearing camouflage fatigues. She was too soft, too pretty, too feminine, her voice too bright.

I wanted to fight. My blood boiled. I'd been attacked. The Chemist sent monsters to my *house*! To Katie's! He came early, hoping to catch us asleep. He invaded our private lives. And Tank sold us for his freedom, breaking our rule about no families. I wanted to break things. I needed justice. A reckoning.

We found Samantha Gear at an outdoor firing range. Where else. A small crowd gathered to watch. She stood perfectly still, her left elbow propped on her left hip, glaring down the length of a sniper rifle. She was still dressed in camo cargo pants and a tight black shirt.

A buzzer sounded. Targets moved. She fired five times, sharp blasts, spinning copper cartridges, and she shattered five mechanical moving targets.

Two soldiers stood in front of me, whispering.

"See how fast she works the bolt? Christ almighty."

"Not even using a scope."

"Scope? How could she? Moving too fast."

"I'm not that accurate when I'm kneeling. She's just standing there. Who the *hell* is she?"

Samantha turned and glared at the crowd. She held up a pair of fingers.

"You boys have two problems!" She started stalking up and down the line of admirers, professional soldiers in awe. "One, you're moving too slowly. You're concerned with silence. Forget silence. This isn't elegant. War isn't elegant. There's no silence in combat! You shouldn't be using a bolt-action anyway. You need the semi-automatic M110. Reloading messes with your mind. When you're worried about silence and about reloading, then you're *worried*. Worried. Guns. Don't. Hit. Targets." Her teeth were grinding and she snarled in their faces. "Your enemy, this new enemy on the television screens, won't give you time to worry. They'll rip you open. Never practice silence. Never practice worried. Practice angry. Practice desperate.

"Next! Your second problem! You're practicing with scopes?! No! Lose the damn scopes! Anyone can hit anything with a scope from a mile away. You don't need to practice that. You don't need to practice with a scope. This isn't Boy Scouts! This isn't Sniper Camp! You need to practice firing at targets sprinting at you fifteen feet away. Practice firing at targets moving too fast to see. There will be NO time for scopes! Scopes make you worry. You won't have time to worry. You won't have time to *fret* over being accurate. Forget about accuracy. Your ass will be dead. You want something to worry about? Worry that you won't even hit them *once*. That you won't have time to fire. That you'll miss entirely. Forget perfection. Forget aiming for the heart. Just hit them anywhere. If you can. Otherwise you're dead."

She tossed her rifle to the man behind her, and said, "Where's your Armory Officer? Where's your Gunnery Sergeant? Speed up the targets.

Triple the speed. Get semi-automatic weapons, not single shot sniper rifles."

Katie whispered to me, "She's very impressive. I didn't know she could do all this stuff."

One of the observers, probably the senior ranking officer in attendance, spoke up. His hair was buzzed and he spoke quietly. "This is very impressive. But I don't recognize you, soldier. You're not Green Beret. And I don't believe you're Navy SEALs. Our soldiers need to use the weapons they've been trained on."

Samantha stared at the emblem on his shirt and said, "That's very cute, Captain. However it's obvious you've never seen combat. None of you boys have. Just arrive here from some safe outpost in Texas?"

"Training matters. Repetition matters. Comfort level matters. Working as one unit matters. And who are you?"

Samantha *Moved*. She had the Captain's firearm out of his holster without warning, and she pressed the muzzle into the soft underpart of his jaw. The assemblage tensed and stepped back as one body. It happened so fast. I groaned.

"Tell me about comfort level now, Captain," Samantha said quietly. "Go ahead. I'm listening. Explain to me how repetition is going to save you." His eyes were wide and he didn't move. More guns emerged, pointed at Samantha. Voices were raised. Radios began squawking. "Here's the point, Captain. Your enemy is ten times faster than you are. You have no time to worry. No time to reload. No time to aim through a scope. Get it?"

More boots came pounding across the pavement. More yells. More weapons. I mumbled, "This is going well."

Katie said, "She's so cool. I hope she doesn't get shot."

"Might be good for her."

Two MPs ran up, guns drawn, and began bawling orders. "Drop the weapon! On the ground! Everyone back! Drop the weapon now!" With recent hostilities on military bases, this could escalate quickly.

"Drop the weapon?!" Samantha cackled. "Drop the weapon! You think your enemies are going to drop their weapons??" She began turning in circle, one fist holding onto the helpless Captain, the other fist pressing the gun into his neck. "Stop me! Someone stop me! How will you do it? There's only one way. Only one way to stop me. What is it?"

They didn't know. I knew. And I hoped no one tried it.

"This is fun. Let's turn this into a lesson. All you kiddos need to learn this. Everyone follow me!" she called. "We need more space."

She marched the Captain away from the firing range, past the pool, across Yorktown Avenue, through a parking lot, next to a hanger, and onto the runway tarmac. Our crowd grew the whole time, swelling to over a hundred. They were nervous, agitated, but interested. Everyone with a gun had it drawn, fifty total. She halted on the airstrip, immediately encircled by Military Police and soldiers with firearms.

"Stay behind me," I told Katie. "I've seen her like this before. It's going to get weird."

"This is Captain Comfort," Samantha called to her audience, turning the poor man in a circle. "He wants to stick to the old way! Just keep doing what you practiced, he said! Repetition will save you! Trouble is…the old ways won't work anymore. You aren't fighting Al Qaeda! You aren't fighting Islamic radicals or any other religious zealot. This is a new animal. There's a new beast in the jungle. And it's faster and stronger than you."

The captain hissed, "Who are you?"

"I've fought the Chosen. I've killed more than you ever will."

"What are Chosen?"

"Who am I, you want to know? Who are the Chosen? I went into Compton with the FBI's HRT. None of them walked out. Brave men. Well trained. All dead except one, and he had to be carried."

"Alright, soldier!" the ranking MP shouted. "There's a lot of us, and only one of you. Gun down."

"Only one of me?" she laughed. "Who cares?! I'm more than enough for you. All of you. Why? Because you'll fight using old methods. I will take you apart, and I'm not even the one you should be scared of."

"Oh crap," I muttered.

She continued, "You should worry about me, but you ought to be *terrified* of him!"

"Katie, back away. I have a bad feeling."

"Because you can shoot me! I mean, *you* can't. But technically I could be shot. But not him! He's too fast! That should give you a hint about how to save Captain Comfort. Bullets won't work. So how can you save the poor Captain? Forget bullets. There's your hint."

"Our bullets work just fine, lady," a growl.

"Oh really??" She howled in laughter.

I sighed. "Oh no."

"Watch!" She raised the gun. At me. She fired three times. Some cerebral mechanism activated, computing time and distance at hyper speed, and fired synapses independently. I saw the oncoming rounds. Saw the disturbance as they cut through air. I *Moved*, twisting away from the bullets, and catching the final shot. The lead hissed and spun briefly in my hand. No idea how I do that. It's like the phenomenon happens to someone else.

The crowd shivered again and moved away from me. I stood alone, glaring at the Shooter.

There went our anonymity. Way to go, Samantha. I tossed the hot metal onto asphalt.

She had their attention now. Well, we both did. She spoke evenly and slowly. "You will barely see them. You will not have time to use a scope. You will be lucky to get off a few rounds. And you will probably miss. So I repeat myself. How will you save Captain Comfort?"

I heard the whispers. *It's the Outlaw! I saw him on the television! It's him!* I was bigger than them. Taller, broader. The presence I imputed on their emotions and their psyche was stronger than normal. I *felt* big.

"You feel safe behind your guns?" Samantha continued. "Put them away. Right now. Trust me. They are doing you no good. Put your guns away or the Outlaw will disarm you. And he can. And you won't like it."

I could. I just didn't want to. Slowly, alternating stares between their superior officers and me, they holstered their weapons. She wasn't an active hostile. She was something else.

"Now you realize just how helpless you are against your enemies. Against the Chosen and Infected. You have one chance to save Captain Comfy. What is it?"

No one spoke. She growled and produced a smooth green grenade. THAT spooked them. And me. Was it real? It better not be. I hoped not. But it was. I knew Samantha. Crap.

"In all likelihood, the Captain here is dead. You can't realistically save him. The one chance you have, and this is important…" She pulled the pin out with her teeth and released the lever. I started to count in my mind. "…you can drop grenades and pray you survive."

One second. The troops backed away.

"You can't hit the Chosen. You can only slow them."

Two seconds. The Captain was white.

"And your best chance is grenades."

Three seconds.

"It might kill you. Might kill the Captain. But you're probably already dead when it goes off."

She tossed me the grenade at four seconds. I *Threw* it straight up. It detonated two hundred yards high, a safe pop.

Samantha released the Captain. He collapsed to his knees. Poor guy. Only human. She disassembled the pistol with one hand and the metal parts fell noisily to the ground. "Any questions?"

"Yeah," one of the guys said. A lot of cameras began emerging from pockets. "Can we get a selfie with you?"

Colonel Jordan wasn't happy with us. He appeared to be a perpetually irritated, thirty-five year old black stalwart. Older and wiser and angrier than his years. And his territory was in an uproar.

Katie was besieged by the women on base. She'd been in gossip magazines, kidnapped on national television, named one of the 50 Most Beautiful People, dated the infamous Tank Ware, and now dated the Outlaw. She took pictures, signed autographs, and answered questions.

Samantha was a hit with the guys. She beat them in arm wrestling. She outshot them. She doubled them in pushup contests, screaming at them the whole time. She turned down a dozen date requests.

After thirty minutes of pestering, I finally relented to a race. Fifty guys lined up to race me across the width of the airstrip and back. I gave them a head start but I still lapped the field. They roared with delight. We played catch with a football until their fingers blistered.

It was fun for an hour. But that was enough. I wasn't a zoo animal. Nor a circus act. I grew weary of ducking uncomfortable questions. Fortunately Colonel Jordan began blowing an airhorn and ordering everyone back to their duties. He allowed Samantha to work at the shooting range, lecturing on new techniques for battling Chosen.

"You two. Get in," he ordered. We obeyed, Katie in the front, and me in the back. He climbed behind the jeep's wheel and we motored back towards housing. "I've got over two thousand men and women stationed here, due to the threat downtown. Over thirty-five aircraft. And more arriving as soon as we complete major repairs. That's a lot of moving parts. And the only way it keeps moving is through discipline, structure, and routine. I don't like when those get disrupted."

I liked this guy. Gruff. Straight to the point. "I understand, Colonel."

"Don't misunderstand. You and I, we have the same mission. On the same team. But I need Los Alamitos to run like a well-oiled machine. Now you two. Both of you. Reach under your seats. Packages just arrived."

We found insulated manilla envelopes. Inside were brand new phones with text messages from Puck.

>> **hey dummy key katie**
>> **i see u left ur phones at ur houses**
>> **puckdaddy transferred all ur data over to these new phones and erased the old ones**
>> **wiped'em clean no worries**
>> **don't lose these!!!**

"Aw," Katie smiled. "Puck's so sweet."

"How'd he do that so fast? It's not even dinner."

"This is the Plus size," she marveled. "It's as big as a tablet."

Colonel Jordan barked, "Speaking of dinner. You'll be eating in your room. I don't need my mess hall turned into a damn zoo."

"Understood."

"And speaking of your room, now that your secret is out, I've taken the liberty of moving you to nicer quarters."

We squealed to a stop in front of what looked like a cinderblock cabin. Katie said, "Thank you, Colonel. We're very grateful."

"Just about every man on base volunteered to stand guard. So both entrances will have three guards at all time," he said with a trace of pride. I didn't bother to tell him those guards would be worthless if the Chemist attacked. But I doubted that would happen in the near future. We were expecting him. "I support you, Outlaw. We fight with you."

Katie and I walked into our new quarters. Two bedrooms. Much nicer.

Katie checked her phone and said, "Oh look. We're trending on Twitter."

Chapter Seven
Saturday, January 6th. 2019

I quickly grew sick of my own face. On every television. On every news website. On every social media app. Katie's pictures were great. I looked goofy.

The Outlaw's secret identity finally revealed!

Blah.

Cellphone footage of our interactions with soldiers at Los Alamitos quickly went viral. Video of me playing quarterback for Hidden Spring High was spliced alongside the game of catch with marines yesterday. My yearbook pictures were dug up and shown in sequence on CNN, illustrating the remarkable change my body had undergone during the previous twelve months. Wow. I *had* gotten bigger. The story of my mother's death got a lot of airtime. Katie and I watched a few minutes last night. She stroked my fingers and said, "You look so good on television. Great cheekbones."

"I need a haircut."

"No, it's perfectly unkempt."

"Next to you I look like Tarzan."

She smiled. "Me Jane."

Carter was furious with Samantha Gear and me. We were exposed and vulnerable. He wanted clearance to send a plane for us but I refused.

"Tell him that I'm his *ally* now. Not his employee," I directed Samantha. We were all sitting on the girls' bed Saturday morning, watching television.

I'd slept in the other room.

Samantha frowned. "Tell him yourself, punk."

"No. Tell him, Puck."

The speaker on my phone rattled, "Tell him what?"

"Tell Carter we don't need his plane. He'll use it as an excuse to control us."

Puck's irritation came through. "That'll be a fun message to deliver."

Katie asked, "Where are you, PuckDaddy?"

"Dunno. Haven't looked out a window in a few days. California somewhere. PuckDaddy should probably track his own location like he does yours."

Samantha scowled at her phone. "The Priest is in the news again. That little whelp grows irksome."

"What now?"

"He's calling for Chase Jackson to repent and surrender himself to their guidance."

"Yeah, well, I'm not gonna."

"Grass Valley, California," Puck mused. "Huh. Wonder what we're doing here. My drivers are curious animals."

Cory texted me when he heard the news about my secret identity.

>> I knew it. You a boss.

Cory *knew* it?! No way. His reaction was much more subdued than Lee's, who quickly touted himself as my best friend and assistant, and had been answering questions on his Outlaw blog and enjoying the notoriety for fifteen hours straight.

Puck reported, "Carter requests you keep him apprised of your plans. And he'll do the same."

I asked, "What are *his* plans?"

Puck said, "Don't think he has one. He's in Norway. Went to monitor an 18 year old Infected kid, but she died before he got there."

Katie said, "That's awful."

I asked, "What happened?"

Samantha didn't look up from her phone. "Relax kids. Happens several times a year. This disease kills pretty much everyone who has it. Remember? We're only able to save one Infected every couple years. And even then, they often don't last long."

"What a fascinating and monstrous disease you have," Katie said, rubbing her forehead in thought. "There *has* to be a cure."

"Katie, tell your boyfriend to quit rubbing my leg."

"What?!" I cried. "I'm not!"

"Are too."

"It's just this tiny bed."

Katie sighed. "Do I need to sit between you two?"

Samantha sniffed. "Only if you'll rub my leg."

"Mine too," I said.

"Aaaaaanyway," Puck groaned. "What's your plan? What should I tell Carter?"

"We have two plans." I held up two fingers that he couldn't see. "Keep Katie safe. And remove the Chemist."

Puck pushed maps of the city to our iPhones and iPad while Samantha and I brain-stormed. Throughout the day we'd text Isaac Anderson and get his input on various details, and to find out what the military's plans were. Trouble was, the military was fractured. No one was sharing information or collaborating on solutions.

Samantha and I didn't have a very elegant plan either. Essentially, the next time Puck confirmed with certainty that the Chemist was downtown, we were going hunting. We'd take supplies and weapons and we wouldn't come back until we had him. Puck illustrated on maps where the military *thought* he hid, and where the positive sightings had been. The military's intelligence was good. They were monitoring the city from every angle and with every known technology. Much was known about the inner workings of the fortress. Except how to storm it and eliminate targets too fast to be shot, without massive civilian casualties.

"I can get you all the equipment you need," Anderson yawned over the speaker phone. "The remaining Navy SEALs are currently training with munitions that don't require high levels of accuracy."

That piqued Samantha's interest. "What kind of munitions?"

"OC spray."

I said, "Huh?"

Katie answered, "Oleoresin Capsicum."

I said, "Huh?"

"Pepper spray."

Samantha tapped the phone against her lips in thought. "OC spray. That's interesting. I bet they're training with goggles. Might work."

"I thought our lungs filter out the harsh chemicals. Deadens the effects. Chosen wouldn't feel it."

Samantha answered me, "The eyes are more vulnerable. OC spray is primarily an eye irritant. Can swell them completely shut. If the SEALs wear eye protection, and can deliver clouds of OC...it wouldn't level the playing field, but it might help. At least slow the Chosen down."

At noon, Katie got up and stretched her arms over her head. "Your war games grow wearisome. I'm going for a jog."

I joined her. Our guard detail, a mixture of Air Force airmen and MPs, snapped to attention when we emerged. A couple airmen eagerly volunteered to show us their usual route. Katie and I set off at an easy pace after them, quickly joined and surrounded by most of our armed guard.

"Protective group, aren't they?" Katie observed.

"They've just got good taste."

"Samantha will have the remainder of the guards in bed with her by the time we get back."

"What??" I nearly stumbled. "But...isn't she...aren't she and my dad..."

Katie grinned, chasing the lead airmen with easy strides. She'd been a runner her whole life. "Yes. They are. But I don't think it's exclusive. It's not like Samantha and your dad can get married or something."

"Yeah but....yeah but..."

"Besides, your father has an on-again-off-again thing with one of his commanding officers. Her name is Annette."

"Nope."

"Oh Chase. You're so beautiful and adorable and naive. Your dad is kind of a hunk. How long did you expect him to stay single?"

"Until forever, obviously. His sole purpose in life is to be my father. He has no needs."

She laughed.

I continued, "So she and my father aren't...romantic?"

"Oh they are. But I think they both know this isn't permanent. Ships passing in the night. Are you sure you want to talk about this? We're being followed by a lot of ears and this is pretty juicy gossip." She indicated our protective contingent. I glanced around and several airmen snapped their eyes forward, faces wooden and fixed. Our group crossed a street and began jogging along side the green Destroyer Golf Course. We had swelled to twenty total joggers.

After a transport helicopter thundered overhead, we could speak again. I asked, "Why can't it be permanent?"

"They live on different planets. Richard's life is here. Samantha's is...everywhere." She had begun taking deep breaths. So far the run wasn't affecting me. "Do you mind if I take your photo with my phone while you jog?"

I said, "I don't care. Does the age thing bother you?"

"Smile!" I smiled. Click. She asked, "What age thing?"

"Infected can live a long time," I explained. This was dangerous territory and I'd been dreading this conversation. "Two or three times longer than normal."

"You mean, does it bother me that when I'm sixty-five you'll still look like a hot twenty-five year old?" she grinned, brightening the world. She could charge solar panels with her smile. "I'm okay with the arrangement."

"Well, when you put it that way..."

She elbowed me lightly. "I'll try to die young, like maybe seventy, so you can start dating hot girls again."

"This conversation has grown weird."

"What bothers me is the suicidal tendencies you Infected have. I've heard you and Samantha and Puck talking about it, about how Infected don't live long because cheating death sounds so...adventurous."

"You have nothing to worry about," I said.

"You don't feel it?"

"No, I do. I feel it. But I have more to live for than the others do. I have you."

"If you keep talking like that, Outlaw, then you can have me right here on the golf course."

The Air Force airmen surrounding us around stifled laughter.

Puck called us that night. "Oh man. Turn on your television."

"Which channel?"

"All of them." His voice came through my speaker phone. He didn't sound happy. Katie shot me a worried look and pressed the remote. The television on the dresser flickered on. Samantha wandered in from the other room. She was sharpening a knife.

All the major stations were playing a video recording they'd just received. Teresa Triplett was on screen. The lighting was bad. She appeared to be in an empty room, sitting on a chair, looking exhausted and scared. She wore a blue robe tied across the middle with a wide red sash.

She spoke. "This is Teresa Triplett, reporting from downtown Los Angeles, within the Empire of the New Age." Her voice was shaky and hollow, and the mic wasn't close enough to her mouth. "I'm here to read a message from Martin Patterson, the man you call the Chemist."

Samantha Gear and I sat on the edge of the bed, just inches from the screen.

Teresa Triplett said in a rush, clearly going off script, "I've been told if I don't read this statement then my roommate will be executed." I groaned inwardly. Not a good idea, Teresa. You might be punished for that later. Her roommate and fellow hostage was the movie star Natalie North. "I'm being treated well. We all are. It is the presence of the United States' military that keeps us hostage. The farther you remove yourselves from our Kingdom, the more freedom the Emperor will grant us."

Samantha grunted as Teresa Triplett read from the paper. Katie had to elbow us aside so she could see the screen. Puck was silent. Most of the world was watching, I bet.

Teresa continued, "Our Emperor has taken notice of the media's Outlaw discovery. This masked terrorist has been identified as a child, a mere high school student named Chase Jackson. Our Father has known this all along, and wants you to know the boy may appear innocuous but in reality he is a grave threat. Dangerous."

Samantha grumbled, "Damn right he's dangerous."

"He cannot be trusted. He poses as a symbol of hope, but in reality he subverts your country and your future. Our Emperor has a message for the more rational citizens of America." Teresa Triplett stopped reading for a moment. She stared off screen and took a deep breath. Her eyes were red and pooling with tears. "Our Emperor seeks to aid America in removing this threat. To demonstrate how committed he is and how urgent the situation grows, he offers a reward to the men and women brave enough to capture the Outlaw."

Puck said, "Oh crud."

"Any person who delivers the body of the Outlaw unto our Emperor shall be compensated with one hundred million dollars and the additional option of becoming immortal, like our Emperor."

Katie gasped. Her hand on my shoulder squeezed hard. "A hundred *million* dollars??"

"Any person who delivers the Outlaw still living shall be compensated with five hundred million dollars, and the option of becoming immortal, like our Emperor."

Samantha stood, her face as grim as death. She retrieved a pistol from the other room and stood between us and the door, her arms crossed. She and I shared the same thought; we might need to fight our way out in a minute.

Five hundred million dollars is not just life-changing. It's world-changing for generations of lives.

Teresa continued, now talking through sobs. "The Outlaw is a vicious murderer. His capture will result in injuries and most likely multiple casualties. He won't be afraid to slaughter any brave soul that draws near. Therefore, if a valiant *group* is required to capture the masked terrorist then our Emperor will increase the reward to fully compensate your patriotic sacrifices."

Noises were increasing outside our door. It was eight at night. We all stared at the wooden door, which seemed to shrink and grow more fragile.

"We know from news channels that the Outlaw is traveling with certain companions. Our Emperor offers rewards for these lesser terrorists, too. You may find these terrorists in southeast Los Angeles. Treacherous and disloyal government officials are hiding the Outlaw on the military base Los Alamitos. Find them. Bring them to me. Or kill them all. Happy hunting, and may God continue to bless America."

Chapter Eight
Saturday, January 6. 2019

My phone rang. Special Agent Isaac Anderson.

"Two things," Anderson barked in my ear. "One. We gotta get you out of there immediately."

"Sooner the better," I said, glaring warily at the door. Fear for Katie's safety was carving holes in my stomach. Rumor of the bounty on our heads spread instantly. Instantly! Like wildfire. We could hear men outside growing rowdy.

"Two. We found him."

"Found the Chemist?" I asked. Samantha turned from the door to eavesdrop on the phone call, her eyebrow arched. I put the call on speaker.

"Roger that. The Chemist. He made a mistake. We've been monitoring as many towers as we can with microphones and infrared cameras. We got lucky. That recording was made on the thirtieth floor of the Gas Company Tower, and based on heat signatures it appears the Chemist was present."

"How do you know?"

He answered, "Infected have warmer blood. Didn't you know? You guys run hot."

"Heck yeah we do."

Samantha spoke up. "Is he still in the tower?"

"The warm body we believe to be the Chemist is still in the tower, yes."

"Level it. Cut the whole tower down."

"Negative. Several hundred civilians are housed there too."

"So what?" Samantha snapped. "Do it anyway. This will result in lives saved, ultimately."

"Samantha," Katie whispered. "Natalie North could be in that tower. He loves her."

"Oh God," Samantha groaned and raked fingers through her hair. "Everyone and their damn feelings. War is hell. Gotta walk through it to win."

Isaac continued, "Navy SEALs are preparing to drop on that tower within thirty minutes. If we're lucky, he's still there."

"No! Anderson, don't send them! I'll go," I shouted.

Samantha said, "Those little boys will get chewed in half. You need monsters. Just get us a chopper."

"SEALs are going in. I fielded a call from the Secretary of Defense, personally authorizing us to escort you two in also."

"Great." She ground her teeth. "Babies for us to take care of. Tell them they need semi-automatic shotguns and grenades. As much as they can carry."

Anderson said, "I'll be there in twenty minutes. My helicopter is already spinning up. But I'm worried about Katie. She can't go with you and she can't stay there."

Katie sat on the edge of the bed, posture erect, beautiful brown hair pulled back, watching me, excited and worried. I said, "I've got an idea."

Twenty minutes later, we pushed out of our private barracks and into madness.

Our protective wall of United States servicemen had grown to over a hundred bodies. A complete ring of armed marines and airmen encircled our small building, three deep. Unified, they faced down a rising tide of greed. Night had fallen and our corner of the base wasn't well lit, but the sounds alone were frightening enough. Hundreds of men and woman massed on Liberty Avenue, armed with flashlights and firearms. They wanted me. They wanted us. Dead or Alive.

The love of money is the root of evil. The promise of unimaginable money to armed servicemen living below the poverty line…causes berserk mobs. That amount of cash doesn't set you up for life. It sets up vast dominions. Builds kingdoms. Creates emperors, and frenzied hordes. We held the keys to these new kingdoms.

There were very few safe places left for us in the world. The Chemist banished them.

The MP at our door grabbed my hand and shook it. He was a lantern-jawed, hard man. "Sir, we need to move quickly. There's going to be violence. We've already arrested five."

Samantha's eyes were afire. "Violence is my love language."

I said, "Cool it, Gear. We need to avoid this party."

Colonel Brown was out there somewhere, hidebound and furious, bawling orders through a megaphone, but the massed bodies began to flow like crashing seas at our arrival. Our guards constricted around us, sweating and casting nervous glances.

The angry crowds surged, calling for our surrender, calling for our deaths. Colonel Brown and his cadre threatened to shoot dissenters. I believed him.

A Black Hawk roared overhead, en route to the base's airfield. Isaac had arrived, our escort to the military's incursion against the Chemist, but the path was barred by crowds that may as well have been waving torches and pitchforks. More and more troops arrived, adding to the numbers of both sides.

"We need to get to the airfield," I told the MP. "Now."

"Roger that, sir." The sergeant turned to his small contingent of Military Police and shouted above the ruckus, "Men, we're escorting these three to the airfield via an alternative and longer route, going around the National Guard building on Saratoga. If approached by an unknown party, we use force. Colonel Brown's orders."

"Yes sir!" they barked.

"Move out."

Our squad moved east, away from the showdown. We pushed through startled guards, moving quick, moving in darkness. Some of the guards broke away and trotted alongside. Behind us, the melee intensified and shots rang out. Samantha stiffened, yearning to go play.

We kept our heads down, going against the tide of soldiers rushing past. Our sergeant brandished a flashlight and he shined it in the eyes of anyone getting too close. The three of us had donned camouflage caps and made eye contact with nobody. Well, except Samantha. She glared at everyone, hands at her holsters.

Our helicopter hummed and rattled on the tarmac in a cone of brilliant illumination. The tower's searchlights lit it up. Somehow, two news crews were here, frantically filming everything at once. Maybe they were military news? No idea. We jogged onto the runway and into the loud rotor wash. I tied on the red bandana, Rambo style, and then pulled the black mask into place over my mouth and nose. The world knew my face, but theatrics are important.

Our squad escorted us to the gunner bay and shook our hands. The three of us climbed aboard and we lifted off. Samantha glared at the cameras and I waved a Thank You to the MPs.

Anderson pressed headphones into our hands and yelled in the mic, "Do you think they bought it?"

"They better. Or I'm tearing this place apart," I said.

The girl beside me kept her head down. She was not Katie Lopez, but the resemblance was there. She played the part well for cameras, which would broadcast our departure to the world. The real Katie Lopez was hidden under Colonel Brown's bed, holed up with two pistols, pinned in with shoe boxes, and probably praying for me. The only three people on earth who knew her location were me, Dad, and Colonel Brown. Dad would arrive to fetch Katie within the hour. My heart would hammer and bruise my ribs until then, but I didn't know what else to do on such short notice. She was safer than the rest of us.

The girl crawled up to sit in the co-pilots seat and act as gunner. I glanced down; the black land below rushed by and sparkled with crystalline lights.

"Navy SEALs en route!" Anderson called. "We have to time this perfectly, otherwise we give the enemy time to deploy rockets."

Samantha gasped in the darkness and began inspecting a weapons cache at our feet.

Mike Matthews, our loyal pilot, yelled, "We land first. Then the SEALs."

"Matthews will remain in case we need emergency evac."

I said, "We?"

"Hell yeah, we. Natalie is in that tower."

Samantha held up a bizarre gun. She might cry. "A sawed-off Benelli with magazine feed? I've never seen this before."

Anderson chuckled over the rotor chatter. "Our armory is full of illegal projects, apparently. Thought you might like it."

I asked, "What is it?"

"A short, semi-automatic shotgun," Samantha replied, looking over the black weapon. "With a magazine for extra shells. Wide and powerful scatter. Nasty death."

"Three magazines at your feet. Thirty shots total. Illegal magnum load. You need more shells?"

"If I need more that thirty, we'll be dead."

"Outlaw, you need a gun?"

"No way. Guns kill people."

He and Samantha shot each other a knowing, frustrated glance. I indicated the Thunder Stick strapped to my back. "I'm here to hit the Chemist in the head really hard with this. That's all."

He held up his iPad for us to see. On screen was a blue labyrinth dotted with red bursts. He had to talk loudly. "This is thermal imaging of the tower. Top of the tower is mostly vacant. Just a handful of heat signatures per floor. Maybe guards, maybe hostages, maybe off-duty workers searching for peace and quiet? Point is, we should land easily."

Samantha asked, "Is this a live feed?"

"No. NSA updates me every five minutes or so. Once we land, SEALs will rappel twenty floors, making a quick descent to the Chemist's location."

Our pilot called back, "Be advised, we're over enemy territory and I got eyes on the SEALs chopper. Gas Tower dead ahead."

Downtown was a vast black hole compared to the surrounding brilliant city. No power for the Chemist, except for flashlights and generators. Chosen and Infected didn't need lights to see at night.

Puck called me and Samantha. We piped him directly into our bluetooth headsets.

He said, "PuckDaddy is nervous."

"Shooter is amped," Samantha replied.

"Contact!" pilot Mike Matthews yelled. "SEAL chopper taking fire!"

"There goes our surprise," Samantha growled. We leaned out from gunner door and into the wind, searching for gunfire on the mammoth towers sliding below.

Puck said, "It's not coming from the Gas Tower. No active heat signatures on the roof."

"There." Samantha pointed to the north. "Two California Plaza." The nearby tower's glass carapace duly reflected moonlight, and from it's zenith came bright gunfire aimed northwest, away from us. "Just firing pistols, but they'll have rockets soon. I can hit them with my assault rifle before they damage the chopper."

"Nah," I grinned. "I got'em."

"You *got* them??"

I leapt before she could stop me.

Chapter Nine
Saturday, January 6. 2019
Samantha Gear

Anderson rushed to the side and stared wildly into the night. "What the hell! Where'd he go??"

I ground my teeth. "I hate when he does this."

I couldn't see the Outlaw but I knew what he was doing. Using his wings. Chase possessed internal compasses and altimeters, capable of instinctive recalculation so quickly it defied belief. I focused on Two California Plaza and the sporadic gunfire bursts. "Watch." I pointed. A black phantom, darker than the night, swooped across the rooftop and the guns fell silent. Enemies eliminated. His feet never touched down. Fast. Efficient. Ferocious.

"How'd he do that?" Anderson asked in awe.

"He's a showoff."

"He's flying."

"He's dramatic."

Puck shouted into my ear. "You've got hostiles running up the Gas Tower stairwells. I'm monitoring infrared cameras."

"Get us on that tower!" I shouted to both Anderson and the pilot, WhatsHisName. "Our landing is getting hotter." Our machine dipped and roared in response. The Gas Tower is a tall, monolithic glass structure, wide and deep except at the top. The pinnacle of the skyscraper tapers to a point, providing a smaller landing surface amidst three gaping exhaust vents.

The Outlaw got there first, just as the first wave of Chemist troopers rushed onto the white helipad. They were helpless against Chase. For three reasons. One, he was too fast. They couldn't aim at him because he moved like lightning. Two, *if* the bullets hit him it wouldn't cause permanent damage because of the ballistic vest and his rock hard skin. Three, he used his Boom Stick to deflect the bullets. Like the Chemist did. I had no idea how the Outlaw did that, and neither did he. He spun away from their crosshairs, swung the rod like a bat and brought them down with crushing blows. It was like watching a tornado wreck trailer parks. He grew more dangerous every day.

Anderson and I jumped out of the Black Hawk and landed on the helipad's big red '12'. I carried an assault rifle across my back and the shotgun in my fists. The disease was an insatiable hunger in my body, thirsting for action and danger, sharpening my reflexes. My hands shook with adrenaline and violence. I wanted to cut this tower in half and ride it down.

The Outlaw stuffed the Rod of Treachery (or whatever he called it) into his vest. His body was swelling and growing. He looked six and a half feet tall, but he *felt* like Everest. "This won't work," he said.

"What won't work?"

"Rappelling," he answered, and the SEAL helicopter came thundering in. "The SEALs won't make it."

"Why not?" Anderson shouted.

"Chosen are climbing the outside walls."

Anderson's eyes bulged. I asked, "How do you know?"

"I can feel them. Sense them. Hundreds are coming."

"Feel them?"

"Close your eyes," he told me. "They have the disease. You and I are sensitive to it."

I tried. I tried reaching out with my senses, exploring for...whatever it was that the Outlaw felt. I could detect the disease when I was near it, but not from a distance. And not under angry helicopter blades.

Eight heavily armed men disembarked, and their transport took off again. Only eight??

"He's right," Anderson announced, looking at his updated thermal imaging. "Hostiles on the inside *and* outside of the walls. They're like monkeys. This tower is lighting up like a damn Christmas tree."

A SEAL asked, "Hostiles climbing the exterior walls?"

"Affirmative."

"We can engage as we rappel."

"No," I rolled my eyes. "You can't. They're too fast and they'll cut your ropes."

The Outlaw said, "Shooter, you take the SEALs and start pushing down through the tower. Release as many civilians as you can."

Isaac asked, "What will you do?"

"I'm going after the Chemist."

Puck moaned, "Ah crap."

Chase continued, "If he escapes, he might travel upwards. If so, Samantha you stall him until I get there."

I growled, "I hate this."

He grinned, obvious through his mask, and said, "And try to enjoy yourself. This should be fun."

He jogged to the security fencing atop the 750-foot tall spire and leapt off. A SEAL swore in surprise. I wanted to go watch his free-fall until he engaged his wings and entered the 30th floor at a hundred miles per hour, but we had a job to do.

"Puck," I said, "keep me updated."

"Roger that, homie."

We hustled down the helipad stairs to the broken penthouse doors. I plunged into the building first, using enhanced eyesight to scan ahead, sidestepping empty cans and water bottles. Isaac and the SEALs wore night vision goggles. The air tasted stale. Angry voices caromed up the concrete stairwell. We didn't have long.

"Puck, any bodies on top level?"

"Negative. There's a cluster three floors below."

In my ear piece, I heard Chase crash through glass. Screaming. Gunfire.

I gripped the gun so hard I thought the barrel might bend.

We descended until we found a big 47 painted on the door and we pushed in. Not a moment too soon. A horde charged past our floor on their trek upwards, unaware we hid on the other side of the wall. I heard them. I felt them. Diseased. Chosen. My skin crawled.

We now had enemies above and below.

Each floor of the Gas Company Tower was a 20,000-square-foot labyrinth. Puck could see the vague heat outlines but couldn't guide us directly to them. He saw a cross-section image, and was only able to alert us when we got close from his point of view. We moved silently, following a trail of trash.

This setting would make a great haunted house. I loved it. I longed to go pump shotgun shells into screaming maniacs hooting above us. I'd get my chance. First, we needed to release hostages.

Wish Carter was here.

We found a mother clutching two daughters in a back office, staring wildly at us. Their sole purpose in living alone on the 47th floor was to discourage American rockets. A candle burned on the nearby table. They wore blue robes with red sashes. The two girls were under seven years old. Their room stank. Mattresses laid in the corner.

"Let's go," I said. "We're getting out of here."

"W-who're you? The F-Father says we should stay."

"Get up!" I ordered. They obeyed. "Puck, update me on the Outlaw."

"He's alive. Going from room to room, beating everyone up."

Chase's voice came through the mayhem. "Sounds boring when you put it that way."

Puck said, "Shooter, there's elevator shafts everywhere. There's one just down the hall. You can climb down the cables."

"Stairwells too full?"

"All stairwells are basically glowing. PuckDaddy recommends the elevator shaft," he said.

I looked at the SEAL team and hissed, "Listen up. We're climbing down the elevator shaft. I need a volunteer to stay with the hostages and escort them up when the coast is clear." Hands went up. I picked one at random. "The hostages are wearing blue robes. I think that signifies they can't be harmed. The Chemist's men won't hurt his property, so don't get yourself killed trying to protect them. They'll live. You stay alive. Hide near the stairwell until it's time."

"Roger," he said.

"Let's move." We pried open the elevator doors, grasped the heavy cables, and slid down three floors.

I heard Puck tell Chase, "Outlaw, you've got company!"

"Whoa," the Outlaw said in my ear. "They have new weapons!"

"Cool, what kind?"

"Tell you later! I'm busy temporarily retreating."

I cursed quietly, dangling 650 feet up in a dark elevator shaft. "This isn't going well," I whispered and winced at the echoes.

We discovered two more groups of hostages on the 44th floor, giving us eight total. All women and children.

Thumping on nearby windows. Chosen were crawling exterior walls, ascending to the top. They hadn't seen us inside.

Puck said, "Outlaw, from my screen, it looks like you're in the same room with the Chemist."

Chase's voice came garbled and ragged. "You're right. Except that bright heat signature isn't the Chemist."

I pressed the bluetooth headset tight against my ear and said, "What?! Who is it??"

Chase responded grimly, "Walter."

"Walter," I snapped. Isaac saw my expression and his hope drained away. No Chemist. "Kill that son of a bitch." Walter was evil. Pure destruction. The Chemist was a maniac, but Walter was a monster in cornrows. Eliminating him would be the next best thing.

There was a violent burst of noise in the speaker. Voices. Grunting. Growling. Air. And then nothing.

"Chase?" I said. No response. My pulse was frozen, my heart refusing to beat until I heard his voice. "Chase??"

"His connection is gone," Puck told me. He sounded stunned.

"What's that mean??"

"Means…I'm not getting any signal from him."

"Can you see his heat signature?" I asked desperately.

"Lost it. My screen is on fire, there are so many bodies on that level. …That floor might *actually* be on fire."

I set my jaw. "I'm going after him."

"You'll run out of bullets long before you get there. In fact, whoa! Hostiles on your level!" he cried into my ear.

The SEALs saw them first and opened fire, deep booms destroying the quiet. Chosen. They came down the hallway like an avalanche, some moving over the walls and ceiling.

"Grenades!" I ordered, throwing one of my own, and then released the devastating power of my shotgun. It kicked and roared, louder than the others. Our black hallway lit up with fire, highlighting faces twisted in rage. Animals. Insanity.

I pulled the trigger again. The firing pin struck brass inside the chamber, creating a spark. Gun powder lit. One hundred steel pellets burst forth at a thousand feet per second. The closest Chosen disintegrated into hamburger, hard skin unable to resist the shot.

Our grenades went off, puncturing holes into landscape and the tide of bodies. I was shot in the shoulder but it didn't penetrate. A SEAL took a round and collapsed. I fired six times, pulling the trigger so fast it sounded like one loud eruption. The six remaining SEALs and I melted the first wave.

"Puck get us out of here!" I shouted. "I need stairs!"

"Behind you! Middle of the south wall. You'll have to fight your way up."

"Follow me!" I turned and fled. We couldn't fight that many. And more were coming.

A Chosen fell out of the ceiling, a white kid about Chase's age. Grotesquely thin. Needed a shave. Corded with muscle. Wearing only jeans. The disease's scent roiled off him. I severed his carotid artery with my knife as he lunged.

We reached the stairwell, a madhouse of screaming. I fired my shotgun, felling two panting gunmen on the landing.

Isaac grunted, "We'll never make it up."

"Got a better idea, Special Agent?" I snarled. I ripped three grenades off the closest SEAL vest and hurled them upwards, picking out different ricochet angles to cover the most area. The grenades bounced out of sight, and detonations shook the walls. My ears rang.

We made it only one level and then the crush of descending bodies forced us onto the 45th floor. One of the SEALs was caught and pulled over the railing, gone forever. Our hostages screamed.

"Far side, other stairwell, move move move!" I ordered, and I stood in the doorway an extra twenty seconds, shredding hostiles exiting the stair shaft. Four rounds. I ejected the magazine, tossed a grenade, and ran. "Puck, any word on Outlaw?"

"No," he said miserably.

We ascended another level and were pushed onto the 46th. This floor had been under construction. Half the level was completely open, a vast plain, all the way to far windows. The city sparkled beyond. Support beams and plumbing and ventilation shafts stood exposed.

A small group of Chosen waited for us, standing ready.

I muttered, "Ah. These are the new weapons Chase mentioned."

These twelve Chosen appeared healthier. Better fed. Stronger. And they were armed with gory gadgets.

Six of them, four women and two men, wore metal gloves which provided the wearer with two-inch razor claws. The Chemist had decided bullets were ineffective. These claws would cut through our skin easier than bullets could puncture, I bet.

Three of them wore heavy boots and bizarre electrical gloves. The gloves were corded with exposed wires and connected to powerful batteries in thick black cuffs. Their fingers sparked and spit. Could be a horror movie.

The final three Chosen brandished metal bats connected to a battery strapped to their back. The metal bats were electrified.

These Chosen and these weapons were Outlaw killers. The Chemist had grown wiser. He'd created soldiers specifically designed to hurt Infected with razors and electricity.

"Everyone stay behind me," I said. "Keep that stairwell sealed. Kill anyone who comes out. This just got fun."

One of the armed Chosen, a Latin American man brandishing a nasty looking bat, called, "We do not want you dead, pretty lady. We want you alive."

"Those are the Chemist's orders?" I asked.

"Straight from his mouth, senoritá. Put down the gun. He wants you to join the family!"

"Is that so."

"And I want you in my bed, mamitá. Let's talk."

"Talking's the worst," I growled. "Why do guys always wanna talk?"

I fired.

They were too far away for shotgun damage. They charged. We released grenades. These Chosen were fast, well trained, and they danced away from eruptions. Only one fell without getting up.

I fired into the face of a bellowing bull with earrings. He died, but not before raking his claws across my abdomen. His steel slashed straight through my skin and muscle.

The Navy SEAL on my right fired and got a piece of a second Chosen. The man fell. His baton connected with a steel girder. The battery released its load into the metal with an enormous *snap*, and floor insulation around the steel beam melted with a sizzle.

This floor, the 46th, had offices on the north half. I laid down murderous fire and we retreated into the main doorway. The SEAL on my blindside was caught at the neck by an electrified glove. Their connection allowed the electricity to ground, instantly killing both men. My nostrils filled with burnt flesh.

An electric suicide bomber.

It would kill me too.

The tower suddenly shook. Through the far windows, a magnificent blossom of fire. Some eruption below shook our structure like an earthquake.

Hopefully that meant the Outlaw still lived.

We backed into the offices and fought the Chosen and gunmen with guerrilla warfare, reducing their numbers through attrition. We hid, making them come to us. They charged into our crossfire blindly, and died. Rivers of blood ran. So did my sweat. The four surviving SEALs fought valiantly. Isaac too. The man was fearless. Mothers and daughters screamed from under tables. We survived until the grenades ran out. Then, tides turned. Their unending numbers rose against us. We lost a SEAL to Chosen with bladed hands. Then another.

Isaac aimed and fired his assault rifle over my shoulder. Click. "I'm out," he barked.

"Take a magazine off my belt," I yelled. Boom! My shotgun pulped his target, and a spent cartridge clattered on the tile floor. "Only two more shotgun rounds left."

"You were right," Isaac commented, tugging an assault rifle magazine off my belt. "You run out, we die."

"I love being right. Most of the time."

We had two SEALs left. And six hostages, and Isaac and me. Plus presumably three hostages and a SEAL still alive somewhere above.

"Save your rounds!" I called. "We're making a run for it! Hopefully we thinned the herd enough to get up the staircase."

Puck murmured something about that not working. But we were out of options. I discarded the beautiful, steaming shotgun in favor of my assault rifle. I still had sixty bullets left, enough to fight my way out. At least to a window. But I didn't want to escape via parachute. I wanted to get everyone home.

Chase's influence on me. Damn him.

"Let's go!"

We burst from our hiding spots and scrambled for the eastern stairwell.

Puck was right. It wouldn't work.

We ran into a hundred enemies. Two hundred. Maybe three. Waiting for us. They were everywhere, even crawling up walls and hanging from rafters. Many marked by traces of powder around noses and mouths, indications of the Chemist's super drug.

We were wanted alive. They didn't kill us immediately.

"Hold your fire!" I screamed to my squad. Shooting would be like fighting waves with handfuls of sand. Pointless. There had to be a better option. Quickly they encircled us. They didn't attack. We didn't fire.

"This sucks."

Isaac muttered, "My radio was destroyed. We got no help coming."

"Shooter." Puck's voice sounded sad in my ear. "Special Agent Anderson has Hellfire missiles aimed at the tower. A lot of them. I can fire them. Just...just say the word. And I will. The collateral damage might be worth taking out that god-awful army."

"And a quick death," I mused.

"Yeah."

"I still might talk my way out of this."

He didn't laugh.

The leader from before, the Latino carrying an electric bat, sauntered into view. He spread his hands to indicate the infinite number of men and women at his disposal.

"Well well, señorita. You ready to talk with me? Or will we just take what we want from you?"

My blood boiled. This man, at least, would die.

I asked, "What are you offering?"

"You will be kept alive and taken to the Father."

"And the hostages?"

"The property you're trying to steal?" he smirked. "They'll be sent back to their rooms."

"And the men with me?"

"They will be fed to tigers. Alive, if you don't surrender. Dead, if you do." He shrugged. "The Father's pets enjoy the taste of human. Be merciful. Give yourself to me."

"Nah."

"Nah?" His eyebrows rose in surprise. "Nah? We will hold you down, perra. My men will take turns with you. Nah?"

I called, "Not tonight. Some other time."

He shook his head in disbelief. His men raised weapons. Probably a hundred guns. I trained mine on his face.

That window/parachute option was looking better and better.

All of a sudden, a loud voice burst forth.

"NO!"

Such a voice! I shuddered at the sound, at the power.

The Outlaw. He stalked onto our floor and his presence sent the enemy reeling. They cowered and ducked, forced backwards. He was enraged and engorged and his fury shone like the sun. I could barely look at him. Chosen shielded their eyes.

The virus was a volcano in him, thrusting its power against our senses. Chosen felt the strength more acutely and they cried out when he glared. The disease in him crippled their own by comparison. And mine.

"Back!" he ordered. The crowd acted as if scalded, and scampered away. He swept enemies backwards with his will. The weight of his anger was a physical force. He bled…everywhere. His mask was gone. His bandana missing. Clothes torn. Rod stuffed into his vest.

A girl clutched his free hand, exhausted. Natalie North. She panted and struggled to stand.

He approached the center of the room, pushing Chosen and gunmen ahead with his gaze. This was the Outlaw the Chemist feared. This was the man Carter knew Chase might become. A man that could break the world. Or save it.

His body called to me. A siren. Drawing me. The Chosen experienced it too. They loved him. Feared him. And hated him. Despised him. Loathed him. How had the Chemist poisoned their minds' against Chase so effectively?

Hundreds of Chosen and gunmen pressed against the far walls and against each other. As they congealed into one mass, however, their resolve hardened. Their courage returned as they collected. Combined hatred swelled. Soon they'd have strength enough to defy him.

"We're leaving," he told us. His words went into my bones like raw power, an infusion of vitality. His voice carried hope. The two SEALs obeyed him. Even they had trouble meeting his eyes.

We didn't speak. Isaac took Natalie North's hand and we jogged quickly towards the door while Chase held back the rising tide of evil. But his power over them waned. Our time ran short.

"Wait!" Natalie North cried, beautiful even in destruction. She pulled out of Isaac's protective grip and hurried back. She released the red sash from her waist and reached waaaaaay up to tie it around his face. Her blue robe fell open but she wore lingerie underneath. The red sash covered Chase's eyes and all his hair, like a helmet which knotted in the back. She ripped two eyeholes in the material's thin weave. "There," she smiled wearily and touched his cheeks with her hands. "The Outlaw wears a mask."

"Thank you, Natalie."

Puck asked in my ear, "What the HELL is going on??"

"The Outlaw is back. Natalie North just gave him a new mask," I replied.

"A new one?"

"Yup."

"What happened to his old one?"

"I don't know. It's gone."

Natalie North walked quietly back to us and took Isaac's hand.

Puck asked, "What's it look like?"

"His new mask? It's red. Covers his whole head except for his nose and mouth. Ties in the back, and the ends dangle down. Who cares?"

"Huh," Puck said. "Like Zorro's?"

"No," I snapped in irritation. "Not like Zorro's. You need to focus."

Isaac said, "Maybe he means Zorro's *first* mask? In the movie, Antonio Banderas wore a mask like that before putting on Zorro's hat."

"Kinda," Natalie North nodded. "More like the Dred Pirate Roberts. Except crimson."

"Affirmative," one of the SEALs nodded. "Exactly like Dred Pirate Roberts."

"Who?"

"Did you never watch *The Princess Bride*?" Natalie asked, smiling affectionately at Isaac.

"The what? No."

"Great movie, sir. A must-watch."

"Samantha." The Outlaw spoke in a fierce whisper that cut like a knife. "Get everyone on the helicopter and take off."

"Roger that, Outlaw."

We fled. The wave of humanity broke, crashing against the Outlaw. I didn't watch. I obeyed. But we could hear his Boom Stick singing. Crushing. I ran, yelling for the Navy SEAL and hostages waiting on the 47th floor. They joined us in our mad dash through darkness. Women and children staggered and we hauled them up. Our crew reached the roof and fresh air. Pilot WhatsHisName plunged his heavy Black Hawk towards the helipad.

There wasn't enough time to land and load two choppers. We'd have to shove into the FBI Black Hawk's rear cabin, which was loaded with equipment and not intended for troop transport. Eight people was a tight fit. We numbered fifteen, including the Outlaw, who had somehow joined us.

The helicopter landed hot and reckless. Forward landing wheels crunched and the fuselage sparked against tarmac. Chase and I threw Natalie and hostages into the rear cabin.

"In!" I ordered the SEALs. They balked and tried to force me on.

"Get in!" Chase ordered and they obeyed.

Men. Typical stupid men.

The horde of gunmen and Chosen arrived, pouring up the stairs. Our transport would be swarmed. Their leader, the man from before, led the charge with a sparking baton of death.

Chase turned, casually spun his Thunder Stick, and *beheaded* the man with one violent hack to the base of his skull.

Beheaded! That was intense, even for me. The helicopter's downdraft sprayed a burst of crimson across the helipad.

Chase held up his hand, like a traffic guard stopping oncoming cars. The enemy screamed and reeled away, collapsing backwards as one body. Their momentum terminated like an interstate wreck.

How did he DO that?! Chase's arm muscles bulged and he groaned in effort, like he physically pushed against…something. He stared them down, daring someone to move. Like last time, this halt was temporary. The

Chemist's forces gathered and rose like a wave.

"GO!" I screamed at Isaac. The SEALs and Isaac pressed into the helicopter, crushing women and children between them. It was close. The men grabbed handholds, and women secured them with arms wrapped around their waists. They fit.

Above us, the Navy Pave Hawk circled. "Puck!" I shouted. "Tell that Pave Hawk to light this place up!"

"You got it!"

The enemy surged. We met them at the crest of the staircase. The Outlaw dealt death with each hack, and I fired my assault rifle as fast as machinery allowed. Their gunmen returned fire and I absorbed hits in my vest and thigh, but we slowed the tide.

Pilot WhatsHisName threw the helicopter back into the sky, diving straight towards stars.

They were safe.

The Pave Hawk ducked, suffering a salvo of enemy gunfire from lower levels. Then, its heavy miniguns roared and unleashed .308 death into the top floors. So loud! Glass exploded. The structure shuddered.

"Outlaw, time to go!" We turned in unison, sprinted to the side of the helipad, chased by a sea of insanity. I angled towards the Pave Hawk and *Leapt*.

Not even close. I couldn't jump like Chase. And if I had gotten close, I'd have hit rotors most likely. Stupid! Stupid Samantha! So high up. The free fall would last…sixty seconds? I couldn't do math with wind howling in my ears. Then Chase slammed into me. He took my hands and carefully placed them at my waist. Of *course*! The flight suit. I'd forgotten, too hopped up on adrenaline, so ready for death. Almost welcomed it. But not today. I hooked gloves into pants, extended the wings and took flight.

Chapter Ten
Sunday, January 7. 2019

Samantha and I flew miles across Los Angeles. We landed around midnight when we saw the lights of an iHop on 6th Street. Both of us famished, I helped Samantha stow her parachute. She announced she was going to kiss Lee on the mouth as a Thank You for the wings and chute. If I knew Lee, he was going to suggest Second Base might be a more appropriate sign of gratitude.

Samantha extracted a bullet from her outer thigh, the way a normal human would remove an air rifle pellet, and secured the wound with a bandage. To avoid recognition, I wrapped the sash around my head in a more common fashion, like a balaclava, and we collapsed into a booth. Everything hurt. The bones in my hands ached. My face felt raw, like someone had scorched the skin with electricity. Which they had. My ribs burned from slash wounds. Claws had raked my neck. My ears rang from Samantha's gunshots. Every time I blinked the darkness filled with muzzle bursts.

Patrons inside the warm diner cast curious glances our way but we weren't dressed dissimilarly from extreme hipsters. Except for the blood. Each of us was splattered with an alarming amount of drying blood. But other than that, we fit in. And our vests. Those were weird too. And my Stick of Treachery. That was also odd.

"Omelets," we told our server. "Five each. Whatever's quickest." She cocked an unamused and heavily penciled eyebrow and sauntered off.

I had texts from Puck.

>> **PuckDaddy is tracking u**
>> **stop flying around**
>> **where r u 2 going**
>> **r u at an ihop ??**
>> **anderson is freaking out**
>> **ur at a ihop i can tell**
>> **ur so weird**
>> **fine. eat and ignore Puck**
>> **not like PuckDaddy has been worried sick**
>> **i gave isaac ur location**
>> **don't think he cares right now**
>> **hes got natalie**
>> **bet hes making out**

I texted Katie. **We are alive. But we didn't get him.**

>> **Aw, I'm sorry, handsome. You'll get him next time. I'm sure you tried really hard.**

I grinned. **I love you.**

>> **Back at'cha! Come find me. I don't know where I am but I have all the kisses for you. =)**

Samantha asked, "Do you have your wallet?"

"No. Left it with Katie. Why?"

"iHop is going to frown on our lack of funds. Tell Isaac to bring us money."

"No way. He just got Natalie back. Let's give them some privacy."

She rolled her eyes. "I am *not* washing dishes to pay for this food."

"I'll text Dad."

She perked up. "Even better idea. I could use Richard right now."

"Oh," I grimaced and my stomach lurched. "Holy...never mind, ew. Gross. I'll just go rob someone."

I ate four omelets, two plates of hash browns, two bowls of fruit, three chocolate pancakes, and drank six glasses of ice water and three mugs of coffee. Samantha ate an extra pancake, just to prove she could consume more. No talking. Just shoveling food. My hands quit shaking after twenty minutes.

"My father doesn't want any part of *that*." I pointed at Samantha as she leaned back, holding her stomach with one hand and loosening her belt with the other.

"I don't care," she sighed. "Don't need him anymore. I'm good."

Puck texted me. **>> puck is sending help ur way, u dummies.**

I replied, **Send money too. We're broke.**

We sat in silence, digesting at an inhuman rate. I sucked on a mint from the counter and closed my eyes, trying to remember how many hostages boarded the helicopter. Not enough.

"So how'd you do all that?" Samantha asked, interrupting my recollections.

"Do all what?"

"Chase." She glared with a piercing, knowing glint in her eye. "You have telekinesis. Or something."

"I have *what*??"

"You controlled the Chosen with your mind."

"Oh. That. No, I just yelled at them and they believed me." I screwed up my eyes and replayed the night's events in my mind. How *had* that happened? I remembered watching the enemy…knowing they'd do as I ordered…understanding the disease in me dominated the disease in them…some preternatural instinct told me so. "It was like, in that moment of time, I was connected to them. Like wolves in a pack. We shared a collective mind. And I was the Alpha. Does that make sense?"

"No. Maybe. But what about the regular guys? His normal thugs? Why did they obey you?"

"I don't know, Samantha." I rubbed my forehead and pinched the bridge of my nose. "I'm too tired. Don't over think it. They might have just been scared."

"Did you kill Walter?"

"No," I sighed, irritated at the memory. Walter was lethal. Quick as a viper. He'd gotten stronger too; I felt it. "I think I broke his shoulder. One of the Chemist's new electro-toys zapped me and he got away."

"Wimp," she grinned.

"You shut up. Those guys hurt. Fried my earpiece."

"Did they get you with a baton? Or the electric gloves?"

"Never saw the gloves. Just guys holding electrified bats. Actually, it was a girl that shocked me."

She nodded. "The gloves are nasty. They touch you, or you touch them, pow. Like a bomb goes off on contact."

"What happens if the glove is armed and they accidentally touch a flagpole or something?"

"Or your Boom Stick?"

"I need thicker gloves." I pulled mine from my pocket. The fabric was torn in multiple places. Lee would receive my commission soon for a new pair. "I didn't sense the Chemist. Or smell him, or whatever it is that alerts us he's nearby."

"I thought Walter was in Seattle. Guess he came in for that damn Teresa Triplett news bulletin."

"Who knows." I shook my head. "They just fly around, destroying the planet at their leisure. And we keep missing them."

She yawned so wide her jaw cracked. "This has been a long forty-eight hours. I don't know how Puck goes days without sleeping."

To our surprise, Dad walked into iHop fifteen minutes later just as our fellow patrons began noticing Samantha's resemblance to the girl on the television screens. The girl worth millions. Dad gave us both hugs and paid our bill.

Samantha climbed into the front of his squad car. I fell into the back, next to Katie. She still wore camouflage, and I rested my head in her lap. Dad put the car in gear and we motored out of the parking lot. Katie carefully removed the sash from my head, unzipped my vest, and examined my various injuries.

She pointed to a cut over my eye. "How'd you get this one?"

"Walter hit me."

"I dislike Walter."

"Me too."

She sucked at her teeth, a cute look for her, and stared out the window in thought. "He's the one who shot your helicopter down in Compton. With a rocket. And attacked you with a knife while I watched from the bus. Right?"

"Correct."

"What about this one?" She gingerly touched an open gash on my shoulder.

94

"Flying through windows."

"I think it needs stitches."

"It should heal in the next day or two," I yawned. "Might leave a scar."

"Scars are sexy. What about this bruise?"

"Gun shot. I think."

"Knives and glass penetrate your skin easier than bullets?"

"Dunno," I murmured from the cusp of consciousness. The quietly rocking car lulled me towards sleep.

"What about this welt near your ear? It's red and puffy. Some of the skin is peeling."

"Electrical burn."

"I forbid you from going into that tower again. Everyone there was mean to you."

"Yes ma'am."

I woke up a few hours later in an unknown bed. Katie was lying next to me, scratching my back with one hand and texting with the other. Other than the glow from her phone, it was dark. Other than the hum from an AC unit, it was quiet.

I whispered, "Wanna make out?"

"No," she replied. "You stink."

"Okay. Good night again."

Chapter Eleven
Sunday, January 7. 2019

After hours of effort, I forced my eyelids open. The nightstand clock read 9:12. Hopefully morning. No windows. The room was small and white and undecorated. Military, most likely. No Katie.

My dad sat on a metal chair in the corner, reading something on an iPad. Small brown reading glasses perched on his nose, comically small on such a big hairy guy. Samantha said he looks like the guy who used to host *Dirty Jobs*.

"When'd you get glasses?" I grunted.

He answered, "Recently," but didn't look up. "Quite a snore you got, boy."

I snorted some air through my nostrils. One side was mostly clogged. "I think something got knocked loose back there." Talking made my head ring, but I felt…okay. The welt near my ear wasn't as swollen as last night. My body ached instead of screamed. Rapidly regenerating body tissue and a high white blood cell count rules. "Sorry about our house."

"S'okay. All the furniture was ugly."

"Mom picked the furniture."

"Beautiful woman," he sniffed at the memory, a smile on his face. "Bad decorator."

"Did we have insurance?"

"Yes. Insurance company should have enough cash for all the Los Angeles payouts sometime next century. Your cousin called. He wants you to visit his fourth grade class. In costume."

"My costume is destroyed. Look. I'm surprised the parachute deployed. And my mask is gone."

I held up the mangled vest. It was burnt and ripped, never to be worn again. Dad turned his face away and closed his eyes. "Son. Fathers don't need to see visual evidence of their sons' brush with death."

"Sorry. Tell him I'll visit his class if I get new gear. And call it gear, not a costume. Makes me sound cooler."

Dad turned off the iPad, slid glasses into his shirt pocket, cleared his throat, and said, "Has it occurred to you that if the Chemist had been there last night then you'd be dead?"

I tried to get out of bed and failed. "What do you mean?"

"From what you told've me, the Chemist is a much more dangerous monster than Walter. And if you almost died facing Walter…"

I took a deep breath and let it out in a blast at the ceiling. "Yeah."

"Son, perhaps….if you are the world's most valuable resource against this enemy, *perhaps* you should exercise more prudence about when to throw your life away."

"Prudence?"

"You heard me."

"I don't consider it 'throwing my life away.' Last night was a calculated risk."

He made a dissatisfied noise. "Did you have a plan? Last night during the calculated risk?"

"Yes. Hit the Chemist in the head really hard."

"But he wasn't there. And if he had been, can you even do that?"

"…I'm not sure," I admitted. And it was the truth. I didn't know if I could. I *hoped* I could. But the evidence sided against me. He had been alive too long; his body was too strong, too fast, and his brain too quick.

Sanguine. That was the word. I was being sanguine about my dismal chances. Katie would be proud of my vocabulary.

"There is no father on earth more proud of his son than I am. But I am compelled to point out things that your…adoring public…won't. You jumped into an enemy-occupied tower seeking a target that wasn't there and nearly died. That wasn't a calculated risk. That was an inch from a disaster. Samantha told me how close she and the others came to dying. Following you."

"Yeah. That was scary."

He nodded, his beefy arms crossed over his chest. "You're doing all this for Katie, aren't you."

"Probably. He threatened her and then put a bounty on her head."

"Are you sure dying during a rushed and miscalculated risk is the best way to protect her?"

I had no answer. There was no correct response. So I stayed silent and prickled painfully with the rebuke.

He said, "Your disease forces you to act unwisely."

"I deal with fight-or-flight episodes often. Samantha does too. The adrenaline makes us jumpy. Craves action."

His voice was thick with emotion and intensity. He leaned forward and rested forearms on his knees. "I honor your bravery. And I know you shoulder more responsibility and consequences than I can imagine. Far too much responsibility. It would crush a lesser person. But it seems to me that if you're going to survive this, you'll need to control the impulses." He found my foot beneath the covers and shook it. "You're doing a great job, kid. And your next step into manhood needs to be self-control. In your situation, you can't afford many missteps."

"You're right, Dad. I know you are. But I'm so desperate to get rid of the Chemist…you know?"

"We all are. But I want you around for the decades it'll take to clean up his mess." He stood and put his hand on the door knob. "This is a marathon. Not a sprint."

"Understood."

"You should shower, too."

"Hey. Dad. Are you and Samantha…romantic?"

"Aggressively so."

"Ewwww, Dad!" I covered my face with a pillow and punched it. "Gross gross gross. Why'd I ask that."

"I gotta go. Duty calls. A third of the force has quit and moved east. Keep in touch."

He left. I crawled out of bed and stretched, loosening all the sore muscles and joints. I took a shower, and pulled on khakis, a blue Air Force polo and my sneakers.

Two airmen saluted when I opened the door into a bright hallway. I returned the greeting as best I could.

"Good morning, sir. I have a list of messages for you."

I grunted, "Read them to me over breakfast."

"This way, sir."

I filled two plates from a breakfast buffet and sat down at an empty linoleum table in a large cafeteria. The conversations had temporarily halted when I walked in. A nearby group of burly and grim giants got up from their table and sat at mine.

"I was with you, sir. Last night," one of the five giants said. He was black and, despite the severity, he had a friendly face. His eye was swollen nearly shut and his nose was busted. "So were these two."

I asked, "You were the SEALs on the tower?"

"And we're home, thanks to you."

"My condolences on the loss of your fellow SEALs. They died well."

He nodded. "We watched you fight. Watched the enemy cower. We're all in, sir. We've requested reassignment to your protection detail."

"You'll have to clear it with my current protection detail. She doesn't play well with others."

"The hot girl with a shotgun?"

I laughed around a bite of eggs. "That's her. She won't make your life easy."

"The only easy day was yesterday, sir."

Yesterday was NOT easy. I glanced at one of the airmen who'd been at my door. "Any idea where my phone is?"

"Yes sir. Ms Lopez has it. She said it was buzzing too much and waking you up."

"Where is she?"

His face paled. "I'm not sure, sir. Sorry. I'll find out. But she told us she'd meet you later."

I nodded and ate some bacon. I love bacon.

"FBI pilot Mike Matthews is at the airfield," he continued, reading off his notes. "He's re-fueled and sleeping in the HRT helicopter, ready if you need him. Air Force is assigning him a gunner."

A cluster of soldiers approached our table, probably just wanting to take a picture. They had camera phones. The SEALs glared at the cluster, stopping them cold. After a long uncomfortable moment, the soldiers took the cue and left.

The kid with notes kept going, "Special Agent Isaac Anderson reports there is a meeting at ten hundred hours. Your presence is required."

"You can get me there?" I asked.

"Yes sir. You don't need to prepare. And the Shooter will also attend."

"The Shooter?" I grinned.

"That's...that's how she identified herself."

One of the SEALs nodded. "Hot girl with a shotgun."

I had nowhere to be for twenty minutes, so I remained at the table, drank juice, and chatted with the stony SEALs. The SEALs related details of last night's fight to their comrades, using salt and pepper shakers and knives to demonstrate relative positions. On their small battlefield, I was a bottle of hot sauce. I approved. They got lost in their retelling and allowed an audience to gather until the cafeteria filled.

They finished their narrative by saying, "The last we saw, sir, you and the Shooter jumped off the roof. Thought for sure you'd be dead. You were wearing a parachute?"

"A wing-suit," I replied. The crowd murmured. Pictures of this wing-suit had circulated online a few months ago.

"Damn small wing-suit."

"I've got a good tailor."

The nervous airman found his voice. "Sir, we need to go. The briefing begins in five minutes."

I drained my juice and stood. So did the SEALs. They surrounded me and followed the airman, shouldering aside the mass of bodies. I did my best not to look overwhelmed in this bizarre parade. Through a labyrinth of corridors we marched silently for several minutes. Underground, I bet. I got lost quickly. Without a guide, I'd die down here. Finally we paused at a fancy elevator guarded by two armed soldiers.

A grey-haired, uniformed man shook my hand and said, "Chase Jackson, I assume? I'm Major General Roberts. Welcome to the Los Angeles Air Force Base."

"I appreciate the hospitality."

"Gentlemen," he addressed the SEALs. "I've been informed that your reassignment requests have been processed and approved. But you'll have to remain here, outside the restricted areas."

"Yes Major General," answered the SEALs. They were standing at attention. Perhaps I should stand straighter, too.

The elevator scanned Roberts' retina and we shuttled deeper into the earth. He commented, "I had the pleasure of meeting Ms. Lopez. She's even more lovely than her photographs."

"I have the pleasure of dating her. And it's been even better than I hoped."

He chuckled. "She reminds me of my daughter. All smiles and optimism. I have a grandson on the way. My first. I'm trying to keep the world intact for him."

"Not a fun time to be pregnant."

"It speaks well of you, son, that men follow you so easily." He raised his chin to indicate the SEALs far above us. "Good men don't blindly follow poor leadership. That helps the rest of us trust you."

"Better find yourself a parachute," I said. "Following me gets weird."

"Parachutes are useless without a safe place to land," he grumbled, turning sour. "The time for parachutes and all safety precautions might soon be at an end.

"I've got a friend who'll be delighted to hear that."

"I met *her* too. She's…intense."

"Yeah. And you probably met her during one of her *good* moods, too."

He escorted me to a wide, wooden-paneled room with a mahogany table and black swivel chairs. One wall was a bank of television screens and computer monitors. The air smelled like money and secrets. Most chairs were occupied with fancy old people who stood to shake my hand as Major General Roberts introduced me around the room. They were all heads of hard to pronounce military directorates. Some wore badges, which would help with name recall. I sat down between Isaac, who appeared to be healthier than he had in weeks, and Samantha, who appeared deeply bored.

I whispered to Isaac, "How many of these folks do you trust?"

"Don't know most. So I don't trust them."

Television screens flickered on. Video conference calls piped in from around the globe. Isaac quietly identified the Secretary of State; Secretary of Defense ("I trust him," he said); Director of the CIA ("Him too."); a representative from the Joint Chiefs; and finally the President of the United States, a handsome and square-faced guy going silver around the ears. He put on reading glasses and squinted at the screen.

"Holy smokes," I murmured. All the bigwigs greeted each other, deferring especially to the President, and made light-hearted smalltalk.

"Remember what Carter said about the President," Samantha whispered.

Isaac whispered back, "We are aware the President's under the influence of a powerful Infected girl, but we don't know how to intervene."

"Blue-Eyes," I said in a hushed voice. "I remember her."

As if on cue, the President peered intensely through his computer screen and broke into a grin. "Ah! Do I spy the infamous Chase Jackson?"

I froze. Like someone sucked out all my oxygen and replaced it with ice water. The President of the United States of America just addressed me by name.

"Uh, yes...yes sir," I stammered, staring around. Where the heck do I look?? He's in a computer screen. Where's the camera?

"I'm a long-time admirer of yours, young man. I'm glad to finally pass along my appreciation face-to-face. So to speak."

"Oh...well...thanks."

"I look forward to hearing your report on last night's traumatic events."

"Yes sir."

A lady across the table frowned at me. "I thought you'd be taller."

"And older."

"So," the President mused to himself, leaning back in a chair. "You're at the Air Force Base in Los Angeles. Not a very isolated location for such a wanted man."

Suddenly, I knew. I knew without a shred of uncertainty that Blue-Eyes was in the room with him, eavesdropping on the video conference. His body betrayed her. He smiled too big. Kept glancing off screen. He was nervous. This was a performance. She controlled him. My hackles rose.

He continued, "I just watched one of the Lopez videos. Has everyone seen those things? Outstanding. Just outstanding. Is she at the Air Force base too?"

"Lopez videos?" I wondered out loud. "What Lopez videos?"

The Secretary of State, a stern women with brown hair piled atop her head, said, "The *Katie Clips*. They're fantastic. I applaud her efforts."

"The *Katie Clips*??" I cried. I looked to Samantha for help but she shrugged.

The room laughed at me, and then took turns explaining. Katie Lopez had over two million followers on Instagram. Two million!? Her followers had grown steadily since she appeared in People magazine. Beginning last month, she had been posting short videos on her Twitter and Instagram accounts, in which she discussed what to do in emergency situations, explained how teenagers could help their country and families, and read short excerpts from famous patriotic poems and essay. Her favorite was Henry Wadsworth Longfellow. Her common-sense suggestions presented with humor, encouragement, and hope, from the girl who had survived everything, were viral gold. The videos were aimed at young girls, but she was so pretty and likable that her popularity grew.

The Secretary of State sighed, "Of course her followers tripled yesterday when the Chemist released his Outlaw bounty. I'd like to meet her."

Major General Roberts chuckled, "Her recent video is about how to kill time while your boyfriend is trying to save the world and you're worried about him. I loved it. I know the youngsters loved it. She's upstairs right now, filming PSAs with the Navy, accompanied by guards I trust. She's going to Stanford?"

I nodded, a little numb. I'm the worst boyfriend in the world. How could she not tell me about this? Better question, how could I not notice?

The Secretary of Defense, a stern man with hollow cheeks, spoke up. Anderson trusted him. "Let's begin the meeting, if we can. Special Agent in Charge, you're the director of the Hyper Humanity Terrorism Joint Task Force. Why don't you guide us through this circus?"

"Certainly," Isaac said and he stood up, clearing his throat. "First, a preliminary clarification. We have two civilians in attendance. For legal and protocol reasons, we are awarding military rank to Chase Jackson and Samantha Gear. Effective immediately, they are designated as GS-12, or the equivalent of a military O-4 rank, with all due benefits and security clearances." He glanced at us and winked. "Congratulations, you two. You just became majors in the military. Only, don't try to pull rank. It won't go over well."

"Okay," I said, dumbfounded and confused. Did I outrank my dad, now? Samantha didn't seem to care.

The President said, "Bravo!"

"I hope you've all had a chance to review my debriefing and the footage from last night. If not, here's a quick summary. Thanks to NSA intelligence, we identified a high-profile target within enemy occupied territory. Specifically, inside the Gas Tower downtown."

On the big screen, silent night-vision and infrared videos of the rooftop battle played. I watched with interest.

He continued, "We scrambled a squad of Navy SEALs with orders to capture or kill the target, and also authorized Chase Jackson and Samantha Gear, codenamed Outlaw and Shooter, to accompany. The mission was not a success. The target, who we believed was the Chemist, escaped. We brought home nine hostages and lost five Navy SEALs."

"Not a success," the President repeated.

We sat silently and watched the mayhem, culminating in the Pave Hawk's ferocious attack, which was blinding when viewed with night vision.

The Secretary of Defense asked, "Incredible footage. Special Agent, can you describe the combat? And the enemy?"

"Yes sir. Same as previous engagements. He deployed an army of untrained civilians with guns, often displaying evidence of drug use. And of course, hundreds of Hyper Humans who are too fast for us. We'd have died in minutes without the Outlaw and Shooter."

"The enemy appears to…fare poorly against the Outlaw and the Shooter."

"Yes sir," he laughed without mirth. "The enemy is not too fast for *them*. The enemy dies. Or runs away."

Everyone at the table scrutinized us, looking for clues. So did the people on camera. Samantha rolled her eyes.

The Secretary of State cleared her throat on screen and said, "Well, I have a stupid question, and I'm not even sure how to phrase it, but how do they…do you…the Outlaw and-and the Shooter…why are they able to…how do they do that?"

Everyone at the table nodded in complete understanding of her inability to articulate the question.

"We have an illness, ma'am," I shrugged. "The same as the enemy."

Samantha shouted at the screen, "We're just better at it."

The Director of the CIA flipped through several sheets of paper. He said, "Mr. Jackson and Ms. Gear, Special Agent Anderson's report mentioned new hand-to-hand weapons wielded by the enemy. Several varieties, including electroshock. Did you encounter these?"

"Damn right, we did," Samantha said. "Almost cut me in half. Took out your SEALs, too."

"The weapons are new," I confirmed. "Infected often fight at close range. These gadgets are designed with that in mind."

The Secretary of State cleared her throat again and said, "Mr. Carter never mentioned the weapons."

I asked, "Mr. Carter?"

"Yes. Your colleague, the bald man known as Carter." She took a deep, unhappy breath and said, "We've met his demands, against my better judgement, and he's consulting on this new threat."

The President sat up straighter and yelped, "He is??"

"Yes, Mr. President."

"I did not authorize this." He was looking above and beyond his camera now, watching something off screen. Watching Mary, the Blue Eyed Witch. My blood boiled.

The Secretary of Defense, the stern and irritated and trustworthy man, said, "I made the decision to work with Carter, after consulting with the Joint Chiefs."

The Director of the CIA said, "I thought it wise, too."

"That decision was ill advised," the President said, shifting in his chair. He shook his finger at the monitor. "You should have consulted with me. Effective immediately, you are to cease communication with him."

"Mr. President-"

"Or! An even better idea. I'd like to meet with him. What is his location?"

I slammed my hands on the table and shouted, "Enough!" Everyone jumped except Samantha, who snickered. The table cracked. I stood up and stalked towards his monitor. "Put Blue-Eyes on screen."

Behind the President's reading glasses, his eyes bulged. "I beg your pardon?"

"Mary. You might call her Mary. I want to speak with her. Now." I stood in front of his screen, fists on hips, glaring. I wanted to crawl through the camera.

"Young man, perhaps you forget who-"

"I know she's listening. MARY!" I bellowed. The room shook. Several of the room's occupants cried out in alarm. I can yell loudly. A hearing aid squealed. "Blue-Eyed Witch, I know you can hear me, get yourself in front of the camera."

The room rang with my voice. All listeners had been stunned into silence. No one could've stopped me if they wanted. Who spoke to the President like this?! He appeared to have been electrocuted or frozen. His face turned white and beads of sweat formed at his hairline. Only his eyes moved.

After a long, tense moment, a girl slid into his lap and smirked at the screen. She was gorgeous and could have been on the cover of any lingerie or swimsuit catalog. Blonde hair, heart-shaped face, intense blue eyes, she was so pretty it hurt to look at her. Her shirt was low cut and belonged in a casino lounge, not the Oval Office.

"Hello, darling," she cooed at me. With one finger she tapped her lips. With her other hand, she stroked the President's face. "You've grown even more…masculine since we last met. I think about our encounter often, you know."

The President's romantic fling with a gorgeous blonde was a poorly kept secret among political circles. It was a shameful and embarrassing affair for America. But allowing her to be in the room and listen to classified conference calls was tantamount to treason. A low buzz of shock came from our audience. I pointed at her and addressed our listeners, "Our President's girlfriend is Infected. A cohort of the Chemist."

"Oh, my love," she purred, stretching out like a cat. "That's quite an accusation. Have you any proof?"

I said, "She holds powerful influence over the men she attracts. She bends them to her will."

Samantha barked, "She's a shoot on-sight target, in my opinion."

"Well, if it isn't the gun-toting tomboy. You've also grown more masculine, I believe, yes? Sweetie, you must come visit. We'll find you a push-up and mascara, and finally the boys will realize you aren't one."

"The disease enhances her charms," I told the men and women ogling her. "The same way it enhances my strength and Samantha's coordination."

"So it's my fault for being born lovable?" She shrugged and pouted. "Outlaw, I want so badly for us to be friends."

I broke eye contact with her and faced the others. Even at this distance through a monitor, she was clouding my judgement. Against reason, my pulse sped at the thought of being with her. I said, "The President is essentially a hostage. If you've noticed a change in him recently, it's because of Blue-Eyes. She is powerful. *He* isn't our enemy; *she* is."

"Well, handsome boys, this has been fun," she laughed, an inviting, intoxicating sound. "But the President and I have a date. Don't we, dear?"

"You can't hide there forever," I said, turning to stare at her again.

"I'll trade you," she winked. "I'll trade his body for yours. Alive. You and I would have so…much…fun."

"Let him go," I seethed.

"Your powers over the weak-minded will not work on me through this technology," she cackled. "Just like mine do not appear to affect you. Pity."

The President jerked spasmodically. He gasped and slapped the computer he'd been using. Their video feed died instantly.

Outrage burst into the room. The President was a stooge for the Infected?? What could be done? Couldn't arrest the President's girlfriend without hard evidence. Had she broken any laws? Had he? I stalked around the room, waiting for my anger to burn off. There's no way to determine how long her effects take to deteriorate?? The Secret Service was loyal to the President. It would be hard to pry her fingers off him. But the SS couldn't be happy about his new girlfriend, right?

"They're in love with her too, probably," Samantha grumbled. "No man around her is safe. And maybe no woman either. I won't let Chase near her, if I can help it."

"Anybody who goes into the Oval Office is compromised," I said. "And can no longer be trusted."

The Secretary of Defense, clearly disturbed, said, "Anderson, I'm starting to understand why you don't release the names of your covert task force."

"Yes sir. I trust very few of you."

The Secretary of State, the lady with brown hair messily piled in a bun, said, "I've been in that office multiple times and met that girl. Does this mean I'm not to be trusted?"

"All due respect, Madam Secretary," Isaac said, "but I wouldn't trust you to tie my shoes. Much less with sensitive information. I have multiple photos of you with Blue-Eyes."

"Careful who you make enemies with, Special Agent."

"Couldn't have said it better myself, Madam Secretary."

"This country is in a hell of a lot of trouble," she snapped and turned off her video screen.

The Director of the CIA scrubbed a hand through his sandy hair and said,

"She's not going to be happy with me. We took the photos."

"Those two," Isaac Anderson announced, pointing at the blank screens of the President and Secretary of State, "are the two I worry most about. *And* the Vice President. Now you can see what we're up against. I essentially trust no one in Washington. The girl has tentacles everywhere."

The Secretary of Defense, looking more and more irritated, grouched, "This is why the individual states need to declare emergencies and marshal their reserves. Our military is receiving conflicting leadership from federal sources."

"The President will never approve of Governors breaking off."

"Well, Christ, the President won't have a say-so before long," the Joint Chief on screen said, speaking for the first time. "These mutants are spilling into nearby cities and towns, leaking out of Houston and Seattle and Los Angeles, according to reports. And the federal government just…watches. More and more cities burn."

Major General Roberts said, "What do you mean, the President won't have a say-so?"

He grumbled, "States and cities have already begun circumventing his authority. And *our* authority, though I can't blame them. Sheriff offices and State Police are tripling their forces without authorization, taking on volunteers. Essentially forming illegal militias. Portland is under Martial Law."

Roberts said, "We're spread too thin. Air Force is pulling out of the Middle East."

"So is Navy. And Army."

"We need more military bodies in America, but the Middle East is going to implode. Evil is going to fill the power vacuum."

The gloom and doom talk continued. Stock market crashing. Oil prices at an all-time high, and Russia threatening to cease exports. China crashing as a result. Military bases abandoned. American forces clashing with each other.

"I don't get it," I said after absorbing as much pessimism as I could bear. I still paced. "We've lost one city. Los Angeles. Seattle and Houston still exist, right? Why is the world collapsing?"

"Seattle and Houston still exist, but essentially do not function. Other American cities are panicking. They believe the vampire and zombie rumors."

Samantha snorted.

Major General Roberts said, "Much of the world flowed through Los Angeles, in some form or another. It's loss disrupted the planet to the scale of trillions."

"Young man, fear of the unknown changes everything. And the Chemist expands unchecked like…like Hitler once did, and he's doing so on the home turf of the most powerful nation on the planet."

Isaac clicked his pen over and over, flexing his jaw. "America is heading towards another civil war, because of Blue-Eyes. We're fighting each other AND a terrorist organization."

I said, "Okay, but-"

"In very simple barbaric terms, we could shoot the Nazis. We can shoot Al-Qaeda. We can shoot ISIS soldiers. But we can't shoot these damn Chosen freaks. They're too fast, and too imbedded among the hostages to use larger ordnance."

The Director of the CIA rubbed his eyes and mumbled, "It's been a hard two months for America. And this past week was even worse. But we should all keep it in perspective. We'll survive this. We can rant and moan like this in private. Once. But then we need to return to work with heads high. We need to project optimism. And to believe it, ourselves."

Roberts chuckled, "We need more *Katie Clips*."

"I'm watching one now," Samantha said absently, staring at her phone. "I hate Katie. She's so pretty."

The Director of the CIA said, "Mr. Jackson, did you know the Andy Babington character?"

I blinked, confused and surprised. Andy's name felt so out of place in this room that it took me several seconds to place it. "Andy? Sure. I know him. Why?"

Samantha looked up in surprise. "*Did* he know him? Don't you mean, *Do* we know him? Something happen to that little prick?"

He answered, "Andy Babington recorded several Periscope videos, bragging about his friendship with the Outlaw. Essentially, he leveraged his relationship with you into a higher celebrity status. The Chemist saw it. The final Periscope video was interrupted by Chosen. He was abducted live, while thousands watched."

My blood ran cold and I collapsed into the chair. Andy and I weren't friends, but he didn't deserve to be kidnapped. There was no predicting what the Chemist would do with him. "The Chemist used the videos to locate him?"

"That's the way it appears," he nodded grimly. "Happened last night. Sorry to be the bearer of bad news."

Under her breath, Samantha grunted, "Got what he deserved."

"Isaac, I have two other friends that might be in danger," I said, suddenly terrified at the thought. "You know Cory and Lee, right?"

"Of course," he said, already dialing his phone. "I'll send a car for them immediately. They should be in protective custody." He walked to the corner of the room, one hand on his hip, and spoke quietly into the receiver.

I said loudly into the room, "Puck, are you listening?"

A voice boomed out of the speakers, "Of course, dummy."

Gasps. Shocked expressions. Who was this?? Who could possibly eavesdrop? I waved off their questions in a reassuring manner.

I said, "Can you text Cory and Lee? Tell them what's going on?"

"Sure. PuckDaddy to the rescue. By the way, you may be interested to know that as soon as she hung up, the Secretary of State placed a secure phone call to the President."

The Secretary of Defense and the Director of the CIA and Isaac Anderson all shared a grim, knowing look. So many secrets. Isaac hung up and said, "Thanks Puck."

"I should probably get a cape."

Isaac said loudly, "Okay, well, this meeting has gone on too long. Let's spend two minutes sharing departmental solutions and then we'll dismiss."

Major General Roberts said, "Seconded."

"I'll go first," Isaac said. "We have several Chosen in custody. No Infected, unfortunately. But our FBI labs will have blood samples to study. We'll know more about our enemy soon. And their disease."

I said, "You want some of my blood?"

"Not yet. Bad precedent to set. If we can't get theirs, I'll call you."

The Secretary of Defense said, "United Nations has called an emergency meeting to discuss the terror threat. Next week. In the meantime, Special Agent Anderson, you and I can discuss the President's...predicament."

"Predicament? You mean the witch?" Samantha asked. "She's not alone. She has help. Carter tried to remove her once and never heard from his team again."

"The FBI and CIA and Secret Service should be able to handle one little girl."

Samantha scoffed. "Great. She's going to be crawling in all your laps soon. If you're not dead."

"You have a better idea?"

"Yes. Kill her. Shoot her from a mile away. Hell, I'll go do it if you keep Chase safe. Which you can't. And while you're at it, carpet bomb Los Angeles. Our problems are growing exponentially. We've got the Chemist on one coast and Blue-Eyes on the other, Walter somewhere in between, and the three of them are ripping your country apart."

"Carpet bombing is not an option."

She snapped, "Do you have *any* plans for removing them from Los Angeles?"

Silence.

I said, "As soon as we have confirmation that the Chemist is downtown, Samantha and I are going in. And staying until we have him. Even if it takes months. I don't think more widespread violence is the answer. Maybe Carter can help remove Blue-Eyes."

"What if you fail to eliminate the Chemist?"

"Apocalypse!" Samantha shouted. "Boom!"

Their faces turned white. The Major General snickered. I scolded her, "That's not helping, Samy."

"What? I'm so boooooooored."

An attendant scurried into the room and handed Major General Roberts a note. He glanced at it and his face darkened. Bad news. The paper disappeared into his fist. He took a deep breath and reported. "We've finished our search of the base, and found several rooms with the Chemist's...super drug. Their occupants are missing."

"In other words, you're housing Chemist insurgents. That base isn't safe for Chase and Samantha and Katie."

Isaac said, "It never was. Too easily accessible to Downtown. I need a more permanent solution. Any ideas?"

Samantha scowled, "My truck is a great solution."

"Nope," I shook my head. "I'm not living in your truck."

Major General Roberts offered, "How about the *San Antonio?*"

"The what?"

"The *USS San Antonio.* The Marine's amphibious transport ship. Big ass warship, parked a few miles off Los Angeles, part of the *George Washington* strike group."

Samantha perked up. "A warship? First good idea all day. I get to drive."

Isaac said, "Okay, Major General, make the call if you don't mind. I'll order the Black Hawk warmed up. Then I'm taking the rest of the day off and spending it with the beautiful and talented Natalie North."

Chapter Twelve
Wednesday, January 31. 2019

We spent two weeks on the *USS San Antonio,* which was state-of-the-art and sleek in appearance, like a wedge of smooth steel. She was primarily a troop transport ship, intended to dump Marines into Los Angeles months ago. Now, thanks to the military and government infighting, the amphibious ships in the Pacific simply kept to their station with hulls full of disgruntled warriors, and receiving no new orders.

San Antonio was a big ship, basically a floating city (though dwarfed in size by the nearby aircraft carrier). Its cavernous cargo holds brimmed with men and helicopters and landing craft. The mood aboard was stony and volatile. Marines stewed and drilled and stewed some more, keeping a weather-eye on the news, impotently watching their country stagger.

Our arrival served as a tremendous boost to morale. The seamen and troops cheered when we landed and saluted us all the way to our staterooms. Samantha and I were treated as Majors in every sense except operational duties. But in reality, they received us more as honored guests, celebrity supernumeraries, the same way Marilyn Monroe or Peyton Manning was worshipped on USO overseas tours. Lee and Cory arrived the following day. All cabins were searched for the Chemist's super drug but none found. Any crew members wanting to collect on the massive bounty would find it impossible; they'd never get off their ship. We weren't safe, but it was as close as possible.

Samantha and I didn't plan on staying long, but the Chemist was sighted in France, and Walter in Portland. Our target was elsewhere.

"So??" Samantha demanded. "Let's go downtown anyway. We could work on cleaning that place out."

"Our goal is to surprise and eliminate the Chemist. If he finds out we're there, he won't return. We'll have ruined our best chance at getting him."

Samantha vented her frustration by drilling Marines on the aft flight deck. She ordered tens of thousands of clay targets and had Marines firing without aiming at disks arcing over the waves. Over and over again. Shotguns, not rifles. I *Threw* golfballs and busted the disks if the marines missed, which always earned cries of disbelief. We were such a hit, the commodore asked us to tour the entire strike force group. We acquiesced.

I *Jumped* from ship to ship. I leapt high in the air and coasted the distance on wings. Samantha accused me of being a circus act, but I enjoyed it. Being cooped up on the ship aggravated me, and jumping released stress. If the soldiers liked it too…well, good for them. We briefed soldiers on combat with Chosen, demonstrated the disk drill to improve their odds of survival, led physical training exercises, and took pictures. Mike Matthews ferried Samantha and Katie. Katie was a resounding smash. The guys clamored for her. She'd become an ambassador of good will. A hot one. Being wanted by the Chemist, and a bounty worth millions, made her hotter. The world knew we were aboard and tuned into her social media for updates.

They cheered for me. Adored Katie. And revered Samantha. The entire ship watched her shooting demonstrations, which included busting apples off ships a quarter mile distant. She trained and drilled and ranted and screamed, and the soldiers soaked it up.

At least until they were called into action. Packs of Chosen and armed Chemist terror groups began surfacing in other states, coordinating attacks on multiple cities at once. First Portland and San Antonio. Next Oklahoma City and Reno. The attacks focused on electrical systems and transportation, crippling response times. Marine companies began deployment to hot spots. Most terrorist groups vanished, but the attacking group at Reno was found and destroyed, even the three Chosen.

The Navy repelled small boats approaching our ship daily. Stubborn reporters or daredevils or crazed fans braved the seas and desperately tried to board, wanting an interview or audience with me, but they never got close. The Navy treated them as would-be pirates and arrested them. Twice the aircraft carrier's escort fighters scared off news helicopters getting too close to our strike group.

Carter surprised us on the ninth day. He'd been assigned a personal helicopter, a Huey, and it landed on the flight deck that morning. He startled me by wrapping Samantha up in a fierce hug. She returned it, and for the first time I realized how big a sacrifice she'd made leaving him for me. They'd worked together for ten years before I appeared.

I saw Russia, a silent giant, in the pilot's seat. He was an Infected from Asia, and on Carter's payroll. A nasty man who'd cut my throat without a second thought. Shadow, Carter's personal body guard, nodded to me from the helicopter's door. Both intended to stay with the chopper. Apparently this would be a short visit.

Captain Travis greeted him professionally, but Carter ignored him. He pulled us into the superstructure and slammed the hatch.

"Appears sea life suits you," Carter grunted, voice caroming in our small metal compartment. He clamped a cigarette between pointy teeth and lit it with a flick of his lighter. "Although staying in one place is stupid. Sitting ducks."

Carter looked different. No, that wasn't it. Smelled different? …no…but something was off.

I asked, "Why are you here?"

He shrugged and spewed smoke towards the security lights. "Was in the area." His voice came low and full of gravel, with traces of an old accent. Probably Australian a hundred years ago. He pointed a finger at me and spoke around the cigarette. "Headaches gone? Any other symptoms?"

Samantha said, "He's fine. What are you doing about Blue-Eyes?"

"Nothing. The witch relocated the entire White House staff to Camp David. I'd need everyone we have to break in there." He grinned malevolently. "Still. There's fun to be had. We're cruising the country and hunting Chosen."

"What about Walter?"

"He's going up and down the coast. Not sure that one sleeps. Thought we had him in Portland. He's dangerous. What's your plan?"

Powerful. That was the change in Carter. He *felt* powerful. The disease in me recognized and responded to the disease in him on a deep mammalian level. Carter was ancient and strong and the illness seeped from his pores, broadcasting power. Most likely, he hadn't changed. *I* had changed. I had grown, matured into my weird skin and its weird receptors. He intimidated me now that I could feel his strength. No, not intimidated. He didn't frighten me. He...pressed against me. He invaded my security. He intruded. He aggravated my sensory apparatuses.

I said, "We're going into Los Angeles. We'll surprise the Chemist if he returns."

"And then?"

"Kill him."

He sneered with disdain, blue tendrils of vapor leaking from his nose. "Still just an ignorant kid."

"And you're still a grumpy old man."

"You *can't* kill him, mate. Not yet."

"Not yet? What do I need?"

He shrugged and resettled into his duster like the close confines bothered him. "Another ten years? Thirty, maybe? I dunno."

Samantha said, "I disagree."

He shrugged again. "Martin's in Europe, anyway. I doubt he'll come back. I might go after him, myself. Want to join?"

"Maybe. Probably. When?"

"Dunno. He's moving a lot. Need for him to settle."

I said, "He's coming back here."

"How do you know?"

"Because I'm here," I said.

Carter looked at me a long moment. He took a deep breath and held the ash and nicotine in his lungs, and held it, and held it, and released the fumes reluctantly into my face. "First smart thing you've said, hero. I admire your testicular fortitude, even if you're not up to the challenge yet."

"I'm ready."

"You're *lucky*. No other reason you're alive, champ. You show all the restraint of a prepubescent brat. No thinking. Just leaping."

"I'd forgotten how much I dislike you," I mumbled to myself. Had Carter been talking to my dad? Because I hated it.

Samantha asked, "You talk with China? Or Pacific? Or Zealot?"

"China politely declines to get involved, the bitch. Pacific won't answer. Can't find Zealot. Crazy old man is probably closer than we think." He nodded towards me. "You staying with him?"

"Yep. Not all of us are sell-outs, Carter."

"Ah," he chuckled. "You are irked that I'm taking America's money?"

"Not at all," she sniffed. "You forced me to hide for the last twelve years, and then you hold a press conference and demand money on national television. Sounds fair."

"Dumb-ass here changed everything." He jerked his thumb at me.

"You're a stooge."

"Here's an idea," he said, tapping his temple and staring at her. "Get your hands on some missiles. All of them. The hacker can help. Stash the kid on a skyscraper until Martin comes to investigate. Then blow the whole damn city. He's vulnerable to fire."

"The government won't-"

"Who said anything about the government? You do it. Collateral damages be damned. Then disappear. I'm building us a fortress in the Rockies to survive the coming end of civilization," he laughed, an evil slow sound. "We'll watch the world rebuild itself and carve out whatever piece we wish."

"We're after different things now, Carter. I want to prevent the end of civilization."

He chuckled. "So did I. For a while. But this might be gratifying. More for us, in the end."

"You want to live in the shadows and get your jollies accumulating a kingdom. I don't."

"And you want to get married and adopt all the babies," he scoffed.

"No," she snapped, chin jutting, chest out. "I just want to live. And that involves taking care of this place."

"I do that."

"No. You manipulate and steal and violently impose your idea of order. You want control. I want..."

"What?"

"Freedom. And in your perfect world, we're all on your payroll. You're the only one truly free."

He had sucked all the tobacco into his lungs and now chewed on the butt. "You make me sound like Martin."

"No. Martin wants to be God. To live in a world he creates. To be worshipped. You don't want to be worshipped. People aren't important enough for you to worry over their opinion. You want your part of the world to move exactly as you demand without anyone knowing you're there."

He arched a brow, spit out the dead cigarette, and nodded. "Bingo. And no price is too large. Stay in contact with me. Maybe we'll all get what we want."

She nodded.

"You," he pointed at me. "You've gotten stronger, mate. I can feel it. You radiate like the sun. Don't let Martin strap you to a table. Or there will be no earth left for me to salvage."

He hugged Samantha again before leaving. Had I read their relationship wrong? Did he love her? As a woman, or maybe as a daughter?

Whatever. I was relieved when his Huey took off, but I had a bad feeling. The Chemist wasn't the only old white guy trying to control our future.

Chapter Thirteen
Sunday, February 4. 2019

By the end of our second week aboard the *San Antonio*, most of the Marines were gone and our ship felt hollow. It wasn't until the ship emptied that I realized how tranquil I'd become. During the previous fourteen days, all my stress and anxiety had been washed away by the Pacific Ocean. Bobbing on the swell and staring at the blue horizon and listening to the waves was cathartic. Therapy for my soul. The undulations balanced me. Part of my happiness could be attributed to the empty ship affording more secrecy. Fewer eyes staring at Katie and me, keeping us apart. More Katie equaled more bliss. Secret kisses from a beautiful girl could turn any dinghy into a floating Eden. But it was more significant than that. I slept better. I smiled more. I felt stronger.

Samantha underwent the change too. She didn't scowl for days. She and I stared at deep waters without speaking for hours on end, long after our other companions grew bored. She took to diving from the flight deck and swimming laps around the hull.

I did not join her. Whales are scary.

This was our first experience on a boat. At least, our first experience longer than a couple hours. Like a baby in a rocker, the constant motion calmed us. Soothed the disease's demands.

"Carter told us that sea life would suit us. He knew."

"I wish I'd known years ago," Samantha said. She and I sat on the bow, legs pressed through scuppers, feet dangling over foaming crests twenty-five feet below. The wind brushed her short hair back, and infiltrated our nostrils and lungs and minds with sea and salt. Her eyes closed and she took deep breaths. "I could have lived on a sailboat between Carter's assignments."

Katie sunbathed on the warm deck behind us, soaking up afternoon heat in a turquoise bikini. A hardback copy of *The Goldfinch* lay open beside her, face down. This was her third book of the trip, all Pulitzer winners. I turned around to ogle her now and then, and to glare at crew members on the sponsons watching her with binoculars.

I loved her. I ached to be closer, to experience all of her, to touch more than humans beings could, to consume each other. I wanted her all to myself. She and I needed our own boat. Just us. Long talks into the night. Long nights with no naval officers. She felt it too. Sometimes our eyes would meet like ships colliding, staggering both of us, throwing sparks I'm surprised weren't visible.

Self-control. I took deep breaths. Dad said that real men had control of themselves. Self-control. Self-control.

It was like trying to ignore hunger.

The two Navy SEALs who'd transferred to our protection detail, Sergeants Cody and Dalton, were with us on deck. Both were beefy tattooed giants with shaved heads; Cody was white and Dalton was black. They went everywhere I did, but sometimes split up to monitor Katie. Samantha, they reckoned, needed no body guard. Which was vaguely insulting. Both wore shades and kept their gazes out to sea, instead of on my girlfriend's bikini.

Since Carter left, I'd been getting up early with Cody and Dalton to exercise. My father and Carter were right. I needed self-control. And discipline. And these two SEALs might have been the fittest duo on earth. And they didn't get that way by just surviving a crazy super virus.

They had brought me to the exercise room the morning after Carter left. Cory refused to join; said it was too early. I couldn't get the treadmill fast enough to challenge me, so I spent my time with weights. I hadn't worked out in a weight room since junior year football season, and the familiar sounds and smells were welcome. After warming up, I was able to bench press over five hundred pounds, squat nine hundred, curl one ten with each arm, and a perform a hundred and fifty pull-ups consecutively. None of these were world records, the SEALs told me, but were more than they'd ever seen. I could do more if the disease was angry. I could do more if I was disciplined and exercised, and not so lazy.

After the second morning, I panted, "Is it weird watching some punk kid lift more weights than you, even though this is your career? I think it would piss me off."

"Nah," Sergeant Cody grinned, wiping his face with a white towel. "It's weird watching your body actually grow in size, Outlaw. That's some spooky-ass stuff, right there."

"I feel like I haven't earned the right to lift this much."

"You took a lot of punishment on that tower, sir. Got shot and got the hell beat out you. Seems to me like you earned it. And either way, glad you're on our side."

Endorphins. That might be another factor in my contentment, I mused, now sitting on deck, trying not to stare at Katie's turquoise bikini while I pondered exercise and listened to Samantha talk about the sea.

Katie sleepily murmured, "The happy version of Samantha is eery. I like her but…it weirds me out."

Puck's voice rattled out of a bluetooth speaker nearby. "Yeah, she hasn't cussed at PuckDaddy for days. I don't like it."

"All of you, shut up. You're ruining my zen."

"Samantha Gear does not have zen, dummy."

Katie chirped, "Chase has zen too. He's been smiling more. I have loved his smile since elementary school." She pushed me gently with her toes. I took her foot in my hand and began massaging. She'd be asleep soon if I continued.

"Gross," Samantha said. "Now my zen is completely gone."

"She right," Cory said. He sunbathed too, though he didn't earn the attention Katie did. "Ya'll white people nasty."

I asked, "Did you hear from your parents?"

"Made it to Toledo," Cory answered. "Want me to come out, soon as its safe. Never gon' be safe, though, you two keep sitting here."

Samantha grinned. "I'll have to get up soon. Captain Travis said we're going to get a storm out of the Pacific. Clouds, rain, larger waves. It will ruin my zen."

"I think that sounds fun," I said.

"Yeah, me too, actually, now I say it out loud. Never mind, Cory. You can't go home."

Lee was currently aboard the *George Washington*, working with a team of Army and Navy engineers. They were replicating the Chosen's new weapons in an attempt to counter them. His creativity and ingenuity, combined with my willingness to be his test dummy, and his elevated status as the Outlaw's personal gadget inventor, was proving useful to their R&D. He already spoke their technobabble language. In many ways, they deferred to him. We heard his excited voice across the water on more than one occasion as some poor soul got zapped.

He loved the new mask Natalie North had created. I told him I no longer needed one. He had frowned and said, "Dude. The Outlaw wears a mask." Besides, he explained, this one prevented my ear piece from falling out. He had also made new wing-suits and vests for Samantha and I. "And check out these additions, bro. See these three pockets? Boom! The first pocket holds a small can of OC spray. Know what that's for?"

I turned the small red bottle in my hands. It was about the size of a restaurant salt shaker. "Yes. It's pepper spray. Spray it in the eyes of Chosen."

"Wrong! Well, kinda. But wrong! It's for tiger eyes! You've seen the pictures of those herculean cats downtown, right? Well. Now you're prepared, dude! Right in the eyes, bye bye tiger, hello wimpy pussycat. Okay, next pocket. This blue canister is full of oxygen. Only good for about five deep breaths. If you deploy the OC spray and worry you might breathe in the toxins...pow! Instant oxygen!"

"Nice. I could use this sky diving, if the air is too thin."

"The bottles are the same size so...don't confuse them."

I pulled out a black device from the third small pocket. "Is this a flashlight?"

"Yes. Not my invention, though. This one comes from the military. It's a high intensity strobe light. Seven flashes a second at over eighty-five lumens. It's ten times stronger than a 747's landing light, bro."

"What do I do with it?"

He smacked his head with his palm. "*Blind* people, dummy! It causes temporary flash blindness. Especially Chosen or Infected, at night, because their eyes are already...all...night visiony...right?"

"Night visiony?"

"You know! They can see in the dark. Their pupils must be wide open and then you shine this baby into them?? That's gonna hurt! I'm trying to find you non-lethal weapons, bro. At least *act* happy."

"I *am* happy! These are awesome. What about a water gun? To short circuit their electro-death-gadgets?"

"We're experimenting with water guns," he nodded sagely. "The problem is, electricity follows the water to its source and zaps the squirter. In other words, the water gun *does* short circuit their gear, but it shocks them *and* you."

"Ah."

"We're building prototypes which fire short bursts of water. Instead of a stream, it releases a single shot. Like a water balloon without the balloon. That way, electricity can't follow the stream. It's all very complicated, Chase. You probably wouldn't understand."

The squall rolled in during our thirteenth day aboard. Storms posed no threat to our mammoth ship, but the roll increased and our world became grey and wet. We stayed inside and watched the news.

Natalie North was on again, relaying her harrowing capture, imprisonment, and escape. She and the other prisoners were treated well, other than general debilitating effects due to stress and lack of sleep. The Chemist said he had special plans for her, but then disappeared. He had an empire to build, she assumed, and no time to spare.

"Have you spoken to Chase Jackson since your release? To the Outlaw?" Natalie was asked.

"No!" she laughed in self-deprecation. "I lost my phone, and thus his number. Chase!" she beamed at the camera and made a pretend phone with her right hand. "Call me!"

Katie winked. "I give you permission. I adore her."

CNN also showed Katie's recent Instagram photo, which sent her dancing and giggling around the metal mess hall with low overheads. Each book she recently recommended had jumped to the top of best seller lists.

Subsequent news segments were less exciting.

Las Vegas burned, once again demonstrating how devastating even small groups of Chosen were. They'd ruptured natural gas lines near the strip.

Andy Babington was still missing. My heart sank at the reminder.

The Priest was in the news again, calling for his following, the faithful, to seek the Phoenix. Join him at the Outlaw compound, he declared, and help locate the Fire Girl, Hannah Walker. His votaries numbered over twenty thousand now, and had begun farming land and purchasing live stock, preparing for Armageddon. He shone like a beacon for religious zealots.

The stock market was a dumpster fire.

Demonstrations were held in every city, denouncing all 'mutants.' That included me.

Another airline declared bankruptcy.

Lines were drawn between military generals. Fort Bragg was in the throes of a full civil war. Americans killing Americans. The Army suffered the most mutinies, indications that Blue-Eyes had multiple Army generals within her clutches.

Gasoline was over twenty dollars a gallon. The trucking industry strained to function, creating food shortages in remote sections of the United States.

Police couldn't control civil unrest in Chicago. Or in Detroit. Or Philadelphia. Rioters rampaged.

The long barricade around downtown Los Angeles thinned due to lack of manpower, and militants streamed unchecked through the border, joining the Chemist's 'noble' crusade and bulging his ranks.

The world accelerated into insanity.

But. Remnants of hope existed.

The FBI found a training center for Chemist goons in Mississippi and destroyed it, capturing several hundred would-be insurgents. This led to the discovery of a dozen newly created Chosen still in their comas. We spotted Carter in the video, overseeing the Chosen's relocation. If they woke up early, he'd cut their throats.

Samantha simmered and seethed, furious with Carter's hypocrisy. He'd threatened to shoot any Infected communicating with the government, and now he aided them to the tune of millions.

A powerful benefit of the mounting fear was that it provided most Americans with a common enemy. The Chemist and his 'mutants' unwittingly fostered widespread unification and resilience. Cities banded together and held their ground, working together to become self-sufficient as rapidly as possible. Population centers created partnerships with local farms and water sources so goods wouldn't have to travel cross country.

If the military and the government wouldn't help them, then they'd help themselves.

Plants manufactured solar panels at a breakneck pace and still couldn't supply the demand. The Chemist couldn't block out the sun.

This massive localization project began just a few weeks ago, and then only in certain cities, but it was picking up steam. In the event of catastrophe and the breaking of interconnecting super structures and systems, the groundwork of survival was being laid. Pockets of order and stability would endure. It was the beginning of massive change. All because of the Chemist and his creations.

The television's carnage and destruction, and the uncertainty and the hope, washed across our faces, reflecting grimly in our eyes. We stared without speaking, watched without blinking. We drank in the news, getting a full dose of our planet's struggle. A struggle we'd help create.

"What are we doing here?" I whispered eventually. "Just sitting on this boat."

"We need to go." Samantha's voice was equally somber.

Katie agreed. "The world needs the Outlaw. Needs both of you."

"We can't wait. Can't just *hope* he'll return to Los Angeles."

"Europe," Samantha grunted softly. "That's where Puck found him last.

The Chemist. Two days ago. Somewhere in Germany."

I took a deep breath and let out a long slow sigh. "Okay. Let's game plan about going to Germany. Follow that maniac all over the globe if we have to."

We switched off the volume when the President came on screen to address the nation and call for peace and tolerance. His face made me want to vomit.

As a group we exited the mess hall. Captain Travis, a hard man with a salt and pepper mustache, intercepted us in the adjoining passageway. He'd been a busy man recently, coordinating the launch of seven hundred marines.

"Would you follow me to the security room, please. I require your input." It wasn't a question but not exactly an order either. We followed him up the ladder to a compartment near the bridge. The deck swayed beneath us, tossing Katie and Cory into bulkheads. Inside the security room was warm and aglow with computer monitors. All areas of the ship were under constant surveillance. Cody and Dalton, our SEAL shadows, remained outside. Captain Travis pointed to three monitors without live feed. No picture. They flickered blue. "Two hours ago, at approximately seventeen hundred hours, this camera malfunctioned. Thirty minutes later, the second camera failed. Then we lost the third. My bosun went to inspect the cameras twenty minutes ago. Haven't heard from him since."

I asked, "He disappeared?"

"Essentially. He's not on camera and won't answer his radio. And then. This." He nodded to the seaman at the keyboard. The seaman punched up a recording on his computer screen. The recording was of the aft well deck. The lighting was poor. "Keep watching. Seaman Burke scanned backwards until he found it. This is a recording of our wet deck at the stern of the ship. Three hours ago. We flood the deck during operations. Watch the gate."

Five seconds later, a shadow slipped over the top of the gate and vanished behind an amphibious landing craft. A *big* shadow.

Katie's breath caught. She knew that shadow. I did too.

"Now," Captain Travis said, voice angry. "I'm not happy. That who I think it is? Saw him on the news."

The shadow reappeared, temporarily stepping into a shaft of light. Seaman

Burke froze the picture and zoomed in. An enormous man was on screen. Smiling. Soaking wet. The security light cast a cold gleam in his eye.

"Yup," I nodded. "That's him. Tank Ware is here."

Chapter Fourteen
Sunday, February 4th. 2019

"What's he doing aboard my ship?" Captain Travis barked.

Samantha's jaw was set, her eyes aflame. "He's going to ruin my zen."

"He's here to kill me," I said. "And reclaim Katie."

"He's like you guys, right?" Travis asked. "He's got your…condition?"

"Except he's stronger. Much stronger."

Captain Travis pushed a button on the wall's squawk box and spoke into it. "Officer of the deck, this is Captain Travis. Sound general quarters. Not a drill. And call the Master-at-Arms to Security please."

Our compartment and the passageways were instantaneously filled with a siren. A voice blared over the speakers, "**Attention all hands. This is not a drill. Not a drill. All hands. General quarters. All hands to battle stations. All hands to battle stations.**"

"Okay," Travis said, crossing arms over his chest. His voice was surprisingly calm after the raucous announcement. Outside and below us came the sound of pounding boots. "Let's assume that is indeed Tank Ware. Is he here to earn the Chemist's reward money?"

"No," Katie answered. She sank into a chair beside Seaman Burke, hands over her mouth. "This is about pride. His parents are already rich."

Travis said, "But his intentions are hostile, correct? Will he be armed?"

I shook my head, watching the silent screens. "His hands are too big to work a gun."

"Then how in the hell does he plan on getting to you?"

"Better question," Samantha scoffed. "Is how in the hell can you stop him?"

"He's strong," I said. "He can probably go through walls."

Captain Travis arched an eyebrow and rapped a knuckle against the grey bulkhead. The metal rang. "You think he can rip this steel apart?"

"Not the hull. But the walls? No doubt."

"And bullets won't penetrate his skin."

He glared at us, debating whether we were joking. "You think he's the Incredible Hulk."

"That's a really good comparison," I said, marveling at the revelation. "I wish I'd thought of that."

"Meh," Samantha waggled her hand. "Not as strong as the Hulk. And he can't jump very high."

Katie's voice was small from her chair. "But he's intelligent. He can think logically. He can plan."

Four men appeared at the door. They wore camouflage and had pistols clipped to their belts. "Sir!"

Captain Travis drawled, "Gentlemen we have an unwelcome guest aboard. Potentially very dangerous. Please inspect the wet deck and report. Arrest any intruders."

"Yes sir."

"No," I said. "Do not arrest. Do not engage. Call me if you see anything."

Samantha added, "And don't split up. Stay together. And get some bigger guns. Those little pea shooter won't do a damn thing."

They stared at us and at Captain Travis in confusion. Captain Travis clearly debated whether or not he bought our story. He nodded. "Maybe better listen to them, Master-at-Arms. Couldn't hurt. This is their crazy-ass territory."

The four Master-at-Arms took a final look at me and departed, boots clunking on the deck. Travis pulled radios off chargers and handed them to me and Samantha.

"Channel three," he said. "CID channel. You'll hear any…problems."

The *San Antonio* took a large wave awkwardly. We all held on as the ship rose and twisted. From somewhere down the passageway came the sound of howling wind and lashing rain.

"His name's Tank? Tank avoided detection and got aboard because of the chop. We can't see in the storm."

I asked, "How do we get Katie off the ship?"

Travis shook his head. "We don't. Not in this weather. Not unless there's an emergency, for the next forty-eight hours."

"This *is* an emergency."

"Better idea," Samantha said. "Let's all jump overboard and scuttle the ship. Detonate one of your missiles. He couldn't survive that."

Travis arched an eyebrow again. "Scuttle the two billion dollar ship? Pass. Besides, we have no missiles that big. And it's just one man."

"One monster. But he's vulnerable to fire and electricity," Samantha said.

"We're fresh out of flame throwers, Major Gear. But I'll check with the Chief about tasers. Meantime, stay here. Keep the door secured. I'll be on the bridge." He stepped out and pulled the heavy door closed. Seaman Burke immediately twisted the lock.

Samantha rummaged through chests and drawers. "Burke. Got a gun?"

"Next room, ma'am. Aft cabinet."

She opened the weapons locker and grumbled her displeasure. I sat next to Katie and rubbed the back of her neck. Her face was pale, hands still over her mouth.

"Maybe I should talk to him," she said quietly. "He's reasonable."

"No he's not. He's a volcano."

"I could go with him. Get him off the ship. You come get me later?"

"You stay with me," I said. "I'm not throwing you into a volcano to appease the gods."

She gripped my hand. Hard.

"Chase," Samantha growled, loading pistols. "We need to go."

"Not yet."

The sounds of her pistol ceased. "What do you mean?"

"You and I are fighting a larger enemy than this. You're too valuable to die fighting Tank."

"I'm not going to die." She rolled her eyes.

"You might. He's not worth it. Let's give them a chance."

For five long minutes we sat silently in our blue metal box, eyes on the screens as they cycled through points of view. The marines were gone but three hundred seamen and officers remained, plenty of activity to watch. The *San Antonio* worked up and down waves, and we swayed. Then, another camera went dead. Four blue screens total. Burke stared in horror. He picked up a phone with shaking hands, waited a moment, and said, "Sir, lost another camera. Just aft of the machine shop." He replaced the phone and rewound the video to watch again.

My radio squealed, startling Katie. Captain Travis's voice. *"Master-at-Arms, status report."*

No answer. No sounds.

"Master-at-Arms, report."

"Sir, this is petty officer Parker. We got separated from Graves. We found evidence of the intruder. A busted hatch. Must have used a small explosive. And a crushed camera."

"Or a big fist," Katie noted.

"Where is petty officer Graves?"

"Unknown, sir. We'll find'im."

Samantha called, "I told you! Stay together! Shut up, Chase, I know they can't hear me."

Silence. Just the faint buzz of power, almost undetectable at the edge of awareness. On the monitors, nothing happened. Burke pointed without comment at the three Master-at-Arms crossing a cargo bay, guns drawn.

Katie's eyes were large and pooling. Her voice came softly, whispering between her fingers. "He never told me he wanted to kill you. But he hinted. A lot. Even his parents were scared of him. They wouldn't always correct him when he got out of line. Their apartment was full of things he squeezed till they broke, like door handles and chairs and baseballs. He liked to bust baseballs. Broke a metal bat once. His mom loved him. Loves him. She's a sweet lady. Very smart. She would hug him to calm him down, scratch his back to put him asleep. His dad wanted to kick him out, but his mom…she unconditionally adored him. He never hurt me. Never got mad. At first he didn't even like me. But the more time we spent together...I don't know what I was thinking. I knew he was a danger. But he started to like me. A lot. Said he loved me. Which means his pride is involved. Above all things, he is proud. We are an affront to his pride, and he cannot abide that."

The cameras continued their cycle across the bank of monitors. Medical bay. Well deck. Flight deck, partially obscured by driving rain. Passage way, populated with scurrying crew. Forward cargo hold. Cafeteria. Kitchen. The bridge. Stateroom passageway. Vehicle deck, mostly empty. Machinery. Rec compartment. Fifty cameras scattered throughout the ship took their turn across the ten monitors, changing in rhythm like a clock ticking.

"How can a big guy like that disappear?" Samantha asked.

Seaman Burke answered, "No cameras in private quarters. And some of the cameras swivel between shots, so he could be timing his moves."

"So many people," Katie said.

"Wait. Go back." I pointed to the second screen. Burke hit a few keys and the picture jumped onto his personal monitor. "The previous camera. The one with hovercrafts."

"This one?"

"Yes. What's..." We all squinted and pressed in closer to the screen, peering at a pixilated pile in the corner. "What's that? Does it have legs?"

"Those are bodies," Samantha said. "Two bodies."

"Look at this," Burke said, taping glass. His voice wavered and his breath fogged the picture. "There's the Master-at-Arms group, on another screen near engineering. Those two bodies aren't them."

"Then who is it?"

"Probably the Bosun and the seamen assigned to the vehicles." He picked up the phone and rang the bridge. "Captain, we may have located..."

He dropped the phone.

On screen, a colossus attacked the Master-at-Arms. Tank stepped out from a hatch and crushed the three petty officers against a wall. He clubbed each man once and the fight swiftly ended. One shot was fired, and its report clattered through our passage seconds later. Most of the ship heard it.

"Okay," I said grimly, standing up. "Samantha, let's draw him to the flight deck and kick him off."

She chambered a round into the Beretta. "We're ill equipped. Take this." She pressed a fancy flashlight into my hands. "It's the Navy's dazzler. Similar to what Lee gave you. Blind him."

Katie made a faint groaning noise. I kissed her forehead and we closed the door behind us. I retrieved the Thunder Stick from my stateroom and we plunged below, Dalton and Cody proceeding us, boots ringing on steel. The ship pitched abruptly, tossing all four of us forward. Water sloshed down the ladder.

From somewhere deep in the bowels of the ship, a roar. And gunfire.

"**Attention all hands. All hands. Intruder aboard. Repeat, intruder aboard. Shoot on sight. Intruder considered dangerous and hostile. Repeat, shoot on sight. And brace for heavy seas.**"

"We're going to make him mad," I called to the SEALs. "Let him see me. He should chase me, and I'll lead him to the flight deck."

"Roger that, sir!"

"I go first. He can't kill me. At least not easily."

We reached the vehicle deck, a vast and empty bay with few vehicles left. The remaining equipment strained against restraints as the ship worked through the swell. As I put my hands to my lips, indicating silence, my phone beeped. I cursed silently, and frantically clawed at the device.

>> HEY! TANK is aboard UR ship!!
>> puck is monitoring the security cameras!!!

I rolled my eyes and cursed again. **We know!**

>> oh man oh man oh man oh man!!!
>> okay okay okay puck will help if he can
>> oh hey btw
>> the chemist emailed you

You're telling me this NOW??

>> ur right! my fault!
>> focus!

I switched the phone to silent mode and we stalked towards the bow. Don't worry about the Chemist. I can deal with that later. Focus on Tank.

We pressed through a doorway. I felt like we'd entered a swamp. The irate disease raging through my veins, flaring in my joints, twitching my muscles, quickening my mind, sharpening my eyesight and my sense of smell and my hearing-my whole body detected Tank. He stank of illness, though the SEALs couldn't perceive it. I *felt* him. The assault on my sensorium turned the air shades of red and green as my brain strove to understand and process.

"Do you feel him?" I whispered.

"Like I'm being choked."

"He can probably feel us, too."

We crept through Tank's fog for fifteen minutes, searching in vain. The SEALs couldn't identify him in the air like we did, but they were on edge, jumpy. Maybe on some unconscious, preternatural level their bodies detected the threat. The surrounding tumult of a working warship masked any soft noises Tank was making as we searched over and under vehicles. We encountered more bodies. None appeared dead, but none would move any time soon either. All suffered from broken bones and bleeding skulls.

Suddenly, he roared. Gunfire. Above us. We pounded up the nearest ladder and raced along the narrow passageway. Lights were busted. Big gouges in decorative panelling. More bodies. Cries of alarm. The ship rolled and Cody slipped, landing on his back. Samantha's teeth ground so hard I could hear them. Tank's fury was palpable.

"We found him in here, sir." An ensign on the deck pointed through a doorway. He lay beside two Master-at-Arms, both unconscious. The ensign's face was white, though I saw no injuries. I flicked on the dazzler, which issued a brilliant green beam into the dark compartment. It was an empty room with four bunks and a hole through the back.

Samantha went in. "He escaped through the rear bulkhead. It's made from a softer alloy."

I asked the officer prone on the deck, "Where'd he go?"

"No idea, Major," he panted, trying to maintain composure. We turned in a circle, glaring every direction in vain. Empty corridors. Only groans. "He was...everywhere. We shot him, sir. Over and over. Then he just...he was gone."

He'd vanished.

"This ship is a city," I growled.

"Maybe the cameras followed him," Samantha said. "Where the hell am I? How do we get back to security?"

"Upwards," Cody answered and we followed him back to the camera room, trudging in defeat. Katie opened the door before we knocked.

Seaman Burke pointed to the screens. Over half of them were dark. "He can go through most of the ship now," he announced miserably. We were never going to find him.

Katie stood at the monitors, staring into them. Her hand pressed the wall to brace against the ship's rising and falling. She spoke without breaking her gaze. "I think Tank went into the cargo hold. He ran that direction. He breaks cameras as he goes. And..." She held up her phone. "He's texting me."

"He's what??" I yelped.

"He must have taken a phone from one of those bodies." She pointed at the video screens. Dozens of men lay unmoving. Or moving slowly. She handed me the phone.

>> Katie
>> I'm here for you
>> Do you still use this phone? Please answer me. -T

Captain Travis burst into the room. His face had lost some of its color and he was sweating. "What the *hell* is going on? I want some answers. Right this very damn second. Christ almighty, that...*thing* has wiped out a tenth of my crew in the last hour."

"That thing is a medically enhanced insane teenager who escaped from a highly secure military prison," I explained. "Maybe you believe us now? He's the strongest person on earth, and one of the fastest too. He can be drowned or burned or electrocuted, but those are the only ways I know to stop him. He's here for her. And for me, too."

He glared a moment, looking like a man who'd just been told the moon was made of blood. "We have a dozen tasers on board," he said eventually. "I'll send for them."

"You'll need to hit him with more than one."

"You two can't subdue him?" he asked.

"We can't *find* him. He's staying away from us."

"This is a mess, Majors. This is a God-awful, unprecedented mess. I don't know how the hell I'm supposed to explain this to Admiralty, but I'm turning the *San Antonio* around. We need resources we can't obtain in this squall."

The phone rang. Captain Travis grabbed it and barked, "*What?*" He listened and rubbed his eyes. "Where's the Chief? Sounds like a electronic malfunction-"

Loud thumps below interrupted him. The ship rang like it'd been struck with a hammer. The reverberations were too deep to be gunfire. Travis stared crazily at the deck, like he could see through it.

I asked, "What on earth was that?"

"Sounds like something hit us," Travis said. "But it came from below, near the keel."

Two more thumps. Samantha swung open the door. Echoes of the blast caromed off steel, faint but sharp. Samantha said, "Those are grenades detonating."

"Seaman Burke," Travis said, a new note of tension in his voice. "Show me the Armory."

Burke hit a few keys and a blue picture jumped onto his screen. "Those cameras were destroyed, Captain."

"Son of a bitch has our grenades." Travis shook his head, living a nightmare.

"Grenades can't puncture the hull," I said.

Our room dimmed. The overhead speaker sputtered. Half of Burke's monitors blinked off and on. Lights in the hall flickered, instants of pitch black, accompanied by a deep digital hum as electronic systems shuffled their loads.

"No," Travis said. "But he could destroy our engines. And power. That bastard's in engineering."

Samantha asked, "This ship have a nuclear reactor?"

"Four diesel engines. Though, maybe three now."

"If that big oaf went to the Armory, you can bet he destroyed the tasers."

I asked Cody, "Can you get us to engineering?"

"Yes sir. Or close at least."

"Captain, how long before you get us to shore?" I walked into the passageway and flipped the Stick in my hands a few times. It was impossibly heavy, but in my condition I didn't notice.

Captain Travis grumbled, "That depends on how many engines I have left, Major. Twelve hours, at least, in this storm. Maybe days."

"He texted me again!" Katie called. "It's addressed to you, Chase. He says if you let me go, he won't destroy the ship."

"No deal. You're worth more than the boat."

"Aw!"

Cody punched my shoulder. "Nice."

I'm the smoothest.

"So," Travis said, trying to make order from the chaos. "If you weren't aboard, he wouldn't be here?"

"Probably not," Katie replied.

"This is essentially a lovers quarrel?"

"Of epic proportions."

More blasts emitted below. Strident ruptures of steam. Metal tearing apart. The radio in Captain Travis's hand squealed, bursts of static and screams. The screams reached our ears unaided a heartbeat later. The fluorescent bulbs popped, and vibrations in the steel decks noticeably slackened. The propellors were losing power.

Emergency lights clicked on, casting us with an eery half-light.

"Gear," I said. "Let's go. We have a giant to slay."

"We lose one more engine, we won't maintain our heading," Travis barked. "The waves will roll us onto our beam and we'll be ass over heels!"

Samantha and I leapt down ladder wells, following the hissing steam deeper into the metal monster's belly. The order and discipline of the *San Antonio* was abandoned; rain water poured down hatches and hot steam issued from below. Inner horizons swayed and lights failed and men couldn't cope.

"Totally lost my zen!" Samantha cried above the racket, and she stumbled sideways as the ship heeled. "Damn it!"

"Just shoot him in the eye! I'll treat his head like a sledge treats a watermelon."

We reached the bottom deck and his voice echoed from the fog. "Do I hear Super Pajamas?" As always, his deep voice was felt as much as heard. It came tumbling out of air vents. He could be anywhere. "And PJs sidekick, Captain Bitch?"

"Hah!" she screamed. "I *like* that name!" She fired her pistol down perpendicular passageways. "Just stick your head out. I only need to see one eye!"

"I was starved for *weeks*!" he roared. "Because of you. Now I'll drink your blood."

Dalton whispered in my ear, "Engineering down that way, sir, but I bet he ain't there no more."

"I just want what you stole, Pajamas," Tank continued from…somewhere. "Release the Latina."

"She left you of her own free will," I answered, creeping cautiously towards the ruined engineering hatch. That compartment was on fire and emitting awful machinery groans. Dalton was right, but I had to check. "Jump overboard, Tank! We can't chase you in this storm. Start a new life somewhere. You're free."

"I want the girl."

"You can't have the girl!"

My phone buzzed. Over and over again. I glanced at it as our group snuck around a corner.

>> okay Puck rules
>> got u a ride!
>> get to the back of your boat
I typed, **what the heck??**
What do you mean?!
>> u need off that ship, dumb ass!!
>> got you a different one!
>> go!

I showed the screen to Samantha, and I whispered, "Do you know what he's talking about?"

Her eyes widened. "Of course! She's here! This…this could work. If we get off the *San Antonio*, Tank shouldn't destroy it, right? Let's go!"

Dumb founded. Flabbergasted. I followed her, stupidly. "Who? Who's here?"

"Text Katie. Tell her to collect our stuff and rendezvous at the wet deck." "What-"

"You two." Samantha jammed her finger at Cody and Dalton. "Go get Katie, get our stuff, and escort her to the wet deck. We're getting off the *San Antonio* just in time to save it."

"Yes ma'am!" They stormed up the ladder, out of sight.

"What. The. HeckAreYouTalkingAbout!" I hissed.

Samantha raised her gun and fired four shots into the fog. Then she held a finger to her lips and led us aft. Tank's angry voice penetrated the thickening mire but his words were muted and unintelligible.

She spoke into the radio. "Captain Travis, this is Major Gear. We're getting off your ship. Prepare to lower the stern gate."

"*Major, that gate lowers and we sink.*"

"You want us off your boat or not, Captain? We'll disembark and then contact Tank. Once he learns of our departure, he'll have no reason to remain. He should abandon ship soon after."

A long silence. The radio clicked twice, as if Travis raised the radio to reply but changed his mind. She shot me an angry, anxious glance. Travis *should* see reason. Finally, "*Roger. We're monitoring your approaching vessel. Will lower the door. Stand by.*"

"Gear." I took her by the shoulders. Her muscles were rocks. "What's going on?"

"Pacific! She's here. I didn't even think to call her. Puck is a genius."

"Pacific," I repeated. "The Infected lady? I've heard you mention the codename."

"She lives on a boat out here. I've never met her."

"You're positive this is a good idea?"

"Hell no, but its better than staying here."

Above and beyond the aft gate, the world was madness. The driving rain obliterated everything except heaving walls of water. We clung on and gaped and wondered how we'd jump ships.

Cody and Dalton and Katie and Cory appeared three minutes later, carrying duffle bags. Cory vomited into the flooded wet deck. Katie kept her eyes on me.

"Gentlemen," Samantha called over crashing waves. She saluted Cody and Dalton. "You will not be welcome on that boat. This is where we leave you."

The two SEALs didn't know whether to be relieved or angry.

Captain Travis radioed. "*Majors, your boat is in position. Will lower gate on your command.*"

"Ready to roll, Travis," I spoke into the receiver. "Thank you for your service."

He didn't reply. Red lights blared over our heads and a siren wailed. The gate jerked and began lowering.

Fifty yards aft, a yacht paced us, tossing a majestic bow wave. I didn't know much about luxury yachts, but the magnificent white boat looked like a hundred million dollars of splendor. The word '*Amnesia*' was painted on the starboard side.

The living sea was a constant threat to destroy us. The *San Antonio* rose on a deep green swell and the yacht dropped below, almost straight down, and then we crested and went over the apex and now the yacht was above us and racing down the wall of foam. Samantha screamed in delight, her body's thirst for danger fully satisfied.

"Sir, this won't work-" Cody roared but the ocean swept in, flooding the bay and drowning us. Cory scrambled after our duffle bags. Katie treaded water, keeping her phone out of the consuming wash.

We ascended another wave and the water sluiced out. Thirty seconds later we leveled. The water rushed in like a tide and so did the yacht. The luxury liner's bow barely fit into our bay. *Amnesia* plunged recklessly inside the *San Antonio,* burrowing her bow (nose) until the two boats wedged tight, nearly crushing us. Metal screamed. Fiberglass splintered. The yacht was obscene and alien and enormous in the tight space. The two vessels were now attached, nose to stern.

"We've got ten seconds," I shouted and *Threw* Katie over my head, onto the bow of the yacht. She climbed under metal safety rails that bent from the

San Antonio impact. Cory and I tossed duffle bags after her and then I raised him. He grasped desperately and scrambled up.

The *San Antonio* began rising on another mammoth wave. *Amnesia* heaved backwards and bucked loose, drawing free before the Navy's larger, stronger warship sheered off her nose. Samantha swarmed up *Amnesia's* side. I *Leapt* over the chasm of sea and landed aboard the yacht, slipping on the fiberglass.

All four of us held fast to handholds, exposed and tossed in the raging elements. The yacht roared powerfully and began pulling away from the *San Antonio*, which consumed the horizon directly ahead.

I slid beside Katie. "We need to call Tank! Let him know we're gone!"

"Look!" Cory cried, clinging for dear life and green all over.

Through curtains of rain, silhouetted by distant bolts of lightning, Tank stood like an angry sea god at the break of the helipad. The strength of his gaze and hate struck like thunder.

Samantha snatched the pistol from her belt and fumbled it.

Tank got a three-step running start, and he jumped the distance. He hung in the air, Thor himself descending from above, bringing storm and fury. I struggled to stand, wetly grasping for the Thunder Stick shoved down my back. The ship tilted and rocked and I fell.

Tank's arms rotated wildly, trying to pull our boat closer, balancing himself midair. He splashed like a four hundred pound cannon ball three feet short of our hull, lost in the surf. Our yacht surged forward, strong propellors churning, and we chased the waves. If Tank rose, he'd slam into our keel.

Samantha and I slipped and tripped and slid our way aft, holding onto the lifelines. This boat was *huge*!

We reached the stern (back of the boat).

So did Tank. The rear-mounted swim ladder hadn't been secured and it bounced on the surface; Tank snagged it before the engines could shoot him into the creaming wake. He glared malevolently at us, his face still twisted with severe burns. He tried to shout but swallowed gallons of salt water. Even so he managed to get a foot onto the swim platform.

I *Crushed* the ladder with the Thunder Stick. The mechanism exploded and came free, along with chunks of the boat. Tank's fingers broke.

Tank fell helplessly into the Pacific Ocean, grasping at nothing. He went under, lost in the rolling mountain range of waves. We plunged northward at thirty knots and soon Tank was left far, far behind.

We panted, hands on knees, streaming with rain, watching the water flood past, not daring to feel relief.

Above us, exposed and beautiful in the convertible cockpit, a woman piloted *Amnesia* with confidence and abandon, smiling at us. Her long gray hair whipped in the gale like a flag. She howled in laughter and delirium, and she bore us on to safety.

Chapter Fifteen
Tuesday, February 6. 2019

The storm lasted two more days. The yacht, named *Amnesia*, churned north to avoid the worst. Cory and Katie remained in their cabins and hugged the toilet. I stayed with Katie until she physically shoved me out.

"You're wonderful. But I'm tired of being aware how gross I must look," she groaned and slammed the door.

Samantha and I sat at the forward rail (bent from the rescue) and took the shattered rain and bow waves directly into our faces. This *had* to be what cocaine was like. I felt happy and high on subconscious levels traveling all the way back to my childhood. The yacht surged and heaved beneath us, and every motion triggered a positive emotional response. I left the bow for food and rest only. Samantha did not. She slept with her feet dangling, soaked with most of the ocean and smiling pleasantly in her sleep.

We still hadn't met our captain. Pacific never left the wheel. She waved at us a couple times, her brilliant smile piercing the deluge, and screamed in delight when her boat went up and over aggressive waves. She had two stewards, polite middle-aged men, who helped us stow our bags and find food. But even these two felt the storm's effects and they stayed below.

Only Infected were insane enough to brave this storm, apparently.

The seas leveled the second day, and our captain finally relented. She handed the cockpit over to a steward and disappeared, indulging in a much-deserved slumber. The waves calmed and so did our emotional high, returning us to normalcy. I was shaky and weak after so many hours of throbbing adrenaline, emotionally drained. I slept.

My cellphone buzzed and woke me at one thirty.

>> the freak storm passed, right?
>> u guys alive??
Yes, I replied. **This boat's amazing. Thanks for finding it.**
>> yw
>> puck rules
>> b careful with pacific tho
>> she's infected
>> and old
>> which means kinda nuts
>> an sometimes she likes to cause trouble
I'll keep that in mind. Thanks again, homie.

Katie ventured out an hour later, appearing five pounds lighter. Cory emerged too, looking like he lost fifty. Katie and I held hands and explored the exquisite boat, which now basked and steamed in pouring sunlight. It measured over half a football field, and the uppermost deck was four stories above the water. Chairs and cushions and polished wooden tables and pools decorated the many sundecks. Inside the superstructure, all was opulence. We discovered a saloon, formal dining room, gourmet galley, living room with overstuffed couches, a full bar, and on and on. She gasped every time we turned a corner until she eventually collapsed on the lower aft sundeck shaded by a large blue Bimini.

"*Amnesia* was built five years ago," Pacific announced suddenly, descending the stern staircase. We were sitting on dry cushions in wooden deck chairs, and Cory and Katie were sipping juice experimentally. Pacific wore a white sundress, and Ray-Bans pushed her long, thick gray hair back. She looked sixty-five, which indicated an actual age closer to a hundred and fifty, and she was quite attractive. She was thin and erect, her skin glowed golden, and her arms and legs were strong. "I ground my previous boat, the *Vagabond*, down to rust and salt. *Amnesia* is a Benetti too. The Italians build the best yachts, don't you agree? This one required two years to build and cost seventy-five million dollars." She spread her hands wide to indicate her world. "Worth every penny."

"Seventy-five million…" Cory mumbled in shock. I bet he was wishing he'd cleaned his bathroom a little more thoroughly.

Pacific walked barefoot to Samantha, who stood to meet her. Pacific took her hands and kissed her forehead and said, "Samantha Gear, Shooter, sweetheart, I'm honored to meet you at last. You're as pretty as a seabird."

Samantha's mouth pulled into a grim line. "You never mentioned that you're hot, Pacific."

"All of us *sickos* are, to some extent. My name is Minnie Elizabeth McClure. Call me Minnie."

"Sweet ride, Minnie. Thanks for the lift."

"Hmmmm." Pacific pulled Samantha closer and leaned in slightly. Samantha responded by arching backwards warily. "Can you feel it, Samantha? Can you feel our illness colliding? We're like tectonic plates, you and I, honey, scraping against one another."

"I feel it, Minnie," Samantha said through gritted teeth.

Minnie's voice was pleasant but soft. "We stay together too long, there'll be an earthquake."

"Then maybe you ought let go of my hands."

"Isn't it funny. You and I have more in common with each other than anyone else on earth. And yet, soon as you came aboard, I'm spooked. You're a shark in the water, Samantha, making my senses buzz. A beautiful great white."

"You're a shark too, Pacific," she replied, twisting and tugging her hands.

"Mmhm," Minnie nodded and her eyes closed for a moment. "One of the biggest, and we're sensing each others vibrations and electricity. It's called electroreception, sugar. It's one reason I live in the middle of an ocean. And it's the reason you can stay here a couple days, and that's all. After that…well, sharks aren't tame, are they?"

"No ma'am."

"Until that time," she said and she pulled Samantha into an embrace, "you are welcome. And you are my beloved sister."

"Thank you, Pacific."

Cory was agape, stupefied, watching this bizarre exchange like he'd study an unsolvable calculus problem. I understood some of it, but still. The two women had a complex bond, far beyond words, not all of it good. The disease did weird things to us.

"But you," Pacific said, turning to me. "From you I only sense…unbridled power. I could get a tan off you, boy."

I stood up and was immediately embraced. Her body was harder than it appeared. "Minnie, we are in your debt."

"Nonsense, honey. I appreciated the adventure. And I get to meet the fabled Outlaw." She took my face in both her hands and peered long into my eyes. Her gaze was probing and confident. And unhinged. "Why doesn't my body respond to yours in the same way as it does hers?" she whispered so quietly the others had to strain. "I am not repelled by you, boy. He told me you were this way."

"He?"

"This is why he wants you." More whispers. "This is why he seeks you above all else. You are…*pulling* me. My whole being. You could pull his entire army behind you." She startled me by pulling our mouths together. She kissed me. It wasn't a romantic kiss. Or even affectionate. It was…experimental. It was curious, and it was brief.

"You're referring to the Chemist," I said when she released me. Better pretend it hadn't happened. My girlfriend watched, after all.

"To Martin. Yes."

"You speak to him?"

She said simply, "He's my husband."

I was too thunderstruck to reply. So was Samantha.

"What's his is mine. So do not fret, I have no need of his reward money. Make yourselves at home, my loves," Pacific said on her way to the stairs. She stopped beside Katie, who was groping for words. She touched Katie's face. "You *are* pretty. You have a face worth launching ships. I wish your story could have a happier ending." Then she turned to Cory and smiled politely. "I'm sorry. You're not important. You understand. Dinner is at sundown."

Cory, who had been rising to greet her, fell back into his chair. We all did.

From: Jean Francois de la Barre
Date: Tuesday, Feb 2nd. 22:19
Subject: The gentleman Andrew

Duval de Soicourt,
Pontious,

I declare Andrew Babington convicted of having taught to sing and sung impious, execrable and blasphemous songs against ME; of having profaned ME in making blessings accompanied by foul words which modesty does not permit repeating; of having knowingly refused the signs of respect to ME; and having shown these signs of adoration to YOU.

What say you?

Pro patria mori

"He's insane," Katie remarked. Her voice sounded tight with repressed grief. We lay on the bed in her cabin, scanning the Chemist's email. It was now several days old. The Chemist had attached a photograph of Andy Babington lying unconscious on a table, surrounded by grisly surgical instruments. "Poor Andy."

I shook my head in frustration and glared at the screen. "Does any of this make sense to you?"

"A little, yes. La Barre was a French martyr, killed for his religious beliefs. I think the body of the email is a translation of the court's decision against La Barre."

I sucked at my teeth in thought. "So the Chemist is calling himself a martyr."

"Yes."

Puck spoke up from my speakerphone. "He refers to you as Duval do Soicourt. I looked him up. Duval is the judge that condemned Le Barre to death."

I made a *Pfft* noise. "The Chemist thinks *I'm* the one persecuting *him?*"

"That's how the email reads," Puck said. "But the dumb-ass condemns

Andy with La Barre's court decision. So he's getting his martyrs confused."

"In this email, the Chemist is both the judge and the victim," said Katie. "It's either clever, or he's insane."

"Puck, you can't tell where he sent this from?"

"No. It has zero digital signatures, a very impressive feat."

"Would sending the email to the FBI help? Could they find something?"

"…for the sake of our friendship, Puck will pretend you did not ask that."

"What does Pro Patria Mori mean?"

Katie replied, "A rough translation is, 'It is good to die for one's country.' That's his one clear advantage over you. He's a zealot. He's willing to die for his cause."

"I'm not willing to die for Andy. Right? Should I be?"

"I don't know." She rested her head on my shoulder and stroked my arm. "Maybe not?"

"Self-discipline," I said. "I won't throw my life away on a small battlefield."

"Is an innocent human life a small battlefield?"

"Unless *you* are the innocent human life, it's tiny."

She shook her head minutely, tears leaking onto my arm. "You've got to stop thinking that way. I'm your weakness." She caught a sob before it escaped her lungs, and she rolled over, pressing the heels of her hands into her eyes. "This is lunacy. I miss English class. I should be getting ready for the spring Model UN competition. I was *totally* going to win this year. Instead, my boyfriend I are debating whether he should die or not."

"Like our own private debate club."

"That's *not* funny," Katie sniffed. "I miss my debate club too. I was the captain of our team. And I was going to be valedictorian!" She pounded the bed with her fists. Her tiny, perfect, nerdy fists. She shouted at the ceiling, "I already had half my speech composed!"

"You had half your speech written in December?"

"Of *course*!" She went to the bathroom, which Samantha called 'the head', and blew her nose.

"Puck, write him back. Ask what it would take for him to release Andy."

"Sure homie," he replied. "Although maybe you could just ask his wife."

"Did you know they were married?"

"Hell no! I about fell out of my chair."

We ate dinner on the forward sun deck and watched twilight advance across the ocean. Minnie's stewards served fresh caught salmon and salads and lemonade.

"I exaggerated," Pacific admitted, shrugging and swirling her glass of wine. The wind came cold from the north and whisked her hair. She'd given Katie a heavy blue, long-sleeved nightshirt to wear. "Martin and I are not married. We are lovers and friends and confidantes. And have been for over half a century, so I figure I've earned the title. He purchased this boat, a surprise birthday present. He used to propose once a year or so, when he'd stop by." She smiled, delightful and longing at the memory. "I could never be faithful, however. Too many skippers in the sea. But when I think of Martin, I think of him as my husband."

Katie asked, "Too many skippers in the sea?"

"Why do you think *Amnesia* was allowed to approach your Navy? It is strictly forbidden." Another smile. "The American commodore, an Admiral from North Carolina originally, is an…*amoureux* of mine. He visits as often as time and tide allows. I have many such affectionate arrangements. It's simply not practical for Martin and me to marry. We both carry the illness. And I cannot leave the water."

"Cannot?" I asked.

"Cannot. The illness broke my mind. I was certifiably insane and shipped off to an Australian penal colony, just before the American civil war. The only restraints strong enough were anchor chains and thick hawsers. The voyage was my first experience on the water, and I was cured by the third day. Something about the motion."

"We feel it too."

"So does Martin, though to a lesser extent. He's a land mammal. So I talked my way out of the chains, killed our captors, took the convicts as my crew…" She shrugged again. "And I've been at sea since. When I step ashore for provisions, which I do personally once a decade and then only out of necessity, I feel the instability in my mind. I'd be dead in days."

"And the storms?" Katie asked.

"I get drunk off storms. So do Shooter and the Outlaw. I could smell it in their pores. The ocean is medicine and I require a constant and heavy dose. A morphine drip preventing madness. Good squalls are a narcotic."

"Speaking of madness," Samantha said, "do you support the Chemist's crusade?"

Minnie answered in a voice surprisingly strong. "We shall *NOT* discuss these things at night. Such topics are better left for daylight. I will tell you what I know. Tomorrow. And offer counsel, because I understand your crusade too. Perhaps good will come of these revealed secrets. Perhaps not. But it will certainly create mischief, which I adore in all seasons."

Dinner finished. Her stewards cleared the table. Cory, still weak from being nauseated, went to bed. Samantha pestered Pacific until she relented and took her to the cockpit for a discussion on navigation and piloting.

The *Amnesia* lay in a calm, bobbing before the moon's long reflection. The stars had exploded tonight. I lit soft electric lamps and pulled back the jacuzzi's cushioned cover. The steaming bubbly water was illuminated with submerged golden lights.

"What are you doing?" Katie asked with a cagey smile.

"I'm getting into the hot tub. And you're coming with me."

"No way, boyfriend." She shook her head. "It's chilly. I will kiss you until sunrise in my cabin, however."

"I've always wanted to kiss in a hot tub. It looks so great in the movies."

She laughed, my favorite noise in the world. "You're not wearing swim trunks."

I undid the clasp of my Navy belt.

She gasped and said, "Chase Jackson you may *not* get naked on Minnie's boat!"

"Relax," I grinned. I shimmied out of my Navy khakis. I still had on football practice shorts and a t-shirt. "Look, we already have this stack of towels waiting."

"You go ahead. It's freeeeeezing. I'll just enjoy the view inside Minnie's warm nightshirt."

"Nope. You're coming." I bounded across the deck and hefted her easily.

She smothered a shriek and hit me in the chest. She pleaded, "No no no no! Let's just go to my room."

"Why not here?"

"Because this is the nicest article of clothing I've ever put on and she said I could keep it," Katie answered in a rush. "Please please, sweet sweet kind Chase, most handsome boy in all the world. It has layers of cashmere and silk and I'll be so sad if you get it wet."

"I'm worth it."

"I won't talk to you for...twenty minutes if you throw me in. The chlorine will ruin it."

"Then take it off."

"I'm not wearing a bathing suit!"

"Are you wearing anything underneath?"

"Of course."

"That'll do."

She held my eyes with hers and her face filled with a charming blush. "Just my bra and underwear!"

"I've seen you in a bikini. Same thing." We were at the edge of the jacuzzi and her arms wrapped tightly around my neck. In her defense, it did feel like a nice shirt.

"It's NOT the same thing."

"Katie-"

"Okayokayokayokay. Fine. Put me down. I'll take off the nightshirt."

"Promise not to run?"

"I promise. You have seduced me. Well, the way your arms feel. *That* seduced me."

I set her down and blocked the escape in case she changed her mind. She gathered the blue fabric in her fists with deliberate care, her arms crossed, and pulled it over her head. My chest tightened and my throat partially closed. I said, "No wonder people follow you on Instagram."

"Thank you. I feel ridiculous." She posed like a runway model on a catwalk and we laughed. It may have been the most indecent and brazen and sexy pose ever struck by a Model UN captain. "Remember, this is a bikini."

"Somehow…it's not."

"Yes it is! But you can't see the back."

"Why not?"

"Because it's a thong, silly."

"Your legs look great. You work out a lot. I'm sure it looks nice."

"I know *it* looks nice!" She backed towards the water's edge. Her skin texture changed from smooth to goosebumps. "But this is a swimsuit, remember? No thongs. I'm SO cold." Katie dipped her foot in the pool and held the rail. She stepped backwards down the stairs, her face dissolving into pleasure.

"Oh its heaven," she cooed. "Oh wow."

"Yeah?"

"Get your big beautiful body in here. Now."

I entered. The hot, effervescent water sloshed over both sides. She placed her hands under my t-shirt, flat on my stomach, and said, "You're swelling. I like it when you do that. You get so tall."

She was correct. My shorts felt considerably shorter. Luckily we'd just eaten; the change in body composition required calories. A lot of them.

Katie pushed me onto an underwater bench and stood over me. I looked straight up to kiss her. Our mouths pressed together for a long, perfect moment. We'd been dating for months and I still enjoyed the first contact, the intimacy.

"You're wearing the cologne," she murmured against my lips.

"So we can find each other with our eyes closed."

"You're a weirdo. Why on earth are you wearing this stupid shirt?" She pulled it over my head and dropped it wetly on the wooden floor slats and kissed me again.

We didn't speak for twenty minutes. Just melted into the other. Both of us happy and scared, trembling with desire and fear, aware this oasis was temporary. There was no safe place left for us except each other, and soon we had to let go of that. So we indulged and forgot everything except the stars and ourselves. Her fingernails cut lines through my hair, scoring my scalp, carving deeper, more permanently into my soul.

Finally she lowered into my lap, forehead pressed into my temple, and grazed the stubble on my jaw with her lips. I said, "I'm glad it's you."

"What do you mean?" she whispered.

"Humans invariably fall in love. When we're young we have no idea who with, you know? We just know it'll happen. I'm glad it's you."

"You'd rather have me than Natalie North?"

"I'd want you for one lifetime rather than her for a thousand."

I felt her lips pull into a smile against my skin. "That's sweet. Did she ever kiss you?"

"She did."

"I get to kiss a boy who kissed Natalie North. I assume I'm much better at it?"

"Of course. You were born for me and our mouths fit. Celebrity made Natalie arrogant and lazy."

She giggled, a bubbly rich sound. "I know that's not true. But thanks for saying it." She sat up, facing me, straddling my knees. Water rivulets streamed from her hair, down her shoulders and collarbone. She punched me playfully in the chest. "Remember when you weren't this big? You used to be scrawny."

I frowned. "No I wasn't. That's outrageous."

"Well. You were normal sized. Now you're like…" She spread her arms. "Pow! You get so wide. And your arms."

"Maybe you-"

She punched me again. Harder. "It's like hitting the earth. Does it hurt?"

"Not really. But that doesn't mean I'm loving it."

"Poor sweetie." She closed the distance and started kissing my neck and chest. "What's it like? Being that big and strong? Is it weird?"

I spoke through deep breaths. "It hurts. What's it like being that small and weak?"

"Do you still want to wait? To have sex?"

"I never *wanted* to wait."

"But you still think we should?"

I didn't answer. I closed my eyes and tried to concentrate.

She asked, "What if one of us dies before we get to have sex?"

I quoted from memory, "*Oh she is rich in beauty, only poor, that when she dies with beauty dies her store.*"

Katie straightened in surprise. Her eyes appeared hazel in the pool's glow and they glittered. "You just quoted *Romeo and Juliet.*"

I continued, "*Hath she sworn that she will live chaste? She has, and in that sparing makes huge waste.*"

"Are you trying to arouse this literary nerd with Shakespeare? Because it's working. Do you know what that quote means?"

"Yes," I grinned. "If you were to die before someone enjoyed your perfect body, it would be a waste of riches."

She groaned and laid her face back against my chest. Her voice was muffled. "That is so hot. Tonight is perfect."

"Agreed."

"I want you desperately, but I keep hearing my mom's voice. Wait until you're ready! Wait until your ready!" She imitated her mom's tone and Spanish accent.

"She's probably right. Losing one's virginity is a pillar of the human experience."

"I told you that. I read it in a magazine in middle school. Think about what happens to people when they experience sex too early. Before they're ready. It profoundly hurts them. It sometimes redirects their life on a completely different path. But I want to do it anyway."

"Me too. But we always said we'd wait."

She looked up and glanced at our surroundings. "I have to admit. I'd rather our first time not happen in someone else's pool with strangers watching."

"You think Samantha's watching?"

Her lips pulled into a mischievous curve. "I'm positive Samantha's watching. But the hot water, the moon, the stars, the muscles, the skin contact-"

"The...bikini."

"-the kissing. It's almost worth it, despite Samantha."

"I bet she's recording us for Puck."

She puckered her cute nose. "Ew."

"What's a bigger waste? Ruining the first time? Or never having it?"

"I don't know. But I know I love you. Thank you for waiting for me."

"Thank you for not having sex with Tank."

She grimaced and shivered. "He wanted to."

"I know."

"He didn't want to wait."

"I don't blame him. You're crazy fly."

She grinned. "I think you have one of the purest hearts and souls on the planet. And I'm just a girl trying to get into her boyfriend's pants."

That was funny. I laughed. Hard.

"No but seriously." She slid off my lap and climbed from the pool. The night was chilly and she wrapped herself within a cocoon of fluffy white blankets. "Our planet is really lucky you got sick. Most people aren't as good as you. Most wouldn't stand against the Chemist."

"Most people don't have as much to lose as me. They don't have you."

"But that's also a weakness, I think."

"What do you mean?"

"You are too concerned with my safety." She held open a towel. I got out and she wrapped me. "It's almost a form of selfishness. You will only die for me. Nobody else matters. Put it another way; the only thing that matters to you is...you. Your wants. You *want* me alive. It's selfish."

"It's love."

"It's flattering. It's endearing. But perhaps it's not enough."

I crushed her against me, surrounding us both with the last towel. I kissed the top of her head. "You're asking me to be willing to sacrifice you, if need be, for the sake of the planet."

"And I know it won't come to that. But I'm suggesting...your willingness to sacrifice yourself isn't enough. You need to think beyond yourself and beyond me. Your purpose can't be me. This is too important. Too many people depend on you."

"I'm not that selfless," I admitted.

"You *must* be."

"Maybe one day. In the meantime, we can agree on one thing."

"What's that?"

"I saw you getting out of the pool. You were right. You and your thong look great."

She tried to suppress a smile but failed. "Earth is doomed."

Chapter Sixteen
Wednesday, February 7. 2019

The next morning we gathered on the aft deck in a circle of palatial sun chairs. The canvas shade overhead tinted us tones of sapphire and indigo, and the sun sparkled so radiantly off the water's surface we had to wear sunglasses. Breeze blew gently from the north and *Amnesia* rose and fell on long shallow swells.

"Why are you helping us, Pacific?" Samantha demanded, arms crossed. This didn't strike me as a productive beginning, but I'd been wondering too.

"Because PuckDaddy asked me to and it sounded like an adventure."

"Sure, yeah, but why are you providing council today? He's your husband and we're trying to kill him."

"I suspect the answer to your question will become clear in a moment, once you hear what I have to say."

Puck spoke from speakers mounted in the deck and bulkhead. "Before you begin your council of war, it may interest you to know the FBI uncovered another volunteer station. This one in Ohio. The patients were injected recently with Chemist blood and are still in a coma. Carter is en route."

Pacific mused, "Do you know, PuckDaddy, I think this is the first time I've heard your voice." She wore a short yellow sundress and held a jar of iced punch. Her legs were crossed serenely.

"Sup."

"Are you black?"

"More like a sexy brown, baby."

"How many patients are unconscious at the volunteer station, Puck?" asked Samantha. Her scowl was in full bloom today.

"Two hundred. And twenty workers tending them."

"Tending them?"

"You know. Keeping them fed. Giving them drugs. That stuff."

Katie shook her head in disbelief. "Where does the Chemist get all of these volunteers?"

"Mad men and megalomaniacs have always and will always attract droves of the weak minded," Pacific said.

"Is he mad?"

"He is both."

"Puck, does the FBI or anyone else have a guess how many Chosen this makes?"

"Puck read the number ten thousand somewhere. I forget where. I'm forwarding your phones paraphernalia discovered at the Chrysalis."

I pulled out my phone and watched the files download. "Chrysalis?"

"That's what he calls these volunteer stations. In your files you can see that the worthy volunteers are referred to as Larva. The Larva are injected and kept in a comatose state. When unconscious, the workers call the patients Pupas."

Katie finished his thought. "And then the survivors emerge as Butterflies, I bet. Ferocious Butterflies. It's a fitting analogy to the transformation."

Puck sounded a little put out that Katie guessed the final stage. "That's correct. Katie. Know-it-all. New Chosen are called Butterflies until they leave the Chrysalis. Then he calls them Twice Chosen."

Pacific raised her hand for attention. "Martin calls them Twice Chosen. But you call Martin's new creations simply Chosen? Yes?"

"It's confusing, we know."

"Chosen is his term for sickos like us, sick since birth."

Samantha grunted, her heels bouncing on the deck. "Yeah, the Chemist doesn't like the term 'Infected.' That's what we call ourselves."

"'Infected' is the term that Carter uses," she noted, rubbing her thumb on the rim of her jar.

"Makes sense. We were recruited by Carter. Have you met him?"

She nodded. "Multiple times. A very crass and blunt man. But not without his merits."

I picked absently at stray threads on my pants, lost in thought. "I haven't decided which man I dislike more."

"Neither are very ingratiating. Martin, at least, has manners. Those two have always had a strained relationship. Had they collaborated, the world would have surrendered without a fight. But. They are fish of different colors."

Katie asked, "How so?"

"Carter never wanted our small society of sickos to be public, dear girl. He wanted control but anonymity. And on that point, I am in complete agreement with him. Martin wants fame and power and recognition." She shrugged delicately, the ice clinking in her fist. "Hard for those two ideologies to co-exist. Neither man is right. And perhaps neither man is wrong."

I asked, "Can you tell us what Martin's goal is?"

Pacific did not answer immediately. She sat down her glass carefully, wiped her hand on her dress, and stared off towards the mainland and the unseen shore. After a minute, "He and I are alike in many ways. We both…profit…from disorder. It satisfies needs within. I *understand* his crusade. We've witnessed too many normal human births and burials for us to fret over deaths anymore. He is the oldest living human. And maybe the strongest. And possibly the most intelligent. He's outlasted billions. And survived dozens like him. By right of survival of the fittest, he feels this should all belong to him, especially now in his waining years. Conceivably, he's right."

"But-" Samantha started.

Pacific talked over her. "He wants to create a kingdom. A new country or state which he rules by right of his abilities and power. He and other Chosen, or Infected, will live openly and govern as they see fit and the borders will be flung wide to his many admirers."

Puck said, "Sounds like a religion."

"A religion whose god is dying," she nodded in agreement. "We are all sick, both physically and mentally. You two appear more stable than most, but most likely that will deteriorate with age. Martin has a couple decades left at most, and what then? His kingdom, his religion, will be left in tatters, destroyed by less powerful sickos. We make poor leaders, inherently."

I agreed. "There's dissent in his ranks already. Walter already hates him. And hates Blue-Eyes."

A ghost of a smile crossed Pacific's lips. "We all hate each other. It's in our nature. Even Samantha, though you are lovely and unoffensive…I desperately want you off my ship."

"Feeling's mutual."

"This is why Martin wants *you*, Outlaw. We don't despise you like we do each other. In fact, it's just the opposite. Something about your body. You are strong, yes. You are fast. You are a Leaper. But above all your extraordinary gifts, you are a leader. A magnet. Martin wants to create something lasting, something beautiful in his eyes, and you are the key to its survival."

"He's tried to capture me before. Does he believe I can be brainwashed or controlled?"

"Ahhh." She leaned forward in her chair and looked us in the eyes. Cory recoiled from the potency of her gaze. I felt as though I'd been blasted with sunlight. She could turn the impact of her presence on and off, like a switch. "Now we come to it, don't we."

"This is so intense," PuckDaddy whispered from his speakers.

"He does not brainwash, so to speak, in the traditional sense. Are you familiar with neural stem cell therapy?"

Of course not. Samantha shrugged.

Katie said, "Sure."

Puck said, "Oh crud."

"It's a foreign language to me," Pacific continued. "I'm a sea captain, not a surgeon like Martin. But he explained it to me and I retained enough. Martin spent ten years experimenting with his own brain cells, creating neurological tissue which can be implanted inside others."

Katie said, "Stem cells."

"Yes. Stem cells. He grows his own DNA inside his Chosen."

Puck mused, "And he does it while the patients sleep, I bet. While the…Larva are in the Pupa stage. The…Butterfly wakes up with the Chemist's disease *and* his DNA."

"And not just within their brains. He implants skin tissue and bone marrow and…well, I forget. Multiple stem cells within each patient. He kidnapped several prominent physicians to perform the surgeries."

Katie snapped her fingers. "I remember their disappearance! I read about it."

Samantha looked more and more angry. "Isaac Anderson mentioned the disappearance too. But I don't get it. What good does that do?"

Katie mused, "He wants to create a utopia for people who can't coexist. The Chosen and Infected sense each other, like animals, and their bodies do not allow them to play nice. But he's figured out a way to trick the disease." She looked to Pacific for confirmation.

"Precisely."

"He's essentially…masking their scents with his own. The disease won't tolerate others with the same symptoms, similar to an alpha predator's territory dispute. But if he implants and grows his own DNA inside the…Butterflies, then the predators will recognize and accept each other. It's like tricking a human body into accepting a new organ which would otherwise be rejected; there's no reason to reject the organ if it has the body's DNA. Am I getting my analogies confused?"

"No, Katie, that was very well explained."

Katie beamed. "I was going to be the valedictorian."

"He's creating clones of himself," Samantha realized.

"Not complete clones. But it's enough to prevent the disease from rejecting other carriers. He's unsure if the condition is permanent. Right now, it's how he maintains order."

Puck rattled, "Chase, this is why the tigers attacked you and not the Chemist. They smelled their own DNA within him but not you."

I nodded. "I remember. He told me the tigers had his DNA. I just didn't get it. But I'm still confused. How would the Chemist use this to control me?"

"The final stage of the Pupa phase is a medically created amnesia," Puck responded. "I'm reading the paperwork right now. Wiping their brains with these hard to pronounce proteins and enzymes and drugs makes the patient's memory foggy and susceptible to reprogramming. I bet he'd try that on you."

"He did that to Hannah Walker," I realized. "Her memory is shot. She couldn't even remember where I live."

"Ah yes. The fire girl. He's quite proud of that one. Performed the surgeries himself."

"Another thing I don't understand," Samantha growled, "is why his Chosen obeyed Chase? On top of the Gas Tower, he had partial control over them."

"Did he? Hah. Extraordinary. I bet meeting the fabled Outlaw is an overpowering experience for them. His body attracts the disease instead of repels it, so they are, at least in part, drawn to him. On the other hand, they sense the disease but not the Chemist's DNA, which identifies the Outlaw as an enemy. He's an enemy alpha predator, an affront, from outside of their pride. They love him and hate him. Plus they operate under orders to attack and subdue him on sight."

"Yeah but-"

She talked over Samantha. "Finally, on top of all that, the Outlaw is immensely more powerful than the new Chosen. They obeyed him because he is king of the jungle. His will subdues theirs. At least initially."

"They're drawn to him. But they hate him. They've been ordered to attack him. But he's the most powerful." Samantha groaned. "What a confusing scrum."

I asked, "What about that super drug of his?"

"Nootropics."

Katie made a *tsk* noise and said, "Aaahhh. That makes sense."

"Explain. I wasn't going to be the valedictorian."

Katie grinned and squeezed my hand. "A nootropic is a smart drug. A mental enhancer."

"Yes. It speeds them up, honey. Plus, Martin uses the drug to…oh, what did he say…deliver a payload of his own genetic code. In essence, it temporarily does for the drug user what the surgery does for his new Chosen.

At one thousandth the price and effort, the drug user will be safe from his aggressive Chosen. And tigers."

She stood and fetched a pitcher of punch. She refilled our glasses, though I hadn't touched mine. While she worked, Samantha glared. "You still haven't explained why you're helping us."

"Isn't it obvious? I don't want an army of his freaks tearing the world apart. Especially because, after he dies, they will be uncontrollable."

I said, "The disease is communicable. That means he's close to death, right? But earlier you mentioned decades."

"Just a guess," she said, returning to her chair. "Modern medicine is remarkable. And so is Martin. I imagine he'll prolong his life much longer than we anticipate."

"Do you want us to kill him?"

"No. I want you to stop him. The world is more interesting with him in it."

She smiled during her response. Like it was funny. I had to ask her a question I'd been dreading. But we were all thinking it. And we all knew the answer already.

"I can't kill him," I said. "Can I."

"No, dear. You cannot."

"You don't know that," Samantha shot back.

"I strongly suspect it."

"We have to try!"

I stood up and walked to the aft rail as Samantha fumed. The Chemist had been preparing for years. Decades. That was obvious. His intelligence far surpassed ours, and so did his ruthlessness. And his organization. And...everything. My plan, in comparison, was pathetic. My plan involved hitting him in the head with a stick.

"I'm not sure, Samantha," I said.

"What do you mean?"

"Every time we attack him, our problems escalate. Our violence creates more violence. And he is clearly superior at it."

"He fights in wars for fun," Pacific commented, smiling pleasantly again with far off memories, the corners of her eyes wrinkling. "He rose to a Colonel in the Russian army during the first World War. He returned with such a satisfied soul."

"Do you see?" I asked Samantha. "We're kids to him. Infants."

"Powerful infants."

"Not powerful enough. I don't even know if he *can* be killed."

"He once commented on this," Pacific said. "He loves literature, especially from Europe. He adores Tolkien, and compared himself to the Ring of Power. The Ring could only be destroyed within the fires of Mount Doom. Martin mentioned that an active volcano might be the only way for him to die, as well. He was contemplating suicide at the time."

"Fire," Samantha nodded and smacked a palm on her thigh. "American missiles get pretty hot on detonation. We can acquire a few."

Pacific shook her head. "He'd hear the missiles coming. But I thought of a different way."

"Which is?"

She chewed for a moment on her thumb, as a little girl would do, and smiled mischievously. "Drop something heavy on him."

We didn't respond. Perhaps our host had temporarily gone mad. This seemed…simplistic and juvenile.

"I'm not joking. His body is solid from centuries of ossification. Bullets just ricochet off, I suspect. But his skull? It has no muscle protectant. It's simply hard. I think his skull could be split down the middle, like a rock, if you…dropped something heavy."

"Like what?" Samantha chuckled. "A grand piano?"

"Like a mountain."

Samantha groaned, rolled her eyes, and flopped back in her chair. "Okay. Great. Thanks for the tip."

"Easier than throwing him *into* one, in my opinion."

"He's so old, though," Puck said. "Hella old. Shouldn't he be frail and weak?"

"No PuckDaddy. We are not senescent like mere mortals."

"Yo Katie, tell Puck what that big word means," PuckDaddy said. Cory, who had been completely silent, chuckled at this.

"Senescence is the process of aging, Puck," Katie grinned.

"We're like reptiles in some ways, PuckDaddy" Pacific said. "Reptiles grow their entire lives and age slowly. They do not cease growing, the way mammals do. You and I will never stop getting stronger and faster, until our organs quit. Thus, Martin believes his body must be thrown into a volcano. Weak? No. Frail? No. Slow? No. Brittle? …perhaps. But if you really want to kill someone, kill the bitch you call Blue-Eyes."

Puck said, "Yeah, she's trouble."

"I'm the jealous type." Pacific shrugged. "I want to gut her like a fish."

"Speaking of other Infected," I said, fingers drumming on the rail. "Do you know China or the Zealot? Do you believe they'd be our allies?"

"Neither of them would aid you in your quest. Australia would have, but I heard of his demise."

Samantha stayed still, her eyes on the floor. Mitch and Samantha had been as close as Infected could be, though she never consented to marry him. She hadn't spoken of him since his death at the hands of the Chemist.

Katie asked, "You knew Mitch?"

"I knew Mitchell, yes. I was very fond of that one. As pretty as an angel fish. We met twice, though he claimed he couldn't remember either. The disease was unkind to his memory."

Samantha stood and began pacing her side of the deck. Her hands gripped thick handfuls of hair and her teeth ground. "I don't want to talk about Croc. That solves nothing. And neither does this conversation. We're getting no where and I want to blow this damn boat into splinters."

"You can," Pacific chirped happily. "It's rigged with explosives."

Katie's face paled. Cory grew very still.

Rigged with explosives.

"Much respect, Minnie," Samantha crowed, inspecting her surroundings with renewed interested. "That's crazy cool."

I asked, "Why is it rigged?"

She shrugged as it was obvious. "I don't want to be as old as Martin. And some days death strikes me as appealing. I want to select the time of my departure. With the touch of a button. But I can usually locate a shark to swim with, which placates my anxieties."

"Oooooh," Samantha groaned, as though suddenly getting a luxurious back massage. Her eyes closed. "That sounds wicked. I want a shark."

"Minnie, how close to shore can you get us?"

"Very. I have an anchorage at Long Beach."

I grinned, examining a map in my mind. "Perfect. I have a plan."

Samantha cocked an eyebrow. "Where we going?"

"We're going to visit the only people I know who defeated Martin."

Blank stares. No one had a clue.

"We're going back to Compton."

Chapter Seventeen
Thursday, February 8. 2019

The lights of Long Beach glowed like a string of Christmas tree bulbs. We closed the distance after midnight, piloted by Pacific. Her steward sat crosslegged at the bow, clutching a spotlight in his fists. Other than his light, *Amnesia* sliced through the waves completely extinguished. Closer to the beach, closer to goodbye.

Samantha Gear and I dressed in our wing-suit pants and bullet-proof vests, and then jackets and backpacks. My Thunder Stick protruded halfway out.

Santa Monica, Long Beach, Newport, Anaheim, and all the surrounding towns within Greater Los Angeles had been partially abandoned during the previous months. Public officials estimated fifty percent remained. Anyone who could afford to leave did.

The warm breeze from land carried scents of vegetation and cooking food. "Can you smell that?"

Katie's head rested on my shoulder, strands of her brown hair tickling me. "Smell what?"

"Land."

"I cannot. You have a superior nose. Must be nice." She squeezed my hand and said, "*Oh God, I have an ill-diving soul. Methinks I see thee, now thou art below, as one dead at the bottom of a tomb.*"

"Romeo and Juliet?"

She nodded. "When Juliet says goodbye."

"Parting is such sweet sorrow that I shall say goodnight till it be morrow."

She kissed my shoulder and raised up to stretch her arms over her head. She yawned. "Wrong scene, handsome. Wrong act. Nice try. You're no valedictorian."

"But I get to make out with one. Even better."

"I know I'm not supposed to be scared for you. Or worry. But I am. You're going to war. You enter the Coliseum to battle with stronger men who fight dirty."

"Yeah but are they as handsome?"

She gripped my cheeks with her hands. She did not smile. Her fingers held me as if I'd disappear if she released, and her eyes shone like the moon. She was terrified, and afraid to express her fear, and it broke me. "I'm serious, Chase. You're walking into a den of lions. I don't know how to say goodbye when I know there's at least a chance…"

I was ravaged. My heart shattered. I took her hand and kissed it because I couldn't speak.

"You know?" she said and a tear spilled. "…when I know there's a chance you won't come back."

"Then don't," I said. My voice emerged as a painful rasp. "Let's live in hope. And not think about the…chances."

"How? I hurt too much."

I pulled her head close, her mouth onto mine. A kiss, transferring and sharing dreams, fears and tears. Then I said, "I love you. I *will* see you in a few days. And maybe, just maybe when I see you next, the world will be whole again."

"And if you die?"

"Then I die for you. And you will marry Lee."

A small peal of laughter escaped within her misery. "Hah. He wishes."

"He does wish."

She took a deep shaky breath. "Goodbye Chase. I will see you soon. The world *will* be whole again."

"You don't believe it. You're still crying."

She wiped her cheeks and chin with the flat of her palms. "Shut up. So are you. I'm trying."

Samantha's voice shuddered behind us. "Jeez, I'm crying too. This is the saddest thing ever. I might shoot you both so you'll never be apart."

The *Amnesia* cut a tight semi-circle until she pointed westward, her stern now facing the shore. The steward lowered the small dinghy. He and Cory boarded. Samantha and I tossed our backpacks down to Cory and then hopped in.

I reached up and grasped Katie's hand. "I love you. I'll come back for you. May flights of angels sing you to sleep. Or whatever."

She waffled her other hand. "Not quite, but close enough, Romeo."

"Isaac Anderson himself will pick you and Cory up tomorrow night or the day after in a Coast Guard cutter. You'll be safe."

"Be careful. To the world, you're worth five hundred million dollars. But to me, so much more. You're a house that I've bought but not yet possessed. A robe I've not yet put on."

I grinned at her gleaming eyes. "Is that Shakespeare too?"

"Yes."

"Is it kinda dirty?"

She kissed my hand and released it. "It is. We need to get married. Pronto."

"I promise."

The small engine roared and our little boat fled to the blackness. The dark yacht and the beautiful girl quickly vanished in our wake.

Samantha continued to wipe her eyes. "This is why you don't get close to people."

"Keep it together, Gear," I chuckled. But inside I felt like a great fissure had opened in my stomach. A lump in my throat threatened to choke me.

Cory tried to comment but couldn't. His face was a mess of tears and his mouth kept tugging down at the corners. He managed to squeak, "Ya'll crazy," between sobs.

Our steward hoisted the propellor and we beached near the Aquarium after one last surge. This late the beach was empty. Samantha and I climbed off. I shook Cory's hand.

"Thanks, brother," I said.

Cory gripped harder, hauled me close and pounded my back. He wheezed something unintelligible in my hear.

"See you soon. Take care of Katie for me."

Samantha and I jogged off the beach. She jammed a pistol under each arm into holsters specially designed by Lee. Her fingers kept clenching like she wanted an assault rifle.

We proceeded north on streets parallel to I-710. Compton was ten miles away, deep into Los Angeles, but after living aboard ships the last twenty days we didn't mind the walk. The earth felt hard and unyielding under my soles. Thanks to our super strange bodies, we could cover the distance in twenty minutes, but we saw no need to hurry. We strolled beside the Los Angeles River and half-empty neighborhoods on the outskirts of Carson. The streets were quiet. Even for one in the morning, the silence struck us as eerie. The recent pounding Los Angeles had endured apparently drained away energy. And hope. And pride.

Pride. That's part of the void I felt. People at night were usually proud. Proud of their car. Proud of their loud music. Proud of their girlfriend or boyfriend. Proud of their social life. Proud of their youth. Of their income. Of whatever. Nights in Los Angeles were vibrant and electric and unquiet.

Or at least they used to be. Another victim of the Chemist. It's hard to be proud and terrified at the same time.

Lee texted me. **>> BRO! Ya boy PuckDaddy just told me what you and the Shooter are doing, dude!!**
>> **I'm still on the George Washington**
>> **Dating a serious hottie. She's an ensign!!**
>> **Kinda dating. She wants me.**
>> **We have a few prototypes ready for you to test**
>> **So**
>> **Don't die, dude**
>> **Say Hi to Samantha for me**
>> **Tell her I'm still single**

"I miss sitting at a lunch table with Lee," I sighed.

"Me too. That little punk grew on me."

Lee and I texted a few minutes more until Samantha took a deep breath. She let it out in a long whoop, turning in circles, arms spinning wide. "Oh

MAN it feels good to be away from her!"

"From Minnie?"

"From Pacific. Yes. Minnie is a name ill-suited for that vicious killer."

"Vicious killer?!"

"Everything about her grated on me. Bleech." She shook her entire frame like a dog shaking off snow. "Being around other Infected is the worst."

"But not me."

She nodded. "But not you. Like she said, that's your greatest gift. You have a natural gravity. I *need* to be near you. Pacific is already missing you, going through withdraw symptoms, I bet. When you're around, everything makes more sense."

"That's so weird."

She shrugged. "But it's true." When she shrugged, her hands automatically went to her weapons. A habitual, subconscious reassurance.

"When Carter visited us, he grated against me. You phrased it well. He grated. Did you feel that?"

She cackled and whacked me in the shoulder. "Yes. I wondered if you felt that. He was flexing."

"He *tried* to grate against me?"

"Yeah, kinda. He controls how much of his power he secretes. I call it flexing. I can't do it."

"Can Minnie flex? A couple times I felt her strength and it nearly knocked me over."

"Yes. Pacific is very precise and disciplined. She unleashed her...let's call it an aura. She unleashes her aura only occasionally and only to make an impression. God I hate her."

I laughed, a muffled sound in the city's oppressive silence. "You're being a little catty about Minnie."

"I don't care. She and I are not compatible. I can be around Carter for weeks before he repels me."

"How does the aura work?"

"No idea. But think of it like sweat. When someone is sweaty, they have a thick scent. You can smell *and* feel that person. The disease works similarly.

Newbies only detect it in their subconscious. Takes a while to develop the sensitivity. You learned more quickly than usual. Sometimes I forget how green you are. You're still a baby."

"Shut up."

"You shut up."

I said, "Tank's aura was like a fog."

"Yeah that kid is rank. Especially when he's in a state of stress. It's gotten worse since the football championship, too. That's how we know he's so powerful."

"Do Chosen always tend to obey the powerful?"

"No idea. Chosen are brand new, remember? Infected don't."

Our cells vibrated. Puck messaged us both.

>> looking good
>> puck monitoring u from satellite
>> lots going on
>> captain FBI freaked when he found out ur plan
>> so did Carter
>> ROCK -> PUCK <-HARDPLACE
>> captain Travis facing court martial mb 4 losing u
>> tank still missing
>> chemist emailed u back
>> says u didn't reply fast enough 2 save Andy
>> probably a lie
>> ur 2 SEAL bodyguards request permission 2 rejoin
>> hannah walker sighting
>> between korea town and hollywood
>> that whole neighborhood evacuated!
>> ppl scared of her!
>> walter back in l.a. NSA got photo
>> so that sucks
>> blue eye bitch has gov't calling 4 ur arrest
>> but not official yet
>> okay
>> thats it
>> puck is tired needs nap soon

We scanned through the updates. Samantha replied, **Nice work, PuckDaddy. You kick ass.**

>> Yeah i do

I grabbed Samantha's arm, stopping her. "You feel that?"

"Feel what?"

"There." I pointed into the darkness beyond a grove of palm trees near the Virginia Country Club. Hairs on my arms and neck stood up and the disease dumped adrenaline into my bloodstream. She stowed her phone and rested a hand on her pistol. I kept staring. "Someone's over there."

"How many?"

"Dunno. I hear them. I smell them. I feel them."

Her pistol came out. She thumbed the hammer back. "Chosen. Let's check it out."

"Don't shoot. I want to talk."

"Oh hell. Hell and death and ugh," she growled.

They found us. Two Chosen. They fell on us from the trees. One boy and one girl, a little younger than me. Emaciated. Hungry. Wearing tattered rags. They were both Asian.

I pointed at the ground and growled, "Sit down."

They howled like I'd scalded them. These two constituted no serious threat. Had I been alone they'd still be unable to muster strength enough to tackle me. Their bodies were new. Relatively weak.

"Disgusting," Samantha sneered, keeping her gun trained. "Like wild dogs."

"That's exactly what they look like," I agreed. "Wild dogs." The boy charged. Dirty hair covered his eyes. I threw him back. "Sit down!"

They did.

Samantha said under her breath, "You're *flexing*. It's gorgeous."

"Can you two speak?"

No response. They twisted uncomfortably, head in their hands, not looking at me. He had shoes. She didn't. She wore diamond stud earrings and a necklace. Their remnants of clothing would have once been fashionable. A lifetime ago in a happier universe, this pair had been trendy, self-possessed, well-kept. Now their hollow stomachs pressed out and sucked in, deep breaths.

"You're grating on them," Samantha observed. "Being near you is unbearable. Because of the DNA."

"Why don't you two eat?" I asked, shouting like they were deaf. They flinched.

"We eat," the girl said. Her voice scraped, a sad lonely sound. "Never enough."

"You still have headaches?"

They both nodded.

I looked at Samantha. Her mouth pressed into a grim line. I spit, "This is his legacy. The Chemist creates and releases the Chosen but doesn't provide for them. They're broken. Like scared animals."

"These two are in worse shape than most," Samantha agreed in a resigned sigh. "Probably couldn't function in his hierarchy. So they fled."

"Have you killed anyone?" I asked them.

No response. Their heads hung lower. The boy tried covering his ears.

Samantha said, "They're fast. They're strong. They're aggressive. And they can't control themselves. Kinda like you during the Spring of your junior year."

"How long have you been sick?" No response. "What will you do next?" No response. "Have you fought the police? Or the army?"

The girl started to cry.

"This is horrible."

Samantha shook her head. "This is *typical*. Most people with the disease look like this before they die. Remember. The fatality rate is near a hundred percent. The Chemist found a way to lower the rate, but it's still awful."

"Do you want to kill me?"

"Yes," they both said.

"Why? Why do you hate me?"

No response.

I threw up my hands. They flinched again. "What the heck do we do with them?"

BOOM BOOM.

Two gun blasts. So loud and sudden and bright I jumped. The boy and the girl both jerked backwards, head first. They slumped into a pile and moved no more. A chorus of dogs began howling, startled and angered by the sudden crash.

"Samantha!" I cried. "NO!" I snatched her pistol and crushed it in my fist. The warm metal bent and warped and melted. I dropped it at her feet. She calmly arched a brow and prodded the ruined weapon with her boot. "What the heck!"

"Chase," she said quietly. "Perhaps you've forgotten what I did for a living before you showed up."

"You just murdered two innocent people! They weren't attacking you."

"Odd use of the word innocent, especially since they admitted to fighting the police and killing people."

"Yeah, but they're sick, Samantha."

"Wrong, Outlaw. They're *very* sick. And they would die soon anyway. And most likely hurt a lot more people before they did."

"They need to be incarcerated. They need treatment."

"There is no *treatment*." She spat the word. "Grow up, Chase."

"What about you?"

She blinked, thrown for a loop. "Huh?"

"What about you? You just executed two individuals."

"So?"

"So violence damages us too. It hurts them. And it hurts us. Executioners used to get drunk so they could perform their duty. It harms our soul."

She crossed her arms and gave me a sideways glance. "Where's this coming from? My soul is long gone."

"No. It's not. I saw it come alive on the boat, in the wind, on top of waves. Your soul is important."

"You gonna become a vegan, too? Perhaps you need to get off your high horse, princess. I saw you behead someone on the gas tower. De-cap-i-tate."

"Yeah but-"

"Yeah but what? You did it to save lives?"

I nodded. "Exactly."

She jammed a finger at the two dead Chosen. "Me too."

I laced fingers into my hair and paced, nearly tripping on the girl's dead leg. "This is different. This wasn't in self-defense."

"I executed them in defense of others. They would kill again."

"We had time to use non-lethal methods. We could have called..." I searched in vain for solutions.

"Called who? You and I are the answer. And what time do you think we have? You saw Puck's messages. The whole damn world is blowing up."

I sat criss-cross beside the dead girl and held her hand and tried not to cry. Samantha, unnerved, fidgeted and kicked at stones. After a minute she said, "Sorry I called you a princess."

"I just don't want to be this way," I whispered. The girl's hand felt so small. Cold. Brittle, even though I knew it wasn't. "I don't want us to kill. Not when there might be another way."

"You're so different from the rest of us, it's shocking."

"Maybe that's why you're drawn to me."

Samantha had no rebuttal. She kept kicking rocks down the dark street.

Chapter Eighteen
Thursday, February 8. 2019

Camino College was being rebuilt. We reached the campus at nine in the morning and watched.

Last August, an American Apache attack helicopter had emptied its arsenal of Hellfire missiles into the belly of the college. At the time, the campus had been serving as a base of operations for the terrorists. The salvo saved my life and nearly killed the Chemist, but the extensive restoration process would last another year. At minimum.

We stood on Cummings Avenue sidewalk. Workers in blaze orange hats and vests hefted detritus onto waiting truck beds. Loads of bricks, wooden beams, ruined masonry and plumbing rumbled away every few minutes. New steel beams arrived to take their place.

"I like this place better during the daytime," I observed.

"Wuss," she sniffed.

"You didn't get chewed on by a tiger."

"Oh yeah!" She threw back her head and laughed. "I forgot. Oh wow. The past thirteen months have been so much fun."

"You have issues."

"YOU have issues."

"There are too many workers here."

She squinted at the skeletal remains of structures and the riot of orange hats. "What do you mean?"

"Construction crews aren't usually this numerous. There are hundreds. Many too young. Many too old. Look over there, little kids distributing water."

"So?"

"This is a volunteer work force."

The longer we watched, the more sure I became. The bulk of the cleanup was shouldered by the local community. Not only that, the volunteers appeared eager. Excited. Happy.

We pushed on through Compton and encountered more evidence of the Chemist's previous occupation. Fortified machine gun nests, partially disassembled. Hollowed out houses. Ruined storefronts. Charred cars pushed to the berm. However, for all the destruction, we saw many more signs of unity and repair. Men swept glass from streets. Children ran with supplies and groceries, and pulled weeds. Women gardened and painted and hammered. Broken windows were patched with plastic sheets. Police helped move furniture. Venders displayed signs offering free food to volunteers.

Samantha her shoved hands into pockets and watched a Buick roll by, windows tinted, music thumping. She turned in a circle on the corner of Poplar and Oleander, peering introspectively at all the activity. "I thought this was supposed to be an unhappy place."

"Supposedly that's why the Chemist moved here. The citizens were too divided to resist him."

"This place feels healthier than the others we walked through. Right? Lakewood practically trembled in fear, tail between their legs."

We continued, following Puck's directions, past streets named after trees, past hundreds of one-story, four-room stucco houses with barred windows. Folks nodded or stared behind fences. Not many white people; we stuck out. Samantha observed, "See all the red bandanas?"

"I noticed."

"Can't tell if those are gang signals or Outlaw bandanas."

"Probably some of both. Wanna ask?"

"Want me to shoot your foot?"

Puck guided us to a house on Magnolia, not far from Compton's small airport. The home was unremarkable from its neighbors except for the high state of tidiness. And the collection of children drawing on the front walk with chalk.

We approached. They regarded us white folk with polite confusion.

"Hi girls! Is Miss Pauline home?"

The four girls shook their heads, white beads clicking in cute dreads. The three boys throwing a football didn't even glance at me. The youngest girl pointed a finger at me and glared.

"Any idea when she'll be back?" I asked.

"Who're you? You the Po?"

I grinned. "No ma'am. I'm just a friend."

"Nuh uh, no you ain't, you trouble."

"I'm the big bad wolf. And you girls look mighty tasty."

They perked up and smiled and laughed and started running around the yard, screaming. Instant joy.

"Samantha," I said. "Go play with them."

"No. Shut up. Kids suck. And you're weird."

I called Puck on my cell. "Puck, Miss Pauline isn't here."

"…and?"

"Where is she?"

"How the hay-yell should I know that? Puck ain't omniscient, dummy. Go find her yourse…nevermind, found her. She's a block away. I kick so much ass."

Miss Pauline was visiting with neighbors. She appeared about fifty, though Katie once told me black women stayed prettier and youthful longer than hispanic women, so she could be older. Her curly hair had grey streaks. She wore an orange vest, and reading glasses were perched on her nose.

Miss Pauline served as the mayor of Compton. The previous mayor, a former police sergeant elected two years ago, vanished during the Chemist's hostile takeover. Presumed dead but no one knew for sure. Miss Pauline stepped into the role to fill the void and was now discussed on the internet with hallowed words usually reserved for the Pope or Mother Teresa.

Making her even more interesting, Miss Pauline had also declared herself the acting Sheriff of Compton. No one objected, not even the police. In a world full of scared people trying to survive, a pure-hearted and sacrificial leader is hard to refuse.

"Well now," she remarked dryly as we approached. "Who we have here? The Great White Hope? Some do-gooder reporters, I suspect?" Her friends on the fence's far side made commiserative noises.

Samantha scoffed. "Do I look like a reporter?"

"Kinda. Pretty white girl like you. Here in the war. What then? Suffering from guilt? Come to make reparations?"

I liked Miss Pauline instantly. No-nonsense, sure of herself, too busy to make niceties. I grinned. "No ma'am."

"Come from World Vision? Red Cross? Got too many of you as it is. What then?"

"You defeated the Chemist. Or at least you threw his militia out of Compton. And you did it without violence. I want you to teach me how."

She stayed silent a long time, resting her weary head on her fist, elbow propped on the fence. She inspected me with pretty green eyes devoid of emotion. Her friends waited silently for her to speak. Nearby dogs snarled at one another in an aggressive territory dispute.

"Boy got some brains," she said finally. Her words were elongated and tired, the syllables overly-pronounced. "Good-looking too. Remind me of Anthony." Her friends nodded.

"Anthony?"

"My boy. Lost him at eighteen. You the government?"

I shook my head. "Not really."

"Not really. Hmph. You know Jesus?"

Samantha made a small noise of disbelief.

I stammered, "Well, I...kind of?"

"Kind of?"

"Well...you know...I like the stuff...he taught."

"You like his message."

"Yes ma'am. And church brings me peace."

"You go to church."

"Holy Angels Catholic Church."

"Oh Lordy," she rolled her eyes at her friends. They cackled. "Got ourselves a Catholic."

"Is that bad?"

"Had to listen to a Catholic for an hour earlier. Refuse to get his hands dirty. So we kept painting and he kept asking the city for money. With his clean hands."

Miss Pauline pulled a flip-phone from her pocket and handed it to her friend. "Message Carl. Tell him I'm ready." Her friend took the phone and started tapping the keys. She cast her gaze back at us. "I don't message. Can't see the keys."

After a minute, an old beat up Crown Victoria appeared. Once a police interceptor, now the car chauffeured Miss Pauline. Carl, a tall bald man, got out and glared.

I opened the passenger door for Miss Pauline. She tugged off the orange vest and said, "Well. Climb in the back, I suppose."

We did, sliding across the cracked vinyl seat covers. Carl eased the car down the street. Miss Pauline waved a hand at her friends and then spoke to us over her shoulder.

"Go to church but don't know Jesus," she said.

Samantha shifted uncomfortably. So did I. I cleared my throat. "You could say that."

"I could say that." She looked mildly at Carl. Carl shook his head, eyes on the road. "Boy, how you gonna drive out darkness without the light?"

No words. My brain went blank. I felt like a little boy being lectured about heart surgery. Nothing I could say was correct. My mouth worked soundlessly.

She said, "Want me to teach you. About non-violence."

"Yes ma'am."

"Why should I?"

"We want to help."

Carl frowned in the mirror. "Miss Pauline a busy woman."

"So are we. But I think we're a good investment."

"A good investment."

"Yes ma'am."

"I believe you. Don't know why. But I believe you. Take us to the spot, Carl," Miss Pauline said. Samantha and I rode without speaking, hands in our laps like scolded children. I'd never seen Samantha so intimidated before.

Miss Pauline had *presence*.

We drove to north Compton, a recovering war zone. American military forces had attempted a rescue operation here last year, ten thousand soldiers pushing in from South Gate. Walter, the Infected sadist, allowed them their progress, suffering sustainable casualties, until springing his trap. He massacred the Army, wiping out eighty percent of the American troops. Entire blocks were leveled by rockets, far too big a project for Compton volunteers to handle. The restoration would take years. Decades.

Carl stopped the car near Willowbrook Park, now a charred wasteland and mass grave site.

Miss Pauline got out with a groan and walked stiffly to the intersection. Not another car in sight. We followed her, boots crunching on gravel. She said, "The Chemist, he took most his gang north. Downtown. Back in November, or whenever it was. With the helicopters. You remember?"

I nodded. "I remember."

"He took most our men. Didn't have many to begin with. Compton been getting better, but still didn't have many men. Lose them to gangs or they just leave. Go looking for work. And what we *did* have, the Chemist, he takes half. Recruits them into his army. So the Chemist, in November, he leave. Gets in his helicopters and he goes downtown. Takes his army. Leaves maybe a hundred behind. A small occupying force with guns. Some of them have the sickness. You know."

"I know the sickness."

"Maybe a dozen have the sickness. All kids. The rest are older men with guns. He leaves them behind to hold our city hostage." She walked around the intersection picking up bits of metal as she told the story. There was no trashcan so she dropped the metal inside a tire. Samantha and I felt like morons, watching her. We started picking up trash too. "So I get my girlfriends. And my girlfriends get their girlfriends. And we don't let the children come. No kids. Just us old women. Hundreds of us."

Samantha dropped a handful of metal shards into Miss Pauline's tire. Silent. Subdued. The noises of the world had receded. A new kind of powerful quiet. There was only her voice.

"And we go. We know where the Chemist's men are. And we go. We praying with each step, real loud, Lord Jesus help us! Help up, God! They hear us coming. We find them. They shoot their guns. In the air. At our feet. It's about dinner time. They shoot their guns and tell us to leave. But they're scared. And we keep praying. Oh yes, Lord, we keep praying." And then, as if the song itself could no longer bear suppression, she sang in rich orotund gospel tones,

"I'm pressing on, the upward way
New heights I'm gaining every day
Still praying as I'm onward bound
Lord, plant my feet on higher ground!"

Pain I didn't know I possessed began uncoiling in my chest, as though strummed by her song.

Samantha's hands shook. Tiny cuts began staining her hands red with blood, and she cried quietly. She could see the end to the story already. I couldn't.

"We tell the Chemist's gangs. Tell them, You can stay or go. If you stay, you have to give us the guns. And never touch them again. All the men have the powder on their faces. Can't think straight. Some start…" Miss Pauline's breath caught. She straightened up and massaged her lower back, staring off at the blue sky, lost in memories. "Some start shooting us. Killing us old women. Awful. But we keep praying. And we get our hands on them. The men with the sickness, they are too fast. They spooked and they run. You know? The ones with the sickness move like demons. Too fast for old women. But the others. We get our hands on them. Some keep shooting. Some drop their guns and run. Then all the Chemist people start to running. All his worshippers and workers and doctors and nurses and the rest. Hundreds of them. Thousands. They grab what they can grab and they get in cars and drive off. Went downtown, I suppose. Spooked off by us women."

Carl might've been listening but I couldn't tell. He walked in circles around the intersection, staring down the roads, a hard man with a hard past.

"Most men drop their guns and cry. And cry and cry and we sang Glory Hallelujah! A few refuse, so we disarm them. That's hard. They fight like the devil. But there are hundreds of us, you know. We handcuff them and walk them out of town. Out of our Compton. Except one man." She wagged her finger at us and made a tsk sound. "Except one stubborn old mule. Oh Lord. There was a hundred men for the Chemist. At the start. We got 'bout sixty back. Maybe seventy. The others ran off or we pushed'em out. All the ones with the sickness, they fled. Found three of them dead later. Killed themself. Sixteen beautiful women lay dead. Some of us injured. It's all over, except that one man. We chase him and chase him. He keep shooting. Finally. Finally, sweet Jesus, we old women surround him here. Right here in this street. About midnight. He gone outta bullets. He throws his gun. He punches and kicks. We surround him. We sing!" She laughs at the memory, husky and rich. "We sing hymns. He curses. He punches us. Us old women. Gave me a black eye! Finally we get our hands on him and he cries!" She laughed and clapped her hands, over-flowing with emotion and memory. "He cries and cries. Cries for days. Jesus set him free. Heart-broken man. Made no sense for us women to die and sing for him. You know. It broke him. The sacrifice broke him. So now, where's that stubborn old mule?"

"Where?" I asked.

"Well, you know. He drive me around in my car. We friends now. My good friend Carl."

Carl still walked circles around the intersection. Only now did I notice the tears. Samantha sat down during the story. Her face was streaked with blood from where she wiped her eyes.

"We didn't kill no men," Miss Pauline said. "No sir. We wanted their hearts. We wanted them back. I don't pretend to know about the sickness. That's up to God. But our men. Well, you know. You can't drive out darkness with darkness. You need the light."

Carl shook his head, like trying to dislodge his grief. "Can't drive out evil with evil. Praise Jesus."

185

Miss Pauline placed her firm hands on my arms and squeezed. I wanted her to hug me and never release. I wanted to be one of those kids in her yard. "You said we defeated the Chemist without violence. You half right. You more right than most. But there was violence. Yes, boy, oh Lord, there was violence. Violence that makes me cry still. But we took the violence into ourselves. We accepted it, instead of throwing it on others. Martin Luther King. Ghandi. Sweet lord Jesus. They won hearts with their broken bodies. We won our men's hearts with love."

My voice sounded strange. Not my own. "I don't know how to do that."

"Do you love the Chemist? Would you die for him, boy?"

"Absolutely not."

"Then. Well." Her palm went to my face. Calloused, rough, and soft as angels. "You aint' ready yet, sweetie."

We ate dinner at Miss Pauline's house. Her friends all brought food for her and each other and the kids and us. The gathering overflowed the house into the yard. Samantha and I sat on the sparse grass, leaning against the fence, watching. Samantha hadn't spoken for hours. Miss Pauline's guests stared at us but didn't approach.

Miss Pauline's reign as mayor caused pronounced consternation among entrenched politicians. She held office at construction sights while picking up trash. She took meetings and expected attendees to pick up a paint brush. That's not how it's *done*. I could see it on their faces as two groups of sharply dressed constitutes were rebuffed at her fence gate. By children.

"Missus Pauline say she'll see you tomorrow at the airport," they were told by a sassy little girl in a white dress. She shook her finger at them. "That's where she be cleaning tomorrow. Now she set down to dinner. Good *bye*."

The people loved her. The establishment didn't. I learned that over my plate of pasta in the span of twenty-five minutes while sitting on her grass.

Carl sat next to me, his plate heaped with pasta. He was a big guy, broad shoulders, strong arms. "Miss Pauline, she like you."

"I like her too."

"Then you ain't dumb. Even though you white."

"Mmm." I waffled my hand. "I'm kinda dumb. But my girlfriend is hispanic. That's gotta count for something."

"She with you, she dumb," he grinned, big and bright and infectious.

"I can't fault your logic. But she's not."

"She blind?"

"No. Beautiful eyes. And you're about to get punched."

He laughed. I'm hilarious.

His phone rang. It rang a lot. Carl acted as her political bouncer. He rose with a groan and paced the yard and talked into it. After a minute, he pocketed the device and found Miss Pauline. She listened and nodded and excused herself.

"Well," she said at the front gate. She glanced at us. "Better come on."

Carl drove, Miss Pauline in the front, Samantha and I in the back. The sun sat on the horizon, casting Compton into shadows. Obviously tired, Miss Pauline leaned her head against the window.

"Ain't no place can change overnight. Or over a year. Or ten years. Compton got a lot healthier. But we still got poverty. Hate. Anger. Divisions. Gangs. You know?"

"I know," I said.

"It's culture. Culture hard to change. Watch Jesus. One reason they killed him, he was changing culture too fast. Why don't God just work miracles and change a place? Because people got foundations. They got beliefs built and established. God don't push. He pulls. He calls. Cause people? They don't like being pushed. You can't change people by pushing."

Samantha shook her head, staring at the ceiling. She'd reached her daily limit of crazy ideas. Samantha had foundations too.

I asked, "How do you pull people? Instead of pushing?"

Miss Pauline elbowed Carl. "See? Boy got some brains."

"Maybe. Not so sure."

"How do you pull people," Miss Pauline sighed. "These people are broken. Especially the young ones. Need healing. And I am willing to die for

187

them. They know it. It shakes them. I will sacrifice. They know. And that sacrifice begins healing."

"Sacrifice begins healing?" I asked.

"Our goal is grandchildren, really. We want healthy grandchildren. These young men, they already got babies. The women got baby daddies they don't know. And we love them. It spooks them. I want to spook long-term changes. You know. Little by little. And our current unification? It's just a start."

"What about the Chemist's super drug? Is that still here?"

"I think we run out. Hope so. Awful withdrawals. The Chemist, one good thing he did, he disrupted the drug flow. The system broke. He flooded Compton with his own brand. For free. Lord Jesus, help us. Drug dealers out of work, all a sudden. Now listen. You two."

She turned all the way around in her seat and locked eyes.

"We almost here. These OGs. Big important men. They got pride. They act dangerous. We cannot speak their language. You understand? We cannot speak with violence. Cannot."

Samantha said, "I'm not sure I follow."

"If they hit me..." she said slowly, keeping her eye contact, "...you don't hit them back."

"What about shooting them?"

"No baby," she said. "That's not even funny. They ain't gonna like you two. Too white. Too many corrupt white cops. So you stay in the car. And don't get out."

"Stay in the car?!"

I asked, "What's going on?"

"Gang dispute. Going to be bad soon. But maybe not tonight. And you will stay in the car."

"Miss Pauline." Samantha struggled to keep her composure. She wanted to explain to Miss Pauline that the two people in her backseat could most likely subdue every trouble maker tonight. She didn't need to endanger herself. But we'd agreed to travel in secret. Incognito. There was, after all, hundreds of millions of dollars hanging over our heads. "We are good at this. We can help."

"Your violence will create more. I don't want to win this fight, sugar. I want to win their hearts. I want to win their grandchildren. And you will stay in the car."

Carl's headlights washed over an angry mob on the corner. The street lights were busted. Forty people, at least, raging against each other, just this side of fighting. Posturing and cackling, men and women, all under twenty-five.

"Miss Pauline," Samantha hissed. "There's going to be trouble. You can't go in there."

"I'm the Sheriff," she chuckled. "Ya'll stay here. Drive away if we don't come back."

Miss Pauline's arrival was an *event*. Clearly adored and revered, she circulated throughout the mob distributing hugs and conversation. Carl stayed tight on her heels, stone-faced even when accepting complex hand-shakes. The OGs, the men with most at stake, stayed back, watching impassively. No chance could they admit they loved Miss Pauline, no chance could they hand her power. She moved deeper into the riot, into the danger, and we lost sight of her. A handful of the disinterested sat on our Crown Victoria, laughing and banging on the windows.

Samantha took deep breaths. "I'm so stressed."

"Right?" I agreed, peering desperately into the crowd. "I'm terrified. For her. This sucks."

"I see a dozen pistols. At least. And we're just sitting here."

I tore my eyes away and scrubbed my face with fingers. "Can we really drive away if it gets bad?"

"Hell no."

"She asked us to. Demanded it."

"She ain't my Sheriff," Samantha sniffed.

"She should be."

Her fingers drummed on the hidden gun beneath her jacket. "An old lady stares down an armed gang. While the mighty Outlaw watches from a nearby car."

The crowd shrieked and tensed. Angry shouts. Something had happened.

Samantha's hand flew to the door handle.

"Wait," I shouted, grabbing her. "Give her a chance."

Our window was cracked. Above the noise, we heard Miss Pauline's stern voice. Couldn't see her though.

"She's alive."

"For how long??"

We waited forever. Hours. Days. An eternity in fifteen minutes. Finally the crowd began to disperse. The uninvolved grew bored and wandered off. Like an onion, the mob peeled away in layers.

A half-hour after she climbed out, Miss Pauline returned to her car. She collapsed into the passenger seat, sweating, drained, eyes closed as Carl gunned the engine.

Samantha might have been nearly as exhausted. "How'd you do that?" she asked.

"I have earned the right to be heard. So they listen. No deaths tonight, Lord Jesus," she sighed heavily. "Still a chance those little babies will know their daddies."

"I don't understand."

"The men and women with the sickness. You know? I can't speak about them. But the men of Compton? My men? You can't solve their gun problem with guns."

We had travelled halfway back to her house when Carl's phone rang. He answered, one hand on the wheel. He listened and hung up.

Miss Pauline said, "Well?"

"Trouble in Northwest," he answered.

"Trouble?"

He shook his head slowly. "You ain't gon' believe it, Miss Pauline."

"What trouble?"

"The Outlaw."

"The *Outlaw*??!" Miss Pauline, Samantha and I all said it at the same time.

"The Outlaw up north," he nodded. "Throwing grenades."

And in the distance, through the partially lowered window, I heard the thump of detonations.

Chapter Nineteen
Thursday, February 8. 2019
Katie

Cory and I played chess on Minnie's boat into the evening while I tried not to dwell on Chase. He had texted me when they reached Compton. I knew he'd be fine. Of course he would. Samy was with him. But still. Ugh.

Cory waved at me, getting my attention. "Still your turn," he said.

I glanced at the board. "You can't move a pawn backwards, Cory. Try again."

He glowered and hunkered over the board. "Stupid white people game."

"I'm not white."

"You half white."

We kept moving the board and chairs so he could stay in the shade. Cory's appetite still had not returned; he'd lost fifteen pounds during our two weeks at sea. I luxuriated in the sun, wearing a bikini at which he tried not to stare. I didn't mind. Boys didn't used to stare.

He moved his queen (way too early-now she was exposed) and drank lemonade Minnie had provided. "You worried?"

"About Chase? I'm trying not to think about him."

"Weird stuff, him being the Outlaw."

"Yes," I grinned. "Very weird stuff indeed. You had no idea?"

"You crazy. How would I know he's the Outlaw?"

"You're his closest friend."

"So. You his shorty and you didn't know."

I nodded and moved my knight. "That's true."

"Think he'll go to college? With you?"

"To Stanford? I wish. But no." I gazed up at the blue awning and contemplated colleges and the future and sweet Chase. "Will I even go? Will Stanford still have doors to open this fall? I have no idea."

"Wonder how much being the Outlaw pays," Cory mused, tapping a bishop against his forehead in thought.

"I believe it's a free public service he provides."

Minnie slowly glided down the stairs, one hand skimming along the rail. She announced, "Time to pack your bags, dear ones. I see your next adventure approaching on our starboard beam."

"Isaac's here?" I wondered, turning to inspect the northern horizon. I lowered my sunglasses but saw nothing. "That was quick."

"The craft is still several miles away," Minnie explained, swirling a glass of rum punch. "I can see it from the top deck."

"Hell yeah," Cory said, trudging towards the stairs. "Bout ready to get back on some land."

I followed him belowdeck. Due to the desperate dash from my apartment that awful morning, I didn't possess much clothing, and most of it was ill-fitting Navy gear. Clean-up only required five minutes. I pulled on the long coverup Minnie had gifted, and laid down on the bed. Most likely our next destination wouldn't be an exquisite luxury yacht. Might as well soak up the last few minutes in my private cabin, which was basically a suite.

I was thumbing through Instagram photos when I heard the boat motoring nearby, and then it attached to our stern. Sounded more like a raft with an outboard propellor than the Coast Guard.

"Goodbye room," I sighed and collected my things.

The sun blinded me again, streaming from above and ricocheting off the ocean. Minnie spoke softly near the rail. I slid on Ray-Bans and dropped my bags onto the wooden deck.

I'd been correct. The new boat *was* just a life raft with an outboard motor. Far too small for long voyages, and definitely not the Coast Guard. Two men stood on the deck with me and Minnie. One of the men looked about my age. He wore Sperry loafers, stylish jeans, a white button-up shirt and a vest. A good-looking, baby-faced guy.

The other man, hispanic, appeared emaciated. His clothes were rags, like he fell over a lot. His hair needed a trim. His eyes were sunken and full of hate. At the sight of me, he flicked a switch on the small metal rod he held and it began humming. The rod connected by cord to his backpack. He was not Coast Guard. He was Chosen.

Minnie sipped her punch and watched me expectantly.

Cory and I had been betrayed.

My heart dropped into my stomach and my knees weakened. *Chase!*

"Katie," Minnie said politely, "have you had the pleasure of meeting…" She held out her hand to the handsome boy. "I'm sorry, I don't know your name?"

The boy stared at the deck and stubbed it with the toe of his shoe. "That's okay, ma'am. I'm not allowed to use it."

"Not allowed to use it?"

"No ma'am." He took a deep breath and glanced between her and me. "The Father says my name is Kid. Until I earn a different name."

Pleasure registered in Minnie's face and she erupted in laughter. "That sounds like the old goat I know!" she cackled. She wiped her eyes and murmured, "Have to earn a different name. So clever."

"Minnie," I said with a voice stronger than I hoped. "What…?"

"Kid is going to escort you into the city," Minnie explained simply. A pleasant smile tugged at her tanned and freckled face. "To Martin."

To the Chemist. I had been kidnapped.

The baby-faced kid looked miserable. The other man holding the electric rod looked hungry.

I asked the boy, "You are Infected?"

He nodded. "Yes ma'am. Chosen, as the Father calls it."

"And you're kidnapping us."

"I have no choice."

Minnie said, "You don't appear up to this task, young man. You have a sour face and no constitution. Why did Martin not send Walter?"

"Walter was busy, ma'am."

"Mmmm. Lucky for you, Katie. That Walter. He's a rotten one."

Minnie was stroking my hair. Shocked and outraged, I whirled on her. "How COULD you?!"

"You have such beautiful hair, you know."

"You betrayed us!"

"Betrayed *you*? Pretty girl, have you listened to nothing I've said?"

I backed away from her. But I had no where to go. I stood on a boat alone with monsters who could truly kill me with their pinky. I restrained sobs and fury. There was zero chance of resistance.

"What do you mean?"

"Did I not tell you that Martin was my husband? My lover and *confidante*?" she asked innocently.

"Did you betray Chase too?" I spit the words. If I knew how to detonate her explosive boat, I would have pushed the button in that moment, so desperate I was to hurt her.

"I spoke with Martin. I told him the Outlaw would be in Compton and traveling without his costume. After all, Katie. Above all things, I enjoy mischief."

She spoke so matter-of-factly. She was right; she'd seen too many births and burials to care about normal people. I knew from conversations with Chase that Minnie was powerful, even if she didn't look it. The power came with age. She was in charge here. The boy'd be strong too, but might made right; the Chemist and Minnie were his bosses. The hispanic man holding the weapon was low on the totem pole, despite being infinitely more dangerous than Cory and me.

I could jump overboard but they'd fish me out. I couldn't drown myself; they'd bring me back to the surface. Nowhere to hide. No way to fight them. And I wouldn't beg. A tear rolled down my cheek.

"No no no," she soothed. She cradled my face and wiped the tear with her thumb. A strong, suicidal urge to bite her lurched in my chest. "Don't cry. You don't know Martin like I do. He doesn't enjoy causing pain. You will not be mistreated. Or perhaps I should say, you will suffer not brutality."

I pointed in the direction of the electric metal rod with my eyes closed. "They brought brutal weapons with them, Minnie."

The handsome boy spoke. "Only if you resist us. We'd rather not use them. Well. At least, I'd rather not."

"And the Coast Guard?"

"I'll be long gone, sweetie, by the time your friend arrives. This way is more exciting. Think of it like a storm."

All was lost. I could get in the raft quietly. Or I could be hurt and then forced into the raft. We all knew it.

Suddenly, Cory surprised us all. He leapt from the upper deck with a ROAR and landed on the evil-looking man. Cory's three hundred pounds crushed and knocked him backwards.

"Cory NO!" I cried.

Electricity sizzled as the rod pressed between two bodies. The clump of arms and legs tipped over the rail and dropped limply into the ocean. It happened so quickly. A burst of light, brighter than the sun, flared and popped.

We rushed to the side. Both men were dead, fully electrocuted on contact with the water, floating face down like big fish.

"CORY!" I screamed.

"Oh my gosh," the boy breathed. He seemed as shaken as me.

Minnie squealed with delight. I couldn't...I didn't...what could I do? My mind grappled with events too terrible to process.

The mayhem kept pouring on. New fresh chaos behind me, but I was too overwhelmed to notice the small explosion. When I look back in retrospect, I understand; I understand he'd been patiently waiting for the right time, for days, exhausted, and this moment, when we gaped and screamed, was the perfect time for Tank to strike. Kid and I turned drunkly, lost in surprise. Metal had ripped. Fiberglass shattered. A small amount of gasoline caught fire, burning instantly with a whoosh.

Tank. Tank Ware had an engine hefted in his hands and over his head, like Atlas. Between his feet, the deck gaped brokenly and belched oily smoke.

My brain tried to make sense of this upheaval, putting surprises in proper sequence. He'd ripped an engine out of the deck??

Tank hurled the metal machine. It caught the boy, Kid, in his chest, shattering shoulder bones and barely missing me. Kid was propelled up and over the rail, and he splashed into the Pacific near dead bodies.

Tank turned his fury onto Minnie but she effortless *Leapt* onto the deck above, careful not to spill her punch.

"Look at you," she screeched in surprise. "I am enchanted! You're as strong as the Outlaw. Maybe stronger! Can the oceans support two such young fish??"

Tank advanced.

"Take her," Minnie said, eyes frenetic. Her wide smile was deranged. I understood for the first time; she was truly insane. "Take the raft. Take the girl. And go. This is so perfect. He'll be furious! Hah!"

"Where you going to run?" Tank asked her. "It's a small boat."

"We could fight each other," she responded, and she squatted, bringing their faces closer together. Tank could reach up and grab her ears. She was either very brave or much stronger than she appeared. "We could smash each other and this boat. I think you'd lose but maybe not."

"I wouldn't lose," he rumbled.

"You're starving, you beautiful mass of muscle. I am not. You're weak. I am not. And the kid in the ocean isn't dead. He's hurt, true, but probably angry. We can fight and you can lose. And the pretty girl would be injured." She held up a finger and aimed it at the raft. "Or. You can go. With my blessing. What a disaster we can make!"

Tank didn't answer immediately. I glanced at Cory. Wake up, Cory! Wake up! But he wouldn't. I knew. I knew.

"Katie. Get in the boat."

I didn't trust Tank. But at this moment, he became salvation. My only hope. I climbed into the raft, my mind still spinning, and began untying the ropes.

"You better hope I don't see you again," he told her.

"On the contrary," she replied, and the way she watched him…her gratification in this sudden, unexpected change of events looked almost sexual.

Tank lowered into the raft, nearly swamping it. I twisted the throttle and the small propellor screamed. With one big thrust, Tank pushed the raft's nose clear and we began bouncing away.

"Go!" Minnie screamed from her smoking yacht, her ruined paradise. "Gooooooo! Go and die beautifully!"

Chapter Twenty
Thursday, February 8. 2019

"The Outlaw is throwing grenades around north Compton," Samantha said, a smirk on her face. "Yeah that sounds like him."

"When has the Outlaw *ever* thrown a grenade?"

"I was joking."

Carl's Crown Victoria barreled through stoplights, trying to reach the scene before police cars did. The police would stop the threat with pistols.

"Miss Pauline," I addressed her over the bouncing seat-back. "This sounds like a madman. With explosives. Samantha and I need to handle this."

"Tell you what," she replied. "I'll let you help this time." Despite her bravery, her hands quaked. She half-smiled at Carl and said, "Times like this? I miss cigarettes."

He didn't answer. Just shook his head, attention locked on the road.

She asked, "Have any on you?"

"Now Miss Pauline…"

"You right, you right." She waved him off and looked out the window. "You right. Don't answer. Don't want to know."

"We here," he said, getting on the brake.

Carl slowly motored up Avalon and we peered down dark side streets, looking for the Outlaw. So weird. This neighborhood appeared to be a pocket of stark poverty. Next level indigence. Many of the houses had been abandoned. Rusted cars on the lawns. Nobody in sight.

A detonation. One street over. The clear and recognizable bang of a grenade. Carl executed an illegal u-turn and headed towards Central.

The imposter stood in the middle of the street beneath a yellow streetlight. Had to admit, that guy looked like the Outlaw. He was big, dressed in a black vest, and wore the right gear. Ski mask and red bandana. He'd slung a satchel across his back, presumably carrying explosives.

All four of us got out of the Crown Victoria at a safe distance.

"Miss Pauline, I think you should remain here," I said.

Samantha retrieved the pistol from under her arm and thumbed back the hammer. "I concur. I promise not to shoot unless forced."

I reached over my head and pulled the Boom Stick free. "We have experience."

"You have experience with grenades," she repeated.

"Yes ma'am."

"Well I have experience with Jesus."

Samantha was about to growl a rebuttal when the imposter Outlaw cried out.

"Chaaaaaaaaaase! Come out, come out where ever you are! Chaaaaaaaaaase!"

His voice sounded eery, haunted, and painful. The lonely wailing of a lonely man in a lonely place.

Miss Pauline wondered, "Who is Chase?"

I said, "That's the Outlaw's first name."

"He knows the Outlaw's first name."

"Everyone knows the Outlaw's first name," Samantha sighed.

"So he ain't the Outlaw."

"No," I agreed. "He's probably here to kill him. And claim the reward."

"Then why he dress like that?"

I said, "Samantha, stay on the sidewalk. Keep that gun out of sight. Don't want to spook this guy. Miss Pauline and I will get his attention. See if we can't talk him out of the grenades."

Miss Pauline grabbed hold of Samantha's wrist. "Don't you fire that gun, baby."

Samantha appeared caught between rolling her eyes, shouting at Miss Pauline, and rubbing Miss Pauline's hand against her face for comfort. Fearlessly, or at least without hesitation, Miss Pauline waddled stiffly away from the car and into the street. I stayed beside her. So did Carl. Samantha vanished into shadow.

"Chaaaaaaaaase!" The guy shouted into the atmosphere, seventy-five yards away. "You're a nobody! Show your face!"

"Why'd he assume the Outlaw would be here, I wonder. Oh Lordy. Pray with me, boy."

I nearly tripped. "Pray with you?"

"Pray with me."

I closed my eyes a moment, heart hammering. "Dear God. Please keep Miss Pauline alive."

"Amen?"

"And Carl too."

"Amen?"

"And the rest of us."

"Amen?"

"Amen."

"What about the Outlaw fellow?"

"What about him?"

She smiled kindly and patted my arm. Then she prayed with her eyes open, "Lord Jesus, we resist the wicked in your name. We cast out the devil from this here street. Grant us safety, Lord Jesus. And that man, that hurting broken man, Lord Jesus, grant his safety too. Amen."

Carl started to pray.

I was out of my league.

When Carl finished, Miss Pauline said, "He's white."

The imposter was indeed white. I'd been assuming he was. They'd been assuming the opposite. What would Katie assume? Or Lee?

"All these white people," Carl scoffed. "With their weapons."

The imposter caught sight of us. "Stay back! I'll kill you!"

"We still coming," Miss Pauline, too quietly for him to hear.

"I'm here for someone! And I'm waiting. For his blood." He raised a grenade in his fist.

Miss Pauline called, "My name is Miss Pauline. I'm sixty-five. And I'm here to talk."

"No talking," the imposter growled. He yanked the pin and tossed the explosive under a nearby Nissan Sentra. I counted. Two. Three. Four. Five. Si- BOOM. The pavement shattered. The Nissan's undercarriage broke and the gasoline eruption cracked the car in half.

The man yanked out another grenade immediately. "The Outlaw is in Compton! Bring him to me!"

"We ain't bringing you nobody, baby," Miss Pauline called. "We gon' talk. And we gon' get you help."

"No talking, old lady." He pulled the pin.

We froze. "It's okay," I whispered. "He's still holding the safety spoon. Don't panic."

"Oh Lord Jesus," Miss Pauline said, tremulous voice traveling up and down octaves. "Help us, Lord, help us."

"I am the Outlaw!" he shouted. "Have been all along! It was always my gig! Always my show! That no-talent hack...he just wishes..." his voice trailed away, dissipating within grief. "Can't even remember it all..."

Samantha got in position. Saw her from my peripheral. She could end this charade anytime.

Miss Pauline took a shaky breath and started forward again.

"Nope," the man sobbed and he threw the grenade at us.

We were fifty yards away. Too far for a normal person to throw a small grenade.

He wasn't normal. The grenade came on a straight line, humming with velocity. Thrown like a hundred mile-per-hour fast ball. Carl called out in alarm, wrapped Miss Pauline up and sheltered her.

I caught the grenade and sent it skyrocketing towards stars, just like the trick at Los Alamitos. The grenade popped in the sky. The Outlaw imposter watched it one second too long. Samantha got there and sent him sprawling with a crisp blow to the skull.

Miss Pauline started running. "Don't hurt him!" she cried. "Don't hurt him!"

Samantha threw her hands up and swore, using words I hoped Miss Pauline didn't hear. She snatched the bag of explosive and kept one foot on the man's neck until we arrived.

"Young man," Miss Pauline said, panting and peering into his face. "Young man, are you okay?"

The imposter wept, hands at his temples.

"Miss Pauline," I said quietly. "This man has the sickness."

"The sickness. You can tell?"

"I can tell."

"Young man, you one of the Chemist? You with him?"

The kid, about my age, nodded. His eyes shone with tears and he sniffed. "I'm sick," he said.

"Go ahead an cry." With help from Carl, she sat on the pavement next to the imposter and took his hand in hers. The boy pressed Miss Pauline's hand hard into his temple. "Cry all you want."

"Still have the headaches?" I asked him. He nodded again.

"The headaches?" Miss Pauline asked.

"Part of the sickness. He hasn't been sick long."

"You," he said. He peered intently at me, staring at my silhouette thrown into darkness by the overhead light. "You...smell."

"That's the sickness too," I said.

"Or maybe you just stink?" Samantha mumbled under her breath.

"You." He glanced at Samantha and back at me. "And you. You two."

"Shhh, boy," Miss Pauline said. "Let the headache pass."

"You two," he said again. "I know you two...somehow..."

A shock of realization. Of recognition.

"Oh no," I whispered. Samantha lowered to a crouch. She pulled off the bandana and pushed down the mask, revealing Andy Babington's face. "Andy," I said, a lump in my throat.

"You," he said. He covered his eyes again and cried. "I hate you. I hate you. Hate you I hate you I hate you hate you so much."

I examined him. He had two fresh surgical scars, puffy and red, at the base of his skull. Small scars on the bottom of both forearms, one recently split open. I bet I could find more too. "Andy, he operated on you," I said, voice tight. "He gave you his disease."

"My head," he groaned. "Hurts so much."

"He usually keeps his Pupas unconscious for months. But you've only been missing for..." I glanced at Samantha. "How long?"

"About three weeks."

"The next few months are going to be rough, Andy. The disease is savage. And I think he did some other stuff to you too. Stem cell implantation."

"Who *are* you?? Shut up, shut up, shut up," he growled. "You're a nobody. I hate you. I hate your body. I hate your voice. Everything about you."

It was the disease inside me already irritating the disease inside him. Two predators in close proximity. "You need to go home," I said. "Be with your family."

"Can't go home," he wheezed. He took Miss Pauline's hand and placed it flat on his cheek. "Can't go home."

Miss Pauline asked, "Why is he in pain?"

"The disease. It's changing his body too quickly. He'll die from an aneurysm soon if he doesn't calm down."

"You shut up, you're a nobody, a nothing, I despise you."

Samantha put the satchel of explosives around her neck. "I see the little prick hasn't lost his charm. I'm going to a safe place to detonate these, in case the Chemist planted a nasty surprise. Back later."

Soon after she left, the police arrived. Two, three, then four cars, turning the night red and blue. Miss Pauline and Carl left to consult with them while Andy writhed.

"Andy, listen to me."

"Shutupshutupshutup."

"You need to go. The police have to arrest you. And then they'll perform tests. The stress will overload your brain and you'll die." I crouched beside him, keeping an eye on the cops.

For once, he remained quiet.

"Understand? Your brain is fragile right now. And you're about to be arrested. You'll die."

He whimpered, "I want to die."

"That's just the pain talking. You'll feel better tomorrow. Will the Chemist take you back?"

"I…I don't know…where'd she go? Lady with the soft hands…who are you…oh god…"

"Did he send you here? The Chemist?"

"…yes."

"For me?"

No answer.

"You need to go home to your parents. Or to the Chemist. Maybe he'll put you under again. You need to sleep as much as possible for several months."

"I can't think…can't see…can't sleep…can't eat…"

"Here they come. Decide now." I touched his arm. He sprang up like a cat, so fast I fell over, which was a good thing because he took a swing at me.

The police shouted in alarm but Andy was long gone, faster than humanly possible.

I was gone too. Moved even faster than Andy, stealing back to Miss Pauline's car without anyone noticing. I flattened on the back seat and stayed out of sight.

Andy. Jeez. I hurt thinking about him. The disease had throttled him, forcing muscles and bones through devastating transformations far too quickly. His brain already displayed evidence of damage; he'd forgotten how he knew us. Operating on instinct and orders without sanity or reason. So much pain. Maybe if he had stayed in the coma longer.

Fifteen minutes later, Miss Pauline and Carl wearily fell back into their seats. My somnolent caretakers cranked the engine and rubbed their eyes.

"You back there?" she asked.

"I am."

Carl said, "You the real Outlaw. Ain't you."

"I am."

"And you worth half a billion dollars," he grunted.

I kept silent.

"Well. Lordy. Let's go find the girl. And you best sleep at my house. Not safe for you anywhere else."

That was the truth. I should text Katie. Have her come stay at Miss Pauline's house. But she could be asleep by now.

I'll call her tomorrow.

Chapter Twenty-One
Friday, February 9. 1019
Tank

"You going into hypoglycemic shock," Katie told me. "Or something like it."

Too fatigued to answer. My mouth was dry and my muscles kept trembling. It was after midnight and we'd been on the raft for hours. On our third and final tank of gas.

Been hungry forever. But now, face down on the wet raft in the sloshing water, bouncing for an eternity, I was also nauseated.

"We're at the shore," she said. She sounded exhausted and scared. And maybe irritated. Always thought she was cute when she got mad. "I think it's White Point. Royal Palms Beach, but I'm not positive. My phone is dead."

I wanted to lift my head but couldn't.

"Here's the plan, Tank," she said. "I'm sending us straight towards the shore. It's a rocky coast and beaching won't be fun. But you're too enervated by the lack of nutrition for anything else. Understand?"

No. The hell does enervate mean?

"Don't fall in. I can't pick you up," she said.

I felt the ocean lift and drop us. And again. Sounds of the shore. The hissing and sucking of rocks and water.

"Here we go…"

The floor of the ocean rose and met us. Round stones crashed against my hands, skull, and knees. The propellor struck and was demolished. We skidded to a stop, the raft's floor half shredded.

"Success," Katie panted, her voice shaky. "I bet that hurt. But you won't drown."

I grunted something. Couldn't open my eyes.

"Okay. Okay," she said. Sounds of her bare feet tripping on stones. Always thought she had cute feet. "Wow, where is everyone? This place is deserted."

A shallow wave embraced my legs and scraped the ruined propellor against rocks.

"You need food," she said, voice receding. "I see lights. I'll be back...ouch, jeez, the ground is so hard...I'll be back in a minute."

Then. Nothing.

———

Life slowly returned, like the volume of a radio increasing slowly over half an hour. My lips tingled. Toes cold. Another splash in my mouth. Something sweet. I gagged.

"Can you hear me?"

"Mmm," I said.

"I've been trickling Pepsi into your mouth. You need the sugar."

"Aight."

"If you can't swallow yet, just swish it around. Your gums will absorb a portion."

More Pepsi. So good. I swished. Swallowed. Coughed.

"I've got water too. And a hamburger."

"From where?" I said.

"Campers. Near the road. Two guys. They said I was hot, so..."

"No ambulances."

"No ambulances," she agreed. "You're a fugitive, I suppose."

"You should eat the hamburger."

"I had a bite. You need it more than me."

She fed me the burger in crumbs. It took a long time. Hours. Parts of my body began hurting but she said that was a good thing. Organs waking up.

"You need more food," she yawned. "But I don't have any money."

"Always knew I'd get you back."

"You have *not* got me back."

I grinned. "You feeding me on a beach, babe. That's the definition of a couple."

"Oh? Well. I'm in love with someone else."

"Naw."

"Yes."

"What's he got that I don't?"

She fiddled with my collar, her finger brushing my skin. "For starters, his clothes aren't soggy rags."

"Like what you see?"

"You've lost a lot of weight, Tank. Maybe…forty pounds?"

"Trimming down for you."

She ignored that. "Did you eat anything after you jumped off the Navy ship? You swam quite a distance with no calories."

I wiped my face but just got sand in my eyes. She knocked my hand away and brushed the grains out. I said, "Ate two fish. Raw."

"Ew."

"And snuck aboard at night. Could only find lemonade."

"Yeah, Minnie likes to drink. How'd you swim to her yacht without dehydrating?"

"That storm. Had plenty of rain water."

"Oh yes. Of course."

"Still. Wasn't fun."

She placed her hands on my temples and kissed my forehead. Bliss. "Tank. Thank you. Thank you for intervening when you did."

I reached up for her but she pulled back.

She said, "I am grateful. But I'm still in love with someone else."

"I've missed you. So much." And then, like a big stupid baby, tears began leaking out of my eyes.

"Well," she stammered, and for a moment her voice trembled, "well, Tank, you…you shouldn't have tried kidnapping me. Twice! You kidnapped me twice."

"I'm the jealous type."

"You're the crazy type."

"Run away with me."

"No." She shifted in the sand, getting more comfortable. Her toes pressed into my shoulder. Soon I'd be able to stand. "Tank, why do you hate Chase so much?"

"He's stupid."

"That explains nothing."

"And arrogant. And ugly."

She sighed. "Never mind. Forget I asked."

"Why are you with him?"

"I love him."

"Why?"

"For a variety of reasons. My heart loves him. My brain loves him."

I frowned. "Huh?"

"I mean…I'm attracted to him and I'm emotionally drawn to him. But also, he has all the character traits I desire in a boyfriend. Or husband."

"Did you cheat on me? With him?" I hated the question. But I'd been dying to know. And now I was too weak to do something stupid.

She didn't answer immediately. Took her time. Too long. "Emotionally, yes. While I dated you, I thought about him a lot. But I remained faithful up to the end, until you got grounded."

"Faithful until I got grounded."

"…yes."

"My stupid parents."

She laughed. Always thought she was cute when she laughed. My vision was slowly coming back into focus. It was dark and we had no lights. Her hair was up.

I said, "So you cheated on me with him. At the end."

"I did. And I'm sorry. But I didn't want to break up with you via text message."

"You owe me."

"What do you mean?" she asked with a suspicious grin.

"Cheat on him. With me."

"I will not." She pressed my shoulder with her toe.

"One kiss."

"No."

"Because of my face? The burns?"

"No. Not because of your burns."

"What if he was dead? What then?"

"Ugh," she said and her head dropped. "I can't think about that."

"Maybe I'll kill him so we can be together."

She kicked me. "No kisses for you."

"But I saved your life."

"And then I saved yours. We are even, buster."

I asked, "Are you tired?"

"Exhausted."

"Me too. Haven't slept in days. Let's sleep under the raft. Use it for cover. And then get food in the morning."

She eyed me skeptically.

I added, "I won't touch you."

She looked around and rubbed her legs nervously. Always thought she had great legs. "Might be a good idea. You and I are both wanted persons."

"By the Chemist?"

"By everyone. He put a bounty on my head. Millions."

"I didn't know that."

She realized her mistake. Should she have told me that? What would I do? Watched me out the corner of her eye, holding her breath.

"Millions," I repeated slowly.

She didn't respond.

"Hm," I said. "Not nearly enough. I'd take you instead of the millions."

She relaxed, relieved. "That's sweet of you, Tank."

"I'm a sweet guy." I removed the outboard propellor from the raft. She laid down next to me and I pulled the raft over our heads. I was still weak and shaky, barely able to lift the light boat. The cover wasn't perfect due to the slashed bottom. But it helped. "Comfortable?"

She faced away from me and drew her knees up. "Don't talk. It's weird."

"Cold?"

"A little."

"Want to spoon?"

"*No.*"

"We used to."

"*No.*"

"Let me know if you change your mind."

Katie fell asleep quickly. She shivered. I covered her with my arm. She didn't push me off.

It's a start.

Chapter Twenty-Two
Friday, February 9. 2019
Kid

Twelve hours after getting slammed by the giant and falling into the ocean, I finally lowered into the waiting Lexus at Queensway Bay, just across from Long Beach, at five in the morning. The Worker who'd piloted the boat to the yacht got in the back.

What an awful night.

And it was going to be an even worse day.

I'd let the girl escape.

And Walter was in town.

Plus, EVERYTHING hurt, especially my chest and neck. Broken bones. Busted lip. Loose teeth.

My chauffeur, a former taxi driver now in the employ of the Father, drove us north using back roads to enter Downtown. To enter the Sanctuary. His Kingdom.

I'd grown up in Beverly Hills. Traffic congestion was as abiding as sunlight in LA. The absence of it was like being in another city. Driving into Downtown, we could have been on another planet.

He stopped at the 717 Olympic building, our home. Two blocks over, a Cleaner crew swept dust from the street, the final stage of restoration at that crash site. Tomorrow the Cleaner crew would move to another. We called them crash sites, where helicopters had fallen or rockets punched holes through high rises. The 717 Olympic, a modern residential tower with teal green windows, had survived unscathed and so we populated it with our Devotees and Guests. The government had the 717 under infrared surveillance, we knew that from informants. Thus, the surplus of warm bodies.

The elevators required too much power for our solar panels or generators or hydroelectric engines, and so, like always, I walked ten floors to my quarters. I no longer noticed the climb. My Devotees, dressed in thick cotton robes, had been alerted. They met me at the door with fresh clothes and helped me change, another oddity I no longer considered.

"Where is Walter?" I asked.

"We have not seen Master Walter."

"He is here?"

"We have heard Master Walter is present in the Sanctuary. Shall we locate him?"

"Oh god no. I need a nap."

I fell into the king bed without removing my slippers.

I was roused at noon. As was prudent, none of our sleeping quarters had windows.

Walter was here. I detected him in the darkness. Walter didn't wash often so he had a scent. An odor. But he also had a presence. His air pulsated. The Devotees were frightened of him but not enough. They didn't appear cognizant of his evil scrim, the spreading stain he left on the atmosphere. They couldn't detect him from another room. I could.

As always, he wore sunglasses and his hair was cornrowed and his mouth twisted with displeasure.

"She escaped," Walter barked. He was furious in perpetuity. "You let her escape."

"We were ambushed," I protested.

"You are weak."

"Tank Ware, the giant, surprised us. Even Pacific, the yacht's captain, she didn't…"

He pulled his knife blade out of my mattress. I hated it when he stuck his knives into my things. "You are worse than a nothing."

"He pulled the boat's engine straight out of the yacht's floor."

That gave him pause. He considered this fact with awe. Walter was a great respecter of power and destruction.

I pressed my advantage. "We weren't prepared. He broke most of the bones in my shoulder."

"Stop sniveling. The virus is wasted in you. You don't deserve its power."

I'd heard that phrase a hundred times. I knew better than to respond.

"Get up. You got an errand."

"Walter, I'm exhausted. Send a Twice Chosen. Or a Worker. My body hurts like-"

"Get up. Or I'll throw you from the window."

I got up, wincing at the shifting and grinding above my heart.

"Babington. He's back. He's resting in a room on the east side. Bring him in."

"I'm surprised he's not dead. I thought for sure the stress would kill him."

"Unlike you, maybe he's no coward. You fail at this, I'mma drum your shoulders with a bat. Understand?"

He stormed out, door slamming and breaking. Again. The third time he'd broken my door.

My Devotees pretended not to notice. I looked in the mirror and winced at the bruising around my neck. "The elevator is almost functional, Master."

"I hadn't heard. Is this one of Nuts' projects?" I asked.

"Yes. Master Scott's been working for days now."

Master Scott. Nicknamed Nuts. He was a reclusive Chosen, a long-time cohort of Father Martin. We called him Chosen. The rest of the world would refer to him as Infected, a term forbidden in the Sanctuary. Nuts was not strong, nor fast. He was smart. Brilliant. An inventor, making millions with patents published through proxies. A man of diminutive stature and fewer words. He hadn't slept in years, or so Father Martin said.

"How will the elevator work?"

"We don't know, Master."

"Master, are you leaving again?"

I had two Devotees. So did Nuts. So did Walter, though he always left them here. So did Mary, the girl in Washington. Her Devotees were male and she took them to Washington with her. The Father said their goal was to soothe our nerves, something he no longer required. Twice Chosen didn't have Devotees, unless specifically granted by the Father. He wanted the Twice Chosen freaks fully wound up. Our attendants were beautiful and had volunteered to attend our every wish. I had fallen in love with a former Devotee. Which made me weak, the Father said. He took her away.

"Yes," I sighed, easing pressure on my shoulder. "I have to leave again."

"Would you like the pleasure of our company before you go?"

"No. No thank you."

I couldn't look at the two women, my attendants. Their warm hopeful eyes and sensuous mouths made me miss her. My previous Devotee. I'd never...been with a woman. I wanted to be with her. Two weeks ago, I cautiously sent out feelers to discover her whereabouts. No luck. Yet.

I said, "Please fetch me a bottle of water and an apple."

"Yes Master." Obediently she skipped off, eager to please. I didn't want to know her name.

"How does the new elevator work?"

"I don't know exactly, Master. I heard the elevator car is to be lifted off the ground by using the combined weight of Workers." She helped me into my favorite blue jacket. It had been *her* favorite jacket too. She'd told me once, months ago. Before disappearing. Or worse.

"So...Workers will just haul on a rope or cord or something?"

She asked, "Would you like for me to find out?"

"No. Thank you. I'll ask Nuts if I see him. You can both take the rest of the afternoon off."

"You are generous but that is unnecessary, Master. We'll be here when you return."

"Please call and have my car ready."

"Of course."

I collected the water and apple and left, walking past a pod of Guests (hostages) scrubbing the hallway walls. The Guests couldn't leave but they weren't mistreated.

Actually, that applied to all of us.

I wasn't meant for this life. I didn't like attention, much less devotion. I didn't like violence. I didn't like being in charge of hundreds. Thousands.

And yet. Here I was.

Often I wished the headaches would have killed me.

Or that I had courage enough to join the Outlaw. A fate worse than death, Walter told me once, as if reading my mind. That would be your consequence.

Workers on the ground level bowed when they saw me. All of them not-so-secretly hoping to be taken to a Chrysalis one day and Transformed. The lobby doors were always open to help with ventilation. As a result, the floors collected extra dust and grim. Workers swept constantly.

Across the street, two Twice Chosen quasi-bowed towards me. Animals. Swift. Fierce. And half-mad. Not sane enough to take proper care of themselves. They were Warriors. The law enforcement. Revered and tended by Workers. I did not fear them. The strong ruled in the Sanctuary. And due to my freakish birth, I was the strongest.

My car arrived. "To the east side," I told the Driver.

"Yes sir."

"We need to collect a package. Mose likely from the East Barracks."

This was when I felt the most exposed. The American government monitored us via dozens of satellites. And if they wanted to, this would be a great time to drop a missile on me. I used to bring Guests with me for protection, but I'd grown numb to the danger. Let the missiles fall.

We angled southwest on 7th and…

There!

Between vacant shops, in the alley beyond, a flash of black and orange. A tiger! Several prowled Downtown, eating rodents and dogs and occasionally human bodies. They were legend, but real. Ghosts in the flesh, haunting the city. The tiger's heavy face regarded me for that instant. Impassive, impersonal, unafraid, like an assassin sending a simple message. I'm here. See you soon.

The Father claimed they wouldn't attack anyone who'd been Transformed on a surgical table. I hadn't been. He'd done *something* to the back of my skull once, but only mentioned it would make the Twice Chosen more accepting of me. Didn't put me under. So the tigers terrified me. I'm vigilant against them. I'd come close to dying more than once.

"Did you see that??"

"See what, sir?"

"Holy...whoa..." My heart pounded and pounded and pounded. "One of those...freaking tigers...ugh."

"Saw one the other day, sir. Shouldn't bother *you*, right?"

"Why does he keep them here?" I wondered with a shake of my head. "Makes no sense. Why build a utopia...and then drop man-eating tigers inside?"

The commute lasted thirty-five minutes. Our car was forced to detour around collapsed streets and rubble and deserted cars. We stopped at the East Barracks, a recently abandoned condo complex. The Warriors had moved into the furnished rooms and operated out of it. As usual, my presence excited them. Rabid eighteen and nineteen year olds had all the energy of teenagers but none of the social restraints. Many of them were naked and in need of serious mental therapy. The place smelled rank after just two months, despite the operational plumbing. My presence inside the small space acted like a Mentos dropped into a two liter of soda.

They needed a leader. Desperately. It wasn't me; I'm no leader. It wasn't Walter; he wanted to burn the world and everyone in it. Certainly not Nuts. It should've been the Father but he constantly trotted the globe.

It could have been Carla. She had possessed leadership skills and common sense. The Warriors had followed her. Until the Father strapped her to the nose of a helicopter and crashed.

I missed Carla.

I suspected this was the true reason the Father sought the Outlaw; the

Outlaw was a commander. A natural chief. With him at the helm, the Father's army would be motivated and impervious. Unstoppable. But now, with no leader and no mission, the Twice Chosen raged like angry elephants. They howled and gibbered and tried communicating with me through their delirium while I searched the rooms. I discovered Andy Babington on a cot in the back.

"What happened to your mask?" I asked.

He groaned.

I tossed him a new bandana and a pair of ear muffs. "Put those on. Cover your eyes and ears. We need to go. Hurry up. I don't want to stay here."

He looked rough. Close to death. His scars were angry and red, but the rest of his pale skin glinted with sweat. He fumbled with the bandana, at length covering his eyes and ears. I hauled him up and guided him through the dirty main level. He tripped on trash. The Warriors watched with interest, sympathizing with their brother who struggled through the familiar pain, and jealous at his special treatment.

He fell asleep immediately in the back of the Lexus.

"Take the long way home," I ordered the Driver. "There's no rush, and he needs the sleep. We both do."

Stay mobile. Stay away from Walter.

"Yes sir." He glanced curiously at the man, the boy, sleeping on the back cushions.

"He's a special project. One of the Father's. I don't know why," I explained.

He held up his hands in mock defense. "I ask no questions."

"Probably a good idea."

He woke me up at five. We'd cruised downtown for three hours. The sun descended towards the Pacific and our street sat in shadows cast by looming towers.

"Well done," I told him.

"Thank you, sir."

Andy felt better. Slightly refreshed, able to remove his blindfold. He followed me into the lobby, lit now with battery powered lanterns. We could afford to light the tower with electricity, but why draw unwanted attention? Anyway, we had millions of batteries.

A short bald man stood beside the elevator, frowning over schematics. He spotted me and scowled, which was meaningless. He always scowled. It indicated recognition.

"Kid," he greeted me.

"Nuts. I hear you've got a working elevator."

"Bah." His furrowed brow deepened. "It ain't the elevator that's working. It's the people. You been remembering your heat shield, boy?"

"No," I admitted. Nuts had built and provided us with radiant heaters which, when directed at the walls in our rooms, would render American infrared sensors useless.

He swore and shook his head.

I said, "Did you hear how Pablo died?"

"Water. Electrocution. Fell off the boat."

"I hate those electric rods, Nuts. Too many accidents waiting to happen."

"Bah," he said again. "War is hell. Get on the elevator."

"It's ready?"

"Get on. Tenth floor?"

"Tenth floor."

He radioed, "Tenth floor," to…someone. Andy and I stepped into the elevator. If this fell, we *probably* wouldn't die. At least I wouldn't. But it wouldn't feel good either.

"You won't crash. Hydraulics prevent it from plunging," he explained. As if to calm our fears, he stepped into the car too. His radio squawked. He spoke into it, "Ready and go."

The car rocked gently. Then again. And again, and we lifted an inch, the car swaying. Another jolt. We began the ascent. This car didn't have operational doors. Or a ceiling. We could see how the system functioned. Our car constituted one end of a pulley. The other end, the counter weight, slowly descended towards us. People. Six of them. Workers, stacked in a make-shift metal elevator car, lit by two lanterns. They laughed and smiled as we passed.

"Those jolts we felt," I reasoned, "were Workers getting into that metal car. They loaded until the weight was great enough to lift us."

"Yep," Nuts confirmed. "Their metal car is lighter. It attaches easily to the requested floor. We ain't got enough amps yet, but we got people. People power."

"And if it breaks, we won't fall?"

"Air pressure prevents it. Like a storm door mechanism. Slowly hiss back down to earth. My own invention."

"What happens to the Workers if it breaks?"

He shrugged. "We get new Workers."

Andy shifted but did not speak.

We exited at the tenth floor, and I congratulated Nuts on his elevator. He said, "Meh. Need to safely increase the velocity," and slowly descended out of sight. My Devotees waited with the door open, allowing the remaining sunlight into our hall.

"Master, your presence is required on the roof."

My heart sank. "Walter?"

"Yes Master. Walter."

He could have texted but we reserved cell usage for absolute necessities. Nuts ran our cell signals to multiple towers and satellites, disguising numbers and routing through daisy-chained servers across the globe, but the threat persisted. The Americans would lock onto them eventually.

Even if they didn't, Carter's computer hacker would. That was an absolute certainty. PuckDaddy. Our constant scourge.

"How is your shoulder, Master?"

I answered, "Hurts a little less each hour. Should be fine in a couple days."

"Do you require anything now?"

"I'm fine. Andy? Need anything?"

"Food," Andy answered. Quietly. My Devotees were gorgeous, and Andy had trouble not staring. Later I would explain that the women were weak-minded, sacrificing everything to enter into the Father's service, chasing unrealistic fantasies. Nothing about them was substantial. Like the Warriors, these wounded women needed a lifetime of therapy.

"Food. Good idea. Grab us some fruit, please. And chocolate."

She turned quickly to obey. Andy perked up when she returned with Hershey bars.

We trudged up the remaining eighteen floors. The roof. Why always the roof? I wasn't a Leaper like Walter. By the time we attained the peak, the sun had been hidden by ocean. Andy panted and groaned and ached.

The view. This spectacular view from the open-aired sky lounge. I still wasn't immune. Los Angeles went *forever*. In all directions. The Sanctuary was a city (a dark one) inside a city that never ended. From this perch, Walter and the Father could hop onto the nearby sky scrapers. The ones which still stood.

Walter reclined on a chair set in the grass, smoking a cheap cigar, boots crossed on the coffee table. But it was not Walter who stopped us short.

Andy caught his breath with a hiss. "Hannah. Hannah Walker?"

A girl sat near Walter, serenely surveying us without emotion. I hadn't seen her in months. Hannah had been a classmate of Andy's in a former life. Lovers, if the rumors were true. She was very pretty. No, that's not the word. She was…attention grabbing. Sexy. Trim, muscular, curvy. And melted.

She wore a thousand dollars worth of scant clothing, breezy white fabric, essentially an immodest robe, like she didn't want the material to touch her more than necessary. Her back was straight. Legs crossed. High-heels. Short blonde hair pulled back and spiked, like a flame. Her face displayed extensively burnt flesh and skin grafts. Blue eyes that didn't blink.

"Hello Andy," she said with a raw voice. "I remember your name."

"I remember you too," he answered. He lowered carefully into the chair next to her. "A little."

"You were…" she started but trailed off, like chasing a dream remnant. "You…"

"We were friends."

"*Are* friends. Still."

Andy smiled. He was a good-looking kid. "Are friends."

Walter and I shared a glance. What the heck? He shrugged.

She asked, "Have you seen Chase?"

"Chase? Who is…hang on. I know Chase."

"I search for him."

"Me too."

"You do??"

Andy rubbed his eyes. Then his temples. "…I think."

"We can search together!"

Walter spoke, an insulting, casual sneer. "Andy. Hey stupid. You're looking for the Outlaw."

"But…"

"The Outlaw."

I was confused. I wanted to ask, aren't they the same person? Are we hiding that? Walter shook his head and indicated the adjacent chair. I sat. He told me, "I decided to simplify things for Babington. His head 'bout exploded two nights ago, when I…explained things. Besides. We don't need these two white wackos getting too friendly. Keep'em apart."

"She smells like gasoline still."

"Yeah," he barked a laugh. "She'd be fun, sept for that. I like crazy ass women. But that smell."

"Why'd you bring her?"

"Found her. Up north. Maybe she can help."

Because I felt reckless, because I disliked Walter so intensely, I suggested innocently, "Should I put Mary on speakerphone?"

The effect happened instantaneously. His grip on the chair's arm tightened and the wood splintered. He ground teeth on the cigar for a brief moment, and he grumbled, "Don't need that bitch."

"Are you sure? The Father prefers-"

Walter banged his boot on the table, startling us all. Andy winced.

"Okay. Let's talk."

Hannah stood. "I'm going to look for Chase."

"Sit down."

She turned on him. So fast, half a heartbeat, verging on violence. Eyes flashing, fingers like talons, skin pebbling into rock. Walter, caught off guard, nearly fell out of his chair, inhaling too much smoke and ash. Coughing, eyes streaming with tears, he held up his hands. Universal symbol for Calm Down.

He was no fool; the girl should not be trifled with. Hannah Walker had been carefully and intentionally rebuilt by the Father himself, providing her with an unheard of complete blood exchange. And other things he only hinted at. Then she'd marinated in the disease for months and months, much longer than usual. She'd awoken a physical freak, a miniature colossus.

When the Father first released her into the Sanctuary, she'd *destroyed* a pod of Warriors. Twice Chosen stupid enough to provoke the cheerleader. Her nails acted as razors. So much blood. Evisceration wasn't strong enough a word. Afterwards, the street looked as though human bodies had detonated from internal pressure. After viewing the massacre, Nuts began building steel claws that day.

If she and Walter fought...I didn't know who'd win.

"Let me try that again," Walter choked with a grin, hands still raised, palms out. "Let's all talk. *Please.*"

"About what?"

I said, "We know you're very intelligent, Hannah."

"We wanna find Chase. Jus' like you."

Her face softened. Literally. "You do?"

Andy Babington said, "Chase?"

Walter continued, "Honestly. We do. We want to find Chase. We want to help. Both of you."

She sat, anger diffused, storm passed. "How do I help?"

"I'm not sure yet. Andy...Andy? Andy!" Walter kicked the table again, getting the boy's attention off Hannah's outfit. "Andy, tell us what happened last night."

"Last night?"

"You went to Compton. Looking for Chase."

"I remember.

"And?"

"I found him."

Walter bolted upright, cigar forgotten. "You *found* him??"

"You did?" Hannah clapped her hands. "Good for you!"

"I found him," Andy nodded. "Him and the girl kicker."

Walter and I shared another look. We had the Outlaw *and* his girlfriend *and* the Shooter in our hands. All of them. Now lost. We hoped the Father never found out.

Walter asked the ridiculous question. "Did you kill either?"

"No."

"Damn it."

"They hurt me. And took away my…I hate him."

Hannah Walker stretched her arms wide and yawned. "You hate Chase?"

"I hate him."

"Why?"

"Just do. …I think."

I asked, "Do you know where they went?"

Andy had been watching Hannah, and so he yawned too. "Where who went?"

"Chase and the Shooter."

"The Shooter?"

Walter snarled, "The kicker, Babington. Focus. The kicker."

"What about her?"

He stood up and flung the cigar over the railing. "This is some stupid…"

He stopped.

We all stopped.

The Father was here. Somewhere close. I sensed him. So did the others. He felt like a thunderstorm. Like a change in barometric pressure. Involuntarily I began to tremble.

He stood in the penthouse doorway. Watching. A darker shade of shadow.

Hannah shrieked in delight and ran to him. A little girl finding her daddy returned from war. I was stunned. She *hugged* him. He *allowed* her. Never seen that. He toyed with her hair, pulling back the short dirty-blonde flames.

"Hello little candle," he said. "I hope you've been a good girl?"

"Oh yes. The very best."

He stepped into our lantern light. Death himself, Dracula in appearance. His visage had grown more grim, his skin pallor closer to matching his gray hair. As always, he wore a duster and leaned on the staff. "If it isn't the Three Musketeers."

I stood and bowed to him. Reluctantly, Walter followed suit and gave a perfunctory nod. The Father offered me his hand and I took it. Such strength! Such power radiated. Like shaking hands with a redwood. Like shaking hands with the San Gabriel Mountain. With the earth's core.

A persistent slipstream at the tower's peak caught strands of his hair, the only malleable part of his person. "Hello Andy."

Andy Babington swallowed and stood and nodded and sat again, like a fish flopping, no eye contact. The virus hadn't had enough time to affect significant changes within Andy's body, but the Father's presence cowed him like he'd developed sensory receptors.

The Father continued, "I'm surprised to see you awake, son. I…assumed…you'd be asleep for months. In fact…" He turned to stare at Walter. "…I ordered it."

The gears turning in Walter's brain were almost audible. He'd woken Andy prematurely. He'd disobeyed orders. Insubordination, pure and simple. He chafed under the Father's control. Strained against him, wanting to be independent, autonomous, have complete command. Could this be the time? To overthrow the Father? Even kill him? The old man appeared so slow and frail. Maybe…

The Father read his thoughts.

The Father *Moved*.

Moved as though he stepped outside of time. The governing laws of physics did not apply. He'd outlived them, outgrown their shackles. The wooden coffee table exploded. The Father's staff shattered it. Or else he used telepathy, it happened that fast. The staff cracked Walter in the face, a sound of metal on rock.

Walter woke up on the floor. His jaw broken. Blood trickling from his lips. He spit out a shattered tooth. Maybe two.

"I invested resources beyond your imagination into Andy Babington," the

Father said, standing still, an old man again, as though he hadn't moved. "He will die now. Most likely."

Andy was crying. Hannah frowned at him with bewilderment and…disgust?

The Father turned to me. The blood drained from my face. He said, "Tell me about your efforts to recapture the girl."

"The…girl?"

"After she boarded the raft with the ogre, Tank Ware. Regale me with your progress towards locating her."

I stayed silent. Close to hyperventilating.

He continued, "The raft is small, yes? Couldn't have gone far? No food? No water? Had to beach somewhere nearby, correct?"

My chest heaved. My neck and shoulder throbbed. I'd failed. I'd made zero effort.

"Or did you come home and…sleep."

"I…" I wheezed. His presence suffocated me. "I slept."

"Do you see?" He raised his left hand, hard as steel, and set it on my purple shoulder. "Do you understand?"

"Do-do I understand?"

"Do you understand why your name is Kid?"

"Because…because I'm not good at this."

"Exactly." He gave me a gentle squeeze, almost fatherly, sending lightning strikes up and down my torso and deep into my shoulder. He let go. Tears formed in my eyes. "At least you're honest."

"Thank you, Father."

"I have located the girl. No thanks to you."

Hannah spoke up, "Located who?"

"Katie Lopez, baby."

"I know Katie!"

"Yes you do. Would you like to help retrieve her?"

"Yes!" Hannah clapped her hands again. Old cheerleader habit? "She and I are friends. She can help find Chase."

"Yes," the Father said, his voice picking up hints of a ravenous hunger.

"Yes. She will help find Chase."

"I will go," she said.

Eager for redemption, I asked, "Shall I go fetch Katie?"

"No, son. You can barely feed yourself."

Walter spoke, his lips unmoving. "Where is she?"

"West. With the ogre, taking shelter on a beach."

"With the ogre?"

"Will that be a problem?"

"No sir. Do you think the Outlaw knows her location?"

"I'm not positive, Walter. But I doubt it. Neither Katie nor the ogre appears to have a working phone. They spent the day in a picnic shelter, scavenging food and avoiding discovery."

Walter finally stood, holding his jaw in place. He healed at a truly prodigious rate and might be whole before morning. "I'll get her."

"Yes Walter," the Father nodded. "Yes you will. I run short on time. The world is ripe for the plucking. And if I get my hands on that boy...that mysterious magical magnificent boy...it will all be ours."

"And the ogre?"

"If possible, leave him alive. This globe has a more appealing future with him stomping all over it."

"Yes Father."

"Take Hannah with you. Should be like having the power of hell at your disposal. I'll have Katie Lopez's exact location forwarded to your phone. And Walter, let nothing stop you. My surgeons are prepped for her arrival."

Chapter Twenty-Three
Saturday, February 10. 2019

I woke up at four in the morning on a blanket beside Miss Pauline's couch. She really needed to vacuum. Above me, Samantha snored faintly on the scratchy plaid cushions. Her arm was draped off the couch's side and rested on my shoulder.

Yesterday had been eerily quiet. We'd followed Miss Pauline, and painted, cleaned, swept, listened to her many meetings, and played with her many unofficially adopted neighborhood kids. Miss Pauline was uncomplicated; she worked and she loved and she wielded power through those two avenues and dispensed wisdom along the way.

"How is this helping defeat the Chemist??" Samantha had hissed at me, holding fistfuls of discarded plastic grocery bags. We both wore sunglasses and hats pulled down.

"Maybe it isn't. Maybe it is. I'm not sure. We'll leave tomorrow."

"And go downtown?"

"And go downtown."

"And shoot everyone?" she asked hopefully.

"And hug everyone."

"You're an idiot."

We had eaten dinner on her lawn again, and slept in her living room again, and now I was awake at four in the morning on the floor, so acutely uncomfortable and worried that I couldn't sleep. I quietly checked my phone. For the thousandth time.

No news from Katie. My heart sank. I hadn't heard from her in over thirty hours. An awful dread constricted my chest. I messaged PuckDaddy.

Puck, Katie STILL hasn't texted me.
>> yeah her phones off
>> captain FBI is out there now with the coast guard
>> near the rendezvous, 5 miles off shore
>> probably just no phone charger on his coast guard cutter
Katie should be at a safe house by now, Puck.
>> it took isaac longer than he thought it would
>> president issued warrant 4 his arrest so...
>> that changed things
The President wants Isaac ARRESTED??!
>> well...kinda its weird
>> puck is following events as much as possible
>> reading between the lines
>> america is so fractured
>> so many chains of command so much distrust
>> half loyal to president
>> half aren't
>> skirmishes everywhere
>> so president issued warrant 4 his arrest
>> probably cause blue eyes made him
>> but who is gonna cuff isaac out here?? nobody
>> he's a hero
>> and now kind of an outcast
>> like u

What a mess. I thumbed through some news on my phone. Mounting disaster all over the globe. And now Special Agent Isaac Anderson was a wanted man. He'd known this was coming. Anticipated it. Planned for it. Make arrangements with powerful and sympathetic allies. But still.

I thumbed through Katie's Instagram, hoping to see new photos. PuckDaddy texted me again.

>> hey
>> wake up samantha 4 me
Why?
>> Carter wants her help

I pushed Samantha's shoulder with my finger. Her eyes snapped open, instantly alert.

"What?"

"Puck wants you," I whispered.

"No. Tell him No."

She says No.

>> ugh

Samantha's phone buzzed. And buzzed again. And again. And again.

She snatched it and hissed into the receiver, "OhMyGosh, what the heeeeeeellll, Puck." She listened, staring at the overhead ceiling fan thoughtfully. Then, "I don't have the right gun." Puck's voice buzzed softly in the quiet room but I couldn't interpret meaning. "Okay. I'm on my way." She hung up.

I asked, "What's going on?" Samantha stood up and stretched. "And holy moly, put your pants on."

She shrugged. "It got hot last night."

"Miss Pauline would *kill* you if she saw this."

"Do you like my blue superman underpants?" She slapped herself on her rump and twisted in a circle. "Your dad does."

"That's…no…that's not funny. I hate you so much. Put your pants on this instant."

She did, hopping silently on one foot, shoving the other into a pant leg. "The Chemist is downtown. NSA got visual confirmation. Carter is going in."

I stood up too, joints creaking. Oooouch. Stupid floor. "What's that mean? How?"

"Puck tracked the Chemist to LA, so Carter came back. The NSA showed Carter the photo. The Chemist is on top of a tower near the residential building where they all sleep."

"Doing what?" I pulled my shoes on and packed my backpack.

"Dunno. Carter and Russia are trying a quick sneak attack. If I get there in time, I'll provide long-range support." She eyed my reaction. But I truly didn't know what to think. Getting rid of the Chemist was paramount. However, this didn't seem like a good idea. Violence just created more violence.

"Okay. I'll go with you."

I wrote Miss Pauline a quick note.

Thank you. For so much. You've changed everything.
-Chase

"Carter's en route," Puck told us through our ear pieces. Samantha and I *Moved* north on Alameda through Huntington Park, easily outpacing the early morning traffic. "You won't make it in time."

"I might get in range and get a shot off!"

This was happening too abruptly. We had no plan, just praying we could outfight him. And we couldn't. But Carter was going to try with or without our assistance. And Samantha was going to assist with or without my help.

"You don't have a rifle," I pointed out.

"Puck says there's an enemy barracks just inside the border. On Newton." She ran effortlessly, long strides eating up the road like a leopard. To anyone standing still on the sidewalk, we looked like Olympic sprinters setting new land speed records. "I can find what I need there."

"Maybe."

"Maybe."

In the distance, almost like a memory, we heard helicopter blades pounding the air. Gotta move faster. We went over the military's Downtown barricade as though riding the crest of a wave. She couldn't *Leap* as far as I could, but the parabola of her flight cleared the machine gun nets comfortably.

We found the barracks via olfactory methods; the disease simmering in the Chosen's collective flesh and their combined body odor called like a siren. The door shattered as I went through, an explosion of glass splinters.

"Carter's at the tower." PuckDaddy's alert piped directly into our ear canals.

"Too soon! I'm not in position!"

Samantha and I ransacked befouled apartments, flinging open bedroom doors, bathroom doors, closets, custodian supply cabinets. "I'm not finding anything!" she cried.

The barrack's sleepy denizens woke and irritably inspected the source of their disturbance. A lot of them. Samantha needed a diversion to buy her more time. I halted my search, standing ankle deep in hallway refuse, and tied on the new red mask.

Natalie North was right. The Outlaw wore a mask.

I pulled the Thunder Stick free from my vest and began spinning it from hand to hand. Just in case Miss Pauline's methodologies didn't work. "Free hugs!" I roared, and I crushed a wall with the stick like playing a drum. "Come out, come out where ever you are! Meet the Outlaw and get a free hug!"

"This…" Puck commented. "…this seems unwise."

I felt concussive throbs in my feet and in my ears. Detonations.

"Be advised, Carter's on top of Wilshire Tower! So is Shadow. Hunting the Chemist. Russia's in the chopper, absolutely laying waste with his rockets!" Puck sounded frantic with hope and energy.

"Got it! Found a rifle!" Samantha called. "Keep'em busy, Outlaw, I'm heading to the roof!"

I strolled into the street, abandoning the apartment building. A heaving mass of bodies followed. Chosen. Of all shapes and sizes. Some of the group appeared to be in complete possession of themselves. Some appeared no more stable than angry wolves. I spotted three electroshock rods. The rest brandished steel claws. Claws everywhere.

They hated me. Rabidly. But it was a fearful hatred. A respectful hatred. And maybe something else too. Far too many emotions for me to categorize. They formed a complete circle around me, hounds baying. Dozens. I kept turning in circles, twisting to glare and impart my will against them. I pointed a finger and they winced, ducking their heads.

"Go back to bed and you won't be harmed," I said. "Or. Put down your claws. And get a free hug."

They raged.

"I'm on the roof," Samantha said. "And Miss Pauline is going to get you killed."

Puck shouted, hurting my ear. "Carter found Martin! Carter found the Chemist! They're jumping all over the tower! Holy craaaaaap!"

"I'm too far! Over a mile away!" Samantha cried. "Outlaw, I'm heading deeper downtown!"

"Okay," I said. "I'll keep these stinkers company."

"No! There's too many! Get out of there!"

As if on cue, they rushed me. Claws slashing. Teeth bared. The Leapers launched themselves, death from above. I blocked backwards, parrying aside steel talons, crushing hands. In frenzy, their claws sank into each other, lethal backswings. Blood flew in ribbons.

I didn't counterattack. I didn't ruin their skulls. Instead I played defense, using my superior quickness. Mistake. The Leapers landed on me. Steel sank into my shoulders. Into my ribs.

Pain and numbness alternated through layers of muscle. Metal within my body, alien, out of place. Blood gushed. Samantha was right. Too many.

"Get BACK!" I roared. Involuntarily, obeying some primal instinct, obeying the law of the jungle, the Chosen rocked backwards on their heels like one big animal flinching in fear. Just enough space.

I *Leapt* from the mountain of my enemies, landing beyond them. Blood issued from underneath the vest, absorbing into my pants and trickling down my arm. I'd grown arrogant. Foolish. Believed myself impervious.

How did Miss Pauline DO this??! Okay. So no hugs today.

The wounds were deep. My pulse throbbed in their depths, each palpitation like touching a live wire. The sight of blood invigorated them.

"That was stupid." Half wheeze, half groan. I fled.

My left arm felt strange, hollow, as though operating on reduced power. I went onto the roof, a desperation *Jump*, and scanned for Samantha. No sign. The vast Los Angeles horizon laid out like an endless commercial maze. Chaos at the peaks but I hurt too much to see that far. My shoulder and ribs drummed with pain. Pain that reached my ears. Pain so loud I didn't immediately register what I was hearing.

Madness. A scramble of voices. Screaming.

"What's going on?" I shouted.

"Helicopter crash landing!"

"Outlaw move your ass!" Samantha sounded like she was sprinting. And cursing. A lot. "They'll swarm Carter's chopper!"

"Where?!"

"North! Follow the smoke!"

"It's too dark to see smoke!" But I saw the glow. I went north. Each jump was murder. A drumbeat of red agony. "What happened?"

"Shadow is dead."

"No! How?"

Puck answered, "Carter is wounded and he retreated to the helicopter. The Chemist caught Shadow and…"

"And what?"

He took a full and shaky breath. "The Chemist threw Shadow into the helicopter blades. Cut him to ribbons. And now Russia is trying to land in one piece."

Chapter Twenty-Four
Saturday, February 10. 2019
Tank

I woke up early. Barely light out.

Katie was staring off into the distance, already awake. She couldn't fall asleep last night either. Too stressed about the boyfriend. Her phone was dead and she couldn't charge it without going into a public place, and that risked exposure. So we spent yesterday scavenging for food and hiding from sight. She kept crying about her friend, the football player who died in the water. She hadn't told Chase yet. Being out of contact with him (and someone called Puck) caused her no end of anxiety.

Always thought she was cute when anxious.

But not when it was about Chase Jackson. The wimp. The tiny little dork, unworthy of such a woman.

Later today I'd be healthy enough to venture out. Both of us had well-known faces, and both of us were wanted by powerful parties. Had to be cautious. We'd find a phone and call my parents. They'd wire me funds, and put us in a hotel until she made further arrangements. Or. Until she decided to stay with me.

Although I had no idea what my future held.

Explosions. To the north and west. Downtown. That's what woke her. And me.

"Hear that?" she asked.

"Yeah. Think it's the Outlaw?"

"I hope not." She closed her eyes and took several steadying breaths. Her knees were pulled close to her chest, sitting on the sand near the public picnic shelter and facilities. "We used to live in a world without the constant threat of eruptions."

"It's your boyfriend's fault."

"It is *not*," she snapped. "He's on the side of peace."

"Peace don't wear a mask."

"Some masks are shields, Tank. Protection for other people. Chase didn't cause this. Chase was caught up in this hellish hurricane just like the rest of us."

"He *is* the hellish hurricane, babe."

"Wrong! He's our best hope out of it."

I held up my hand, calling for silence. She glared and puffed up her chest in affront. But I'd heard a noise. There was a partial moon and the earliest indications of morning. Enough light to see by. We weren't alone. Shadows moved silently around us. Ghosts gliding across benches and over the sand. Maybe a dozen. Katie saw them too and gasped. Intruders.

I got to my feet, rage building like a stove. I wasn't strong enough for this yet. Not enough food. Been hungry forever. My fists clenched so violently my knuckles cracked. Katie remained seated.

A man approached. A black man. With cornrows and a foul stench. We glared at each other. "You know me?"

"Don't know. Don't care," I said.

"I'm here for the girl. You get to live."

"Can't have her."

"One way or the other, yes I can."

"You'll have to kill me," I growled. I wanted to break him. And then do it again.

"Don't want to. But I will."

"You'll try."

He chuckled in the dark. I could sense him more than I could the others. He was the strongest. The most dangerous. "You stronger than me, Tank. I hate it. But there it is."

"Damn right I am."

"But you know what I got?" He held out his hands. Several of his gang ignited handheld rods, which sparked and crackled with waves of blue. The electricity was audible.

I hate electricity. So much. Been shocked one too many times. I fought away the fear.

I said, "Gonna need more than that."

He smiled, a flash of white teeth. "Throw all the shade you want. But we don't gotta do this. You don't gotta die. The Father won't hurt her."

Katie spoke out of her anger. "That's what Kid said too."

"Kid stupid, but he wasn't lying."

"I know you," she said. "I saw you fight the Outlaw. And you lost."

I had to laugh at her bravery. Impressive girl. "You lost to that shrimp in a mask? Weak, homie. Weak."

He glowered. A new noise caught our attention. A song. Someone was singing. A raspy lullaby, walking down the brick staircase from the parking lot beyond, drawing closer to the sand.

I knew that rasp. I knew that smell. The tang of gasoline. The cheerleader was here. She'd attacked me three months ago. Set herself *on fire* and burned me. Badly. It would have killed an ordinary man. My skin came off in sheets.

Fear. Fear uncontrollable, like a wintery blast took hold of my heart. She was an alien. A freak. A demon. She'd caused so much pain. So strong. So loud in my ear. Even my tongue had caught fire.

Nobody moved. Except the cheerleader. She kept trilling as she kicked off her shoes and undressed. She shimmied out of her white pants. Folded them carefully, delicately, and handed them to one of the ghosts. "I don't want to ruin these."

My heart thundered. Couldn't speak.

She was about to pull her shirt off when she noticed Katie. Her song stopped. "Katie."

Katie was crying. Always thought she was cute when she cried. "Hello Hannah." She tried to smile. "Hannah Walker. I'm glad you're okay."

"I'm here to rescue you, Katie."

"Why?"

"The Father needs you. And the giant won't let you go. And we're friends."

"He's lying to you, Hannah. Sweet Hannah. He's not your father."

The cheerleader tilted her head quizzically, but just for a moment. "Come away, Katie. There's going to be a fire."

Katie's voice came out in a sob. "No. No please."

The black man started shaking a can. Slowly. A half gallon metal can. I knew the type. Came from a hardware store and contained a pre-mixed solution of gasoline and oil. The oil made it burn hotter and longer. Back and forth, he shook it, and then twisted off the cap.

"No!" Katie said again. She stood up. "I'll go with you."

"Katie. Get behind me." The words were a struggle.

"Tank." She put her hands on my chest and pushed. I didn't move. She wept in frustration. "We can't run…you're too weak. And we can't fight. There's too many. They'll electrocute you and then burn you to death. So…I'll go."

"No."

"Yes! They'll abduct me either way. This way…this way you get to live. And two of the Chemist's messengers said I won't be hurt."

"You won't be," the cheerleader said. She bounced on her toes. "You're going to help us."

"I'm going. With them."

"Katie…" I started to cry too. The humiliation, the pain, it was almost worth dying over.

"Tank, you need to stay alive. So you can come get me." She wiped her eyes with her fingers.

"I will. I swear I will."

She turned and glared at the black man. "You won't hurt Tank."

He nodded. "The Father wants him alive, if possible."

"And you won't kill me."

"Little girl, if I killed you, he would legit skin me. Alive. No I ain't gonna hurt you. And he won't neither. He ain't like that. Mostly."

Katie took a hesitant step towards Hannah. Hannah opened her arms and smiled. A pretty smile, if bizarre. Ghastly. The cheerleader didn't understand all this. She was a six-year old child playing with friends in the sand. The higher machinations eluded her.

"Katie..." I said.

"I know," she replied. "I *know*. But neither of us are supposed to die on this beach. We sacrifice here and now, and our stories continue. Let me go, and live."

She went. Hannah embraced her and the two girls ascended the stairs, holding hands. One final look at me.

The black man stayed, glaring, ready to subdue all my stupid and violent notions. But I had none. I was exhausted from standing. Behind me, two of his goons touched their electric rods together. Pure energy sparked, a brilliant connection, spitting white flares.

Katie disappeared beyond the palms, and the black man struck. So fast, too dark. I couldn't dodge. He hit me in the face with something, temporarily dislocating my jaw. Bright spots and flashes roared in my vision like jelly fish. I dropped to a knee, strength soaking into the sand like water. I had nothing left.

"You follow me," the man hissed in my ear, "and I'll make you swallow one of these electroshock cattle prods."

As silently as they arrived the ghosts departed, taking their stink with them. I felt the black man leave, like a change in the silence, and the air tasted less tainted.

Katie went with them. Gone. Into the hands of a madman.

And I stayed on one knee. A failure. In every sense imaginable.

Chapter Twenty-Five
Saturday, February 10. 2019

Russia flew like a wizard. He prevented Carter's Huey from spiraling out of control despite shredded rotors, and crash landed on 1st Street, not far from Natalie North's old building. The landing gear struck hard, a shower of sparks, but Russia kept the fuel tanks intact and prevented an inferno.

I arrived ahead of the horde but just barely. We had mere minutes before massacre. Samantha was there already, scanning rooftops and windows with her rifle in a state of perpetual rotation. Windows everywhere.

The sun was almost up, fingers of pale light streaming overhead. It'd be so cool if Chosen were vampires about to be vaporized by the dawn. No such luck.

"Outlaw!" she cried. "Russia's safety harness is jammed. And…" Her face paled and the barrel of her weapon lowered. "Damn, what the hell happened to you?"

"I got careless."

"You got cut in half."

"No sweat. It doesn't look as bad as it feels." I ducked under the spinning and mangled rotor blades and ripped off Russia's harness using only my right hand. My left could no longer make a fist. Fabric and metal surrendered, and he spilled out, his face a mess of minor cuts.

Russia was a barrel-chested grizzly bear of a man, bulky but lithe. "You look bad," he barked in brusque syllables.

240

"You don't like the new mask?"

"I am in your debt. Thank you for rescue."

"Help me with Carter," I said, sliding the gunner bay door back on its busted track.

"Or." He pulled his pistol out and chambered a round. "Or leave Carter. We make escape."

Samantha ceased her vigilance. Briefly. She glanced between us, weighing this new idea. Leave Carter. He was injured. He'd slow us down. And he'd almost certainly leave us to die if the situation was reversed.

Infected are monsters. No honor. No loyalty. Lone wolves living solely on survival instincts. I despised them all in that instant. Despised myself.

Samantha shook her head. "Forget it, Russia. Chase would die first."

"I couldn't get far anyway." I shrugged and nearly passed out from pain. "I've lost too much blood. Just need an open grave to fall into."

Samantha said, "What's your plan?"

"I know a nearby place to hide. But you'll need to be a diversion."

"I'm diverting as heck." She slung the rifle over her shoulder and pulled out two pistols. She grinned in delight, death with an appetite for danger. "What do you need?"

"Puck, where are the inbound hostiles?"

Puck responded in all our ears. "Moving hard from the south. Hundreds. PuckDaddy is so scared."

"Samantha, get their attention. Draw them after you. Head east. We only need five minutes. Stay alive. Then lose them, and I'll talk you to our hideout."

"Roger that, Outlaw." She was already bounding away, the only one of us moving without injury. She let loose a war cry, an ear-piercing paroxysm, the disease finally allowed to vent.

I grabbed Carter by his jacket and hauled, sliding him out like a heavy slab of beef. He landed on one foot, woozy, bleeding from his head.

"What happened to you?"

"Broken femur, kid," he moaned. "Busted skull."

"I wanted to leave you," I said. "Russia wouldn't hear of it."

"I heard your discussion. Ears work fine. Russia's right. You shoulda left me."

"We gotta move. Now."

Carter leaned on me for support, absolute torture, and we started hopping west. With one functional leg, he moved at a pace reached by a normal human jogging.

"Russia, we need to reach my hideout unobserved."

"I understand." The big man flourished his pistol. He wouldn't miss.

After two blocks of painfully slow progress and Carter's grunting, Puck reported, "Wow, their entire army is after Shooter."

"I bet she leads a merry chase."

Her voice came howling through our ear pieces. "SHUT UP, Outlaw! Puck, which way??!"

"Oh jeez, uh, south. No, east. Either way. But you better speed up."

"Uuuuugh. I'm not a runner. Or a leaper. This sucks!! Not as much fun as it sounded!"

Carter, Russia and I arrived at our destination without incident. A large storage unit warehouse, three stories high. Pitch black, it looked vacant and haunted.

I was sucking wind and light-headed. The wounds were open, leaking blood and energy. Bright bursts like snowflakes filled my mind. I gulped down a lungful of oxygen and detected a new scent, rich and earthen like rotten fruit.

I knew that scent...from...

Russia clicked on a flashlight and aimed the piercing cone of light into the dark metal maze. We weren't alone. A powerful tiger stalked from the corridor, heavy head directed at us, baring his canines. His yellow eyes blinked at the flashlight, which Russia nearly dropped.

He said something in Russian and raised his pistol.

"No," Carter snapped wearily. His face was white with fatigue and fear. "Look at that bastard. You'll just piss him off. We'd need an elephant gun."

"You have better idea?" he asked. His voice shook and he shuffled backwards.

The alpha predator advanced. The finest killer Mother Nature could manufacture, further enhanced by human malice. His pelage showed signs of filth and emitted a stench. Not enough bodies of water nearby to wash. And he was hungry.

I angled my head towards Russia without taking eyes off the beast. "Get behind me."

"Yes. He eats you first."

I had a can of tiger spray in my pocket. Put there by Lee for this exact impossible occurrence. Fill his angry eyes with poison. Don't confuse the bottles! The animal crouched six feet from us, loading his hind legs with weight and gathering forelimbs underneath. There would be a leap, claws, teeth, and ripping and blood.

My hand didn't work. I didn't dare release the Boom Stick with my right, but my left hand fumbled at the pocket. No luck. Fingers slippery and unresponsive. Like trying to pick a lock with noodles.

The tiger tensed and roared.

I roared back.

I became an explosion of sound. Carter flinched so violently at the noise he fell over, and the tiger locked eyes with me. Our wills collided like planets. Biological forces surging. Our shared disease forged a bridge of understanding, subterranean communication.

I held the stick straight out, near his nose. *We are not prey.*

Yes, he answered. *Yes. Prey. And enemy.*

We are not.

Invader. Hate. Hunger.

Find easier prey. You will be injured.

...no.

Yes.

A collision of Kings of the Jungle. I wasn't backing down. His stance shifted, subtle but noticeable. From offensive to defensive. From fury to wary. His ears flattened, pupils dilated. I pointed down the street with the rod. "Go."

He snarled and released a series of coughs. His muscles shivered. I raised the rod, ready to strike. Poised, both. We waited.

Go.

Survival instincts won out. He couldn't be sure of victory. He turned with a woof and padded down the sidewalk towards Grand.

"Tiger is scary," Russia whispered, his breath hot on my neck. "Outlaw is terrifying."

"You need to teach me that trick, boy," Carter said as we hauled him to his feet.

"Let's get inside. In case he changes his mind." I was soaked in sweat and fear and adrenaline, a great stone sitting heavy in my stomach.

We entered the haunted labyrinth. And its miasma. The outer storage units had been pried open, their contents ransacked. The deeper we penetrated, the more subdued the surrounding world became. Our wheezes and shuffles echoed through the metal hallway.

At the very back we reached my unit. Natalie North bought this place for me about a year ago. I hadn't visited since last summer. I release the lock and raised the door, which rolled loudly into the ceiling. The hideout was undisturbed. It contained a bed, a desk, lockers of supplies, a refrigerator, a television and other necessities.

Carter eyed me with respect. "Look at you, hero. Boy got secrets."

"Everyone in."

Carter hopped to the bed and collapsed. Russia unsuccessfully tried the lamp, but found a functional battery-powered lantern. I rolled the door down.

I spoke into my mouthpiece, "Okay, Samantha. Time to come home. Ready for directions?"

"No," she panted. Her breaths came in blasts, distorting the sound. "I'm too far. Too tired. Completely gassed."

"What's your plan?"

"I'm not...not sure yet."

"PuckDaddy has a plan!"

"Go ahead, Puck. I'm all ears."

"Keep going east. You're near the boundary. I'll alert the military barricade. Maybe someone there will be manning machine guns."

"Sounds good," she puffed. "On the way."

I sat on the chair, my whole body on fire, listening helplessly. Run Samantha. Run faster.

"That's not the best part. Oh man, PuckDaddy is a genius!" he chortled.

"What's the best part?"

"Your ride is almost there."

"My ride?!"

Through her microphone we heard the pop of weapons. One machine gun. Maybe two.

"Barricade dead ahead! They're shooting at *me*!"

"I told them not to shoot the hot girl!"

"Tell them AGAIN!"

I closed my eyes and prayed. Get out of there. Dear God, get her out of there. Russia and Carter were also silent, listening to the same drama. I wish it was me, not her.

"Okay, I'm past the barricade. They're still coming. What kind of ride am I looking for?" Samantha wheezed.

"Richard Jackson's squad car."

"Richard??"

"My dad??" I yelped. Nothing would ever make sense again.

"Yeah, he's been trying to help you guys for days. I alerted him an hour ago, concerning your status. He's been circumventing the southern boundary."

"There he is! I see him!"

"Hah!" I cried aloud in the confines of our small storage unit. "Good old Pops!"

We heard the squeal of tires. The sound from her mic changed as she got inside and the door slammed. Still panting, she told Richard he was the best looking man she'd ever seen. She might have kissed him, based on the audio cues. I rolled my eyes.

"Okay," she reported. "We're safe. Heading out of the danger zone at seventy miles per hour."

I was so happy tears leaked down my face.

"Ah ha," Russia said, his voice an expressionless rumble. He stood up with fistfuls of granola bars and bags of trail mix. "We are saved."

Chapter Twenty-Six
Saturday, February 10. 2019

Carter's leg looked dead. Like it'd been dead for days, it was so purple and green. Martin shattered it with his stupid staff. He wrapped his thigh in a sheet and compressed it with his belt and a pillowcase tie-down.

"I don't heal as fast as some," he grumbled. He was sweating from the pain. "Won't walk for a few days."

Unlike Carter, I was a quick healer. But still, my wounds were gruesome. The neck wounds went deep, puncturing the shoulder and penetrating into my chest and narrowly missing heart and lungs. The rib slashes weren't as deep, more like long vivid canals of exposed muscle and bone. I poured disinfectant all over them.

We consumed ibuprofen, though Carter said our bodies were too effective for them to work properly. Heightened metabolism burned the pills up or something weird. We ate handfuls anyway and slept.

I woke up at five in the evening, twelve hours later. My body screamed as new flesh and scar tissue strained and broke. I drank a bottle of water and ate two bags of dried fruit. Our supplies would last less than three days.

Russia was gone. He left a note on my phone.

>> going home

>> no longer fun
>> i will not forget my debt, outlaw

He'd never been my friend, not really. But first Shadow and now Russia. We were losing allies fast.

Against an enemy we couldn't beat.

Still no message from Katie. I ground my teeth in anger and fear. Cold sick fear. Something had gone wrong.

Puck, any news from Katie?
>> no
>> sorry homie. that sucks
What about from Isaac? Talk to him?
>> i messaged him as soon as his boat returned
>> said he'd call puck after a meeting
>> should be soon

I beat the phone against my head and waited.

And waited.

And waited.

Listening to Carter's snores. He had a fever. He'd anticipated an infection, but said not to worry. Wouldn't be lethal.

Lee texted me. I missed Lee. He was remotely piloting drones for the Navy. **They have way more drones than pilots, bro!** He was now a Navy Civilian Serviceman, whatever that was. He was a genius. The Navy knew it, and so they found a way to sneak him into their corp of engineers. His drone had been using recon cameras and night vision to track Carter, Russia and I during the helicopter escape, but we'd vanished out of view behind a tower.

So dude really, he texted. **Where'd you go??!**

I'll show you when this is over.

I waited still.

Waited some more. Got up and started pacing, unlocking stiff joints.

On a whim, I texted Natalie North.

Natalie, do you still use this number?

Her reply came instantaneously. **>> YES!!!**

>> OUTLAW!!!
>> I'm immensely relieved to hear from you! =) =)
Guess where I am?
>> I give up.

At the hideout you built for me. The storage unit.
>> Really??!
>> Awww, that's so great. I'm useful!
It saved our lives today.
>> I have value! Hooray! Self-actualization!
>> I'm very glad I could help.
>> I should be rewarded with kisses. Hundreds of kisses.
Buuuuut...
>> I know, I know. I have a boyfriend or whatever.
And I have a girlfriend. Whom I love.
>> sigh I know. And she's a knockout.
>> She's got Hollywood legs. I'm envious.
>> Fine. No kisses. =(
I wore the mask you made. Wore it today.
>> I saw! There's a couple videos on the news.
>> You're jumping rooftops. So dashing!
>> The video is dark and jumpy, but...
>> It looks like you were bleeding heavily??
I was. But no longer.
>> The whole planet is FREAKING out.
>> I'll tell them you're still alive.
>> What happened??
>> News report said another helicopter crashed?
Long story.
Have you communicated with Isaac recently?
>> He texted that he returned, but that's it.
>> His world is upside down now.
>> I miss him.

And then Puck called me.

I felt the incoming signal before the phone buzzed. Dreadful, brutal premonition. I'd been anticipating this call for hours. Days. Forever. I already knew what he'd say. Between the first and second vibration, my mind processed the heartbreak I knew waited. I shouldn't have left her. It was my fault. I'd abandoned her, exposed her. My soul threatened to hemorrhage.

My thumb trembled. Pressed Answer.

I didn't speak. But he heard me breathing.

"Chase," Puck said.

I made a noise. A miserable sound.

"Chase. I have…I have really bad news."

"Just tell me."

"Captain FBI is back. Isaac. He just called me. Pacific wasn't at the rendezvous. The Coast Guard searched for hours but only found…he…Isaac had the FBI identify the body to be sure. It's Cory. He's dead."

I closed my eyes, a motion which caused the overflow of tears. Not Cory too. Not Cory too.

What *happened* out there? Something terrible.

"Okay. What else?"

"Right before I called you? The Chemist phoned. He's on the other line. Wants to talk to you."

"Put him on." I said the words mechanically. The Chemist. Of course the Chemist. Just hurry up. Just hurry up and tell me. I already know. Just tell me.

"You sure, bro? You sound…scary."

"Puck. Put him on."

"…okay. Here you go."

The line clicked.

The Chemist spoke. I hadn't seen the man or spoken to him in months. But his voice was carved into my ears, indelible grooves which only his timbre filled. The way a childhood nightmare could never be completely forgotten. He spoke with educated, measured syllables. He spoke like a gentlemen. He said, "Katie Lopez is alive."

My legs gave. I fell hard.

"She is lovely, your girlfriend. A beautiful and intelligent nymph. We ate a small lunch together."

I knew it.

Somehow I knew he had her. A gulf of sorrow swallowed me whole. I hurt all the way to my birth. He didn't deserve to eat food with her. I folded at the waist, bending until my forehead rested on the concrete floor.

"I cannot let you speak to her, dear boy. But she asked me to pass you a message."

I didn't answer.

He said, "Would you like to hear it? Then you can trust she's alive?"

"Yes."

"She says...

This bud of love, by summer's ripening breath,

May prove a beauteous flower when next we meet.

Good night, good night. As sweet repose and rest

Come to thy heart as that within my breast."

I wept. A sniffling mess.

He continued, "I knew the reference immediately. It is Juliet saying adieu to Romeo. Did you know?"

"Yes."

"I believe Katie is telling you Good-Bye, Outlaw. And telling you not to fret, and that you'll meet again. Perhaps in the afterlife. Such a remarkable girl."

"What do you want?"

"Let me first tell you what I do *not* want. I do not want to harm Katie. Is her birth name Catalina? Or Katia? No matter. She is an angel. I want her to live a long, long time."

"Go on."

"I want to barter. I am willing to release the girl."

"In exchange for me."

"In exchange for you," he confirmed. "You surrender tomorrow night. On top of the Wilshire Tower. I release Katie. And then I will execute you on live television."

"I agree."

"Don't be hasty, Chase Jackson. The stakes cannot be higher. I do not hide your fate from you. You will die as the world watches."

"I know. I agree."

"Ah, young love. Never was a story of more woe. Does it matter that Katie does not want you to sacrifice for her? I know you will anyway. But her Shakespearian quote indicates she's at peace. She wants you to live. She loves you and she's ready to die."

"She will *not* die."

"You will surrender tomorrow night at…say, eleven? One hour before midnight?"

"Fine. You will not harm her."

"You have my word. No suffering. Speaking of suffering, how is my old friend Carter? I thought we had him, and then he simply vanished. You assisted him, I presume."

I hung up. The phone vibrated instantly with an incoming call.

"Dude," Puck said. "Dude. I have no words. Whoa. I'm…I'm so sorry. I have no idea how he got his hands on her."

"Not your fault."

"You won't actually…let yourself be executed. Right?"

It took me a second to recognize what was abnormal about this phone call. The absence of typing. Puck wasn't working his keyboard. Only talking. I said, "I don't know. But Puck. Don't tell Samantha. Or Lee. Or anyone. Especially not Dad. Give me a chance to think. Okay?"

"Sure, Outlaw, you got it. Anything."

"I want…I just need to…to process this. Okay?"

"Yes. Definitely. That computes."

"Okay."

"Okay."

I put the phone away.

And experienced a blast of raw loneliness. Pure existence, in all its terror and unfairness.

Not Katie. Anyone but Katie.

Chapter Twenty-Seven
Saturday, February 10. 2019
Samantha Gear

Richard and I sat on the hood of my truck and drank beer at dusk. From our view on the rise in his neighborhood, we watched the sun set behind towers nine miles distant. Chase was still in there. Somewhere.

Beer didn't affect me like it did Richard. Or like anyone normal. My body metabolized alcohol as soon the blood stream absorbed it. I experience a slight lessening of tension, but that was the fullest extent. I drank anyway because the benefits went beyond corporeal. Cracking open full cans and crushing empty ones and the implicit lowering of defenses tended to bond humans in unseen ways. It acted as glue. So weird. But I doubted that's why Richard bought a six pack. He drank because his boy was missing.

His phone buzzed a lot. It grabbed his attention briefly but he didn't answer. It was never Chase.

"Don't you guys have software that track each other's phone?" he asked.

"Yes. But his phone is off."

"Right," he sighed heavily. "I keep forgetting."

"Puck said he's sleeping. I'm sure he's fine." Chase *had* to be fine. Because I felt great. Like a brand new human. I'd showered for the first time in…hell, I don't know. Clean clothes. Clean hair. Clean teeth. The only thing missing was the Outlaw.

He continued, "No word from Chase. Or Katie. Or Special Agent

Anderson. Or the bald guy." He waved a hand vaguely indicating he'd forgotten the name.

"Carter."

"Or from Carter. Something's wrong. I *feel* it."

I finished my second can and collapsed it in my fist until it shrunk to a small warm ball of aluminum. "His wounds are significant. They'll take several days to heal."

He lowered his head into his beefy hands and took several deep breaths. Oops. I forgot. Parents care about their kids. He said, "Describe them for me again."

"Richard, probably better not to dwell. Besides, I-"

"Samy. Please tell me."

I patted him on the back. Because that's what nice people do. At least in the movies. "Okay. But remember, I wasn't there to see exactly what happened."

"Where were you?"

"On some rooftop, watching the helicopter disaster. Chase played defense. Have you seen the handheld blades the Chosen use?"

"Look like Wolverine's claws."

"Yeah, kinda. Based on his appearance, I'd guess Chase took a slash to his neck, and one to his abdomen. Near his...left kidney. Deep cuts, judging by blood loss."

"And those will heal?"

"Yes. Should."

"Why do these blades penetrate?" he asked. "Bullets burrow into your skin without piercing, correct? What's the difference?"

"Small caliber slugs don't pierce if they hit muscle. You're correct. Assuming our skin is hard. I think the metal is sharp enough to slice through, while a bullet relies on impact and brute force. Skin and muscle can absorb and redistribute the force, but not so with a knife blade."

He placed a trembling hand on my knee and squeezed. "You told me once he could...command them? The Chosen? Like they couldn't think straight, but they'd obey him."

"Think of it like a momma bear with her cubs. She's in charge, but…the cubs don't always do as they're told. And speaking of bears, when is the last time you shaved?"

He chuckled and ran fingers over bristles along his jaw. "Been a while. No time. Over half the force is gone."

"Gone? Gone where?"

"To greener pastures."

"They just *left*?!"

"Look around." He indicated the neighborhood. I hadn't noticed before. Two cars and twenty empty driveways in sight. Zero traffic. No children laughing. "Everyone is leaving. More every day. We're too close. Cops have families too."

I protested, "Yeah, but they're outside the barricade."

"The barricade is mostly abandoned. A leaky sieve. Only one out of every three stations is manned. And have you seen what those…freaks can do?"

"I have."

"Did you see the mall footage? The two Chosen that got into the shopping center?"

"Oh god. No. What happened?"

"Everything. It's as bad as you can imagine."

"How many people died?"

He shrugged, an unhappy bunching of his shoulders. "Still don't know. The two Chosen had nails like razors, and…" His voice caught. "It'll be months before all the carnage is cleaned."

"Carter told me once about nails like those. Happens to girls with long fingernails in their late adolescence."

"What now? How do we fight this?"

"I'm going back downtown in a couple days. Finish what we started. My hope is still in Chase. In the Outlaw."

"If Chase's still alive.".

"He's alive. I wish you knew how special he is, Richard. I mean, you know. But I know in a different way than you do. He's light-years ahead of the curve. So advanced. He's the only one of us that operates out of selflessness. The rest of us are mean and suspicious and live out of survival and greed. Not him. Only Chase is strong enough to resist the disease, to think about others, to protect the innocent. Chase is the eye of the storm, and we just swirl around him. He's alive. Which means we've got a chance."

Chapter Twenty-Eight
Sunday, February 11. 2019
PuckDaddy

Fox News was broadcasting the President's walk to Marine One on the south lawn. Where is Blue-Eyes? There. There she is, the bitch. The crazy hot bitch.

Mental note. Check the President's itinerary. Find out where he's going.

Incoming texts from Zealot. Weird. Haven't heard from him in a while. Still in Africa, weirdo? Better stay there, bro. America getting crazy.

Yawn. Big yaaaaawwwwwn. Kinda tired. Need to rest soon. Where are we? I swiveled to glance out the window behind me. It's morning? Where *does* the time go.

I texted my driver. **yo!! where r we? running low on supplies. stock up in next twenty-four hours homie**

I could look up our location myself. But I like having servants.

Okay. Back to debugging. Stupid code. Stupid stupid beautiful code. The iPhone's sandboxing methodology is SUCH an irritation. If only everyone was stupid enough to jailbreak their phone, my life would get a lot easier. Samsung got the right idea. Basically an open door…There! There's my mistake. Bah. MINUTES wasted looking for that extra digit.

Still no text from the Outlaw?

Don't think about it. Don't think about it.

>> We're skirting Bakersfield, sir.
k thanks
u better not be texting n driving

that junks real
o and don't forget poptarts
puckdaddy hungers

Incoming texts. From Carter's beta security team, infiltrating Atlanta's CDC headquarters. CDC was operating as the nation's hotspot right now, working in conjunction with the FBI to find solutions to Hyper Humanity. I'd commissioned Carter's secondary team to place phreaking devices which would speed up my long-distance observations.

Looking good, looking good. Window of CDC security deactivation is GO. Atta boys.

I'm SUCH a baller.

I had a half gig of digital military reports to read, staying abreast of the constant and radical changes taking place at the speed of sound within the government. One thing was for certain; the United States of America would be in a state of civil war soon. How big and bad was yet to be determined.

France wasn't far behind. Trying to cover up the existence of freaks. Of Chosen. But the freaks were in Paris. And London. And Germany. And Russia. And China. Not an infestation, like America. But still. Chaos would soon reign.

Chaos. Carter's speciality.

If he EVER woke up.

My screen blipped. Facial recognition software. Such a powerful program, but MAN it ate the batteries and cycles. Worth it, though. Totally worth it.

Who'd we find? Walter. We found Walter. At a traffic light in a Humvee with his crew. Wearing his shades. Always his shades, which is why I located him easier than others. In…where was he? San Jose??! He was in Los Angeles twelve hours ago!

Might be able to isolate his cell signal now. Doubtful. But maybe. PuckDaddy leaps buildings in a single bound!

Walter, what a barbarian. That dude HATES the Chemist. Hates hates hates him. Never wants to be in the same city. I intercepted eleven of Walter's texts last month between phone transfers. High comedy.

Surprised the Chemist let him leave. Tonight is a big night, after all, right? Tonight. Holy crap, *tonight*.

Don't think about it. Don't think about it.

If Chase dies…

Chase was my best friend. Kinda my only friend. Everyone else acted as a co-worker. I was their operator, essentially, but not a friend. Shooter had gotten nicer recently. Like she learned how to be a friend by watching Chase.

My RV hit a pothole or something. All the monitors swayed and my chair creaked. Something had been rolling around the floor behind me for days. I'd get around to picking it up. Sometime. Probably a can of soda.

If Chase dies…then what?

I might just activate the explosives attached to the fuel tank. We'd all be dead anyway.

Phone call. From Captain FBI. I activated my headset.

"What's up, FBI," I said. "You talk with the Outlaw?"

"Just hung up."

"What'd he think of our plan?"

"He hated it." His mic blasted with noise, like he exhaled all his air in frustration. "Sounds like he *wants* to die. There's got to be other options."

"The Chemist isn't giving us enough time to plan, dummy."

"Katie is great. I get it. She's the best. But…"

"Would you sacrifice yourself to save Natalie North?" I asked.

"Of course. Or any American civilian. But this is different. The *planet* depends on him."

"Not much we can do. He's going up there. We can either take advantage of it, or not."

"I've exhausted resources worth ten million just to keep him alive…"

A long pause. During which we both calculated risks and odds and responsibilities. While I waited and calculated, I was also scanning webpages at the speed of one per second. He asked, "Are you positive you can launch those rockets?"

I answered, "I can't *activate* them. Not even mighty PuckDaddy can remotely crank the engine. But if the rockets are activated, I can enter coordinates and launch."

"How?"

"In addition to my other responsibilities, Puck acts as an off-sight consultant for several weapon manufacturers. I've built backdoors in…in a lot of stuff."

"It's treason. On a grand scale. Launching American missiles at Americans on American soil. At the frickin' Outlaw, for Christ's sake. It's a big damn deal. They'll invent new ways to hang us."

I probed my neck experimentally. "Wonder if that would work."

"Innocent civilians might die."

"Yeah," I admitted. "I bet Chase didn't like that part much. He's not quite as…cold and logical as the rest of us."

"The governmental infighting has been skirmishes between military forces. Until now. This is something else entirely."

I shook my head and opened the mini-fridge under my desk. Empty. Gah. Times like this call for Mountain Dew. "Won't matter if we can't activate that rocket launcher."

"My strike team is ready to deploy. We'll activate. If you're looking for a HIMAR system, Los Alamitos has several trucks."

"Okay. Lemme check. Stand by…" I started flying through systems and reports. "After you activate the power, will you be arrested?"

"Possibly. We don't plan to remain on-sight and find out."

"Okay. Okay. Here it is…let's see…four MTVs, two of which carry the HIMAR. Both armed with rockets instead of the big ATACM missile."

"Perfect." A pause. "Perfect. That's all we need."

"Sure you want to do this?"

"Hell no I'm not sure. I want Chase to behead that guy and go home."

"He refuses," I grumbled. "Says violence can't win this war."

"Then what are we doing with these rockets?"

"This was YOUR idea!" I practically shouted.

"We're the only two with the intel! Only we know he's dying tonight! If we can't talk him out of it, we can at least blow the Chemist to the gates of hell." His voice sounded feverish, off kilter, like he'd been trouble-shooting the same software for forty-eight hours straight.

I moaned, "Carter says the Chemist can hear rockets anyway. This won't work."

"Not if he's busy with Chase. He might not be listening."

"Uuuuuugh. This sucks. So much."

He laughed, a soft throaty sound. "So much. I'm planning to start a civil war with help from PuckDaddy, a man the FBI's Cyber Division has spent millions trying to apprehend."

"I always thought that group was cute. I even left them clues."

"Where do you live, out of curiosity?"

I grinned, my cheek brushing against the mic. "Screw you."

"Puck, all kidding aside, if it's discovered that you launched the missiles, you'll be as wanted a man as the Chemist. There will be no safe places left for you."

"Nah. I'm not worried."

"You should be."

I leaned against the chair to stretch my lower back, and stared at one screen in particular with bleary eyes. It was a masterpiece. "I already got it solved, homie. If we launch those rockets, I can make it look like the order originated from within the White House."

Chapter Twenty-Nine
Sunday, February 11. 2019

The big cat was back. I felt him. Like he was radioactive and I possessed an internal geiger counter. He paced back and forth beyond the metal barrier, testing the air, searching. I tuned into his movements and detected soft footfalls and heavy breaths.

We couldn't see each other which diminished the primal exchange of information. But I knew his hate had dissipated. His presence was exploratory. Carter and I didn't smell like the Father. Or like the Chosen. Or normal human bodies. So what the heck were we?

How could I explain to Katie how big these animals were? In dimensions he appeared about the size of car. Not as tall as me, but wider. Maybe weighed a thousand pounds. What sick surgeries had the Chemist performed on the tigers? And how many more did he have? If Puck and Anderson wanted to fire rockets, these man-eating tigers would be an acceptable target. As sad as that was.

What Puck and Isaac Anderson didn't understand was that this wasn't a battle to break the Chemist's body. But to break his heart.

I knew of no other path to victory. And after watching Miss Pauline change her community, I'd decided perhaps no other paths should be considered. The Chemist *had* to be stopped. Unequivocally and aggressively stopped. But breaking his body wouldn't cause the cessation of his evil. We needed the Chemist to do that himself. Lo and behold, he'd presented me with the opportunity to convince him.

He didn't want me to die. That thunderbolt of a realization kept hammering me. He practically tried to talk me out of it.

Don't be so hasty.

The stakes cannot be higher.

Doesn't it matter that she doesn't want you to die?

She wants you to live!

Don't let me kill you, he seemed to say.

Katie. Why did he capture Katie if his plan isn't to execute me?

Because…he wants me to show up. He wants me to break my promise. To fight. To lose. In front of a global television audience. And then to be his captive, soon to be brainwashed.

He needs the drama. He needs me to discredit myself. Needs me to be the villain. Needs me to be weak, like him. *See*, he'll tell the world. See?! He's a liar! The Outlaw is a coward! He can't even sacrifice himself!

I would lose if I fought. And so would everyone rooting for me. He couldn't be beat. Not when he was expecting the battle. Evil can't drive out evil. I couldn't know for sure but I bet it hadn't occurred to him I even *could* keep my end of the bargain. Warriors don't lay down their lives! Kings don't sacrifice!

He was wrong.

He didn't know love. No one loved him.

I would show him love. Show him I loved another human being enough to die. I would express it to the fullest measure. And in doing so, show him I thought he was worth bargaining with. And worth my kept promise. And it would break his heart.

Or else he'd totally kill me. That could happen too. But I doubted it. Not after watching Miss Pauline. Which is why I told Puck and Anderson NO ROCKETS! It would undermine everything.

I expected to live through the night. But just in case, I'd typed messages Puck would deliver to everyone I cared about. Especially Katie.

He'd never deliver those messages though. That's what I kept telling myself. I'd lay down my life and it would work. The Chemist wouldn't be able to follow through with his threat. He'd be broken by the willing sacrifice. He'd be shattered. He'd stop this crusade. That's what we needed most. We needed our enemy to voluntarily lay down his weapons. To renounce evil. We didn't need more violence. The problem had grown too big. We need a fresh beginning. Reconciliation. And it had to start with him. Tonight.

From outside my storage unit, the tiger snarled. More like a cough. A warning? Then a voice. A human voice. I hurt too much to fight. Or run. Speaking of running, whoever owned that voice should run. Or get bit in half. A man's voice. Echoing off metal doors. Softly at first, then growing close. "What is it, boy? What have you found?"

Not a man's voice. A woman's. A husky rasp. Even muted by metal, I knew it. I stood from my chair with a silent groan and backed further into the dark storage unit.

"Why are you back here?" Hannah Walker asked the big cat. "Is this where you live?"

I stumbled on Carter's bed. Carter. Still asleep. I sat on the bed with him and pressed my back against the far wall. Maybe our scents would mingle. He was sweating still. Now I was too. A cold sweat, trickles instantly running down my back.

Hannah Walker. Not here. Not now.

Samantha told me that Carter and Pacific could restrain their aura. They could flex, and they could restrain. But how did they do that? I concentrated my whole being on silence. I didn't exist. I became a hole. An empty space. A nothing. I hope.

Was the tiger...purring? I couldn't see them, but in my mind's eye she was scratching the cat's ears and neck and in return receiving a pleased, soft rumble. Of COURSE the tigers loved her and hated me! It made perfect sense; nothing else was going right.

At my door, directly outside. "Did you find something? Such a good boy. Where are your friends? Do you sleep here? My big boy."

The rolling door wasn't locked. Not that it would matter if she wanted to get in. But she might notice this unit had been opened. She might notice footprints in the dust. I was weak. Wrecked. Unable to resist her.

"You'll find Chase. I know you will. The Father said you would. Such a big, big, handsome, good, sweet boy. I want to take you home. Want to sleep in my room? Want to come with me? Want to go looking for Chase? Let's get you something to eat. Come on. Come on! Good boy. Good booooy."

The sounds retreated. Hannah Walker walked back out of the building, tiger in tow. Going. Going. Gone. My heart hammered, pulsing painfully in my wounds. That was close. Close to disaster.

I needed food. Chocolate. Suddenly famished. Only food enough for a few more meals. But that'd suffice. I'd eat once more and leave the rest for Carter. Quietly and stiffly I dug out the last chocolate bar and a bag of peanuts.

Puck texted me.

>> bad news outlaw
>> teresa triplett (the reporter) just updated her blog
>> she's still a captive
>> she announced the live streaming execution 2night
>> Execution of an Outlaw, she called it
>> the...poop is hitting the fan

He was right. Incoming calls and texts lit up my phones, both Chase Jackson's phone and the Outlaw's.

Dad. Samantha. Lee. Isaac. Russia. Natalie North. Former teammates. Numbers I didn't recognize. Samantha again. And again.

My eyes unexpectedly filled with tears. I would receive no message from Cory.

Puck, I'm turning off my phone.
Tell them I love them.
And tonight, love will win.
And if it doesn't...I tried. For them.

I powered the phone off.

Chapter Thirty
Sunday, February 11. 2019
Kid

10:55 pm.

Five minutes to go.

I shook like a leaf. Partially from chilly winds whipping through the exposed steel beams. Partially from adrenaline and terror. But mostly from a deep, profound sadness.

Now that I stood atop the Wilshire, I understood why the Father chose it. At 1,100 feet, this tower reached further towards the moon than its peers. Impossible for snipers to get a shot. Harder for the American military to get photos from the ground. The lengthy, monolithic sides were glass and unscalable. Up here, he reigned with impunity.

The recent helicopter attack had wrecked much of the upper levels, which worked to our advantage. The Father had hidden equipment here among the destruction and no one knew. Not even me, until an hour ago when preparations began in earnest.

Three stationary cameras were mounted and filming, and banks of lights blasted the night into oblivion. Everything centered around the expansive and shallow rooftop pool, empty except for the tall object inside, still covered by sheets. One end of the pool had been crushed by rockets, so it was a large rectangle without a fourth wall, open to the air. The mysterious object had been set near the missing wall, dangerously close to the exposed drop off. One wrong step and I'd fall a thousand feet. But that wasn't what worried me. I couldn't even look at the dreadful thing covered with red sheets. I didn't know. I didn't *want* to know. An instrument of death.

Teresa Triplett, the pretty reporter, sat in the corner with a laptop and chronicled everything she saw. She remained out of the light, out of view, because she couldn't stop crying. She'd ruin the perfect broadcast.

A dozen Twice Chosen stood with us, here to work cameras and aid in theatrics. And for protection. The hands of six Twice Chosen glinted with long slivers of steel, talons sharpened with lasers and capable of splitting a human hair. The Father, despite his mania and apparent glee, was nervous. He shivered too, just like me.

"What if it's a trap?" I asked.

"Of course it is," the Father snapped, his teeth chattering. "He comes to kill me, nothing else."

"You will let him?"

"Don't be dense," he said. "He will fight. He will be humiliated. He will be maimed. And then…"

"And then?" I asked, realizing too late he was quietly crying. Oh wow. Oh wow.

"And then he will be *mine*."

"What if he arrives with explosives?"

"Then I slowly kill the girl until he discards them. Honestly, Kid. When I contemplate your deep stupidity, I'm forced to miss Carla. Her treachery may be more desirous than your idiocy."

"What if he doesn't show?"

Another sigh. "Then he is humiliated. Exposed as a coward. And we televise her slow death, forcing his appearance. But he will show. Now hush."

"What if the military drops a big bomb on us?"

For a moment I thought he would hit me. He thought about it. But the moment passed. "That depends. If the Outlaw is present when the bomb drops then perhaps…perhaps I will die with him. Of my own volition."

"Why??" I gasped.

"I'm not sure. It strikes me as poetic. Now, Kid, if you speak again, I'm going to slit your throat."

I did not speak again.

Please don't die, Outlaw. Please don't die.

Someone has to kill the Father. Someone brave.

The seconds ticked by, ticking ticking ticking. The world was shrinking to the size of a snow globe, nonexistent outside our circle of artificial light. I felt like we were quickly using up the universe's remaining oxygen and I gulped mouthfuls to stave off lightheadedness.

At 11:00 pm, the Father snorted air from his noise like a bull, left his place outside the light and moved towards the pool. As per my orders, I followed him into the glare. He moved down the concrete steps, now in full view of the active cameras.

The Outlaw got there first. He fell from the sky, pulled by something beyond gravity, like a comet descending out of orbit. He landed and the tower shook. Which was impossible. But it did. The Father rocked back in surprise. The upper crust of the pool's cement cracked with the impact. Of our dozen Twice Chosen, exactly half turned and fled. So powerful was his entrance, his presence, that they simply couldn't withstand it.

He towered over us, body fully engorged as it often became in times of stress. He took up space in ways that made no sense. His skin was striated with muscles and rivers of dried blood. He was immense. He was magnificent.

He wore no mask and the full collision of his gaze shattered me. I staggered. Put your mask on, I almost begged. Too intense. The mask shields *us* from *you*! He looked at the Twice Chosen and three more retreated shamelessly. Turned and ran, abandoning steel weapons. What would it be like to experience the Outlaw if I didn't have the disease? I felt like I was being mildly electrocuted, like he created a constant thunderstorm. Surely not everyone felt that.

The Father was holding his breath. His hands tightened on the staff. Today, for the first time I could remember, he wore gloves. Expecting fierce combat. Now he laughed, "He plunges from the heavens like a god! Such an entrance!"

The Outlaw glared at the cameras, at the lights, at me, and at the Father. "Let her go."

The Father nodded to me. I nearly fainted. On unsteady legs I left his side and approached the Outlaw. He watched me with no interest. Not unkindly. He'd never been unkind to me. In fact, at every opportunity he'd tried to rescue me. He allowed me to pat his legs and boots and vest.

"You may leave him his weapon," the Father called, indicating the rod shoved into the back of the Outlaw's vest.

Other than two phones in his pocket, I found only one thing of interest. Tubes were shoved into small vest compartments. I removed one tube and examined it.

"Pepper spray," the Father laughed when I presented it to him. "I can smell it. This is how you arm yourself?" He shook the small canister and tossed it from the tower. It wouldn't land for a long time.

"I'm here to die, Martin," the Outlaw responded. His voice was strong and frank, as opposed to the Father's fluted, overly formal tones. "Prove to me Katie is alive and free."

The Father indicated the cameras. "First, dear boy, a few preliminaries. For the sake of our viewing audience. For the sake of your jury. You are here to pay penance for your sins. You are found guilty of disturbing the peace, of crimes against humanity, against me, of defiance, of insubordination, of murder, lying, deceiving the good people of America. Of the earth. Shall I go on?"

The Outlaw stood as a rock. No reply. No expression.

"By surrendering tonight, you admit your guilt. You place yourself into my custody. Under my authority. Under my discipline. Under my judgement." The Father paused to allow the Outlaw a chance to speak. Silence. "Have you nothing to say, Outlaw?"

"I'm not here as the Outlaw. I'm here as Chase Jackson, a boy who loves a girl you kidnapped. Release her. And take me in her place."

The Father blanched. For a brief moment, he floundered. This wasn't going according to plan. He wanted the Outlaw enraged. Out of control. Wild. Disrespectful. Combative.

He continued, "Release her. I'll confirm her safety. And then…do what you need to do."

The Father chuckled. "You will not run."

"I will not. I'm getting the better end of our bargain."

"Very well." The Father raised a radio, with fingers clearly shaking. He spoke into it. "Katie Lopez is to be released immediately."

The Outlaw asked, "Where?"

"She shall be driven north on Grand, out of my Sanctuary, and delivered to a place of your choosing."

Below us, far far below, an ambulance began to wail. The Outlaw searched us for meaning, for clues. "She's in an ambulance?"

"Yes."

"Why? Why an ambulance?"

"It's perfectly safe."

The Outlaw made a phone call and put it on speaker. Ringing. Someone answered. "Outlaw! Holy...you're calling me now?! If the Chemist doesn't kill you, I will!"

"Samantha," he said calmly. "I need you to drive to the northern barricade."

"I'm already here, waiting on a helicopter."

"Stay there. An ambulance is driving Katie out. Please intercept it and confirm Katie's safety."

"No! Not if it means you're going to die!" the voice roared.

The Father cackled but it was fake. False bravado.

"Thank you, Samantha. Call me when you have her, please." He hung up.

Then began the longest eight minutes of my life. And possibly of the Outlaw's. Of Chase Jackson's. The siren faded into the distance, lost in high swirling vicissitudes. He remained stoic but his eyes leaked in desperation. I'd never seen a man my age care so much about someone else. He couldn't be older than nineteen. How could this girl mean so much? The Father tried baiting him into conversation but was rebuffed with wintery silence. Somehow, someway, the Father had lost control of this engagement.

"I should tell you," he said as time drew near, "that Katie Lopez is not alone. I released a physician to accompany her. Doctor Whitmer, one of the world's foremost neurobiologists and surgeons, is in the ambulance also."

This new piece of information was almost too much. Chase came closer to panicking. "Why? Why does she need a doctor?"

"Just to be safe."

His phone rang. He answered it on speaker. "Samantha," he said. His voice thickened with emotion. "Give me good news."

The voice which answered was panting and rattled. "I checked the vehicle. There's no explosives. Katie is here. She's unconscious. She's being attended by a physician."

"Why is she-"

The voice continued, "She's safe. She's alive. But Chase...ugh, I'm sorry. It...it looks like the Chemist performed the same surgery on her that he did on Andy Babington."

The phone exploded in the Outlaw's fist. Veins throbbed in his neck and arms. His body trembled and purpled. "That wasn't part of the deal," he thundered in quiet, awful agony. "Why did...why...*why*??"

"She has not suffered," the Father responded pleasantly. "Not in the least. And your friend Samantha is wrong. It is not the same surgery. This one is far, far more advanced. Doctor Whitmer will keep her asleep for months, and she will awaken as a new being. A god. A goddess who will live for hundreds of years. Not that you'll be around to see it." His smile widened in wicked antagonism.

For a moment, we stood on the edge of a knife. The Outlaw raged inwardly. He fumed and cried. The Father tensed for glorious battle. This had been the final straw. The last torment necessary to tip the Outlaw into blind wrath. Chase shook his head back and forth, like a dog killing the prey within his jaws. In addition to all his other battles, the Outlaw also wrestled with insanity. "You. Should not. Have done that. She'd done nothing wrong. Nothing...nothing..."

The Father moved his staff off the ground, balanced in both fists, ready to defend.

Then, slowly, the moment of crisis passed. The Outlaw crossed through every violent, painful human emotion and emerged on the other side in tact. He took deep breaths and wiped away tears. "Okay," he said. "Okay."

"Okay *what*, Outlaw? Ready to spring your trap?"

"A deal is a deal. I surrender."

Chapter Thirty-One
Sunday, February 11. 2019
PuckDaddy

I called Captain FBI. "Anderson, you watching this?"

"Affirmative. Streaming live on my phone. Like seven billion other people."

My heart was overheating. Brain running too fast, verging on overload. "Chase isn't going to fight! The Chemist is going to kill him."

On screen, one of the Chemist's henchmen approached that weird, tall *thing* in the empty pool. I recognized that henchman. He was Infected. Chase called him Baby Face. The henchman grabbed a fistful of red sheets and tugged. The covers slid off to reveal the contraption.

Oh crud. That really sucks.

The Chemist beamed in triumph. The Outlaw didn't react.

Isaac was in my ear and he asked, "Ready for activation?"

"Light'em up, baby. Let's kill that bastard."

Three hundred miles away, Isaac Anderson and his faithful team turned on the HIMAR system and fed power to the rockets. My screen instantly populated with controls and diagnostics and information. Propelled death at my fingertips.

"Activated."

"Bingo!" I shouted. "I've got clearance."

I heard new noises through my headset. A strident blare and urgent voices.

He said, "We're retreating, Puck. Alarms going off. You've got…five minutes? Before Colonel Brown kills your launch."

"I only need two."

Chapter Thirty-Two
Sunday, February 11. 2019

There's only so many ways to kill an angry Infected. The simplest are fire, water, and electricity.

I'd been expecting electricity. I was wrong.

Baby Face pulled the sheets off, like revealing a statue. But it wasn't a statue. It was a tall submersion tank filled with water. The device reminded me of a magician's act I'd seen; the magician went into the chamber and we watched through transparent walls as he undid handcuffs before running out of oxygen.

I should have guessed. The Chemist craved drama. Craved an audience. Slowly drowning me for three minutes was perfect. The tank had a hydraulic cap that would seal me in.

"Turn, Outlaw. And look upon thy death."

He was quoting Shakespeare. Because he knew Katie and I did. I could hardly hear him over the rush in my ears.

Don't watch this, Dad. Someone take his phone away.

My plan, so far, wasn't working. He was shaken. I could tell in a thousand ways. But still he proceeded.

"For the crimes aforementioned, Outlaw, I sentence you to immediate death by drowning. You will enter the water and stay until dead."

My voice operated on its own. "Very well."

"Have you any last words?"

"Yes." I approached him. He flexed, prepared for the expectant trap. But there was none. I stood close. He wanted great television, he got it. "I forgive you."

No response, other than a spark of disbelief far down the well of his irises.

I continued, "I forgive you for capturing Katie. For destroying my home. For destroying Los Angeles. For destroying me. We weren't meant to live this long. And it's hurt you. You're weary and exhausted and lonely and scared and angry, and I know, and I forgive you."

"You...*forgive* me?" he spat the words and flecks of his spittle landed on my face. He laughed, a forced choking sound. "You don't GET to forgive me!" He struck. He swung the staff so fast it broke the sound barrier like a whip.

I caught it in my one working hand, a sound like iron bars colliding. The other still didn't flex well. The impact rang both our bones near the point of shatter. He winced in pain. In horror. In fury.

"I'm done fighting with you," I hissed. "I'm done dancing on your strings. You don't get to take my life. I *give* it to you."

I shoved the staff back at him and went to the tank.

"You don't forgive *me*! You are not the judge!" he screamed. Behind the tank, I saw chains and medical equipment. He'd anticipated fighting me, hurting me, subduing me, and knocking me unconscious with his drugs. I ascended the ladder. The tank was thick and heavy and the cold water sloshed over. "You don't willing go to your death! I SEND you to it! I send you into the tank!"

His plans were spiraling. His motions frantic. I sat on the tank's ridge, eight feet off the ground, and lowered my boots into the water. I transferred the phone from my pants pocket to a watertight compartment in my vest. I said, "Not to sound corny, Martin. But I wish I had more lives to sacrifice for the people I love. You can't take from me that which I willingly give away."

"Oh! OH! You believe you're a martyr??" he howled, tears streaming down the wrinkles of his face. "You think your death will provide...some sort of catalyst? You amuse me, boy. This death is too good for you. Come down and fight, if you're a man."

"You're in no position to name-call, Martin. The whole world is watching and realizing you're just a bully. And a sad one."

"You. Will. Die!" He slammed a button on the tank's control panel. The heavy metal lid rotated upwards with an electric whine.

I still believed in my plan. Still held out hope for success. But I was afraid. The kind of fear which shocks your mind into awareness and perspective. I felt the weight of a world watching. I keenly recognized my existence. I tasted the air and enjoyed the inflation of my lungs, the thump of my heart beat, the crystal stars and the wind stinging my eyes.

I took one deep breath, two, three, and plunged into the tank. The lid closed and sealed itself automatically.

How long can Infected hold their breath? Probably longer than normal.

It was like sitting in a fish tank. The lid and water blocked out much of the light. The world beyond appeared as warped penumbra. He screamed. Or laughed. The sound came from miles away and reached my eardrums wholly muted and distorted. I saw him as a malformed shadow, flickering back and forth. Whump! Whump! He beat his hand flat against the outside wall.

The fear vanished, left outside in the oxygen. I was already dead. So many people had died already. I was no better a man than them. And perhaps mine would be meaningful. There was freedom in giving your complete self to a righteous cause, in sacrificing for others.

Still. I hoped he changed his mind. Quickly.

The tank's large dimensions allowed me to sit criss-cross on the floor. The rod in my vest counteracted the air in my lungs and kept me pinned to the bottom. I pressed my face to the wall and peered out. Whump! Whump!

Tables had turned. It was no longer the Outlaw on trial and facing judgement; it was the Chemist. He fumed and stalked back and forth, aware billions were witnessing him slowly execute an innocent man. He'd desired combat, not sacrifice. But what could he do? He was stuck. Martin knew this constituted catastrophe. The world had been scared of him. This would change everything. Now they'd hate him.

Sixty seconds passed. My blood flowed freely without any strain yet. He'd fallen silent and motionless, all his bluster and pride exhausted. As my death neared, his shoulders slumped further.

He collapsed onto the pool floor and pressed his forehead to the tank wall, exactly mirroring me. He spoke. I couldn't hear him. Must be whispering. But I could read his lips.

Why?

Why do you do this?

I don't understand.

Chapter Thirty-Three
Saturday, February 11. 2019
PuckDaddy

I wept loudly. Painful sobs tightening my whole body in iterations. My driver heard the noise and pulled over. I told him to leave me alone.

PuckDaddy cries alone!

I couldn't stop staring at the screen. Chase sat in that awful chamber, his head angled down, arms across his midsection, eyes half-closed. He'd been in there two minutes! Was he already dead? The Chemist sat across from Chase. Taunting him? Maybe. The camera mics picked up indecipherable whispers. This didn't look good for him. This was a PR nightmare.

Can't do it. I can't launch the rockets.

I tried. I tried sixty seconds after Chase jumped in. Tried after ninety seconds. It wasn't an electrical or mechanical malfunction. My heart couldn't bear the responsibility. My fingers became defiant. And my brain couldn't overcome their rebellion.

I refused to turn off the monitor. Chase wouldn't die alone. PuckDaddy would be with the Outlaw until the end. As best he could.

On an adjacent screen, a warning light switched on. I almost didn't notice. The HIMAR system. It was being operated.

Go ahead, Colonel Brown. Shut it off. I don't have the fortitude to commit treason and kill my best friend. Not today.

But no. This wasn't Colonel Brown. Who in the world...?

On the television monitor, the Chemist stood up. We could see his face for the first time. His jaw was set. His eyes glistened.

Back to the computer screen. The HIMAR system wasn't being deactivated. Coordinates entered from a third party, a remote log-in. Like me. That could only be... A firing code entered! My eyes widened in surprise.

Three hundred miles away, at Los Alamitos, the night would be shattering with light and fire. The heavy truck recoiling against solid fuel ignitions as its payload, guided projectiles, screamed off into the Los Angeles night.

A dozen Successful Launch messages appeared on my screen. Rockets inflight.

I verified their target; Wilshire Tower.

Chase.

Chapter Thirty-Four
February 11, 2019.

At the foundation of my awareness , some subconscious clock informed me that two minutes had passed. My lungs hurt now. Instead of too little air, I felt like I had too much. My lungs threatened to burst. Increasingly hard to fight instincts to breathe, to surface and inhale.

My vision swam. The Chemist became harder to hold in focus. He'd been whispering forever. For my whole life. The man across was crushed. Utterly defeated. He'd aged twenty years.

Stop, he whispered.

Stop this.

Please come out of there.

Please.

...

No more.

Okay.

Okay. I get it.

You win.

You win.

I struggled to make sense of this. My eyes had been partially closed, zeroed on his lips. I glanced upwards to his eyes. He nodded and smiled grimly. A man who'd made a decision. A flood of information passed in that instant. He couldn't win. Couldn't let me die. He knew it. He would surrender. And he appeared relieved to admit defeat.

He stood. Readjusted his grip on the staff. He was going to shatter the tank!

I pushed away from the slippery wall with limbs barely responsive. All clarity from the outside world washed away. He melted into a watery blur.

My back against the far wall, I waited for the crash. Lungs aflame.

Beyond the arc of my aquarium, now twenty-four inches distant, something happened. Blurs flashed. Faint noise. No crash.

Realization dawned; a scenario worse than any I'd dreamed up was occurring. A precise and perfect disaster.

"Nooooooooo!" I roared, a rush of bubbles, using the remnant of my oxygen.

Chapter Thirty-Five
Saturday, February 11. 2019
Kid

It was not the Outlaw who drowned. It was me.

He'd been in there for almost two minutes. The second hand of my watch moved with lazy torture. I hadn't drawn a breath since he went under. Close to collapse. Stars winked in my vision.

Voluntarily. The Outlaw *voluntarily* went in. I trembled with confusion. With despair.

Our only hope suffocated. On purpose. I was in pain from desperation. No one else could stop the Father. It had to be the Outlaw.

The Father kept whispering. I couldn't hear it all. "Okay." I heard that one. "Okay."

The Father stood.

I released my air with a blast and sucked in life. A luxury the Outlaw couldn't afford. With the fresh oxygen, my memories bore me back to the yacht again. I'd visited that memory so many times.

I had lain in the back of the yacht holding my broken shoulder while the lady drank wine and giggled. "Call me Minnie," she'd told me. The chaos, the broken plans, the unforeseen turn of events made her drunk. She laughed for an hour after Tank Ware and Katie Lopez escaped in my own raft. She was barely coherent. "You have the disease but you're not strong," she chirped. "Not mentally, at least. No wonder he picks on you. He bullies you.

My Martin. You'll have to kill him, you know." I couldn't respond. Too much pain. Climbing back onto her boat had nearly finished me. So I laid in the sun and dried and throbbed and listened. "But you can't. Not unless you crack his skull. By dropping a mountain on his head. Good luck with that!" she cackled.

He bullies you.

You'll have to kill him.

By cracking his skull.

Good luck with that.

I never commanded my body to move. Way too terrified for that. My muscles moved on their own, perhaps furious with my cowardice.

The Outlaw couldn't just *die*.

Before I knew it, I had the Father in my arms. He never saw me coming. Too surprised to resist. He was grotesquely thin, winnowed by centuries. A rebar skeleton.

He screamed and scrabbled at my hands, breaking the bones inside, but we were too close to the missing wall, to the precipice. The one side of the pool exposed to the night. I hefted the Father, Martin, the Chemist, the Scourge of the Planet, and leaped.

He fought me during the descent's entirety. Screaming I was an idiot. That I'd made a mistake. But I didn't care. I wasn't Kid any longer. I'd stood up to the bully. If I died (and I probably would) I would die as something other than a coward.

Drop a mountain on his skull, she had told me. I couldn't do that. But as it happened, he landed skull first on Figueroa Street.

Chapter Thirty-Six
Saturday, February 11. 2019

Blurs wrestling.

The blurs vanished.

I knew the details without seeing them clearly.

Over the edge. Gone. In a fit of violence, which he assumed would aid me, Baby Face betrayed and murdered the Chemist. And himself. Just as the Chemist had surrendered. Just as the sacrifice won. All the evil could have been undone. All the divisions could have begun reconciliation. Now…who knew?

I felt no relief at the Chemist's demise. Just a profound sense of loss. Of missed opportunity.

Of lightheadedness. I was near asphyxiation. Time to go.

A new face at the tank. A woman's. I pressed near. Teresa Triplett. The reporter. An angel with a brilliant liquid nimbus. I was too numb to be shocked. She shouted something. I heard the noise and read her lips.

The button is broken! He broke the button! It won't open!

The tank's cap wouldn't unlatch. The Chemist had punched it too hard. Maybe I could pop the top off. I braced my feet on the tube's bottom and *Jumped*. No use. Not even close. I possessed zero strength. And jumping through water allowed no applied force.

The world saw the Chemist fall. Help would arrive soon. Could I wait? No. Again, not even close. I had seconds.

I punched the glass. But it was curved and slippery and my hand simply squeaked across. I punched again to no effect. Teresa Triplett whacked the glass ineffectually with something. Whang! Whang! All it did was hurt my ears. I fumbled desperately for the Boom Stick but couldn't grasp it. No energy in any finger.

Then, from some other universe in which people existed, my pocket buzzed. I felt the vibration. Inside its water-tight compartment my cell had received a text message. Curiosity for that instant made me forget I was dying. I dug at the pocket with numb digits, pressed apart the plastic zipper and removed the phone. Pressed the home key and the screen turned on for a tenth of a second. Just a tenth of a second for seeping water to short-circuit the phone's motherboard. One brief burst of power. But that was enough. I saw the message from PuckDaddy.

>> INCOMING ROCKETS!!!!!

Incoming rockets. That jerk. I told him no rockets. My irritation registered like it was someone else's emotion. Distant. Unattached. I was dead anyway. Oh well.

Whang! Whang!

Except Teresa Triplett was up here. She would die. I had no way to convey her plight. And she'd never escape in time. That was sad. But I had no options.

No options. And no oxygen.

No oxygen.

Oxygen…

Oxygen! I had a canister of the stuff in my vest.

I patted my chest. Lee's tube was still there. The Chemist had taken the OC spray but left the oxygen. Don't confuse them, Lee joked. I groped and fished in the thin pockets. Pulled something out. A flashlight. Dropped it. Went groping again with unsympathetic fingers.

Got it! Carefully I removed a small blue can of pressurized air. Popped the top. The nozzle went into my mouth and I depressed the trigger with my tongue. Sweet, sweet, beautiful, delicious oxygen flooded my lungs. Filled them to the point of pain. My heavy mind cleared. Headache receded. It was probably imagination but the oxygen felt palpable as it circulated throughout my body. Another breath. Another explosion of life. Energy. Strength. Hope. One more deep inhalation and the canister gave out.

It was enough. Full power. I brought my knees to my face. My back against the rear wall. Boots flat on the front curvature of the tank. I pressed. Essentially doing a sideways squat. The glass didn't even resist. Starbursts appeared. The structure buckled. Great cracks opened at the upper and lower seams. The tube remained structurally intact but shattered into a mesh of slivers and chunks. Water gushed out like a dam breaking.

I easily pulled the Thunder Stick free. The water had emptied to my waist. I shoved the stick upwards and blasted open the hatch. I *Jumped* out and landed wetly beside Teresa Triplett. "Incoming missiles," I gasped, and we fled.

The rockets made a sizzling noise as they approached from the west. We reached the crest of the pool as the first struck. It released its payload like a punch, vaporizing a path through the upper levels of the Wilshire and coating everything with fire. The Wilshire Grand rang from peak to foundation.

We jumped into infinity as the second and third rocket detonated. And the fourth and fifth. The tower shuddered and swayed and was engulfed, rapid oxidation melting metal.

My parachute opened with a snap. The wall of heat thrust us up and away into the stars. Into clean air. The chute wasn't meant for two people. The impact would be significant. But we'd survive. We sliced in a wide arc over downtown Los Angeles, curving gently northwards. Towards the barricade. Towards everyone I loved.

Chapter Thirty-Seven
February - May. 2019

Katie's ambulance took us both to the UCLA Medical Center, just north of Santa Monica. Dr. Whitmer, an abducted surgeon living in captivity for the past eighteen months, clearly struggled with the tsunami of emotions experienced by all released hostages. Except he still had a job to do, a patient to preserve; he had assisted the Chemist with Katie's surgery and he felt responsible.

An hour later, at one in the morning, Dr. Whitmer, Dad, Katie's mom, Samantha and I gathered in the hospital room around Katie's bed. Her beautiful brown hair had been shaved off to allow for multiple surgeries. The sight of so many incisions nearly overcame Ms. Lopez. I knew the feeling. I bordered on nausea and violence. Katie could have been a corpse by appearances.

"Katie Lopez received a more thorough procedure than any previous patient," Dr. Whitmer explained. He was clearly exhausted and running on fumes. Four other physicians stood in the room with us taking notes. "She was given a full blood transfusion yesterday. In other words, every drop of blood in her body was produced initially by the Father."

"By the Chemist," I said.

"Correct. He never allowed me a chance to examine his illness. But whatever *it* is, she now has. The Father...err, the Chemist is a truly gifted physician and neurosurgeon. Was. *Was* gifted. He grafted stem cell transplants into the muscle tissue and bone marrow of each appendage. Multiple spinal cord neural transplants. And, as you can see, the brain. Stem cells were taken from the Chemist himself over the past eighteen months. I performed many of the extractions myself."

Ms. Lopez spoke out of her heartbreak. "Why? What does this do?"

"As I said, he was a genius. And he didn't allow me access to his methodologies. His understanding of medicine and cell engineering is ten years past anything I've studied, ten years past anything in clinical trials. His transplanted cells will begin to repair and replace Katie's own cells. His goal is structural amelioration. Her body isn't as strong as it should be because her illness was only recently introduced. For comparison, the Outlaw's body had eighteen years of preparation. Not Katie's. So he's assisting her body with the coming transformations. We did this to a lesser extent with all his Twice Chosen."

She rubbed her eyes and shuddered. "I do not understand."

"Think of it as rebuilding a car. The Chemist gave Katie his illness, which is like dropping a race car engine into a Honda Civic. The Civic will tear apart under the power of the new engine. So he rebuilt the Civic too. Making it stronger."

I was holding Katie's hand. So cold. So lifeless. I asked, "What about the brain surgeries?"

"He inserted his own brain cells. His own DNA. He wanted to grow new circuitry inside her mind. The brain surgery took twelve hours and he performed it all himself. I can't stress this enough…his mind functioned on another level. I'm under-qualified to fully understand or explain. We all are."

Dad asked, "Now what?"

"Now we keep her unconscious to protect brain tissue. Protect her psyche, for lack of better phrasing. Full body reconstruction is difficult for the patient. She'll need two hundred precent of her usual nutrition intake. I've performed this surgery hundreds of times, and monitored the results. Patients will wake when they're ready. If we force them to wake up…it's never a positive outcome."

One of the faceless physicians behind me asked, "Time frame?"

"Ninety days. Give or take a few weeks. Maybe longer for her. The surgery was traumatic. The longer the better. Preserves sanity. Mostly."

Samantha asked, "What do you mean he wanted to grow new circuitry inside her mind?"

Dr. Whitmer shrugged, eyes bloodshot. "I'm afraid to speculate."

"Do it anyway."

"Judging by these two incisions here, it appears he operated on the medial temporal lobe. The limbic system."

"Which means?"

"Memory processing," he said. I'd been afraid of that. We all had. He continued, "Maybe. Again, he understood this in ways no one else does. These small incisions here, the frontal cortex, could be any number of cognitive functions. Behavior. Personality. I'd like to run a battery of neural scans to find out what he did. We could fill books with conclusions based on her condition when she wakes. But..." He didn't finish. He was on the verge of collapse.

I said, "Doctor, one more question from us. The Chemist and I spoke on the roof. About Katie. He said this surgery wasn't like the others. Katie's was far more advanced, and she'd wake as a goddess. Was he lying?"

"About the goddess? Well, the Father was prone to dramatic hyperbole. But this surgery was unique in two ways. One, she received a full blood transfer instead of an injection. This was only performed one time previously, with Hannah Walker. The cheerleader. The Chemist was very pleased with those results. And two, the other unique aspect...He wanted Katie to wake up stronger than his previous patients. More powerful. We hadn't attempted it before, and we are both unsure of its success."

"Attempted *what*?"

"The muscle and bone marrow transplants? I inserted stem cells from *two* different individuals. From the Chemist himself, and from an individual named Tank Ware."

Samantha swore. My head swam. My stomach heaved. Dad caught me before I fell. Katie had Tank's genetic code growing in her bones.

Dr. Whitmer continued, "The Chemist claimed Tank Ware possessed the strongest muscle and bone tissue on the planet. And somehow he got his hands on Tank Ware's DNA. A significant amount of blood and muscle tissue. This type of gene therapy is Star Trek type stuff. Light years away from us. Simple immunorejection could crash the whole project."

I heard no more. I sank onto the sleeper couch beside Ms. Lopez and we existed in a shared stupor until morning.

Martin Patterson, the Chemist, was dead. His body was recovered off the street below the Wilshire Grand. His skull and his body had cracked open upon impact. The body of Baby Face could not be found.

News of the Chemist's death did not provide the result for which we all prayed and hoped. Walter did not throw down his weapons. Blue-Eyes did not release her control over most of Washington DC. And the Chosen went berserk, like their hive queen died. Any party hoping for an easy reclamation of Los Angeles was quickly disillusioned. The Chosen had previously been unruly and dangerous soldiers in a poorly organized army. However, now leaderless, they formed lawless bands of vengeful freaks.

I watched the world lurch from inside the hospital. I'd left Katie once and she paid the price; never again. Far off conversations with the Chemist and with Carter ran through my mind. *Unconditional love protects us.* On Maslow's Hierarchy of Needs love was foundational, only slightly less crucial than food, shelter and safety. Katie needed unconditional love. Her body and mind would undergo hell, but I'd be present the entire time. Vividly I recalled how soothing Katie's physical touch was, how the headaches fled before her affection, how she kept me sane, kept me alive.

I didn't leave her room for days at a time, not even when Ms. Lopez relieved me. I massaged her hands, her arms, her feet and legs. Her incisions healed and I rubbed lotions on the wounds to prevent hard scar tissue. I bent her knees and elbows to keep the joints from freezing. I dripped water into her mouth hourly. Moistened her dry lips with vaseline. I talked to her incessantly. Or sang. Or read books out loud. Dr. Whitmer demonstrated how to apply splints to obstruct contractures, and how to administer low doses of neuromuscular electrical stimulation to prevent atrophy. But, he told me, the disease caused so much muscle growth that she'd need very little physical therapy when she woke.

I could do this. For ninety days, for Katie, I could do this.

Samantha remained furious about my surrender to the Chemist, but she stayed to keep rabid paparazzi out. Katie's capture and release and my skyscraper shenanigans revamped the absurd fanatical frenzy. After a week, however, she grew sick of this lifestyle and left to join Isaac Anderson and his crew of resistance fighters. They operated independently of the Federal government, though with growing underground support from its members and resources. America appeared on a crash course with civil war, breaking neatly between those loyal to Washington and the President, and those recognizing the federal government had been usurped by a mad woman. Isaac and Samantha grew in notoriety and within a month were the figureheads of the resistance. Thanks to Puck's help, the world learned the White House had indeed ordered the launch of rockets against American civilians, against the Outlaw, on American soil (Blue-Eyes herself issued the order, but that was impossible to prove).

The conflict was growing on too many fronts to count. Walter held a sizable chunk of the wild Chosen in partial abeyance and he set about burning the world down with abandon. The Pacific Northwest lived in terror. His numbers swelled unchecked because Blue-Eyes kept Americans busy in cold war against each other. Officials estimated over twenty thousand Chosen roamed freely, often with adoring attendants toting guns.

Carter healed and paid his respects. I'd grown so bored and lonely that his visit was welcome. He moved with a vague limp, though nothing else had changed. He smelled of cigarette smoke.

"Katie has always been a better person than the rest of us," Carter said, brushing her arm with surprising tenderness. "She deserves better."

"What will you do now?"

"Are you kidding, mate? There's a war brewing. Which means a fortune is up for grabs. You've always got a place in my crew. I owe you a favor anyway."

I grinned for the first time in days. "Good to know."

"You can't stay here forever, you know. You're a target."

"I'm staying as long as it takes."

"You'll go crazy, kid."

"Maybe."

Natalie North came a few days later. She brought flowers and pretty gowns for Katie to wear. All the hospital staff followed her around. We hugged for a long time, happy to be friends and allies in such a broken world.

"Wherever I am, you and Katie have a home," she told me before she left. "Call me."

Lee visited soon after. He'd grown into a man during the past few months. Taller, stronger, wiser. He cried over Katie. We cried together over our fallen friend Cory. Lee'd been made an E6 military rank, a non-commissioned civilian officer, and traveled with an Army engineering team to demonstrate electroshock weapons for subduing Chosen.

PuckDaddy swung by during Lee's stay. We visited with him in his brand new roving computer lab. Puck and Lee regarded each other with a friendly yet suspicious rivalry, curious and cautious at the same time.

"Had to update," Puck explained his new ride, which could have been a spaceship. "This baby runs on electrical power primarily. Oil is getting harder to come by. But it has less range."

Lee asked, "Who is your driver?"

"Same guys. Why? You looking for a job?"

Lee recoiled as if slapped. "Dude! What? No! No, I'm…I'm so busy saving the world, that…dude, no. Gotta catch a flight out of Fresno later today. I'm a globe trotter, baby."

"You played Tetris for an hour on your phone last night, dummy. Not too busy."

"BRO! No! You…no!" Lee dropped his phone on the ground and jumped on it. "You do not get to spy on me, you glorified computer nerd. Chase! Tell him! How about I pop your tires with the bad-ass classified weapons in my car?"

Some parts of the world hadn't changed after all.

I didn't notice the reduction in hospital staff until mid-April. After watching nurses change Katie's bandages, shift her to avoid bed sores, swap out catheter bags, feed her through a gastrostomy tub, and change her IV solutions, I managed most of it myself now. That was illegal, but they no longer objected. On April 17th, sixty-six days after her release, I realized I hadn't seen a nurse in twelve hours. I stretched and went into the hall to investigate.

Empty. The adjoining rooms were vacant. The nurses' desk was a wasteland. I didn't find anyone until I left our wing and ventured into the hospital's main patient care department.

"Consolidation," a harried nurse explained. "I haven't slept in days. We're operating on a skeleton crew. Over half our staff is gone and we're shipping out patients as fast as possible. We left Katie where she is for the moment because you're giving such good care. Dr. Whitmer should come by soon."

I returned to the room. Looked in the mirror for the first time in days. Maybe weeks. I was thinner. Hair longer. Badly in need of a shave. I'd been in such a routine, so caught up with Katie and her treatment, that I hadn't noticed...anything. I read to her eight hours a day and we watched reruns and east coast baseball another eight, and then I slept. Ms. Lopez came and stayed several hours every few days. Dad visited once a week. That was the extent of our company. The media had long since realized how boring our situation was.

I plugged my new phone in to charge. Hadn't glanced at it since...what day was it? Turned the television to CNN.

Los Angeles was being abandoned. And not just downtown. Huntington Park, Inglewood, Montebello, Glendale, and other surrounding areas were emptying. The circle of abandonment enlarged daily. Chosen and gangs of gunmen ran amok. No wonder all the nurses and physicians were leaving. Beverly Hills had begun evacuation and that was only four miles away.

Millions moved. A never-ending flow of humanity. Vehicles loaded with belongings got in line and slowly disappeared east. Highways backed for miles. Thousands of families walking, abandoning cars with no gas. It was one of the great migrations in human history, a massive undertaking lasting months.

Katie's mother arrived later that day. I dashed to UCLA's campus library for a fresh set of books. No librarian. No patrons. I browsed shelves entirely by myself.

Dr. Whitmer never returned. A nurse brought me a long email printout from him with instructions for care over the next thirty days. He had returned to Chicago to be with his extended family. I couldn't blame him.

Katie's body had begun a significant transformation. At night I heard her bones grinding. She sweated and cried out and I whispered to her and bathed her face and neck with a cold cloth. Her muscles flexed and twitched incessantly. She'd clearly grown an inch taller. Maybe two. She was no longer bald, now sporting a cute brown dome of thick fuzz. Her nails became harder to trim. The IV needle sometimes bent instead of penetrating her skin.

Five days later, at two in the afternoon, a man I'd never met staggered into the room. He adjusted his spectacles and his tie and said, "Okay, Mr...Mr. Outlaw. Katie Lopez is our final patient. We're ready for transport to Las Vegas."

"Who're you?"

"I'm the hospital administrator. *Was* the hospital administrator, I suppose. We're locking the doors permanently at five."

"Katie and I are staying," I said simply.

"They told me you'd say that. But I have an ambulance prepared."

"Dr. Whitmer instructed me not to move her. We're staying. Besides, I've provided one hundred percent of her care for six days now."

"The evacuation is mandatory by police order."

"The police have no authority here, Mr. Hospital Administrator. I appreciate your help. Really, I do. But we're staying."

He made me sign release forms. He took me to Katie's secure medication cabinet. Then the large medical supply rooms. We examined the pharmacy and the cafeteria kitchen. Katie and I had a surplus of supplies; we could live here for years if necessary. But it wasn't. I just needed thirty days.

He placed a set of keys in my hands. Wished me luck. The nurses hugged me. And then they were gone. A fortune of medical gear abandoned in dark rooms and dusty hallways.

"You and me, baby," I told Katie. "Thirty more days. And you'll wake as a goddess. Not that you weren't one already."

I stocked the adjacent rooms with cans of food from the kitchen. I raided all the drink machines and refrigerators for water bottles. Katie groaned and twisted and stared with vacant eyes.

Dad offered to come get us. Ms. Lopez insisted on it. Isaac arranged a helicopter. Samantha sent me texts in all caps. Lee informed me I was stupid. So did Puck. No, I told them. We're safe. And happy. And Katie will wake up soon. We'll find you.

The power shut off one morning in early May. I'd anticipated this. From local hardware stores I'd brought back three gas powered generators and stored them at the nurses station along with fifty gallons of gasoline siphoned from ambulances and the hospital's emergency reserves. Our wing of the third floor had become a survivalist paradise.

I only needed to run one generator to power our small fridge, an electric stove, two fans, the television, and Katie's IV machine. We didn't need air conditioning; we had the southern Californian climate, a pleasant breeze, and open windows. I kept another generator running down the hall for a large freezer full of emergency supplies and the solution I used for mixing Katie's liquid diet.

I read her Emily Dickinson's entire collection. And then, because I was exhausted from all her emotions, Edgar Allen Poe's. Our life was peaceful. Quiet. It would have been romantic if my date wasn't asleep. I got lost in the routine of food prep, waste disposal, administering medicine, physical therapy, checking on supplies, and reading.

The news no longer interested me. I would help as soon as Katie woke and became mobile. America wasn't lost, despite mounting casualties. In fact, our country was handling the turmoil with impressive resilience. The infrastructures held. The food supply never stopped. The electrical grid kept humming. The gas shortages were problematic but we'd been preparing against it for six months. Communities condensed and held ground against the terrors of the night. Volunteer militias provided additional security. The military skirmishes escalated in severity but took place away from civilian populaces.

That all changed when the White House ordered the first nuclear missile launched at the resistance in Arizona. The warhead was small; only fifty tons. But it signified a change for the worse.

I quit watching the news then. The incoming cable signal would probably give out soon anyway.

In mid-May, Samantha brought me a care package from Lee and Puck. Two new Outlaw costumes, vest and pants. Two satellite smart phones. And a powerful laptop.

"How's she doing?" Samantha asked, placing her hand on Katie's forehead. "Wow, she's burning up."

"Dr. Whitmer said the fever is typical. Not to worry unless it gets above a hundred and three."

"She's taller. Stronger."

I grinned. "She's going to be a handful."

"Are you worried? What she'll be like?"

"Because the Chemist's other creations are often crazy?"

"Yeah. I mean, Hannah Walker vacillates between adoration and insanity. And Andy is…who knows. Maybe dead now. And all the Chosen hate you. Right? Want to rip your throat out. Because of his DNA, they perceive you as a threat."

I shook my head and squeezed Katie's hand. "Not Katie. I've been here the whole time. She's heard my voice every day. I know she'll be different. It's going to be hard. But we'll get through it."

"Glad to hear it. She should be waking up soon?"

"Any day. Hopefully."

"Good," Samantha said with a sigh of relief. "Good. It'll be nice to have you back."

She left soon after.

We weren't alone. I'd been hearing noises from the bottom floor for two days. Chosen or homeless drifters or whoever, I didn't care as long as they left us in peace. Soon there was more activity in the surrounding neighborhood. Scavengers. Chosen. Former occupants. A fire two miles distant sent smoke coiling into the blue.

The intruders probably belonged to the Priest and his band of followers, now two hundred thousand strong. The Outlawyers. Somehow they'd established a working relationship with the Chosen and lived in symbiotic peace within Los Angeles.

I prepared an ambulance for departure, just in case.

One hundred and four days after Katie's surgery, I woke earlier than usual. 7:30 in the morning. I'd fallen asleep in her hospital bed, as I often did. The sun sat low over the San Gabriel Mountains in the east. I extracted myself, stretched, yawned, and brushed my teeth in her sink.

Something was different today. After a hundred routine and mundane mornings, I noticed any change. Something *woke* me. I cast around the room and hallway. No intruders. Whatever it was, I detected no immediate danger.

Katie's breathing had altered. Shallow. Rapid. She stirred restlessly. That began two days ago. I took it as a good sign. She would wake soon.

But there was something else…

I walked to the open window.

Three stories below, in the parking lot, over a hundred Chosen watched me. Some sat criss-cross on the blacktop. Some rested on haunches. Some stood. Black, White, Asian, Latino, skinny, strong, well-fed, emaciated, men and women, all of them staring directly at our window. Wide eyes. Curious. Like expectant pilgrims at the foot of their paragon. Subjects before their king.

No weapons. Simply waiting. I examined them for five minutes, predicting trouble. Looking for a leader. For a cause. For a clue. They patiently inspected me in return.

I waved. No response. No sounds of any kind. Complete silence. No cars, no airplanes, no birds, no barking dogs. Just kids my age staring as if spellbound. "Kinda creepy," I yawned and turned from the view.

And nearly fell.

Katie was sitting up in bed, blinking against sunlight with big brown eyes. No, they were hazel in this light. She shifted her shoulders awkwardly, stiffly. She glanced at the needle in her arm. At the bed. At the room.

At me.

Her lips twitched. In a smile.

"Hello," she whispered.

The butterfly had awoken from her chrysalis.

My beautiful Katie had come back.

The End

Dear reader,

Thus ends the Outlaw series. I hope you enjoyed it.

The story of Chase and Katie, however, is not concluded.

If you'd like to stop reading about them, now is a perfect time. The Chemist has been defeated. Katie is saved. Good will prevail. All is perfect. Close the book and be at peace. They can live happily ever after within the hallowed halls of your memory.

But if you'd like to know what happens next, read the following pages.

You've been warned.

Epilogue One (of Three)
Monday, February 13. 2019
Two Days After The Chemist's Death
Kid

My skull had fractured upon impact; fortunately I'd landed on top of the Father. But that didn't prevent me from rupturing my spleen, puncturing a lung, breaking all my ribs, both femurs and my left humerus. (Plus my fingers were already broken) Despite the cushion of the Father's body, I'd have splattered all over Figueroa if I hadn't been Chosen, or *Infected* as the Outlaw referred to us.

Nuts found me and brought me home that night. The surgeons set my bones, patched me up, and replaced all the lost blood. They used what they had. The Father's blood. I have NO idea what that means for me long term.

The Father was dead. But I didn't experience the relief I'd anticipated. No one did. No one danced in the streets. No celebrations. No new rapturous freedom. The Twice Chosen freaks lost all ability to function when the news broke. Nuts and I sat in my room (me in a wheel chair) and watched them rampage. The building across from us burnt on three different levels. Why do we destroy stuff when we're angry or scared?

"Idiots be wrecking the plumbing next," Nuts sniffed, arms crossed, brows furrowed. "Took me weeks to set up."

I winced against my constant headache. "I read somewhere that adolescent elephants become destructive and break everything they see until a mature elephant appears and sets them straight."

Nuts said, "That's why I saved you."

"It's not me, Nuts," I sighed and grunted at the stitch in my lung. "It's never been."

"God help us all if it's Walter." He stood and rolled me away from our view. "Come on, Kid. You've been putting this off too long."

"Nuts," I groaned. "I don't know what to do about the women. I can't help."

"You're their *only* help."

He wheeled me to the elevator. The hallway appeared spooky in lantern light. We boarded, he spoke into his radio, and we descended. Descended past the lobby level into restricted areas.

"Nuts, what do you expect me to do? To say?"

"Figure it out."

The lower levels of our tower had been cleaned out and expanded where possible. A small fraction had been devoted to macabre labs and sterile operating rooms. But the remainder was an absolute secret. Only a handful knew. His most trusted.

Five hundred people lived down here. And another five hundred in a nearby tower's basement, identical in every way. One thousand of the Father's most prized possessions. He called them the Inheritors. The Inheritors spent twenty hours a day here. Only four hours above ground. Four hours allowed in the sunlight. Four hours in the secret gardens. They weren't mistreated. In fact, much energy had been spent on making them as comfortable as possible. But confinement is hard.

In the beginning there were a thousand people in the basement. Two thousand total, between this tower and the adjacent one. Approximately five hundred had already died. Five hundred from *each* tower. Fifty percent. The Father had predicted sixty, so we're doing something right. He is pleased with fifty. *Was* pleased.

Nuts rolled me across the concrete floor towards the sealed double doors. One of the chair's wheels squeaked and echoed off the distant walls. "Nuts," I said desperately, "I'm not ready. I can't. You talk to them."

"I don't talk. I fix. I build."

He punched in a code. The heavy doors clicked and moved inwards with an electric whir. We entered.

The room was low-ceilinged and vast, painted in pink and yellow colors intended to be cheerful but which appeared drab under fluorescent bulbs. On the far side of this room, doors led to sleeping quarters. Kitchens. Bathrooms. This was the play area. Toys everywhere. Rocking chairs. Televisions. Books. The faint smell of urine.

The women were awake, all two hundred and fifty of them. They paced. They wrung their hands. They drank. They waited for news.

I couldn't lead these women, even though I was Infected and they weren't. What did that matter? I was younger than them. I wasn't a leader. Not wise. No vision. No confidence. Plus, there was only one of me. There were two hundred and fifty women here. And two hundred and fifty in the other tower.

And every woman had a baby. Five hundred mothers, five hundred children.

Most of their babies slept. Of the two hundred and fifty babies housed here, about fifty of them bounced in their mother's arms. They cried. They nursed. They sucked on a bottle.

The babies were of all races and nationalities and between the ages of one and eight months. They had two things in common. One, they were unlucky enough to be born in or around Los Angeles during the previous year. Two, at birth they had been given a small injection of the Father's blood.

The implications staggered me. Nineteen years ago, give or take a year, the Father and a man named Carter had injected forty babies with tainted blood. Nineteen long years ago. Of those forty, only seven survived the virus. The Outlaw, Tank Ware, Carla, me, Walter, Troy and Melissa. Those seven were enough to shake America's foundations. Carla, Troy and Melissa were dead. I should be.

Just seven. Out of forty.

What would happen with five hundred Inheritors? Five hundred Infected babies. Their destiny sealed. Madness boiled inside. Madness and fate. Doomed to power, possibly as powerful as the Outlaw himself. Possessing the combined might to forever break the planet.

This was the Father's long-term plan. Infected babies growing up in the loving arms of their mothers. Growing up to rule the world.

The mothers knew the Father was dead.

They wanted answers. Wanted hope.

I had none to offer. We needed a leader.

Epilogue Two (of Three)
One Hundred and Four Days After Katie's Surgery

Katie was sitting up in bed, blinking against sunlight with big brown eyes. No, they were hazel in this light. Almost green. That was new. She shifted her shoulders awkwardly, stiffly. She glanced at the needle in her arm. At the bed. At the room. At me.

Her lips twitched.

In a smile, I thought.

"Hello?" she whispered.

"Katie!" I whispered back. I bottled up my excitement and fifty other emotions. Dr. Whitmer cautioned against early stimulus. I went to her bed slowly. "Are you...can you...can you hear me?"

She closed her eyes and moaned. Her face had changed. The muscles and skin hugged her skull in harder edges. She still looked like Katie, but a Katie who won triathlons.

She moved in a dream state. Not fully awake. Operating on long dormant impulse. A shudder wracked her body. She tried to speak but couldn't. Her arms raised in a half stretch and she took a deep, deep breath through her nose. Paused. Her eyes snapped open again. Sharpened. Examined me. Frowned. Her mouth moved soundlessly.

"Don't move," I said. "I'll get you something to drink. Take it easy. You've been asleep for months. We need to call your mom."

I went to the window for a bottle of water and my phone. The Chosen still watched expectantly. Except now they all stood. Every single one. On their feet. What were they waiting for? I was at a complete loss. A shiver ran through the crowd and they began generating a noise. A murmur of corporate excitement, a faint stridulation. Some of them were hopping.

I caught a reflection in the glass of the open window. A reflection of myself. And of Katie. She had moved out of bed. Silently. Now standing behind me. Trailing tubes and sheets. She was glaring at me without recognition. Glaring with wild eyes that no longer belonged to Katie Lopez. That belonged now to a stranger.

She struck me in the lower back. Doctors told me later she pulverized my 4th and 5th lumbar vertebra and sacrum bones with that kick. Had my adrenaline been pumping, blood racing, muscles tensed by the disease, ready for combat, I could have absorbed the impact. Instead my spinal column snapped neatly in half. I was propelled out of the window, spinning like a broken toy. I fell three stories, landing on and collapsing the ambulance's roof. The ambulance I'd prepared for rapid departure.

The Chosen reacted like howler monkeys, jumping and screaming in delight.

Above their din, an alien noise erupted. A roar. High-pitched and ferocious, louder than the others. I felt it in my bones. Felt the ambulance roof tremble.

It was the enraged howl of an alpha. Of a goddess.

Epilogue Three (of Three)
November 2019
Former Special Agent Isaac Anderson

We meet in secret because we're outlaws. The President actively searches for us. Because we've broken away from the government. Because we commandeered almost half his resources and manpower. Because we've attempted to abduct or eliminate the Blue-Eyed Witch three times. All failures.

We're forced to operate in shadows. We gather in a vacant high school two hours outside Los Angeles. Feels similar to the middle school we met in almost a year ago. A lifetime.

The taskforce I've gathered is part resistance, part American government. Traitors to the President. Saboteurs against Blue-Eyes. All of us have seen combat in the prior months. All of us have killed our American brothers.

We're in way over our heads.

"We've got a lot to cover," I say, turning on the battery-powered projector. "Let's get started."

But I can't muster the energy. I'm exhausted. Like everyone else. It's been a long day. A long month. A long year. The American public is on our side. The majority roots for us in secret. But that's no substitute for sleep.

We have nuclear warheads. And we're divided on what to do with them. We can't even bear to bring the subject up.

Someone asks, "Where's the Shooter? She's usually here."

"Samantha's busy," I answer. "She didn't tell me. Something with

PuckDaddy. Or Carter. I forget which. I trust her."

"Any update on the Outlaw?"

I smile wearily. There, at least, is some good news. "Chase is up and running. Finally. He might be stuck with a limp, but considering our physicians expected him to be paralyzed the rest of his life…"

"How soon will he be back in the field?"

"Soon. Although we shouldn't expect much help from him. Not in the near future. He doesn't plan on joining the Resistance. At least not yet."

The room rings with shocked silence. Dashed hopes. And quiet outrage.

Someone finally blurts, "*What?*"

"Don't get me wrong. He's our ally. But Chase only has one thing on his mind."

He scoffs. "He's going after the Crimson Witch?"

I slam my hand on the table. The room jumps. "We are *not* calling her that. Not ever."

"You prefer The Butcher?"

I answer, "No. Not even that. Not around me. I don't care what she's called on the internet. I don't care about the photographs. Don't care about the rumors. Pick a different name."

The man asks, "What's she call herself? Carmine, or something. What does the Outlaw think he can do? His girlfriend tried to kill him, for crying out loud. Broke his back."

I rub my eyes and admit, "I don't know. But Katie Lopez deserves better than these nicknames."

"Deserves better? She killed all those people. She's ruthless. She and her growing army are…hell, I don't know what to call them."

I don't answer. I have nothing to say. He's right. We all know it. I know it. I stare out of the dusty window westward towards Los Angeles, towards Carmine. Towards Katie Lopez.

The man grumbles, "We *need* the Outlaw. And he's going to get himself slaughtered."

"Maybe," I say. "But he believes he can make her remember."

"Remember what?"

"Everything."

The sage of Chase and Katie continues in…

Carmine

Rise of the Warrior Queen
Book One

The world is breaking under the strain of Chosen, powerful human beings crafted in a lab and driven insane by a mysterious disease.

Nineteen-year-old Carmine is determined to keep her corner of America intact. Possessing little memory of her former life, she is the unquestioned leader of the Chosen. She knows the genetically modified outcasts can be the planet's salvation.

Carmine has few allies, however. She is misunderstood and alone in her quest. The world views her as a beautiful monster, the surviving governments want to control her, and sinister warmongers seek to enslave her people. As society collapses, Carmine confronts enemies she can't defeat and romances she can't remember.

Click here **http://eepurl.com/b1e2r9**
to get a preview!

MANY thanks to the readers who left Amazon feedback over the past year. You helped launch my career. I'm beyond thankful.

Many thanks for the Goodreads ratings too.

Text me. I reply to as many as I can. (260) 673-5450

I took minor shortcuts with Californian geography and with military procedures and with modern medicine. I know I did. They simplified the story, else we'd get bogged down. You already have my apologies, but you can yell at me anyway if you like. =)

Find The Outlaw on Facebook
Find me on Twitter or Instagram

A big thank you to everyone involved
  — artists Anne Pierson and Damonza.
  — beta readers Sarah, Liz, Becky, Will, Anne, Megan, and Debbie.
  — Polgarus
  — to my friends and family for the encouragement
  — especially to my wife for letting her husband chase dreams. You are everything.